To Paul & Helen,
With Best Wishes!
Enjoy—

Frank Macdonald

Tinker & Blue
a novel by
Frank Macdonald

BY FRANK MACDONALD

A Forest for Calum, CBU Press 2005, 2011
Longlisted for the International IMPAC Dublin Literary
Award and finalist for an Atlantic Book Award.

A Possible Madness, CBU Press 2011, 2012
Longlisted for the International IMPAC Dublin Literary
Award and finalist for an Atlantic Book Award.

T.R.'s Adventure at Angus the Wheeler's, CBU Press 2010
Illustrated by Virginia McCoy.

Assuming I'm Right, Cecibu 1990
Adapted for the stage.

How to Cook Your Cat, Cecibou 2003

Her Wake, 2011
Best Canadian Play, Liverpool International Theatre Festival.

Copyright © Frank Macdonald, 2014
This book is a work of fiction. The characters and events depicted are products of the author's imagination.

All rights reserved. No part of this work may be reproduced or used in any form or by any means, electronic or mechanical, including photocopying, recording or any information storage or retrieval system, without the prior written permission of the publisher.

Cape Breton University Press recognizes the support of the Province of Nova Scotia, through the Film and Creative Industries NS, and of Canada Council for the Arts Block Grants Program. We are pleased to work in partnership with these bodies to develop and promote our cultural resources.

Library and Archives Canada Cataloguing in Publication

Macdonald, Frank, 1945-, author
Tinker and Blue : a novel / Frank Macdonald.

Issued in print and electronic formats.
ISBN 978-1-927492-94-9 (pbk.).--ISBN 978-1-927492-95-6 (pdf).--ISBN 978-1-927492-96-3 (epub).--ISBN 978-1-927492-97-0 (mobi)

I. Title.
PS8575.D6305T55 2014   C813'.54   C2014-904134-9
C2014-904135-7

Cape Breton University Press
PO Box 5300
1250 Grand Lake Road
Sydney, Nova Scotia B1P 6L2 Canada

www.cbupress.ca

Tinker & Blue
A NOVEL BY

FRANK MACDONALD

CAPE BRETON UNIVERSITY PRESS
SYDNEY, NOVA SCOTIA

For Tom and Beth Ryan
and all the wonderful years

In Memory:
Sextus Feehan
(1943-2009)
who would have known all the stolen stories

One

It had been Blue's idea that he and his best friend Tinker Dempsey drive out to San Francisco to look at hippies in their natural environment, Haight-Ashbury. At nineteen and twenty, their respective ages, Blue believed the time had come for the two of them to follow generations of Cape Breton Island tradition and cross the Canso Causeway, if for no other reason than to find a few stories they could tell as their own when their wandering ways brought them back home.

Ever since settlement, Cape Breton Island had doled out her children to the world – some to the priesthood and convents, ministries and to politics, some to the mines of northern Ontario and the factories of Toronto, some to the skid rows of Winnipeg and Vancouver – and rationed a large portion of its population to work, legally or illegally, in the Boston economy. Historically, Cape Breton was a migrant labour pool for the boom towns and prosperity of the rest of the continent. This constant coming and going kept the island well informed – if unaffected – about trends and traditions elsewhere in North America. For all that wandering, neither the island nor its people had made any serious impact on San Francisco, which was the reason Tinker and Blue decided their destination would be that far off and fabled land.

Tinker and Blue were now driving their fourth-hand 1957 push button Plymouth across Kansas heading for California.

"Fruits!" Blue had concluded four years earlier for the enlightenment of the gang of guys who had gathered in his mother's living room to watch the Beatles' appearance on *The Ed Sullivan Show*. It was a theory he had a hard time hanging on to in the ensuing years as gypsy herds of long-haired hippies began wandering north to Canada, to Nova Scotia, crossing the Causeway onto Cape Breton Island, buying abandoned farms and setting up communes. The long-haired hippies clearly travelled in the free-flowing, free-loving company of beautiful girls, taking part in a sexual revolution that hadn't quite cracked the Catholic cocoon that surrounded Blue's own nightly longings.

Adding to his confusion was the summer return of guys he knew like brothers. They had left Cape Breton with creases in their pants and parts in their hair and returned wearing braids and bandanas, patches on their arses and no knees in their jeans, and speaking a new jargon.

But none of them had ever been to 'Frisco.

―

Travelling for days on the wrong side of the Canso Causeway, Tinker and Blue grew homesick, remembering for each other the good times, humming fiddle tunes, singing the island's favourite sentimental songs, and butchering their way through scores of Gaelic choruses.

Tinker Dempsey, being half Irish, possessed a fine voice, and was fond of singing "real" Irish songs, always informing his listeners that the song he was about to sing was from the old country and not that popular made-in-Boston junk.

Blue had no voice at all, which didn't disturb him as much as it did his listeners. To avoid the barbs of his best friends and worst critics, Blue abandoned singing other people's songs and began writing his own – gems wrestled in rhyming couplets from the depths of his own soul. Who better than he to render his songs in the fullness of their beauty. Discovering the poet within, Blue bartered a broken bicycle for an un-strung guitar, which he eventually did string, learning three chords, "You know what the other fellow says about three chords, don't you, Tinker? That's all Hank Williams ever knew," he was fond of pointing out, and waited for destiny to discover him.

Armed with birth certificates and baptismal certificates, they crossed the border and began their journey across the United States of America, roaring their haphazard harmony above the ping-ping-pinging of the Plymouth's engine. The birth certificates bore all the vital information relevant to the day and place of their births, everything that is except the nicknames they travelled by.

In Cape Breton, where nicknames stick like barnacles, Tinker Dempsey was a natural. His Acadian mother had christened him Aloysius Dempsey, but four years later, when he had disassembled the family's only alarm clock, his father had unintentionally re-christened his son, complaining to anyone with the time or interest to listen that all his son ever did was tinker, tinker, tinker.

Tinker went on tinkering with things mechanical whenever an object of interest fell into his hands. Gradually, his interest reached the car motor stage, and a mechanic in his hometown took the willing young man under his wing. Unfortunately, the mechanic who taught Tinker to tinker with engines was himself self-taught – and he had not taught himself particularly well. But what he knew he passed along and together they crippled most of the vehicles in western Cape Breton.

A neighbour who had brought his aging third-hand Plymouth into what local people called Charlie's Guesso Station to have it serviced, returned several times to retrieve it only to find some new part of its anatomy strewn across the garage floor. Eventually, getting a glance at the growing bill, he abandoned any hopes of ever operating it again, bought a second-hand Chev, and Charlie claimed the Plymouth as salvage against the unpaid bill.

With a lot of head scratching and puzzling random pieces together, Charlie and Tinker managed one afternoon to turn the key and hear the motor turn over. Charlie, whose mechanic business had a lot of unpaid receivables from irate customers in its desk drawer, traded the Plymouth to Tinker in exchange for oft-promised but rarely produced wages. Tinker thought it was a hell of a deal.

Blue had acquired his name because virtually everything he owned and wore was blue. There was no sound reason for this fetish that Blue could explain except that he liked the colour, which for Blue was the only sound reason for doing anything.

As the approaching Kansas night finally lulled them into quiet reverie, Blue strummed his guitar and hummed the melody of "The Red Lobster," his one-hundred verse work-in-progress. Cocking his battered blue hat down over his eyes, he allowed one of the verses to rise to his lips.

> Your beauty traps me
> like a lobster in a pot
> And I turn red
> when the water gets hot
> But you wanna crack me
> break my shell
> So what I gotta say is
> Go to hell
>
> Red lobster, red lobster
> Don't you dare sob, sir
> 'Cause love is you, and love is her
> You're the meat. She's the but-tur

So far, Blue had composed thirty-seven verses of "The Red Lobster," fashioning it, as he was always anxious to explain, after the Gaelic songs sung on Cape Breton, some of which tended to go on for a night and a day in a language few understood any longer, and to which the rest were culturally conditioned to appreciate. Blue had a scribbler full of other songs composed in moments of pure inspiration.

—

They had cleared one state after another, driving into a series of sunsets while erasing the world behind them with a cloud of black exhaust from the oil-hungry Plymouth which ate away at their not-so-well-thought-out grubstake. July, they were beginning to realize, wasn't the best time for this business. Summers in Cape Breton did nothing to prepare them for the real meaning of heat. A couple of weeks of breezy beach days and evenings that required nothing more than a sweater was the way they handled the season in Cape Breton, which had never known too much of a good thing – work or weather. The Kansas heat itself, with a bit of polishing and editing, was already shaping up to be the first story in an anthology of tales they planned to carry back home with them, one of the many they would be telling friends in tag-team fashion come next summer.

What Cape Bretoners sought most on mainland North America was not wages so much as stories. They spent their entire time away from the island telling strangers stories about Cape Breton, then returned home to spend the summer telling stories about the strangers they met while away. Those stories, when told to people they met elsewhere, were credited with being more imaginative than true, but at home all stories were accepted as gospel, their success or failure judged solely on the telling. Even in the modern society of 1968, a good storyteller wouldn't go hungry or sober on Cape Breton Island.

2

Driving through the various states, the litter of hippies hitchhiking along the highway never let up, but the drives they offered were carefully considered: people with haircuts who resembled themselves; people they could talk to without gawking like a couple of old women. But their curiosity was growing. So were the clouds that loomed ahead of them, promising a soothing shower of summer rain. The first splashes on the windshield were large, followed by a not so soothing, pelting downpour that they followed into darkness.

The lone figure with his fingers forming a peace sign struck a lonely image in the headlights and without discussion Tinker pulled the Plymouth to the side of the road. A moment later, a hippie with wet matted hair sat in the back seat among suitcases, Blue's guitar and fast-food cartons.

"Wow, man, like, I was thinking the Good Samaritan and then your headlights were there. I knew there was good people in this vehicle. Like, you're angels, man."

Blue reached across and poked Tinker in the ribs, which served in the darkness for the eye rolls they normally communicated with when passing mutual judgement.

"Everybody's an angel, man, that's what I've discovered so far. Angels don't come from Heaven, see. What happens is, people turn into them for a moment without even noticing. They just do things angels get the credit for doing. Like stopping for me. You could have passed by but you didn't. Why? Angels, man, the world is full of them. How far you going?"

"'Frisco." Blue tossed the word into the back seat nonchalantly, as if it was the name of a village just down the road from home. He took the opportunity to peer into the back seat at the dark form occupying it. Even night didn't disguise a wet hippie.

"Comin' from New York, man?"

"Cape Breton," Blue answered, clarifying who they were.

"Where's that, man?" the hippie asked, which resulted in a "stupid Americans" poke in the ribs for Tinker again.

"In Canada," Blue answered. "Eastern Canada. Nova Scotia. Know it?"

"Canada! Wow! You really got your shit together up there, man. I got lots of friends ducking 'Nam in Canada. Maybe you know them?"

"I don't think so," Blue replied. "It's a big country. Bigger than the United States, you know," quoting the passenger a fact of national pride.

"No, I didn't know that, man. Life's an endless learning. Wanna do some weed?"

"Huh?" Blue asked with a head snap while the Plymouth jerked under Tinker's shocked reflexes.

"Weed, man. Mary Jane. Marijuana. Wanna do some? I have a Colombian right here, already rolled. It's all I got to offer to this trip."

Tinker and Blue, who thought nothing of losing the occasional weekend to a trunk load of beer, drew the line at drugs. In fact, this was as close to an addicted hippie as they had ever been.

"Ah, well, I don't know if I feel like it. What about you, Tink?"

Tinker was having a hard time finding words to match Blue's relaxed panic, but managed a "Nah. Not while I'm driving."

"I respect that, man," the hippie said. "Mind if I light up?"

"Lotta cops on the road tonight," Tinker lied self-protectively. "We were stopped twice already."

"Oh, wow, man, the pigs! I'd hate to get busted again. What I'm going to do is smoke this joint so that if they do stop us again we're clean, man, clean. Any problem?"

The logic was irrefutable in the stunned state with which Tinker and Blue were trying to handle this unexpected turn of events. A match flared in the back seat and an unfamiliar smell rolled through the car in a cloud of smoke.

"Where you headed?" Blue asked, trying to glimpse the face of the addict in the back seat. He had already opened the cubby hole and taken out a screwdriver which he placed on the seat between him and Tinker. Things might get rough once the hippie got high.

"Up there somewhere." A shadowy hand pointed generally in the direction they were travelling. "It's not the destination, man, it's the journey." He drew and exhaled heavily, his breath hesitating, holding itself between those functions. Blue smoked Buckingham plains but this smoke was stronger, filling the air, bothering his eyes with its thickness, choking him. A rolled-down window let in too much rain. He rolled it up again.

"There's places to go just to go through the places that take you there," the hippie continued, wandering through a monologue that involved details about commune living, hitchhiking and more angels.

Soon Blue, half choked with smoke, began having a hard time following the hippie's drugged thoughts and the pattern of rain on the windshield was far more interesting than anything he had seen since they left home.

Suddenly, the world exploded in a sustained flash of lightning that exposed a gruesome scowl of sky. Rain fell with a force unimagined in the worst Cape Breton autumns, bouncing a foot off the pavement as it pounded down, and the wind began to rock the moving car.

"Christ, this is a blizzard without snow," Tinker said, leaning heavily across the steering wheel to peer through the ocean washing against the windshield. Suddenly he slammed on the brakes, jolting them to a stop, and began staring into the night.

"What is it?" Blue asked, trying to find out what Tinker was seeing.

"Nothing," Tinker replied, easing his foot down on the gas, the car moving slowly ahead. "I just thought I saw a herd of turtles on the road."

Tinker's words drifted over to Blue who gathered them in and studied them until comprehension occurred some moments later.

"A turd of hurtles?" Blue asked, sensing the inaccuracy in his remark without actually recognizing it. Tinker did, and fed the line back to him, which made them both giddy.

"You thought you saw a herd of turtles?" Blue said, finally and correctly. "That's the funniest thing I heard since John Alex John R. John C. tried to put the harness on himself when he was in the DT's." Turning to the hippie, Blue explained, "We got this guy back home, eh, John Alex John R. John C—"

"Who are they, man?" the hippie asked in studied interest.

"They? No, no, John Alex John R. John C.! He's one guy, eh, John Alex. But we call him John Alex John R. John C. because— Why do we call him John Alex John R. John C., Tinker?"

"To tell him apart from John Alex John R. the Butcher, of course," Tinker answered without taking his eyes from the rain-splashed highway where strange creatures might be lurking in ambush.

"Yeah. Well, the point is ... help me out here, Tinker. What was the point here?"

"The point was ... ahh ... leave me alone. I have to drive."

"Right! Turtles. Keep your eye out for those turtles, Tink." Convulsions of laughter exploded from the two of them.

"Laughing is good," the hippie observed seriously.

"Know what else would be good?" Blue offered. "Food. I'm frigging starving." Turning to the hippie he apologized. "Sorry we have no food to give you. We made a loaf of baloney and mustard sandwiches at a picnic park this afternoon but two hours later they turned green as snot. My mother could cook Sunday dinner in the heat in this part of the country, boy."

"I don't eat dead animals," the hippie replied.

"So is it hard to take a bite out of a live cow?" Tinker asked, this time snapping Blue in the ribs.

"All life is sacred, man," the hippie explained. "Eventually we'll all know that. The only reason we're alive is to learn that all life is sacred."

"But to stay alive you got to eat," Blue said, moving into a philosophical mood. "Man can't live on bread alone, as other fellow says."

"Have some sunflower seeds," the hippie offered, digging into his pack and pouring some into Blue's palm. Tinker declined.

Blue chewed on the seeds, thinking as he did so that it was about the worst thing he had ever eaten, but his raging appetite wasn't discriminating. He put his hand over the back seat for more.

"Just what a guy would need after a hard day in the coal mine, Tink. A handful of sunflower seeds. Who could think of roast beef after a feast like this," he remarked as he began chewing again.

"You eat a lot of meat, man?" the hippie asked.

"Three times a day where we come from, bacon and eggs in the morning, beans and baloney at dinner and hamburg and potatoes for supper. Chicken on Sunday," Blue mumbled, his mouth full.

"That's a lot of bad karma, man," the hippie warned.

The storm raged over them in a series of frightening flashes and thunder claps.

"Nature, man! Wow!" the hippie remarked from the back seat. "This your guitar, man?" he asked, shifting to make himself comfortable among the baggage and garbage that was collecting there. The Plymouth had an acre of trunk with a hole in its floor almost as large, so the back seat served as a closet for Tinker and Blue as well as a crowded bed for one of them who wanted to sleep while the other drove.

"Yeah," Blue answered, rising out of a lazy haze of half thoughts that had overcome him. "I like to pick a little country once in awhile. I write my own songs, you know."

"Country? Country Joe and the Fish, man. Yeah. I know where you're coming from. They're far out, man."

"Do they play the Opry?" Blue asked, trying to place the unfamiliar name.

"They play everywhere, man," the hippie replied from somewhere that sounded like the edge of sleep.

They were coming out the back end of the storm. Blue was humming the tune to "The Red Lobster," looking for more elusive lyrics. Tinker treaded the highway well below the speed zone, scouting the ditches for turtles.

Sometime later, Blue woke to the hippie's voice, excited by the rising dawn.

"Mornings, man. I love the morning. Let me out up ahead. I'm going to have a sun shower."

"If I go up to Canada, I'll look you up," the hippie promised as he slipped himself and his pack out of the back seat to stand on the shoulder of the road.

"Just turn right at Toronto and you can't miss us," Blue said, walking around to the driver's side to relieve Tinker who climbed into the back seat for a snooze.

"Peace, man," the hippie said, raising the two-fingered salute that accompanied the salutation.

Tinker and Blue lifted fingers awkwardly in reply and drove off down the road.

"Whaddya think of your first hippie, Blue?" Tinker asked, shifting bags and the guitar case to make a nest for himself.

"I wouldn't touch a drug after meeting that guy, Tinker. Give me a beer any day. What do you think happens to you when you smoke that stuff?"

"Ahh, Christ," Tinker said suddenly. "That friggin' hippie went and spit his sunflower seed husks all over the floor back here."

"Seed husks?" Blue replied. "What the hell do you mean, seed husks?"

3

"Go west, young man, go west, as the other fellow says, and look at us, Tinker, here we are, almost there," Blue remarked. "So this is Kansas, huh? Looks different in the movies. Tougher. They have tornadoes here. I read one time about a little girl who got caught in one ... no! ... it's a story about a girl who meets a lion and something else..."

"Sounds like *The Wizard of Oz*," Tinker said from behind the steering wheel.

"Right! That movie we saw when we were kids. And there was just this little guy behind the wizard, making people believe in magic. I remember now."

"Wouldn't it be great to visit a different world, Blue? Where people look like us, I mean, not creatures from outer space. I think about that sometimes, visiting a different world," Tinker admitted.

"Not me, boy. I like the world just the way it is. Farmer told me that when he was in Italy during the war, it was like a different world. The Italians don't eat potatoes, Tinker. Spaghetti! That's all. I don't mind eating a can or two a week myself, but I likes me meat and potatoes, as the other fellow says. I'd hate to go somewhere that only had spaghetti to eat."

The guitar was welding with sweat to Blue's belly as he banged out the chords to "The Wild Colonial Boy" which Tinker flawlessly bellowed for the third time through without stopping. Blue's voice moved in to support him on the chorus but Tinker was unaffected by the discord. At summer beach parties and kitchen gatherings where Tinker was always coaxed by friends and even adults to lead the singing, Blue always considered himself an indispensable part of the duo. Tinker, unable to discourage his friend from the enthusiasm of that conviction, had trained himself not to hear the amusical contribution – the way people living beside the ocean no longer hear its eternal roar.

They had been picking up and examining hippies along the way, comparing those specimens to what they knew of the more predictable world where men didn't spill over into the women's domain of abundant hair and sandals and abrupt shifts in fashion. Some offered joints or an unappetizing handful of dried mushrooms or spitball-sized bits of paper called "orange barrel" or "blotter," but Tinker and Blue forsook them all in favour of a cold beer.

Blue was getting more and more comfortably involved in dialogues with the backseat passengers, whether they travelled with them for an hour or a day. He had long ago put the screwdriver back in the cubby hole, convinced that there was no lurking danger in their passengers that he couldn't handle with his own two fists. People who live on sunflower seeds, he noted to Tinker, probably couldn't go two rounds with either of them.

"You know what I think, Tink ... Think, Tink ... Think, Tink, Tink, Tink," plinking the sound on his guitar. "Hey, that's not bad. I'll have to use that in a song. But know what I think, Tink? I think these people are really frigged up. Must be the drugs. Why else would they want the Commies to win in Southeast Asia so they can invade California next?

"After Vietnam, bang! bang! bang! Right across the Pacific and we're next. I learned all about it in Modern World Problems. Made an eighty in it, too. My best subject because it was interesting. My homework was right there on the front page of the *Herald* every day. I just had to glance at it on my way to reading the comics. You should of took it, boy. You'd know more about the world than you learned in chemistry and math."

In high school Blue had tried to reason with his friend. "You can't bullshit your way through trigonometry," he had argued, trying to protect his friend from the pitfalls of high school that included math, science and French. But Tinker, who planned eventually to join his mechanic mentor, Charlie, in Charlie's dream of inventing an engine that ran on oxygen, understood abstractly that a knowledge of math would be beneficial. He persevered and passed, much to Blue's dismay, and they graduated together.

What had set Blue reflecting on his front-page intelligence of the Vietnam war was his conversations with the hippies they picked up, which always found their way back the war. Blue, without a lot of support from Tinker, tried to reason with them about what was at stake if the Communists won the war.

"We have this guy back home, eh, Farmer. He's not a farmer, though. He's a horse trader, but, to quote the other fellow, they call him Farmer because he planted so many seeds in Cape Breton he's going to have more descendants than Abraham. Well, Farmer was in the Second World War with the Cape Breton Highlanders and he told me if it wasn't for our soldiers we'd all be Nazis. I talked to him about Vietnam because he was wounded in Casino and everything so he knows all about war. Farmer said the Commies are just as bad as the Nazis, and there's billions of them in China. In Korea, eh, the Chinese sent more soldiers than the Allies had bullets. They just kept piling up like yellow snow, Farmer said. He wasn't there but he talked to guys who were. We beat them in Korea, so now they're trying to sneak through Vietnam. If they come across the Pacific and the Russians come over the North Pole, which is the big plan, Farmer says, then the world won't be safe for capitalism."

The rides weren't long enough for him to convert anybody with the logic of what he had learned in Modern World Problems and from Farmer, who had taught Blue much of what he understood about the world.

"I bet if it was Canada over there in Vietnam you and I would be full of medals by now, not hiding in a haystack of hair, eh?"

Tinker's thoughts rose slowly out of the deepening silence imposed on him from the heat and the weird menagerie they had been accumulating and discharging over the miles.

"What if they really are burning babies over there, Blue? Everybody says—"

"Hold her right there, buddy! They have a word for that in Modern World Problems. Propaganda! The Communists are geniuses at it. They spread lies and make people believe them. Do you think our side would do anything like that? Even if some crazy soldier wanted to, do you think the President of the United

States would let him? He's the frigging President of the United States, for God's sake. He's even more important than the Prime Minister."

"But everybody we talked to—"

"Everybody we talked to was a frigging hippie, Tinker! Think! Except for waitresses, we haven't talked to a real human being since we crossed the border.... Oh, oh! Look! Let's pick those two up."

Two hippies were standing with heavy packs piled between them on the side of the road on a straight stretch of highway that allowed Tinker and Blue to study them as they approached.

"I can't be sure, but they might be two girls," Blue said with excitement as Tinker glided the Plymouth to the shoulder.

One of the hikers ran over to the open window on Blue's side of the Plymouth.

"Hi!" she said, a warm smile spreading across the most beautiful face Blue had ever seen. "We're going to Colorado. Can you help us?"

A garbled sound that passed for "sure" forced its way through Blue's lips.

"Great!" she said, running back to get her friend and their gear.

"Is Colorado on our route?" Tinker asked as Blue watched her easy gait take her back to their roadside camp.

"It is now, even if we have to go in reverse to get there," Blue cracked, watching the girls pick up their packs. He opened the door to help then when he saw the third figure rise and stretch from its slumber.

"A German shepherd! They got a frigging German shepherd with them, Tinker!" he almost shouted as his well-intentioned open door closed like a suit of armour between him and the lolling-tongued dog that trotted over to sniff the tires.

"This is great," the girl said as she and her friend reorganized the crowded back seat around to accommodate their massive packs and even more massive German shepherd.

Blue watched the curtain of waist-long dark hair ride across her back as she made domestic arrangements to their quarters and settled in beside her friend.

"Lay, Barney!" she commanded, and the dog collapsed at her feet, sniffing sunflower seed husks.

Blue was grateful for the big, friendly name that removed much of his terror of the German shepherd. "Lay, Killer!" or "Lay, Tiger!" might have stopped his heart, which, with the exception of the time he saw Danny Danny Dan's funeral, was racing far faster than any activity that internal organ had engaged in before, spurred on by a beauty he could only have imagined as the fictional subject of one of his best songs.

"I'm Karma. This is Kathy."

"I'm Blue and this here's Tinker," Blue said as Tinker gawked into the back seat through the rearview mirror while easing the car back onto the road.

"Blue is such a wonderful name! I paint so I use a lot of blue," Karma said. "Someone once told me that before the New Testament there's practically no reference to the colour blue, that it's like blue appeared out of the clear blue. Do you think that's true? Some people think that blue was the colour of Christ's eyes, that Jesus Christ brought the colour blue into the world with him and left it behind to assure us he would be back. His mother is always wrapped in blue when you think about it. I think Jesus is so cool! Not like church religion or anything, but like the new Buddha."

Blue felt Tinker's blow to his ribs and glanced at his friend with a glare that rejected Tinker's amusement.

"God's the captain of a whole fleet of churches, as the other feller says," Blue said.

"Oh, are you Christian?"

"Nope, Catholic."

Karma, who described herself as an artist, and Kathy, who wanted to write plays, were on their way to the Human Rainbow Commune in northern Colorado, a slight detour of three or four hundred miles, which Blue offered to make without consulting Tinker who, the first time he had a chance to talk to Blue alone, related two significant observations: "We're getting low on gas money and those girls aren't wearing any brassieres!"

The latter observation severely weakened any financial argument against the detour, so Tinker caved in to Blue's rationale that nobody else was going to pick up two girls with a German shepherd, omitting the part where they had gotten from New Hampshire to Kansas without the Plymouth. Blue also preyed on Tinker's pride. Tinker, like Blue, was the product of a culture whose favourite past-time was telling stories and whose central myth was hospitality. He also sensed that back home this would someday become a story grounded in a generous gesture of their hospitality. So Tinker joined Blue in exporting their Cape Breton hospitality to northern Colorado. An hour later, Kansas was behind them.

Along the way, Tinker and Blue fought over the rearview mirror, which Blue kept adjusting to his benefit instead of the driver's. Growing less shy, he eventually abandoned the rearview mirror and began craning his neck, then shifting to rest on one elbow, finally turning to kneel on the seat with his elbows on the back of it, staring at Karma and trying to find a place to start a conversation. He saw nothing of the Colorado landscape except for the mini-images of it reflected in Karma's dark eyes. Kathy, who was quietly writing in a journal, he barely noticed; Tinker, now the sole owner of the rearview mirror, was picking up that slack.

With his butt on the dash and his chin resting on one hand while the other reached down and stroked Barney's ears, Blue tried to pretend that his only interest in the back seat was the dog.

"I'm so glad Barney's not biting you," Karma said, watching Blue's hand caress her dog. "Barney is my spiritual seeing-eye dog. Animals sense things about people that people can't tell about each other. Like if he growled at you or Tinker, Kathy and I wouldn't have gotten into this car."

"Does he bite many people?" Blue asked, casually retrieving his hand from its close proximity to Barney's mouth before the dog sensed the flock of unspoken fantasies flitting like swallows across Blue's thoughts.

"No, but he growls a lot. I totally trust his instincts. Barney looks after me."

"Like your guardian angel, you mean?"

"Exactly," Karma said brightly. "Do you believe in guardian angels?"

"Well," Blue said thoughtfully, dropping his hand back to Barney's head, "the way I see it is that we're all angels. What I mean is that people turn into angels when they do something for someone else. They may not even notice it themselves. Say, for example, that if Tinker and I had passed you on the road instead of stopping to give you a lift...."

Blue's theological musings were interrupted by Tinker's coughing fit, so severe he had to pull the Plymouth over to the side of the road and get out and walk away from the car. Karma became alarmed when he began rolling on the ground a hundred feet from the car, his arms gripping his sides, but Blue, telling her not to worry, assured her, "I'll fix him!"

Tinker's laughter had ebbed to a head-shaking chuckle a few minutes later as the two friends sat on the shoulder of the road watching Karma and Kathy play with Barney on a patch of grass.

"You see that dog, Tinker? Well, he just met his Santa Claus. I can be as nice as the next guy when I want to, so shake hands with the nicest guy in the world at this moment. If that dog gets car sick he can throw up in my shirt pocket."

—

Blue gazed wistfully at the graceful scene across the road, snapping memory photos that he would never forget. Karma, dressed in torn jeans and peasant blouse, jewelled in turquoise and silver, had an Indian mystique that reminded Blue of "Running Bear," one fine song if he ever heard one. He would never hear it again without drowning heroically holding Karma in his arms.

Tinker, with more interest than obsession, watched Kathy and worried that Blue might actually engineer his scheme of setting them up with these two girls. He was often paired off with some girl who posed a threat to Blue's plans to take her best friend home from a dance. By doubling them up, Blue got the two things he wanted most, the girl and the back seat of the Plymouth. They would park at the beach with WWVA, Wheeling West Virginia, on the radio, and make their moves, beginning with Tinker and Blue telling jokes to each other while fumbling for something bright to say to the girls who sat with their hands on their laps, thinking impenetrable thoughts.

The next step, according to the manual, was to make some mild yawns with wide stretches of the arms until one arm came to rest with innocent casualness across the shoulder of the date. From there, they depended on the music to soften the girls up. "Sixteen Tons" was no good at all for romancing, but "Mary of the Wild Moor" worked wonders. Dead mothers, half-frozen babies and old men ripping out their hair had a way of making girls mellow enough to kiss. Blue had even added that song to his repertoire for that very reason.

But passionate kisses and brief caresses were no preparation for what Tinker might be expected to know if Blue manoeuvred himself into the back seat of the Plymouth this time. And despite Blue's streetcorner chit-chat with the guys, Tinker knew that Blue was in the same sorry state of inexperience as himself. Tinker could account for every night of Blue's life since they were in grade nine and thought it unlikely that his best friend had been any more successful before then. He was counting on the fact that neither girl had shown the least bit of romantic interest in either of them, a point that Blue had overlooked, to save him from his own ignorance.

While Karma and Kathy prepared a picnic of apples, oranges, raisins and sunflower seeds, Blue coaxed Barney across the road to the field where he tossed a stick. Barney watched curiously as the one-way boomerang arced through the air and landed in the grass an arm's throw away.

"Fetch, boy," Blue commanded while Barney gazed up at him, tail wagging in the slow rhythm of uncertain friendship. "Go on, now. Get it!" Blue instructed with as much success as his own teachers had had in instructing him. Finally, he half led, half dragged Barney to the site of the fallen stick and tried to shove it in the dog's unwilling mouth, causing the tail to stop its movements in favour of a low growl from the other end. For the next several minutes Barney followed Blue back and forth across the field as the human threw and then retrieved the stick while the dog tried to make sense of the activity. The futility of trying to teach a three-year-old dog new tricks finally dawned on Blue, and he walked back to the picnic site with Barney at his side.

"Kind of makes those dead animals we passed on the highway look appetizing, doesn't it?" Blue remarked to Tinker as he examined the spread of food while Karma and Kathy were filling a canteen with fresh water from a spring.

"This is great," Blue said to Karma as she quartered the food into shares and passed him his. He passed on the sunflower seeds.

Tinker, playing Russian roulette with his own fears and feelings, stretched out beside Kathy, leaning on one elbow, flicking raisins in the air, catching them in his open mouth which kept him from having to use it to converse with the attractive girl who seemed as much at a loss for words as himself.

"This is so beautiful," Karma said, absorbing the world around her with a slow sweep of her eyes.

"It certainly is," Blue agreed, absorbing Karma with the lingering gaze of his own eyes while devouring an apple in three greedy bites and tossing the core over his shoulder.

"I suppose that's all right," Karma remarked, watching the gesture. "Apples are biodegradable."

"Sprayed with DDT, you mean?" Blue inquired, but before Karma could reply to his confusion over her choice of six-syllable words, Barney dropped the apple core in Blue's lap. He tossed it again and Barney snagged it out of the sky and brought it back to Blue. After a half a dozen futile attempts to be rid of the apple core Blue stuck it in his shirt pocket, but not before noticing Karma's awe over the neat trick he was able to teach her dog – picking up litter.

Gathering up all traces of their presence more conscientiously than Blue and Tinker might have done if they were alone in the spot with some take-out burgers and fries, the four travellers re-entered the brown and rusting Plymouth, the two front-seat drivers following the vague directions of the back-seat passengers as they made their way toward the Human Rainbow Commune.

5

Reaching the Human Rainbow Commune required the service of six separate roads once the main highway had been left behind. Each road diminished in quality as it lured them to the cooler heights of the eastern slope of the Rocky Mountains until the Plymouth came to the end of a long rut, parking amid an anarchy of architecture. Wooden igloos and log cabins, a swayback barn and an outhouse formed a semblance of a meaningful circle around a small commons, stained darkly at the centre by bonfire ashes. People moved about with listless ease, an attitude evidently adopted and copied by a few goats, one cow and two horses that Blue estimated were worth maybe ten bucks as pet food.

Karma and Kathy coaxed Tinker and Blue out of the car, introducing them to a rollcall of names that ranged from Bob and Mary to Capricorn and Tulip. The bead-and-bangle fashion show overwhelmed Blue who found himself standing on a mountain somewhere high above the civilized world where nothing familiar existed, no streets or stores, flagpoles or monuments. It reminded him a little of when Tinker would drive a carload of friends to the top of Cape Mabou with a case of beer, parking in an abandoned hayfield where they could get hammered without worrying about the cops. This was on a much larger scale, one Blue found as difficult to grasp as the height of the mountain he was standing on.

Nor could Blue figure out what was holding things together. No one was in charge of the commune, according to Karma, just a bunch of people appreciating their lives. He appreciated his with plumbing.

They were just in time for supper, a point several people made, and which told Blue just how strapped for news they were up here, but it was an invitation his own hunger was grateful for until it was time to eat. Pots and dishes of food were brought from the living quarters that were circled like wagons against the wildness around them. A community table was set and laden with food, but with nothing he or Tinker recognized. Blue sampled a grainy substance called tabouli and with undiplomatic frankness gave his opinion of it by imitating a barf before he moved on to the bean salad before finally settling for a pound of heavy brown bread with butter.

"Know what this place needs, Tinker? A good squirt of ketchup," Blue remarked to his friend who was spooning out his second helping of tabouli. "You got guts eating that stuff, boy." But Tinker wasn't feeling conspiratorial. "It's not that bad, you know," was all he said as he wandered away from Blue to accidentally turn up somewhere in Kathy's proximity.

Without Tinker's company, and Karma nowhere to be seen, Blue wandered over to the only other familiar thing he could cling to, an ancient bay mare. For the first time since they had crossed the Canso Causeway, Blue missed Farmer, missed driving around in the horse trader's truck watching him cheat a living for himself. Blue became a one-person audience for Farmer when he was only twelve years old and had earned what few bucks he could while serving an informal apprenticeship over the next eight years. But Farmer, by his own admission, was among the last of a dying breed. "The trouble with these modern times, Blue," the horse trader once lamented, "is that they've taken a great profession like horse trading and turned it into a used car lot." Blue knew he could never sell cars, and horses were quickly vanishing from the Cape Breton landscape. He assessed the mare, his quick hands feeling its legs for heat or pain. Then turning gentle, those same hands stroked the mare's mane.

A hippie approached him, asking if he liked horses.

"You bet, boy. This one yours?"

The black hippie, about his own age, froze, studying Blue's smile for a hint of menace.

"I thought I left all that shit down there," he said with a sweep of his hand that took in the whole world. "Don't call me 'boy' again," the order enforced by an assertive fore-finger.

"Anything you say, buddy," Tinker said, mystified. "Where ya from?"

"South," the hippie whom Blue now recalled was named Cory, replied.

"The South! No wonder you're hiding up here. I read all about that stuff in Modern World Problems, segregation in Alabama and apathy in Africa and everything."

"You mean apartheid?"

"Whatever," Blue went on. "It made a guy wonder what he'd be like if he lived in one of those places."

"I have an idea what you'd be like," Cory said, wrapping his words in a soft smile.

"Yeah? Well, I wish to hell I knew, but when I thought about it, all I knew anything about, really, was home. Cape Breton. Where I come from. And we're clannish." The word caused Cory to raise curious eyebrows.

"If I'm walking down a street in Toronto, eh, and I see one of you guys, or even if it's a Chinaman or a Frenchie, and he's wearing a Cape Breton tartan shirt or necktie or something, well, I'm going to stop him and we're going to get a bottle and maybe sing Charlie MacKinnon songs or something, and tell a few stories. I bet we find somebody we both know back home before we get half way down the bottle. I mean, the island's big, but it's not *that* big! Even Farmer, this horse trader I know back home, well, he sampled all the colours and he says there's no difference. Of course, he was talking about women.

"That's not to say there aren't guys back home I can't stand. Punched a few of them, as a matter of fact, but there's really nobody on the island I hate. Even the Campbells and the MacDonalds sort of get along. So on studying that issue in Modern World Problems, race and colour and stuff, I came to the conclusion that segregation was stupid. Got a good mark on it, too."

"Doesn't sound like any place I've lived," Cory said, rubbing the mare's muzzle.

"Best place in the world. Ask anybody who lives there. You plow that field with her?" Blue asked, studying the large garden and the ancient plow lying nearby.

"Her and the other one," Cory said. "We bought the pair of them in the spring from a man down the hill for two hundred dollars."

"You paid two hundred dollars for these minkers? The man's name wasn't Farmer, by any chance?"

"No. Mister Wood. He was happy to find a home for them."

"I'll bet he was," Blue said.

"Oh, he was. But I don't like living things being bought and sold, and I don't like people who do it for a living, like that friend of yours. Farmer?"

Blue thought about this for a moment.

"That's your history speaking, I bet. But back where I come from you can't eat tourists in February, as the other fellow says. In the summer, Cape Breton is this really great place. On the side of the island where I live we have the warmest water north of Florida, and the whole island is full of mountains and rivers and people you know, but it's like I just said, you can't eat tourists in the winter. You have to do whatever it takes to make enough money to get by on. As for Farmer, that's his living. So it depends on how you look at it, I guess, but if everybody was like you, feeling sorry for the horses, what good would they be to us?"

"Not any good, at all," Cory answered. "That's why I'm glad to see horses working on farms or racing at a track. It gives us a reason for keeping them around, because when people have no use for something, they get rid of it, or lock them in a ghetto."

"Well," Blue answered thoughtfully. "You might have something there. Wherever I see a tractor I never see a horse."

"They're just so beautiful, man. My image of freedom is a mustang running wild. Nobody owns it. It just is."

"Maybe," Blue said, "but if I were to walk off with this nag tonight, though I can't imagine why I would, you'd say I stole it, wouldn't you, because somebody owns it, right? You. Or all of you hippies here.

"Don't get me wrong. I like horses, and I've seen some fine-looking ones in my day. Farmer got two thousand bucks for one once," Blue said, "but a free horse ... there's no such as a thing, as the other fellow says, no such as a thing!"

Behind them, in the growing darkness, a bonfire, fed by deadwood, roared to life. Cory and Blue walked back together, leaving the mare to forage for herself. Cory pointed to the star-punctured sky above the mountain stillness while Blue, who had never imagined mustangs without the perfect toss of his own lasso, glanced back at the misshapen form of the mare and shook his head.

6

Around the bonfire, some of the commune members stared off into a world of their own lost thoughts while others passed around joints which Blue and Tinker rejected, or sipped from a wine bottle which they did not refuse. Some people murmured to each other, and one girl sang to herself until her song spread its influence around the circle, drawing some people into its soft chorus while others paused to listen.

Blue took a swig from the bottle and passed it to the one who called himself Capricorn.

"Good stuff," he said.

"Tulip made it," Capricorn told him.

"She makes her own wine?" Blue responded, looking at the hippie sitting beside Capricorn. He was impressed. "You'd be a big hit with some people I know back home. They drink 74. Ever try it? Sweet but cheap, as the other feller says."

When the bottle made its way back to him again, it was down to its last taste. Blue drained it and tossed it over his shoulder only to hear it drop at his feet a moment later. Barney panting for a pat, lay at his feet.

—

In a gasoline alley near Cheyenne, their friendship had been cemented. Blue found himself alone when Karma and Kathy went to use a laundromat and Tinker opened the hood to investigate an unfamiliar tick. Across the street, a hamburger joint beckoned him in, so Blue, not wanting to alert Karma to his carnivorous ways, nor disturb Tinker at his obsession, quietly slipped over and entered. When he came out with a fistful of meat between buns, chomping on his first bite, Barney was waiting. Half way through the burger, Blue broke before the unrelenting and pitiful stare of the dog. "Probably feeds you sunflower seeds, eh, boy?" he said, surrendering the last half of the patty to Barney. While Barney swallowed, Blue crumpled the napkin and made a bad jump shot toward the garbage bucket, missed and left it there. Barney retrieved and returned it, forcing Blue to walk over and drop the evidence in the can. When they got back into the car, Barney leapt into the front seat, propping himself between Tinker and Blue, and the rest of the way they travelled in that formation, Blue's arm around Barney, his thoughts surrounding Karma.

—

Capricorn was older than the rest, Blue guessed. Perhaps even thirty. His hair hung in two long braids down his chest and a buckskin jacket protected him from the cool mountain air. He wore sandals. When he stood up to feed the fire, Blue watched him, and decided that, whether he admitted it or not, Capricorn was in charge here. Blue saw a subtle deference in everyone's approach to him, and despite the ease with which he answered questions, solved problems, and spoke of non-violence and harmony, the sinewy stealth with which he moved suggested to

Blue that Capricorn could survive anywhere, on any terms. The terms chosen confused Blue.

The second bottle of wine circled the bonfire and when it reached Blue barely any of it was gone. If these people are trying to get drunk, they're not very good at it, he thought, opening his throat for a generous share of the bottle's delights. He passed it to Capricorn.

"What's going on here, buddy?" he asked.

As if he hadn't heard, Capricorn stared into the fire, the bottle, still untasted, in his hand.

"It's about being a part of something, not being apart from it," Capricorn said finally without shifting his focus to Blue. "There's an unpopular teaching that you'll find among the greatest people who ever lived – not the most powerful, but the greatest – that says that we are responsible for what happens on this planet, and to it, and to each other. Buddha said it. Christ said it. Ghandi said it. King said it. And it bothers a whole lot of people that there are other people who listen to those words, who want to be a part of that vision, that truth."

"Yeah," Blue said. "Tinker and me are a part of something. We're a part of Cape Breton, two little chips off the old block, as the other fellow says, eh, Tink?

"We'll always be a part of Cape Breton, boy, but how long will you be a part of this?" Blue asked, the thin air and wine revving him a bit.

"We're here now. That's all that matters. At this moment, everything on the planet is perfectly safe from us," Capricorn explained. "I've done enough damage to it already."

"I could tell you weren't born no frigging saint," Blue said. "What's ya do?"

"I've shed that concept of myself and I have no interest in reviving it," Capricorn said, standing to bring the conversation to a close. He played with the fire, forcing it to flare again.

Blue looked around the bonfire, reminded of bonfires from other summers in a more familiar setting. Driftwood piled upon the sandy beach of his hometown, him and Tinker and the rest of the gang bantering out of a life-long knowledge of each other, urging girls over the beach for a kiss and a quick feel.

—

Yeah, we were a part of something there, Blue thought, something as good as this anyway. So we hunt and fish a little, and buy and sell animals – eat them, too. And Christ, punching a guy in the head isn't violence, not when he's your best friend or your cousin, and back home everybody's either or. And we don't write protest songs; we dance to a music that's a thousand years old. The priests and the politicians might have the power but the fiddler is the king of the island – and when he's done playing there's stories to be told, or old wounds to be argued again, some of them as old as the music. When your people and your culture's been slaughtered on the fields of Culloden and the remains of it is gathered up just like Cory's people – except that we weren't even worth the buying and selling part – and shipped to a new land to try to piece together what they could from what was left, you have to admire what they did, because you're the result, and if it ain't perfect, well, that's just too frigging bad!

—

All he knew here were Tinker, sitting across the fire from him beside Kathy, and Karma who moved around speaking to everyone, not ignoring him but treating them all as if they were as special to her as he wanted to be.

"Give us a song, there, Tinker," he said, but Tinker shrugged off the request, saying he didn't know any songs they might like to hear. It wasn't until Kathy prodded him that Tinker relented, breaking uncomfortably into "The Wild Colonial Boy," and it wasn't long before Tinker's natural enthusiasm forgot his foreign audience and he was deep into the role he loved. Tinker's Irish rebel songs didn't offend anyone at the Human Rainbow Commune that Blue could notice, although he had hoped that Tinker's singing would drive home the differences between them and the hippies. Instead, everyone, including Capricorn, became caught up in Tinker's energy and quickly joined the rousing chorus of "By the Rising of the Moon." Blue, sullen, refused to contribute his own voice, oblivious to the mercy of that decision, nor any of his own songs. Instead, he watched Karma, who smiled at him when their eyes met but who seemed to lose track of him immediately after looking away.

The fire burned down without anyone re-feeding it, and people began wandering away to their own places. Blue watched Karma wave good night and disappear into the darkness, then watched it swallow Tinker and Kathy. Blue stood up, said good night to the straggling remnants of the night's festivities and walked to the car. He stretched out on the back seat with Barney on the floor beside him and fell asleep waiting for Tinker to return.

7

Tinker's non-committal smile told Blue nothing of the night he had spent, but the morning sun, baking the interior of the car, was already too hot for Blue to pester the truth from his groggy friend in the front seat. The air outside the car, cool and refreshing, evaporated the wine-rage of the previous night. The commune appeared to be already several hours into its day as Blue walked to where Capricorn and Cory were working on the construction of another hut, offering his help. They sent him to eat first, pointing to the pot on an outside stone fireplace covered with a grate.

Blue was delighted to discover that the pot, nearly empty, contained porridge laced with raisins and walnuts. He plopped a ladle-full into a bowl, ate and went back to the construction site. From the rafters, surveying the commune, he could see no sign of Karma but he could see Tinker, who the heat had also beaten out of his sleep, roaming around a van in the yard.

"Your friend said last night that he was going to have a look at the Volkswagen this morning. It quit last week and nobody can get it going," Capricorn said.

"Well, you're lucky there," Blue informed him. "Tinker's a mechanical genius. Ran a garage back home for three weeks and everything. Someday, he's going back to Cape Breton and buy that same garage."

Blue, realizing that he was the third man on a two-man job, jumped down from the hut, explaining that he would see if Tinker needed a hand.

"I like the way he works, man" Capricorn said. "He's been tuning himself in to that van for twenty minutes now. Seems to want to get to know it before he starts. Very Zen, man."

Blue joined Tinker as his friend strolled around the van, his hand feeling its way while he studied the vehicle.

"Blue, where the hell do you suppose the motor is in this thing? Charlie was right, you know. He told me that the Volkswagen was Hitler's last revenge. Opened one of those Bugs once and the motor was full of suitcases. The engine was in the trunk, if you can believe that. But look at this thing. No nose and no trunk. If I can get into her, though, I know I can fix her."

Karma and Kathy joined them, and the way Tinker moved toward Kathy told Blue more than Tinker's silence had. A sense of betrayal rippled toward the back of his mind to be dealt with later. Karma was what he wanted to deal with now, although he was baffled about what that thought meant and oblivious to the contradiction.

It was Kathy who unlocked the mysteries of the Volkswagen van for Tinker, showing him what she had seen other people do, lifting a panel in the back of the van, giving him access to its internal organs which he pounced upon immediately, pulling loose every part that could be removed by hand before he started tapping its stationary parts with his ballpeen hammer.

—

Being a product of Charlie's scholarly attentions, Tinker used a hammer to gain access to problem areas more frequently than conventionally trained mechanics. The hammer, Charlie had tutored him, was the neglected tool of the trade, yet it was the most fundamental tool known to mankind, being the one that most faithfully represented the stone-age club. "It got us from there to here and a man should never lose track of his roots," Charlie said. When more modern concepts like wrenches and screwdrivers failed, the hammer could always be counted on.

—

Karma's general invitation to go for a swim was turned down by Tinker who had work to do, and Kathy who offered to stay and help, but not by Blue who was prepared to swan dive into a bonfire with her if she asked.

As Karma and Blue walked away, followed by Barney who was happy to have a moment of undivided loyalties, Kathy sat in the grass watching Tinker's oily hands work their wonders, removing parts of the engine she thought were as permanently attached as her head to her neck.

"That's the Germans for you," Tinker narrated. "They make an engine that won't quit and when it does they dare you to fix it. Our cars now, the ones from Detroit and Windsor, they make them to break down so they'll be easy to fix, but the Germans have to spend a lot of time inventing an engine that won't breakdown just to fuck people around when they do. Sorry about that word – I was ten before I found out it wasn't Gaelic."

"Oh, I've heard the word before," Kathy said.

"You'll never hear Blue use the word, though. He used to. As a matter of fact I picked it up from him. But there's this guy who used to be from back home, Long Lauchie they called him. Well, he had this curse he'd say all the time, 'Lightning Jesus.' Every time something went wrong, Long Lauchie'd say 'Lightning Jesus.' He used to work in a hardrock mine in Ontario and one time he was grabbing the skip, this big iron bucket for taking up the ore, but what he didn't know was that there was a thunder and lightning storm going on up on the surface. By Jesus, just when he grabbed the bucket, a bolt of lightning hit the headframe, came down the steel cable and fried him.

"When Blue heard that story, well he just gave up saying the F word. Said that if Long Lauchie was struck dead by lightning for saying 'Lightning Jesus,' then Blue didn't want some priest or the police coming to his mother's door to tell her how he died – though, there's far worse ways to die," Tinker said, sharing a secret smile with Kathy.

Tinker was more used to singing while he worked. Except for Charlie's hovering guidance and Blue's awed approval, no one had ever just sat there and watched him work before, but, remembering the new and wonderful experience Kathy had led him through the night before, this was something he wanted her to know about him.

"I know this guy back home, eh, Charlie. He taught me everything I know. Well, Charlie was up in a big hospital in Halifax for three weeks one time. This car blew up in the garage, but that's another story. Anyway, Charlie was walking around the hospital and he saw this guy in an iron lung and it gave him an idea. He figured that if an iron lung could breathe for a guy, why couldn't it breathe for a car? That's what keeps us going, right, oxygen. If you breathe in the oxygen in the front end, Charlie thinks, and breathe it out the back end, it would give you propulsion, which is what makes things move.

"When I explained to Blue about this front-end-back-end business, he said it sounded like we'd have to train the car to fart which I thought was kind of funny, so I told Charlie. Charlie thought it was a great idea. What's a fart, he says, but gas? If you take the oxygen in, he says, and turn it into gas and ignite it then you get jet propulsion. That might be the missing key to our idea, he told me, but said not to say anything to Blue because he'll expect to get a cut of the royalties, Charlie thinks. That's about the only important thing I never told Blue, but I'll give him some of my money when the cheques start rolling in.

"Charlie's been writing to hospitals all over the place for a long time now asking if they have a spare iron lung he could have. He's in a good place for looking, too. When tourists stop for gas and the licence plate says New York or something, Charlie always asks, 'Do you have any hospitals back where you come from?' and gets an address and writes them. Once we get the iron lung, though, Charlie figures we'll have to invent a stomach for it because nobody but a cow has a spare one of those."

To Kathy, Tinker and Charlie's theory sounded no less mysterious than $E=mc^2$, which she had studied and comprehended about as well as ninety-nine per cent of the world's population. What excited her, though, was not the physics of the challenge Tinker and Charlie had set for themselves, but its ecological implications.

First, she had to define for Tinker the meaning of the word "ecological," as he tried tracking her through an elaborate explanation of the fragile eco-systems endangered by fossil fuel consumption, of multinational conspiracies to foil development of cheap or even free solar energy.

"You want to give this planet one of its greatest gifts, Tinker, an engine that runs on oxygen. Maybe it could even be adapted to factories and everything. That would force oil companies and coal companies to stop raping the earth and poisoning it with its own bile."

"I wasn't thinking of putting anybody out of work," Tinker said as the scale of his own mind was revealed to him. "If I put coal companies out of work I could never go home again. Coal's all we got in Cape Breton, really. Pulp and fish, of course, but in the town where I come from, we're down to our last coal mine and barely making a living at that. They'd skin me alive if my invention closed that mine."

"But you could put everybody to work building the engine you and Charlie are inventing. It's your engine. You can build it wherever you want," Kathy argued.

"You've got something there, I suppose," Tinker said, trying to imagine his father, who was in his thirty-third year underground, giving it up to go to work for his own son.

"But Tinker, promise me you won't talk too much about what you are doing. It could get you into a lot of trouble. The FBI works for the government, and the government works for the multinationals and they don't want people like you threatening the establishment. They'd love to get their hands on people like you and Capricorn...."

"Is he inventing an engine, too?"

"No, he's inventing something even worse as far they're concerned, a spiritual revolution. The FBI are looking for him. There's this one agent ... well maybe Capricorn will tell you about it himself, but those same people, along with the oil companies, will be looking for you if they learn about your invention."

—

Karma, Blue and Barney stood looking up at a waterfall which dropped thirty feet into a deep pool before the river journeyed on along its rocky course. Beyond the grassy riverbank a wall of trees protected the natural chamber, catching the warmth of the sun and holding it there in a stillness that was enhanced by the torrent of water roaring above them. After absorbing it in silence for a moment, Karma turned to Blue.

"Ready?" she asked, slipping off her blouse and jeans in an easy gesture that left her standing naked beside the river, preparing to dive.

Blue, his shirt off, froze in embarrassed wonder watching Karma turn from him and propel herself into the air, arcing into the water, a mirage disappearing before his eyes, surfacing suddenly at the far side of the pool, waving for him to join her. Blue's thumbs hooked into the band of his underwear but no force on earth could give him the strength to follow through. Instead, removing the rosary that he wore around his neck like a medal, he raced to the river's edge and jumped, hoping to bury in the depths of the water the awkward tent that had misshapen his cotton fig leaf.

—

One April, when he was twelve, during the spring break-up of polar ice that covered the Gulf of St. Lawrence all winter, Blue and some friends spent an afternoon riding the loose pans of ice like rafts, propelling them with clothes-props. When rafting turned to jousting each other, Blue was knocked from his ice raft into the water. He walked home in pant legs stiff as stove pipes and suffered from hypothermia. The water in this river was warmer, but not much.

—

Karma swam over to where he treaded water while listening to his own chattering teeth, and began talking about how refreshing it was before leaping and disappearing like a trout in front of him. He was not too cold to take in the glimpses of her that her playfulness exposed, and when she lay back floating like an offering to the sky, the length of her hair spread across the surface of the pool in a dark ripple. He grew aware that part of himself was torn between the throb of desire, and the desire for that same part of his anatomy to shrink into itself before it froze to death.

Still, he tried to copy Karma's gender-indifferent enthusiasm, but all his imagination and energies could not un-focus themselves from the fact that he was frolicking in a river with a bare-naked girl who didn't seem to notice anything peculiar about their circumstances.

Karma swam away from him, surfacing and disappearing as she moved toward the waterfall, feeling her way carefully up its rocky ledge to stand under the cascade, arms stretched above, inviting the river to wash over her. Blue listened to the joyful laughter thread its way through the river's own rugged voice, tempering its fierceness. Inside her massive shower, Karma turned slowly, lost in delight, while Blue watched, strangely distracted from his general points of anatomical interest to appreciate the shimmering aura of beauty that was Karma herself, a wholeness that overwhelmed him with a longing for something more than he had ever imagined before.

Karma stepped out from behind the veil of water to stand above him, smiling, then dove, the dive taking her under him where he could feel a gentle electricity from the trail of her hair brush against his chest. She swam to the bank and hoisted herself onto it; Blue, turning blue, gratefully followed.

Karma dabbed herself with her blouse, dropped it, walked over to where Barney was shading himself in the meager shadow of a large, flat rock, and sat on it.

"Would you mind if I meditate for a while?" she asked Blue who, drying himself, discovered his own lustful resurgence and crouched on the grass to conceal it.

"No," he answered, watching her position herself on the rock, hair draping over her breasts, ankles moving effortlessly across their opposite thighs, hands resting on her knees, thumbs and forefingers forming perfect circles, lids dropping over her brown eyes, silence emanating from her.

Blue lay on his belly, studying her, no longer needing to make it a covert activity. The chill of the water played only a minor role in the trembling that now shook his body and threw his thoughts into a confused upheaval of fears and desires. Nothing in Farmer's encyclopedic revelations about what women really want seemed to apply here the way he thought it did in the back seat of the Plymouth where his confidence had always been reinforced by the certainty that he would be offered a little but refused a lot by the girls he dated, girls who did not lounge around the Plymouth, meditating in casual nudity.

Over and over again, Blue's imagination rose from the spot where he lay and wandered across the clearing to the rock where Karma sat, not knowing whether to talk or to touch, to caress or take her.

Karma's eyes opened slowly, staring into his own which had been caught at their hungry task.

"Do you want to do it?" she asked.

"Do you?" Blue gasped with disbelief. "Yeah, sure, if you want to." He struggled to remain calm as Karma stood and walked toward him.

"Here," she said, positioning him. "It's easy, really. Just cross your legs and put your hands like this," she instructed a disappointed Blue. Taking her position in front of him, Karma told him to close his eyes and go very still inside.

Closing his eyes was the last thing Blue wanted to do, but he was so grateful that she hadn't recognized his misinterpretation that he slammed his lids shut like a little boy forcing himself to sleep.

The sun poured over his shoulders as he sat there wondering what was supposed to happen, and whether or not it was a pagan activity that he would have to confess along with the litany of impure thoughts that he had already racked up that day. If nothing else, it relaxed him more than he had been relaxed since they had started this hippie adventure at the river's edge. The greatest appeal of just sitting there was that he was in Karma's presence for as long as it went on, an appeal reaffirmed by a series of just-to-make-sure peeks. Ending the moment with a slow walk back to the commune was what he wanted to delay, so he was prepared to sit there until the next Ice Age.

When he looked again, Karma was watching him, her meditation obviously over. Smiling softly, she reached across and put her hands in his, allowing a subtle transfer of control to take place, one that he tested with a slight pressure, pulling her toward him, ready to allow her resistance, and to pretend that he had never tried anything at all, but there was no resistence. Karma's mouth grazed his, her lips soft, her hands tracing first his face, then his shoulders and arms, while Blue's hands, with a knowledge of their own, followed her lead all the way into realms he had never explored before.

Later, still undressed, Blue sat on the riverbank. Karma, lying on her back, her head in his lap, toyed playfully with his disheveled hair. Blue clung to the moment while trying to sort through a tangle of thoughts. He had lost track of the number of times Farmer had left him alone in the truck to smoke the horse trader's tobacco while he disappeared into a house for twenty minutes or half an hour, returning to the boy with a wink and the promise that "Someday, we'll have to get you some of that." It was a promise unfulfilled during the years when Farmer teased Blue about the boy having to marry his own hand. Farmer's harem of widows and unhappy housewives, Blue believed, would eventually result in himself discovering the pleasure of servicing women in heat, as Farmer described them. A few drinks and don't take No! for an answer was all he needed to know, really, according to his mentor, and the rest would come naturally. He looked at Karma and felt a vague gratitude.

—

Tinker had reassembled the Volkswagen's engine into an approximation of itself and turned the key. A cheer rose from across the commune as its residents heard the dead van groan, grind and finally roar to life. Behind the wheel, Tinker nodded to himself with satisfaction. Then, looking through the windshield his smug pride turned to a smile as he saw his buddy whose usually groomed and duck-tailed hair was parted in the middle and hanging down well over his ears.

8

"You know what's wrong with those people, Tink?" Blue said, picking up the thread of a favourite theme as the Plymouth rolled down a western slope of the Rocky Mountains. "They don't come from anywhere. Me and you, we got a home. One thing about Cape Breton, you can scrub at it all day with Javex and not get it out of your system. It's like the coal dust around the old man's eyes, there for life. That's a good thing to know because if we run out of money we can wire somebody back home to send us a hundred bucks which we'll probably have to do, and we'll get it, because if you ask, you shall receive, as the other fellow says.

"Take Cory back there. Says he's from down South. What does that tell you, Tinker? Nothing, because everything south of where you happen to be standing at the moment is down south, right? And Capricorn comes from New York but never wants to go back there, he says. Now what kind of a way is that to talk about your hometown? And Karma, she's a child of the Universe. Figure that one out. Her past life isn't important, she says, as if her soul migrated like a dead Buddhist into an ant or a butterfly. It's fine for her to be a child of the Universe as long as she doesn't need help from home, I suppose, but if she does, who does she phone? Who's the Father of the Universe? The Lord may work in mysterious ways, to quote the other fellow, but he don't wire money, Tinker. He don't wire money."

A few days into their visit at the Human Rainbow Commune, Capricorn asked Tinker and Blue about their plans. It was a friendly chat which didn't fail to make the point that if they were planning to stay they would be expected to accept the commune's vision which included, among other things, the recognition that the earth belonged to itself, as did each living thing occupying it.

"We don't expect you to grasp that primary principle overnight," Capricorn told them, "but we try to help each other work in that direction by owning nothing ourselves and sharing what we hold in common. If you want to come along with us, and believe me, it's a tough trip, man, you're welcome. If not, then perhaps you shouldn't exhaust our hospitality. Think about it, ok?"

The Cape Breton summit was held in the front seat of the Plymouth where Blue discussed with Tinker the obvious to him fact that they had just been thrown out of Human Rainbow Commune.

"I don't think that's what he meant," Tinker reasoned. "He just said that we could belong if we want, either in or out. It's up to us. What do you want to do?"

Blue was angry over being ripped apart by choices he didn't want to make. The image of waking beside Karma put him in direct conflict with everything else he knew about his life, which didn't include weaving baskets in a commune.

"I bet that bastard wants Karma for himself. That's why he's doing this, you know."

"Capricorn and Tulip are together, Blue. And you and Karma. And Kathy and me. Maybe we should try it."

"Look, Tinker," Blue argued, "we're Catholics. We can't get involved in all this sharing shit. Sure, the sex part might be a sin but we can dump all that in one confession. It's the rest that scares me. Think about this, Tinker. Commune. Commune-ism. Communism! Communists are atheists, everybody knows that."

"I'm not so sure, Blue," Tinker replied, his words eluding his feelings.

"Well, how sure are you about this, old buddy? Did you hear what that hippie said? He said nobody here owns anything, everybody owns everything. That means the Plymouth, Tinker. How do feel about that?"

Tinker ran his hands tenderly along the rim of the steering wheel as if it was Kathy's skin. There was nothing else in the world he owned that meant as much to him as the rusting vehicle he had brought back to life with his own two hands and Charlie's help.

"Well, what'll it be, buddy?" Blue asked. "Me or this place, because I'm going down the road."

They had left the following morning, but first Blue had to drag Barney out of the car where he stubbornly insisted on joining them. Then Capricorn told them that he was sorry about something called the bad vibes that he felt from them. "Every soul has its own timetable," he assured Tinker when they shook hands. Blue mumbled something that passed for politeness.

Kathy and Tinker took their goodbye a private distance from the gathering of hippies who flashed hand signals like umpires and said "Peace" and "Love" as if one syllable could soothe Blue's hurt feelings.

Karma squeezed his hand as the Plymouth began to move, then released it as easily as if she were freeing petals to the wind. Barney chased the car for miles before they managed to lose him in dust and exhaustion.

"It's just you and me now, buddy, the way it's suppose to be," Blue said, trying to draw his friend back from a distance of thought that didn't confide itself to Blue. "Next stop, San Fran. It's going to be great to plant our feet in the real world for a change. How we doing for gas?"

"We'll be alright," Tinker smiled. "Full tank. Ever since Charlie's accident I make it a policy not to work on anybody's car if they have gas in the tank, not if I can help it. I syphoned their Volkswagen back there but the only thing large enough to hold all that gas was the Plymouth. Never got around to putting it back."

"Same old Tinker," Blue said, punching his friend on the shoulder.

—

"Tinker?" Blue asked, wandering back from recent memories. "Do you think Karma is presumptuous?"

Tinker rummaged around in his mind for Blue's point, which was not always what he said.

"You mean promiscuous?"

"Whatever. I mean, I really like her, eh? I'm not going to be boasting about this. When we get back to the John Beaton's Corner she's not going to be anybody else's business. I don't care what that Caprihorny says, everybody owns something and I own this, but you were there, buddy. You know. What I can't figure is why a girl like that would have anything to do with a guy like me. She's about the most beautiful thing I ever saw except for my own mother and as a good son I have to lie about that. I mean, I've seen the women Farmer bangs. I'd be in and out of the house in twenty minutes, too. But when I get to thinking about all the women in Cape Breton who wouldn't touch Farmer with a ten-foot pole, what it comes to is the best and the most of them. Why is that? Sure, I know some women can't stand the smell of a horse, but most of them just can't stand the man. I like Farmer, you know that. But if Karma knew him I bet she would've made a big circle to get around me. I'm not rotten or anything, but I'm not exactly a hippie's delight, if you know what I mean.

"Christ, I couldn't even talk to her. Made me a good listener, though, but trying to follow her conversations was like trying to follow the flight of a bat. I think she really believes all this peace and love shit, I mean *really* believes it. A girl like that would have to believe a lot of strange things to believe in me, and that's what she said, Tinker, that she believes in me. The apostles didn't believe in Jesus Christ in three days, I bet, but she says she does, and that as soon as I find myself I'll believe in me, too. Find myself! Now you tell me, Tinker, what the hell does that mean? If anybody is lost, it must be Karma because whoever she was in her *previous life* didn't drive around in the back seat of a rusty Plymouth, I'll tell you that, so her head must be really screwed up to screw somebody like me."

"That's what I thought," Tinker said with a laugh. "Look, she liked you. What's so hard to believe about that? Hell, I even know you and I still like you. Kathy liked me. I don't care why, I'm just glad she did, but you know what scares me, Blue? What if my time with her was the best time I'm ever going to have in my whole life?"

"You know what I remember most about Kansas, Tinker?" Blue asked.

"Meeting Karma, I suppose."

"Nope. How cool it was in Kansas. It was barely a hundred degrees back there. Cool as a cucumber, as the other fellow says. Where are we now? Utah? Boy, this place is for the birds except that it would cook them in mid flight," Blue said. They drove through a night heat that hadn't noticed the sun's departure, forgetting to dip by a single degree according to the sweat still covering them, making him homesick for the cool evenings of other summers.

"Tinker, what do you think of this plan? We get out to San Francisco, get somebody to take our pictures with some frigging hippies for evidence and then we head back home where we belong?"

"Sounds good to me."

Strange things live
On the floor of the sea
But nothing so strange
As what you do to me
From under my rock
Like a lobster I crawl
When you snap your fingers
or give me a call

Red Lobster, red lobster
Don't you dare sob, sir
'Cause love is you, and love is her
You're the meat. She's the but-tur

"Verse thirty-eight, Tinker. I'm making my way to the one hundred mark."

Blue was stretched out in the back seat, feet stuck through the window into the night. He had been soothing himself with the company of his guitar, something the mere act of driving did for Tinker.

Tinker passed few judgements on Blue's musical aspirations. He let "The Red Lobster" grow without forming an opinion on it, as the diplomacy of friendship dictates. He was just grateful that Blue wasn't interested in coaxing Tinker's Irish voice to share his compositions, but there are times when a friend has to risk the friendship itself if it means anything at all, and an hour earlier, Tinker had done just that. Blue's new composition-in-progress, "My Karma," only got as far as

With my Karma
On my arm a
million dollars
Couldn't make me happier
But without her
Life couldn't be crappier

before Tinker, trying to keep a straight face, told his friend that there was no way a love song could survive when it had to depend on crap, which was as close as he could come to telling Blue the truth about his song. Blue sulked for a few moments, strumming his guitar, occasionally humming a phrase that ended in "sappier," "trappier" or "snappier," until "My Karma" was announced stillborn, buried and forgotten, the best idea Blue had since he suggested going home, Tinker thought.

9

Another day and a restless sleep in the Plymouth and Tinker and Blue were making their way across the Mojave Desert under a full moon, canvas bags of water hanging in front of its grill as suggested by a mechanic when they stopped to gas up from the diminishing funds. The car filled the sandy silence with a rattle of exhaust, a pinging piston and Tinker's voice sounding out the words to Tom Jones's "Delilah."

"How can you sing at a time like this, anyway?" Blue asked him, himself in a near panic from the incredible heat. He spent his time rolling down his window only to have the hoped-for cool breeze pound into the car like a blast furnace, and rolling it up again to become trapped in a smothering stillness of heat.

"You know what the other fellow said about the levels of hell, eh? That they get hotter and hotter the deeper you go. I though Kansas was hell, then Utah, but cripes, man, this desert...."

For several miles, Blue was terrified that the Plymouth would break down and they would be caught in a swarm of snakes. All along the highway, dead snakes were common as porcupines slaughtered on the roads of Nova Scotia. Blue acknowledged few fears but snakes were first and foremost among them.

It was Tinker who finally realized that they were not dead snakes littering the road but retreads burned off of vehicles that had preceded them. It was a milder consolation, but not much milder. They were riding on retreads themselves, one they bought from Charlie and three they stole from the back of his garage the night before they left. In Kansas, the tires softened on the hot pavement and Tinker and Blue joked about it, but it had been civilized back there. Out here there was no obvious help.

Under the silvery blue moonlight the desert stretched out on either side of them, a featureless grey monotony of heat. They had become so accustomed to the sameness of it that at first it seemed like a midnight mirage of snow, an expanse of sand bleached white under the moonlight, peopled by cactus that raised their arms in surrender to the merciless heat. It stirred both imaginations to the memory of movies where all the deserts looked like this, the real West.

"Bet a lot of people died out there," Blue noted. "Wagon trains, war parties, Indian hunters. Wouldn't it be great to see a band of Indian ghosts? From in here, I mean. Maybe they've been riding across this desert for a hundred years, caught between their village and their Happy Hunting Ground, not knowing which one they're looking for because they don't know they're dead. I like Indians, Tinker. Know why? Because they remind me of my own people.

"When you really think about it, we had a lot more in common with them that we did with the Limeys. You see, nobody in Europe cared about the Scottish Highlanders because they couldn't make any sense of them. I mean they lived up in the mountains, wore their hair long, walked around in strange clothes, and spoke a language nobody could understand. Remind you of anybody?"

"Those hippies we stayed with?" Tinker asked.

"Jesus, Mary and Joseph, Tinker! Are you getting crazy? Hippies! For the love of Christ! Are you listening? I'm talking about Indians here. Indians, not wackos. Anyway, the only real difference, I suppose, was that they called the Highlanders barbarians and the Indians savages, which pretty well means the same thing anyway, which would make no difference at all between us and them, would it? And the Highlanders lived in clans and the Indians lived in tribes, which is about the same thing, too, so there you have it.

"Then when the Limeys convinced our clan leaders that there was more money to be made raising sheep than raising MacDonalds and MacDougalls and MacDonnells, they sold us out, gathered us up and shipped us over here so the sheep could feed on our land. Then when we get over here, what happens but they take the Indians and gather them up and put them on reservations and gave their land to us, and they still expect us to love the Queen. No way, boy! I always cheered for the Indians in the movies, even when I didn't know this, so that says we know a hell of a lot more than we realize even when we don't know it, right?

"That's why I'd like to see some Indian ghosts, but to tell you the truth, I'd be scared to be walking out there when I do. It's not like bumping into a ghost on the back roads back home. Our ghosts are friendly, eh, not like those ones that scare the shit out of you in the movies. In Cape Breton they just walk around startling people sometimes, but not scaring them. You know what I think? I think they don't want to leave Cape Breton. I mean, every ghost you ever heard of in Cape Breton is somebody's relative, right? When you know your ghosts they don't scare you, but they sure as hell can make the hair stand up on the back of your neck. Did I ever tell you about the time I saw Danny Danny Dan's funeral?"

"No, I don't think so," Tinker said, making himself comfortable behind the wheel, ready to hear it for the hundredth time.

"Two summers ago, eh, there was this party at Port Ban. You were there but there's no reason for you to remember it because all you did after a few beers was pass out, wake up, throw up, pass out, wake up, throw up, but you wouldn't give the keys of the Plymouth to anyone. Everybody else decided to stay and sleep right there on the beach but I had to give Farmer a hand moving a horse in the morning so I walked up the cliff from the beach by myself. I had a little skate on so I wasn't worried, but when I got to the top and onto the Sight Point Road I was getting pretty sober, sober enough to realize where I was.

"Look, Tinker, and you probably know this yourself, but I bet there's more ghosts on that road than anywhere else on the planet. That's where my people first settled, so the ghosts go back two hundred years, some of them. I don't know about the Irish or the Acadians, Tinker, but I don't think that us Highlanders like to be dead. Too many of them keep trying to come back, so I plan to put off dying as long as I can myself.

"But I digress, as the other fella says. Anyway, here I am on the Sight Point Road, a dirt road, twenty feet wide at it widest, trees shaking hands from either side of the road so it's like walking through a black tunnel. It doesn't help matters that there's not a house for miles with anyone living in it, just the dark shapes of barns falling down and empty homes, and each one of them claiming at least two ghosts each.

"Well, I'm trying not to think about just how much I know about this road – it's amazing how much a fellow learns when he's not wasting his time in school. That night, trying not to think about all the information I picked up over the years, I realized that I knew a hell of a lot more about my family, my people – and Cape Breton, for that matter – than I thought I knew. I say 'family' Tinker, because, just for your information when we get to him, Danny Danny Dan would of been a first cousin to my grandfather on my father's side. His father and my great-grandmother would be brother and sister, see.

"Anyway, everything's going great until I get this spooky feeling. Okay, I was feeling spooky anyway so I get this extra spooky feeling. At first, I thought it was just the shadows of trees moving in the breeze, then suddenly these shadows take shape. Look, Tinker, we're out in the middle of nowhere and if these tires go we're as good as dead ourselves so I have no desire to die with a lie on my lips. What I am going to tell you is the absolute truth, so help me God!

"Two black horses were pulling a wagon, not one as snazzy as Dracula's or anything, but it was no hay wagon either. It was a funeral wagon. They were moving slow as death along the road with this guy driving who had a face so white it should of been in a coffin itself. I don't know who he was because he didn't look like anybody we know. I'm frozen on the side of the road as it moves by and this cold spot of air moves across me. I don't think I'm even breathing now. The coffin is on the back with a cross on top of it, no flowers, just a cross and I know from hearing the story before about other people who saw the funeral parade that inside is Danny Danny Dan. It all just moves along as slow as a clock hand, and soundless as a graveyard.

"Behind it, there must have been a hundred people, maybe everybody who ever lived there at the time, and they just passed by, one sad white face after another, men and women and children, lots of black clothes and you know how uncomfortable farmers look in suits, well, they looked like that. And I'm standing there with every hair on my body standing up like they had their hats off for the passing funeral, and I'm sweating scared but a part of me is standing there as calm as you please looking for my grandfather or grandmother's face because they were at that funeral, you know, but I couldn't tell because they would of been young then and I only knew them old.

"It felt like it took forever to go by but it didn't. The sliver of moon hadn't moved an inch in the sky that I could tell. Nothing awful happened. It was awful enough as it was, considering how scared I got. But it told me something I can never not know again, Tinker. It told me that there's more than we know going on all the time.

"The story behind the funeral, because I talked to Monk about it later and he knows more about this stuff than anybody, was that Danny Danny Dan wasn't dead. There was a sickness in his family that faked death. When he said that, it scared the shit out of me worse than the funeral did because I'm a relative, right? But when Monk and I traced the family back it was something that came down Danny Danny Dan's mother's side of the family, not his father's which would be my side of his family, so when I die I'll probably be dead.

"What Monk said was that Danny Danny Dan was alive in his coffin but couldn't tell anybody. The funny thing about it, Monk noticed, was that the only person who wasn't a ghost at that funeral that I saw was Danny Danny Dan. That's why his funeral still haunts the Sight Point Road, because he was buried alive. Remember Ray Miland in the *Premature Burial*? Well, you didn't hear me laughing the last time I saw that movie, boy."

—

When Blue took the wheel from Tinker near dawn the Plymouth had begun a slow ascent into cooler heights as they rose out of the darkness and the desert, leaving behind them a history of desert ghosts they hadn't encountered, and they smiled tiredly to each other when they crossed the California state line.

10

"Well, there she is, Tinkers. Alcatraz! The most famous island on this side of the world."

Tinker and Blue were sitting on the dock of the bay. Their location wasn't lost on them, Otis Redding's song of the same name having pulsed itself through the car radio, off and on, all across America. Blue had spent much of his time scanning the dial for new country and western stations as each faded behind them. Tinker, when Blue slept through or chattered on against the music of his own choice, slipped the dial to music he found less predictable, more challenging to imitate. Blue scolded him for it, citing the dangers of rock and roll, which had the girls dancing so far away from the boys that when you tried to ask to take one of them home you had to holler so loud that three girls in the general proximity of the question might say yes. "Then what do you do?"

But driving across the States, "Dock Of The Bay," considering their destination, even had Blue singing into the handle of the same screwdriver he had once employed as a weapon to fend off drug-crazed hippies. From their seventy-mile-an-hour front-seat stage, Blue would reach across with the mic, holding it before his friend, saying, "Take her away, Tink," and Tinker's voice joined Redding's in a commendable harmony. On the actual dock of the bay, though, it was Blue's voice Tinker had for company as their homesick hearts were poured into the words that Tinker sang and Blue fumbled with, recreating out of his own poetic soul new lines for those he didn't know.

They had been in San Francisco for more than a week, each day exploring a little more of the city than they planned to, Blue charting their course with a street map and a dyslexic attitude toward details such as east, west, right, left.

In the Mission and Market area they found a room for twenty-two dollars a week in a hotel where, on the first night, they barricaded their door with a badly battered three-legged dresser, a security lock against the mob rule that seemed to govern the place.

Whole families huddled in some rooms, rummies who could afford a room occupied others, and an oddly high number of senile old men and women were residents of the remaining rooms. By day tolerable, by night terrifying, the room was affordable for the moment and so became their home away from home for a while. On the other side of the door family wars were being fought, the domestic screams barely covering the sound of someone throwing up in the hall or two men arguing and threatening to "Cut your god-damned throat with this bottle as soon as it's empty."

Each morning, Tinker and Blue were awakened at six o'clock by a pounding on their door, accompanied by the unmistakable sound of a mouth bugling reveille. The call to consciousness moved from door to door and for the first two mornings the boys arose in the belief that they were obeying hotel regulations until the seedy clerk at the front desk told them not to pay any attention to General Jones, an old man trapped inside a one-day loop of boot camp regulations. The old soldier was lost somewhere between the Second World War and his discharge, the clerk explained, but was harmless.

A couple of days later, Blue, desperate for a leak, was pulling the bureau away to go to the floor's only washroom when General Jones began rousing the young recruits. Blue came into the hall as the stiff-legged old man hobbled to the next set of army barracks. Blue saw the old man drop something and ran in the dim, night-light darkness, to retrieve and return it. It was a turd, and as Blue stood paralysed with shock over the sickening turn of events which he held in his hand, he watched another one fall from General Jones pant leg.

"Aw, Jesus, Tinker, we got to get out of here. We're on the skids, boy," he complained to his friend who reminded him that by the end of the week they would be out of money and out of the hotel, so his complaints were academic.

The two goals they had set for themselves they hadn't yet achieved. They had not found Haight-Ashbury despite having been pointed in that direction several times by those whom they asked, only to have Blue improvise on the advised approach with a short-cut of his own. Because they had not gotten there yet, they could not point the Plymouth toward home.

The second goal, like the hotel rent, was also academic. With or without visiting Haight-Ashbury, their planned return home posed a few problems related to the financial feasibility of crossing a continent on a pocketful of change. Wiring home for money was something they discussed and even expected to do when the going got tough, but faced with the reality of it, their pride forced them to delay. It was one thing, they agreed, to be stranded and desperate in the middle of a desert. People back home had seen enough movies to know what that was like, a situation that would have probably placed them in a slightly heroic role once the guys back home heard about it. Being stranded in San Francisco lacked that desert romance, so all telegrams were placed on hold.

After the first couple of days of swimming against the traffic on one-way streets, four-way stops, red lights, amber lights, green lights and numerous threats on their lives, Tinker and Blue opted for a walking tour of the city, roaming the urban hills to exhaustion, fuelled by vendor hot dogs. Always they were drawn back to the water, stunned by its commerce.

The Gulf of St. Lawrence, the arm of the Atlantic upon whose shores they grew up, looked much the same to them as it did to the Highlanders who squatted on its shores two hundred years before. They were familiar with its northern Atlantic moods: grey and foreboding in autumn, besieged by an armada of polar ice floes all winter, its spring palette of blue hues shifting slowly toward summer, and summer itself when a couple of hundred people from the town enjoyed the two-mile length of sandy beach that stretched between the rise of two mountains. They were also familiar with a rare treasure of the eastern continent, an ocean sunset.

The expanse of water back home was sprinkled with lobster boats or ground fishermen at their work and, occasional enough to be noteworthy, a Montreal-bound tanker would be sighted on the horizon. They had known the ocean as a place for children to enjoy.

They couldn't have imagined San Francisco Bay in a million summers with its noisy, oily traffic of monstrous ships gliding through the sunlight or emerging like phantoms from the fog to bellow their way through a congestion of ferries and cruisers and barges. Except for the tourist shops that did more business on one wharf than the whole Cape Breton tourism industry put together, it was no place for children. In San Francisco, the ocean was put to work full time, like a mine or a forest. Their fascination with it brought them back again and again.

Tinker looked across at Alcatraz, the gnawing worry in his stomach becoming a constant condition. Blue had always managed the financial end of their partnership, scheming dance fares and gas money with skill, but Tinker suspected that Blue was too far out of his element now. Because of this, he had scanned the want ads of newspapers he picked up from park benches, but found that there was only a market for certified mechanics and, he suspected, certified Americans. Passing the days walking the streets of San Francisco, "just picking 'em up and laying 'em down, as the other fellow says," brought them closer to flat broke than Tinker cared to think about.

"We got to do something about money, Blue," he said, punctuating his remark with a spit that he watched squirt from between his teeth, arc out and fall to the water below. "Maybe I should call the old man."

"We're in the richest state in the world, Tinker. If we can't make her here, boy, we may never leave home again. You know what the other fellow says, don't ya? The world is our oyster, Tinker, and I'm partial to pearls if you know what I mean."

"I don't like oysters," Tinker replied, streaming another spit into the Pacific.

11

Haight-Ashbury, when they finally did stumble upon it, explained a lot to Blue.

"No wonder we couldn't find it. Look at the way these Americans spell Hate."

No masquerade dance they had ever attended prepared them for Haight-Ashbury, and they had seen some weird costumes come out of the Halloween imaginations of the people back home.

"No doubt about it, Blue," Tinker said. "This is the hippie mother lode. It's not so bad when you see them scattered all over the place, but a crowd of hippies like this looks like a grade one art class went crazy with their crayons and then the whole works came alive."

They walked along through the swarm of people, nudging and pointing out for each other their own winning choices from among the braids and ponytails, ponchos and beads, the faces painted with peace symbols and petals, the clash of colourful clothes that had turned goodwill stores into the fashion centres of the decade, the shiny-eyed people sitting on the sidewalk smoking drugs and offering a drag to complete strangers. They walked through clouds of incense and marijuana and music spilling out of every window, Sgt. Pepper joining Bob Dylan and a dozen other performers in a mass jam session of albums, their popularity in competition with street musicians who played in front of a cap or hat sprinkled with a few coins and loads of encouragement from those passing by or stopping to listen.

"It would be nice to find out where they keep all that free love we keep hearing about," Blue said, his own progress through the busy street peppered with winks at the prettiest girls. "There must of been a hell of a bonfire here when they all burned their bras," he remarked to Tinker whose head was swivelling from one beautiful fantasy to another. "I may not think much of a guy who would burn his draft card but I got nothing but respect for a girl who burns her bra, boy."

A boy in long, straggly hair approached them for a hand-out and when Blue apologized for having nothing to offer, he just sneered the word "Tourists!" at them and walked away.

"What the hell does he mean, tourists, Tinker? Do we look rich? Are we driving over the Cabot Trail? Hell, we're not even Americans! I've got a good mind to go back and clock that guy."

They sat on a step and within a minute a voice from behind them said, "Hi." They turned to see a girl in a granny dress, wearing round spectacles, standing in the doorway. "Would you like some soup?"

She brought them two bowls of soup, asking only that they think good thoughts of the earth that provided the vegetables for the soup while they ate, and to just leave the bowls behind when they were done. The soup was hot and tasted of things unfamiliar as they sat there spooning it into their mouths, letting the street's swirl of colours and music wash past them while they watched, Blue commenting that it was the biggest un-chaperoned teen dance in history. "These hippies are caught up in a Godless communism and they don't even know it, Tinker," Blue said with a sad shake of his head.

"Kathy said there was no such thing as a hippie, Blue. What do you make of that? She said that's somebody else's word for something they don't understand."

"Tinker, Tinker, Tinker, you're so easily led astray. I have to keep a close eye on you, boy. Look, there are Liberals and Tories, Catholics and Protestants, Cape Bretoners and the rest of the world, and hippies and us. Even Saint Thomas believed in Jesus once he put his hand into his side, didn't he? Well, how much proof do you need?"

"I don't know, but when I talked to Kathy, you know, like it was weird at first, but after a while she just got to be like another person. I didn't think about a hippie every time I looked at her even with the way she dressed or talked."

"I bet you didn't, buddy. I know what you were thinking of. With Karma, eh, the more I got to know her the weirder she got, but the more I liked her anyway, but the one thing I know for sure, Tinker, is that she's a hippie. She'd blend into this street like flour into my mother's biscuits. Everybody belongs some place and she belongs here, but not us, old buddy, not us. If we belonged out here with these hippies, I'd be freezing my arse off in a river in Colorado right this minute."

In the silence that followed, Tinker felt relaxed, as if the soup had soothed for a moment the gnawing in his stomach. He let his thoughts stop taking charge of him for a while, freeing them like children for the summer from the school of his own conflicts, and let them drift, forgetting about the poverty of their pockets and the war zone of their hotel. Inside his own silence the throbbing energy of the music and the flow of people on the street, moving as if life itself were something to be danced away joyfully, filled him with the ache of a stranger who did not know how to belong to a world not his own.

Blue surveyed the scene with the eye of a survivor washed up on a foreign shore and who now must learn how to forage for food in an unfamiliar forest. Not much of what Farmer had taught him applied here, where the rules were not clear enough for Blue to manipulate to his own advantage. They were broke and he tried not to cast himself in the desperate role of the hippie who had asked them for money. Standing on a street corner bumming spare change was a wino's economy. Some of the winos back home were artists at that particular existence, setting up shop on John Beaton's Corner or some other high pedestrian traffic area like the Co-op parking lot, hustling people they knew with a new story every morning. But bumming was not Blue's field of expertise, nor did he want it to be. So he examined everyone and everything on the street looking for another point of entry until a wide grin of self-satisfaction erased the lines of concentration from his forehead.

"Come on, old buddy. We got work to do," he said, ribbing Tinker from his reverie with an elbow.

Blue confided nothing to his friend as he led him back along the street, rushing past potters and leather workers, silversmiths and street artists, reaching the end of the hippie population and heading toward the skid row familiarity of their hotel.

In the room, Blue stood in front of the cracked bureau mirror running his comb in unfamiliar directions through his hair until it hung in the style Karma had once imposed; he had returned it to its customery ducktail upon departure from the Human Rainbow Commune. Picking up his guitar he turned to Tinker.

"Come on, buddy. We're going to infiltrate the enemy, to quote the other fellow."

12

"Cripes, Tinker, I wish people would stop dropping drugs into my hat," Blue complained as he shifted aside a couple of purple cigarettes and a small rabbitturd of hashish to count out a dollar and seventy-three cents in very small change. For three days, they had been propped against the brick wall of a building teaching Sgt. Pepper and Bob Dylan a few things about music. Blue, studying the trickle of change into his blue hat, read the tide of its ebb and flow, noting that Tinker's songs took in revenue at a rate of ten to one to his own singing. He finally settled back like what's-his-name, Brian Epstein, to chord and plot the course of their partnership which would take them all the way from their meagre beginnings in hippie Heaven to the golden halo of spotlight that fell on the stage of Ryman Hall. Destiny. Sometimes a man can feel it against all the odds.

Occasionally, Blue left Tinker to sing a cappella while he did a reconnaissance of the competition and concluded that they weren't doing any better or worse than most, except for a classical violinist who at his sidewalk location introduced Bach to the Beatles, where the two got along famously. The violinist had the unfair advantage of possessing only one arm, managing the bow with an ingenious contraption which he operated with his teeth. Why a guy who would have no trouble getting himself a disability pension would go through all the trouble of learning to play the violin with one arm and thirty-two teeth was a mystery to Blue, and he resented the pisspot full of money the fiddler's top hat was taking in. Despite the unfairness of that competition, Tinker and Blue averaged enough to eat, buy Blue's cigarettes, and put a few dollars toward another week of luxury in their home-sweet-home away from home. The profit margin beyond those immediate needs was assigned to their gas-money-home account, current balance: zero.

Tinker's repertoire didn't include a lot of the popular stuff sung in this particular corner of the planet. His renditions of

Irish rebel songs, Scottish ballads, Cape Breton classics and select choices from the country and western charts disoriented those who stopped to listen. They said, "Wow!" a lot and walked away befuddled by this crack in their Universe where old wars were celebrated while the people on the street were trying to stop a current one. It broke the symmetry of this make-love-not-war neighbourhood.

To please his audience, Tinker pulled out of the air around him the melodies and words that appealed to him, practising what he could remember back in their room. "Pretty heavy into this love and peace business there, aren't you, Tinker?" Blue said in his review of Tinker's new material while acknowledging that it made them more money than "Molly Bawn."

Tinker, as usual, chose the words he sang carefully. He didn't care if a song was sentimental or rowdy or filled with rage or warm with love so long as he believed the story. Unlike Blue, he had written no songs of his own that he needed to sing; they had already been written for him. What appealed to him here in San Francisco, and what he found in common with Cape Breton, was that music ran through the core of what newspapers called the counter culture just like it ran through the culture back home. People defined themselves with it, recognized each other through it. Music was really the only way into this counter culture, he realized. His hair hid all but his lobes now, and his red polka-dot handkerchief was tied around his thigh instead of poking a small pennant of itself from his back pocket, but without the music he wouldn't learn much at all about where he was.

Hoping he wouldn't offend the well-meaning gestures that rained drugs into his hat, Blue told the monied people who stopped to listen, "Thanks for the quarter, Mac, and listen, for another one you can have your choice of those purple cigarettes there." It turned out to be a brisk trade once Tinker and Blue discussed its ethical implications, reasoning, like the hippie in the back seat of the Plymouth, that the quicker they got rid of the drugs the less chance they would have of getting arrested for them. According to Blue's high-school Economics class, they were simply unloading an inventory of commodities that their company had no interest in carrying. That argument carried them through a couple of days until Tinker woke up sweating from a nightmare of being arrested as a drug pusher, a profession which, unlike its first cousin, bootlegging, was universally scorned in Cape Breton. Blue had to call upon all his theological and business knowledge to assure his friend that there was nothing wrong with bartering the products that fell by chance into his hat.

"Listen, Tinker, you know a lot about motors but you don't know anything about running a business. I studied all about it in Economics and here's how it works. I have something and you want it. We make a deal. Transaction completed. Sure, sometimes it might be a little illegal but in business, if you don't get caught everything's okay. Even the Church will tell you that. Look at the Mafia, for God's sake. They're all Catholics right from Italy and you can't get any more Catholic than that, and the Mafia makes the most perfect Catholics of all because they're organized just like the Church. They go around cementing people to the bottom of rivers and all that, but it's just business, Tinker, because they still go to church every Sunday and give gobs of money to the priests and get forgiven.

"The Church understands this because when they used to go off on crusades and kill a couple of million pagans, well, it was just Church business. It had nothing to do with Jesus Christ or the Mass or anything the Church believes in. It was just business, buddy, looting and pillaging to build cathedrals to the greater Glory of God. They tell you to love your fellow man, but if you can't, they'll forgive you. That's what the priests are there for, to make everything all right."

Tinker went back to sleep praying not to get caught and reminding himself that if he had to confess to being a drug pusher he had better do it here in San Francisco before he went back home where the priest always recognized his voice, called him Tinker, and told him to say three Hail Marys every night for the strength to stop indecently assaulting himself.

The next morning they went back to business as usual.

"According to Article One, Section Two, Paragraph Three of our union contract with this city, there will be no singing in the rain, Tinker," Blue announced as he emptied the contents of his blue hat into his pocket, placed the hat on his head and snapped close the buckles of his guitar case while a scattering of rain peppered the sidewalk. Warm and refreshing in itself, they recognized it as a prelude to a more dismal downpour.

Tinker and Blue stood wondering about the nearest shelter when they saw her coming, carrying her own canopy of sky, twirling her umbrella into a dazzling swirl of meaningless colours. The abstractly painted umbrella was a living thing covering its semi-globe with joyfully unpredictable movements. The hypnotic spin of oranges and blues, greens and whites, flowing through each other like phantoms, was oddly beautiful in a city gone damp and dreary.

"Let's follow her," Tinker said. A curiosity he couldn't explain rose like a road one will wonder about for a long time if it isn't followed.

Blue knew that it was a foolish idea to walk around in the rain following an umbrella, but he couldn't find enough conviction in himself to argue against his own curiosity. He decided this was as good a time as any to pamper Tinker's infatuation with hippies.

"All roads lead home, as the other feller says," Tinker said with a Blue-mimicking shrug that started them off, re-enacting the boyhood pleasures they took in following the town's fire truck, or the First of July parade or some mumbling drunk, amusing themselves with mimicry. Fire trucks and parades were predictable fun, but following drunks was an unscripted adventure because the whole world was an obstacle to them. Sometimes they wore shoes, sometimes they went in the sock feet of a man who had just escaped from his wife through the bedroom window. Sometimes they pissed on the sidewalk, oblivious to the mid-afternoon audience shopping along the main street, sometimes they pissed in their pants. Sometimes they hummed to themselves, sometimes they snarled at the world. Always, it proved to be worth the effort because it usually ended with a story for them to tell their buddies.

They trailed the maddened rainbow past a cluster of hippies communing with the damper side of nature, along empty blocks vacated by the more sensible freaks, meeting nine-to-fivers scurrying for a roof to put over their heads. Soon they were beyond the influence of Haight-Ashbury and the world began to look more like it was supposed to look, streets and cars and people dressed liked people.

13

"What did she look like?" Blue asked, trying to recall the features of the umbrella person they were following.

"I don't know. I just saw the umbrella."

"Vision time!"

The psychedelic umbrella revived Blue's interest in a game that they had laid aside years ago, a game he had created himself, one in which he and Tinker took turns creating a "vision" by choosing the most attractive features of all the girls and women they knew in town, composing an imaginary perfection of beauty. It made them virginal connoisseurs of the town's beauty, an expertise that never got them very far, not even when they threw in the Plymouth as added bait, but walking along wondering about the girl under the umbrella, Tinker asked the first question.

"Eyes?" Tinker asked.

"Karma's," Blue replied.

"Smile?"

"Karma's."

"Hair?"

"Karma's."

"This isn't working very well, Blue."

"If I'd of known I was going to have to live with her anyway, I'd of stayed in Colorado. Do you know how many times I've seen her since we got to this city? Every time I see a girl with long hair, that's how many times. She's like Danny Danny Dan's funeral, gone just when I think I see her. If I don't get my best song out of this, Tinker, I never will."

The rain had stopped as they followed the umbrella around a corner, slowing as they watched it hurry toward, then disappear into, a forest of placard and peace signs demonstrating in front of an army recruitment centre. A denim brigade was hurling slogans at the Pentagon outpost, indicting it for crimes against humanity. Beyond them, an assembly of America the Beautiful gathered, disturbed, restless and angry with the criticism.

Tinker and Blue stood at a detached distance, polite visitors not interfering with domestic tensions. News cameras really didn't make this stuff up, they realized.

"Maybe we should get out of here. This thing is going to blow and if we get caught in it we could get deported," Tinker warned, watching the crowd of roughly two hundred, totalling both sides.

"That's one way to get home, I suppose," Blue jibed back, "but we got to see this. We never had a riot back home. These hippies are going to get the shit kicked out of them."

"I know, but I wish somebody would tell me why," Tinker remarked.

"If that's all you want to know, buddy, I'll tell you. It's about freedom. It's about the moth and the butterfly, as the other fellow says. The butterfly just flies around enjoying the heat from the sun, but the moth is foolish and flies into the flame. They're both free, right? But there's a right and a wrong way to be free.

"Look, it's like going to a dance in Glencoe and the fiddler is playing and there are five or six sets on the floor. Now, everybody is dancing to the same music or trying to. But down in the corner of the hall you get a hippie set and they're stomping and screeching and hollering. Nobody says much about it, but it's a piss-off. They don't have enough respect for the music to learn how to dance to it. Well, it's the same thing here in the States. These hippies are pissing a lot of people off because if they get control ... well, imagine six or seven sets of them in Glencoe. It wouldn't be a dance, it would be chaos and the Communists love chaos. They set the fire then suck the moths into it."

While Blue argued eloquently for the rights of man according to established theories of "Them and Us" as expressed in Modern World Problems and confirmed by Farmer's wartime experiences, the protest in front of the recruitment centre rose to new tensions. The civilian militia, composed of rained-out construction workers and men old enough to have fought in the nation's earlier wars began heckling the hippies who were heckling two soldiers with stoic faces who stood watching from inside the recruitment centre door. The shouting became a mishmash of indistinguishable noise as accusations from both sides collided in mid-air like fighter planes in Battle of Britain movies. Hippies with fingers raised in a mockery of Churchill's Victory "V" provoked a response of closed and threatening fists from their unhappy audience.

A crewcut workman stepped into the DMZ between the two sides and began walking back and forth in front of the long-hairs affecting a limp wrist and swivelling his hips in an effeminate exaggeration of what he figured was the protesters' sexual orientation. A roar of hilarious approval rose from his supporters, encouraging him on. Suddenly he grabbed one of the protesters whose hair fell almost to his waist and threatened to kiss him with heavily pursed-lips. The protester, unable to wriggle free of the loving arms that enfolded him, exploded in a rage completely out of sync with the purpose of his non-violent mission in front of the recruitment centre and shoved his undesired suitor away from him. The man stumbled backwards, almost falling. Enraged by embarrassment over the hippie's surprising strength and the laughter rising from his own supporters, he charged the hippie, connecting with a right hook that sent the younger man sprawling into a protesting mass of his peers. Other hippies moved to the front line to protect their wounded warrior, a movement mistaken for an attack by the anti-protesters who swarmed toward them.

Within seconds, the demonstrators were surrounded by a pushing and shoving, punching and kicking mob of angry people who were not afraid to stand up for their country and be counted while they dropped hippie after hippie for the count. But within the time it takes for four police cars and a wagon to wail its way across two city blocks where they had been discreetly parked, the law enforcement agents arrived like the U.S. Calvary to the rescue.

While most of the hippies broke from the melee and ran in whatever direction they hoped freedom might be waiting for them, the uniforms moved with billy clubs among the long-hairs and the short-hairs, arresting and dragging people off to the wagon, tapping with their clubs those who offered passive resistence. Not one ally of the State found himself among the stack of protesters piled on top of each other in the police wagon as peace was restored to a San Francisco street. Policemen spoke and laughed with the men who glowed with pride over their courage and with the two recruitment soldiers, and within minutes the street was as empty as any heavy rain could have accomplished.

Tinker and Blue had attracted no attention at all, and with the street to themselves they walked along surveying the spoils of war; soggy cardboard signs, a sandal, a hundred shiny beads from a broken necklace, dark smudges of blood. Blue picked up a twisted umbrella and examined it. It was an ordinary umbrella, black nylon, its surface hand-painted with the colours he and Tinker had followed. Up close, it wasn't nearly as impressive, the lines not particularly straight, the colours not particularly true. He didn't know what had happened to the girl under it, whether she had fled to freedom or had been carted off in the paddy wagon. He turned to show it to Tinker who had picked up a beaded bandana, examined it, then put it on his head to keep the clumps of wet hair out of his eyes. Blue shook his head and shoved the umbrella into a trash can.

—

Tinker sat in the Plymouth behind their hotel, examining his new headband in the rearview mirror. He liked it. He turned his attention to the sound of the engine, listening for any sound that called out for his assistance. They had not moved the Plymouth for several days to save on gas money. He had worried that the Plymouth, left unattended in a parking lot filled mainly with over-flowing dumpsters, would become too much of a temptation for skid-row bandits. The Plymouth couldn't tell him how many times it had been examined by such creatures and judged to have been stripped and abandoned already. The only vestige of self-esteem the Plymouth possessed anymore was Tinker's uncompromising appreciation for it. Salty Cape Breton winters had devoured dark holes around its doors, through the trunk floor, around the headlights. Bitter winter temperatures had cracked its padded dash and seats. But Tinker loved it in sickness and in health, saw only its undying determination to go on despite the ravages of time and weather. He had promised the Plymouth that when they got back home he would spend a week at Charlie's garage removing its acne of rust with body work and fresh paint.

The rain and the periods of no rain which had kept the city opening and closing its umbrellas all afternoon compromised now into a steady drizzle. Blue was up in the room working on a new song and Tinker had no desire to leave the solitude of the Plymouth. He needed to escape from Blue's logic which always managed to out-manoeuvre his own even when he felt unconvinced by his friend's command of how the world works.

What had bothered him most about the scene he had witnessed on the street earlier in the day wasn't the politics of the Vietnam war, which he hadn't really cared about or studied with Blue's intensity, but the people involved in the fight. There was almost no one among the hippies, as far as he could tell, who was much older than either of them. And among the other side, there was almost no one who was as young as them.

Blue had his own Highland history and he hoarded all the stories he could gather about it. If you know where you come from, then you know where you are going, Blue was fond of saying. Or was it the other fellow? Tinker's knowledge of his own history was less factual than Blue's, but more lyrical. There were the Irish rebel songs and famine songs from his father's side of the family, and he had even memorized "Evangeline," Longfellow's love poem about the expulsion of the Acadians which his mother told him in her Acadian accent was a sentimental American's version of the darkest time in history for her people. But the Highlanders and the Irish and the Acadians did not escape their past by escaping to Cape Breton. They each brought their pasts with them, stories, songs, ten-generational memories of their families. In the past, each of those generations had known their oppressor. Tinker didn't even know if he was being oppressed.

What he did know was that there was a revolution going on in this country between people who wanted peace and people who wanted war. It reminded him of Monk who was known all over the place back home as a deserter from the army during the war. Monk lived in the woods back of town for almost two years toward the end of the war, hiding on the military police or any soldiers home on leave who didn't think much of his cowardice. He made the best moonshine on the island in his makeshift home in the hardwood forest, a talent that played a major role in the fact that he had never been betrayed even by those who hated that he had deserted, their logic being that if Monk was arrested he wouldn't be sent back to the war but to jail. Since neither the war nor the local population would benefit from his incarceration, Monk was left to his self-imposed solitary confinement in the forest.

A dozen different versions of Monk's desertion circulated the island, among them stories claiming that he was a coward who ran in the face of battle, or that he met a girl he wanted to marry in England and she was killed in the Blitz, making him not care about anything anymore, or that he sympathized with the Germans.

Monk's version was much simpler.

Blue had once invited Tinker along with him and Farmer during a horse sale once, and when Farmer got the money from the sale he drove directly to Monk's place. It wasn't in the woods anymore. Following the end of the war amnesty, Monk moved to a small un-farmed farm outside town. They all sat around Monk's kitchen table, which was the only room Monk lived in, and Farmer poured himself shots from the bottle of shine he had purchased from his former drinking partner. The key to Monk's exceptional shine, according to Farmer, was that when he set a vat he always added his rosary to it to protect it from the impurities that ruined a lot of other people's moonshine, not to mention ruining some of the lives of the people who drank it. Monk, who hadn't had a drink since an encounter with the Virgin Mary, spent a lot of his time selling shine to Farmer while at the same time trying to save him from the habit of alcohol.

The talk that November day was about the Armistice Day parade which was a few days away. Farmer was trying to coax Monk into joining the rest of the vets in the parade "just for the hell of it." Monk wasn't interested, nor was he keen to relive the war which was strong on Farmer's mind. All through the conversation, the question was forming itself then retreating from Blue's lips until he finally blurted it out. "Why'd you desert, Monk?"

Monk looked at him as if Blue asked him if he thought it would rain that day.

"Well," Monk said, scratching his three-day stubble, "I enlisted for three years and when my time was up they told me I was in for the duration. Never asked me a darn thing about it, just told me. I didn't think much of being played with like that so I left. The way they came after me, you'd think that as soon as Hitler heard I wasn't there to stop him anymore he was going to send submarines up the Margaree River and take over the whole country. Getting taken for granted like that told me that those officers didn't think any more of me than the gun I was carrying. I did what I had promised to do when I enlisted, then I came home."

"You should of stayed, buddy," Farmer said. "You'd be sitting pretty on a pension right now. I can't figure it out myself. I was with you. You weren't no damned coward. That's what bothers all of us at the Legion when it comes up. Why the hell did Monk run? There's not a guy who was over there who thinks you were scared."

"I would have stayed," Blue said. "You too, Tinker."

"Maybe," Tinker answered, "but if they told us in June after a whole year of school that we would have to keep going for July and August I'd go to the woods too."

Monk turned to him and stuck out his hand. "Put her there, buddy." Then turning to Farmer while he shook Tinker's hand he said, "This is the first man who's ever heard what I was saying." For Tinker, it was the first time in all his fourteen years that anyone had called him a man.

—

The people in front of the recruitment centre chanting "Hell, no! I won't go!" wasn't the same thing as Monk going to war, doing what he said he would do, then coming home. Monk had no trouble living with himself. Not now, anyway, although Tinker could remember when he was drunk all the time, and people said it was because he couldn't live with the idea that he was a coward. But Tinker, listening to Monk talk about it, wasn't so sure about that, because Monk had told him a lot more about himself later on. He would like to talk to Monk now, hear what he had to say about people who wouldn't go to war at all, not even against the Communists. The difference, Tinker guessed, was that the people who chased Monk for leaving the war were the ones who were in it themselves. This afternoon's fight on the street was between the young people who wouldn't go off to war and the other people who wanted them to go while they stayed home and watched it on television.

Confused by his own thoughts, Tinker turned his attention to the steering wheel, revved the Plymouth's engine in neutral and matted it down an imaginary road toward home.

14

Tinker Dempsey sat on the sidewalk strumming Blue's guitar. Chording for himself was the limit of his interest in the instrument, but it felt like company, which was more than Blue had been as their days in San Francisco stretched into weeks. Leaving Tinker to hustle their daily bread, Blue found numerous excuses to explore the territory, waving and nodding and winking his way along the street, greeting people with a "Hi, cousin!" or calling out a first name when he knew it. Bit by bit, he had introduced himself, Tinker, Farmer, Monk and most of Cape Breton Island to anyone in the Haight-Ashbury area who stood still long enough to listen. He dispensed stories about "This guy we have back home, eh?" and gathered items of interest to bring back to Tinker.

"Tinker, old buddy, I was walking by that vegetable restaurant up there and potatoes being pretty near a vegetable it reminded me of the time a crew from home went picking potatoes on Prince Edward Island. You heard that one, didn't you, about how they got into the wine the first night they were paid and began playing baseball in the middle of the field and by morning had smashed about an acre of potatoes right out of Yankee Stadium? They were heaving their hungover guts over the side of the ferry the next morning on their way back to Nova Scotia. They say it was the most people ever fired at one time on PEI except for the day after an election.

"Well, I see this guy sitting on the step of that restaurant so I figured if he liked vegetables he'd like that story. His head moves as slow as cold molasses when he looks up at me and I realize that this guy is on whacky tobaccy or acid or speed or all of the above, as the other fellow says. Then he says to me, 'Are you really there, man?,' like I'm something he'd see in the DTs or something. I told him my name was Danny Danny Dan and kept on going."

The streets of San Francisco held less fascination for Tinker than for Blue. Singing on the streets wasn't nearly as much fun as singing for the hell of it or tinkering with a transmission. When he first started strumming Blue's guitar the tips of his fingers hurt, and he saw that the calluses of his mechanic's career, along with the tattoos of grease and oil embedded in them, had turned clean and tender. Except for the radio, his hands hadn't taken anything apart since the Volkswagen van in Colorado. The radio had been a three-dollar pawnshop bargain bought to liven up the evenings in their hotel room, which it did until Tinker became curious about the metropolis of tubes and transformers that resembled an amber city skyline. Reassembled, static monopolized the air waves. Their next radio was filled with transistors protected inside a case of seamless plastic, Blue's idea.

For Blue, the days and weeks hadn't disappeared into a boring rhythm of street songs, hotdogs and the nightly racket in the corridor beyond their hotel room. Instead, he was slowly adapting to the foreign landscape, enjoying it, turning it into ballads on the pages of his scribbler. The biggest surprise the city held for him wasn't the strange food, one-armed fiddlers or weirdly arrayed hippies, but the revelation that Tinker was shy.

At first, Blue put Tinker's reluctance to join him on people-meeting escapades down to a lack of interest in the city. He even thought Tinker might be a little scared of it, hovering in the background when they did find themselves among other people. He could understand his friend's behaviour among the unknown, the hippies for example, but Tinker acted the same in the hotel.

Occasionally, they joined some of the winos in one of the rooms, sharing a bottle or two. This was so familiar, the passing of the bottle, the men telling their stories, listening to Blue's stories with actual comprehension, that it made him homesick. But even in this almost-like-home atmosphere, Tinker held back when he wasn't hiding behind a song. It took Blue a long time to put two and two together, to think the unthinkable, that off the island where he was born his buddy, the same guy who once wore only his long underwear and a necktie to a high school winter carnival dance, was shy. Blue had been planning his remedy for a week.

Walking along the street, he stopped to remind those people to whom he had already spoken, and recruited those he had missed. Gerry, the one-armed fiddler shrugged a "Why not," Patsy and Sasha, leather-crafting sandals and shoulder bags said, "Sure," and Daisy, the girl who had given them a bowl of soup their first day in the neighbourhood, was pleased with the prospect. The scheme was shaping up for Blue but just as he was about to activate the gathering of musicians and street artists, hustlers and speedsters, whom he had secreted around the corner, out of Tinker's sight, his instructions faltered and he fell silent, listening.

Blue's ear isolated a faint new noise which had joined the collision of sound that was the soundtrack of San Francisco: rock music and traffic and screaming seagulls. After a moment spent assuring himself he wasn't being haunted by homesickness, he raised his hand to the gathered crowd to hold them there while he ran off to explore the origins of the unmistakable sound.

He followed the thread of sound, thinking all the time that he must be crazy, until he turned the corner and saw a guy his own age in sandals, jeans, tie-dye shirt and glengarry holding under his arm like a trapped insect the bladder of his bagpipes, the pipes themselves flaring out their beetle-on-its-back legs while the boy's fingers ran along the chanter like happy children, releasing the notes to "Strawberry Fields."

The oddity of the creature on the corner, hippie and Highlander, piper and rock star, had stopped a small crowd, their faces a gallery of bemused expressions. Blue shouldered his way to the front of the listeners, waiting for the tune to finish. The drone of the bagpipes had played in the background of his growing up and had been, like the inflections of the Gaelic, generally rejected by his modern generation in favour of more exciting instruments. Travelling with Farmer had exposed Blue to a smattering of both the Gaelic and the pipes. Standing in the company of the utterly ignorant, Blue marshalled his vague knowledge into the stuff of authority so that when the young piper finished his piece to the awkward applause of his audience, Blue tested the musician's repertoire to see if it equalled his own.

"Do you know 'Lord Lovat's Lament'?" Blue asked while people tossed their offering of coins into the tin can at the piper's feet.

The piper did a double-take but being openly pleased by the presence of a connoisseur amid his audience began preparing his pipes for the tune. As Blue adopted the stoic expression of the hard to impress, the music flowed from the instrument with a graceful sadness that reminded Blue of what he had heard about the tune, that it was composed for Lord Lovat while he watched from the deck of a transport ship as Scotland receded from his sight forever. He listened to the oddly brisk lament thinking that the first time that lament was played on dry land it was on the shores of the New World where Highlanders were washing up by the thousands after the Clearances. Cape Breton maybe.

A small silence, like a final note in the tune, followed the piper's performance, giving Blue time to rise out of the reflective spell cast upon him by the piper.

"You from the Cape?" Blue asked him.

"Where?"

"The Cape. Cape Breton. You can't play like that and not be from the Cape, boy ... I mean, buddy."

"I'm from Seattle," the piper said.

"Get outta here," Blue said. "Seattle! What's the world coming to, as the other fellow would say. How can you play like that and not know the island?"

"What island? I've been in a pipe band since I was eight."

"They'd get a big kick out of you back home, boy. An American playing the bagpipes. Next thing you know you guys will be playing hockey. Can you play anything you want on those things?"

"Pretty well."

Blue told him what he wanted and the piper replied that Blue's request was about as simple as requests got, and pocketing his money followed Blue to the corner where the others were still waiting.

"I'm Blue, by the way," Blue offered his hand.

"Nathan Goldstein."

"Get outta here!"

15

Tinker had seen pictures of the fife-and-drum and the ketchup-stained bandages leading Fourth of July parades in the United States and this wasn't one them. This September parade was led by a hippie piper, a one-armed fiddler, a couple of strung-out street guitarists, several girls in granny dresses dancing to the music of their own tambourines, followed by a beggars-and-thieves chorus of about forty familiar faces from around the neighbourhood. Under normal circumstances, Tinker would have sat back and watched the music ensemble pass on its way to protest some foreign or domestic injustice, but normal circumstances were absent from this assembly which was being parade-marshalled by Blue who carried a case of beer under each arm while directing the pace and participation of everyone in the choir, their discordance worthy of Blue's impassioned prompting. The parade made its way toward Tinker just as he recognized the melody.

"You know what the other fella says, don't ya, Tink? Next to Jesus Christ's, the most important day of the year is a guy's own birthday. Happy birthday, buddy."

While others heaped their best wishes on top of Blue's, Blue ripped open a case and began snapping the caps off the beer bottles with his belt buckle and passing them out to the party people. Tinker took one and joining a toast to himself, tipped the bottle to his lips.

"Forgot all about it," he said. "Where did you find a piper?" he asked Blue.

"You're going to love this," Blue answered, beckoning the piper closer. "Tell him your name." The piper told him.

"Wouldn't they get a kick out of that back home, Tink? Know what they'd call you back where we come from, Nathan? Scottie! That's how we adopt foreigners, see. There's fiddlers back home that play Scotch music who aren't really Scotch, so we call them Scottie. There's Scottie LeBlanc and Scottie Fitzgerald. Damned good, too, just like you. Scottie Goldstein, that's who'd you'd be back in Cape Breton. You should come back with us. Play at the Broad Cove concert."

"No Jewish people where you live?" Nathan inquired.

"Oh, yeah! We have one. He owns the clothing store."

Nathan Goldstein rolled his eyes and Tinker, running interference, asked Nathan, as Blue had before him, where he came from, how he learned to play the bagpipes and requested a tune as a birthday gift. "Anything fast. Don't make me cry," Tinker joked.

Nathan Goldstein chose a lively march and the gathering grew quiet, some to listen, some because their conversations couldn't compete with the fiery music.

"You release those notes just as smooth as a hen scooping oats from the ground, to quote the other fellow," Blue exploded when the last wisps of sound had been whisked away by the September breeze. "There's quite an instrument," he continued, addressing the whole gathering. "We got this fellow back home, eh? Farmer. He fought in Italy during the war and he told me about this time when some Cape Breton Highlanders were pinned down by the Germans. It didn't look very good so the major sent a message back to headquarters that he needed two tanks or one piper to get his men out of there. That's the kind of effect bagpipe music has on Scotchmen. Farmer told me that that story is so true he didn't have to add anything to it."

Nathan sat beside Tinker. "Is everyone Scottish where you come from?" he asked.

"You must have heard the one about Saint Peter giving the new souls the tour of Heaven," Tinker said. "He takes them to a place where everybody is just sitting in the sky, meditating. 'This is Nirvana where the Buddhists stay,' he says. Then he takes them to an oasis where there are old men and eternal virgins and Saint Peter tells them that this is where the Moslems spend eternity. Then he takes them to another place where people are just sitting by the River Jordan singing hymns. 'This is where we keep the Baptists,' he says. Then they come to this big high stone wall and Saint Peter puts his finger to his lips and they all tiptoe past. When they get past, one of the new souls asks what's behind the stone wall. Saint Peter whispers, 'That's where we keep the Catholics. They think they're the only ones here.'

"Well, it's kind of like that with the Scots in Cape Breton, Nathan. They think they're there all alone. But there's plenty of other kinds of people too. Me, I'm Irish.

"Look, I don't play this thing very well but I'll trade you a song for the tune you played." Keeping the theme constant he began the words to "Will You Go, Lassie, Go." A short way into the song soft notes from Gerry's violin joined him, and Nathan produced a chanter and added that to the growing orchestration.

"Great voice," Nathan complimented when Tinker had finished, and Gerry added that he liked to come by and listen to Tinker when he wasn't playing himself.

"You should drop into the Aquarius Café sometime," Nathan advised him. "It's not far from here and anybody can play. They just have a mic and an amp. You go in, you sing or play, you pass the hat. It's a great place to hear some good sounds. Lots of people got their break there."

"Where's this place?" Blue chimed in, listening intently to the instructions.

The street party carried on into the early evening as music, information and stories criss-crossed like girders of a bridge spanning a chasm. Food mysteriously appeared and the beer disappeared, cigarette and marijuana smoke stained the air, temporary bands composed of bagpipes and violins and guitars and tambourines formed and dissolved, songs of the day and songs centuries old sharing the same sidewalk.

"Nathan, old buddy," Blue said, giving the piper a slap on the back during a lull in the singing, "I can't thank you enough for what you did for old Tinker here. He's as homesick as he is lovesick. He thinks I don't know that," Blue continued, convinced that he was whispering. "About being lovesick, I mean, but that's another story, to quote the other fellow. Anyway, the way you play those pipes is enough to make a grown man cry. Not that there's anything wrong with a crying jag, mind you. Hank Williams makes me think about crying all the time. But you know what I mean? You must miss Seattle enough to make you want to cry sometimes."

"I can't honestly say I ever broke down and wept for Seattle," Nathan said with a smile.

"No? Well, look at her this way, buddy. You guys have been waiting for the promised land for as long as there's been a Bible, right? Well, we Cape Bretoners got ours, and let me tell you, Nathan, my man, it's worth the wait. I can't wait to go home myself."

"Where is this place, anyway?" Nathan asked, and Gerry and a few others murmured their wondering as well.

"They don't teach you Americans any geography at all, do they?" Blue scoffed. "I haven't met anybody on this side of the border yet who knows where Cape Breton is. Well, Cape Breton is this island just off the coast of Nova Scotia which is in Canada and Canada, are you listening, students, Canada is in ... North America, just like the United States, and we got more pipers there than a horse has kicks. And fiddlers, too, Gerry. The best in the world.

"You should come back with us when we go. All of you," Blue added with an invitational sweep of his hand. "What would be great, eh, is if we got a bus and filled her up with gas and all of us and headed for home. You'd like that, I bet. There's tons of hippies there already so you'd be right at home. And so would we, huh, Tinker? How about it, buddy? What do you say? We trade in the Plymouth for an old school bus and head east like three times three times three wise men?"

"I'll never get that drunk," Tinker said, picking Blue's hat from the top of his friend's head and shaking it to demonstrate how empty it was. "You get the bus and I'll drive the Plymouth 'and I'll be in Cape Breton afore ye!'" Tinker sang, teasing his intoxicated friend.

16

"Kind of reminds you of the inside of a coal shed, doesn't it?" Blue said, scanning the interior of the Aquarius Café.

The café, complete with low ceiling and exposed pipes, was located in the basement of the address to which they had been directed. The walls were painted black and most of the inadequate lighting came from clusters of candles flickering slow shadows across fluorescent stop-the-war posters while layers of cigarette, marijuana and hashish smoke made lazy swirls in the wake of anyone passing by. Tinker and Blue sat on tin folding chairs at one of a dozen small, round tables, drinking syrupy coffee and waiting for Tinker's turn on the stage.

The stage was a tiny, six-inch elevation in one corner of the café, equipped with a stool and a microphone that was unnecessary in the close basement quarters. They listened to singers singing anti-war songs, poets reading anti-war poems, political activists chanting anti-war slogans and dropped change into the cup every time it came around.

"If you don't get up there soon and get us our money back we're going to wind up on the losing end of this deal, Tinker," Blue cautioned as another donation left his hand. "It's cheaper to go to church."

"I don't know about this, Blue. Everybody that's gone up there has been singing their own songs and they're all against the war. I can sing a few that I picked up on the street, but they're not my own."

"Make you a deal, Tink. You go up there tonight and get our money back and I'll write you some anti-war songs of your own for the next time."

"You sure you can do that?"

"Christ, Tinker, how hard can it be? Do you know how many words rhyme with war? Sore, more, door, floor, gore, nor, snore, chore, bore. It'll be a breeze, buddy. Just be glad they're not singing anti-orange songs."

| 81

A girl with a sweet, angry voice sang of napalmed children and when she finished Blue opened his guitar case and followed Tinker to the stage. Tinker sat on the stool and nervously began "Last Night I Had the Strangest Dream." Blue, playing behind him, remembered the really important thing about this particular anti-war song, the reason Tinker had decided to learn it.

"Fellow from back home wrote that. Ed McCurdy," he shouted between verses. "Halifax, actually."

Tinker moved through his small selection of popular protest songs, his rendering of them casting a spell across the café. Recognizing that this was the ideal time to profit from the war, Blue lowered his guitar and left Tinker to finish unaccompanied while he walked among the tables with his hat extended. When he came to their own table it was occupied by Nathan Goldstein and a friend, along with Tinker who had finished his gig. Blue pulled up a chair.

"Not bad," Blue told Tinker, whose performance was being complimented from all corners of the café. Blue's review was for the collection.

Nathan shook Tinker's hand, said hello to Blue and introduced them to his friend who wore pigtails and Benjamin Franklin glasses with a cracked lens.

"What's the name again?" Blue asked.

"Peter?" Nathan's friend replied.

"Don't ask me. I'm asking you," Blue said. "Peter, you said?"

"No. Peter?"

"Acid, right?" Blue said, turning to Nathan for confirmation.

"No," Nathan answered. "It's Peter? Explain it, Peter?"

"Well," Peter? began slowly, collecting his thoughts. "Descartes was correct in proving his own existence. I think, therefore I am! Brilliant. I couldn't have said it better myself. But proving your own existence is only the first step. You can say 'I am,' and still know nothing except that. So the question that truly brings us to the centre of being, of existence, of the Universe is 'Who am I?' I am still questioning myself. Peter, my parents' choice for a name, really says nothing about me. Peter?, the question you see, keeps my quest eternally before me. Descartes laid the foundation, but someone must build a tower of truth upon it. Wouldn't you agree?"

"Like putting da cartes before da horse, you mean?" Blue said, kicking Tinker under the table.

"Precisely!" Peter? said, his eyes glowing with excitement. "The cart before the horse! Very colloquial but very insightful. We're kindred spirits, I believe, fellow philosophers," extending his hand to Blue.

Blue fired a panicky glance at Tinker who was already on his feet and heading for the washroom, shoulders shaking.

"You've got more than that in common, Blue. Peter? is a writer, as well," Nathan said as Blue rose from the table.

"Great," Blue answered. "Excuse me, guys, but I got to see a man about a horse, as the other fellow says."

"That other fellow's name wouldn't be Descartes by any chance?" Peter? asked, winking at his own witticism.

—

"Tinker, will you shut up and listen to me!" Blue said, standing at the urinal. Tinker was sitting in the washroom's only cubicle, barely able to breathe, laughter rolling out of him. "Know what I think, Tink? When we go to leave this goddamned city we aren't going to be able to get out because there's going to be a big cement wall all around it and written on that wall in letters big as Giant MacAskill are the words 'San Francisco Asylum.' If people aren't shitting on the floor of the hotel they think they're God. Did you hear the guy? I am who am! That's right out of the Bible, boy. And Moses playing the bagpipes. Jesus, Tinker, we gotta get home."

They returned to the table where Nathan and Peter? were listening to another voice rising melodically against the war in Vietnam. Peter? ordered a round of coffee while explaining that freelancing articles to various magazines paid the bills while he worked on his philosophical dissertation. He inquired about Blue's writing.

"I'm a songwriter myself," Blue told him, tapping the guitar case that leaned against the table.

"Spoken like a true wordsmith," Peter? replied.

"The poet?" Blue asked.

Peter? looked at him oddly, then smiled.

"Oh, Wordsworth! That's another pun, right? A wordsmith, I said. You must have heard that used before to describe a writer. A wordsmith, someone who works with words the way someone who works with hot iron is a blacksmith."

"Oh, I get it," Blue said. "A wordsmith. There's a sense of real work in it, isn't there? I helped Iron Angus, this blacksmith back home, shoe a few horses in my time. Blacksmith, wordsmith. I like that. Tinker, don't let me forget it."

"But the important thing," Peter? observed, "is that you described yourself as a songwriter, not a musician. A musician is primarily concerned with music; words are a secondary consideration, but when a man says to me that he is a songwriter, emphasis on 'writer,' then I know that this man is interested in articulating thought rather than feelings. Feelings are fine, of course, and music may soothe the savage beast, but it cannot make the beast argue intelligently for itself or its species. Without words there is no philosophy, and without philosophy there is no hope of understanding Man's essential nature. But what about a sample of your own words, Blue? The stage is free, I see," Peter? said.

"Yes," Nathan encouraged. "If you don't go, I'll be up there with my pipes emptying this place. The acoustics here are not what you would call Hebridean."

Blue, smiling, pulled off his blue hat and threw it into Tinker's lap. "Watch me fill that thing for you, buddy," he said. "I'm working on a piece that you might be interested in," he said to Peter?, taking his guitar from the case and turning toward the stage.

For the first time since retiring his talent on the sidewalks of San Francisco, Blue let the lyrics to his masterpiece-in-progress pour out of him in public. The words to "The Red Lobster," including its latest addition, verse fifty-four;

You reach out and grab me
Like the long arm of the law
Squeezing me hard
With your lobster claw
You wanna hear "I love you"
Squeak outta me
But all I gotta say
is "Show some merceee"

Red Lobster, red lobster
Don't you dare sob, sir
'Cause love is you, and love is her
You're the meat. She's the but-tur

The patrons of the Aquarius Café were unfamiliar with the musical forms employed by Blue, both in his lyrical construction and in his rendering of lyrics. Some listened politely and some not at all and some departed, but Blue didn't notice because his song was directed at the table where Tinker, Nathan and Peter? were seated.

It was their request that caused him to be up there on the stage instead of hovering in the background, engineering Tinker's career. Tinker, of course, had heard it all before. Nathan had obviously heard nothing quite like it before. Peter? pulled a notebook from his pocket and scribbled while listening to Blue's forty-minute memory feat. In spite of Blue's coaxing, no one dared join him in the chorus. He carried the whole event off by himself.

"That's as far as I've gotten with it," he explained as he returned to his seat in the near empty café. "There's forty-six more verses left to write."

Anything that Tinker or Nathan might have felt obliged to say was drowned in the tidal enthusiasm welling out of Peter?.

"It's epic, Blue, courageously epic. I was jotting notes just to keep track of the thoughts inspired by your music. You're not insulted that I call it music, I hope."

"Not at all," Blue answered. "You know what the other fellow says about music, don't you?"

"Remind me."

"The other fellow says music's nothing but organized noise. Well, some people organize it one way, I organize it another."

"Wow!" replied Peter?. "But music is as close as I can come to describing what I have just heard while at the same time I realize that music is exactly what it wasn't. Oh, man, it's so far out there on its own it could originate on another planet. You've read Plato, of course? *The Republic*?"

"Ahhhhh, yeah, I think so," Blue lied. "The condensed version. *Reader's Digest*. Pretty good story."

"You're pulling my leg, right?" Peter? asked him. "*Reader's Digest?* Condensed version? Never happened, did it? I would have heard. I'm sure I would have heard. Then, of course, I never heard *The Republic* called a story before but I suppose you're right. Plato was just making it up in his own head, wasn't he? But do you remember what he said about music?"

"That he liked it?" Blue replied tentatively.

"No, that in the perfect society music needs to be controlled. Plato said that society must have control over the development of its music because, listen to me now, because Plato saw that the winds of change and protest will always appear in music long before people become consciously aware of it. So the Republic must protect itself from the influence of music by allowing only a shadow of it to exist.

"And he was right! Plato, I mean. Because do you remember the first time you heard the Beatles? They were singing 'Yeah! Yeah! Yeah! I wanna hold your hand.' Cute stuff, but not poetry. Still, it mattered. Why? Because of the music. Even when we didn't know why, the Beatles' music still mattered," Peter? pointed out. "It spoke to our restless souls, man. We wanted to find out things for ourselves, about ourselves, things Second World War movies couldn't tell us. And look at us now! The Beatles and so many other songwriters have caught up to the music, putting in words the ideas that make our parents puke.

We're out here making it happen, and the music is leading the dancers.

"But, for all their brilliance, the fact remains that the Beatles are still experimenting within established forms of melody, finding new ways to use established harmonic relationships. Your material, though, Blue, assaults the concept of harmony itself. It threatens to produce anarchy in the spheres. It's wonderful, man. Don't you agree?"

"Well, I won't say that you're not right, but as the other fellow says, I'll have to give it some thought before I sign anything."

Peter? invited them back to his place where a party was already in its fourth day, according to him, and apologized because they would have to walk several blocks to get there. "My van broke down," he explained.

"A VW?" Tinker inquired and, finding out that it was, assured Peter? that there was nothing to worry about. He was an experienced Volkswagen mechanic.

"Whaddya think, Tink?" Blue asked as he emptied the contents of his hat, put the thirty-two cents in his pockets and picked up his guitar. "Follow any of that philosophy business?"

"Lost me just about the time he started to talk," Tinker replied.

17

Hendrix was pulsing out of speakers wired into every room in the apartment, but that was the only visible energy as far as Blue could see. The bodies themselves were slouched on a collection of makeshift pillow furniture which was strewn around the rooms. People made listless, glassy-eyed waves of acknowledgement to the four newcomers. Bead curtains separated the rooms but the rooms were pretty much all the same, beads, posters and incense. In the stereo room a black light searched out a phosphorescent Universe for the entertainment of those afloat on the good ship LSD. Blue wondered what would happen if he threw a fake grenade in there.

"Smile."

Blue turned toward the voice and a flash exploded like a grenade in his face, giving Blue some idea of just how much a fake grenade would be appreciated.

"Have to have pictures, you know," Peter? said, holding a camera in his hands. "Just make yourself at home," he added, entering a room to get rid of the camera.

Blue wandered around, reading the walls, trying to distinguish in the subdued lighting whether he was nodding to a girl or a guy. The party, he realized, presented the first possibilities since Colorado. He wanted to remind Tinker of that.

Tinker was into the van engine before he was into the apartment, the latter only to find a light he could string outside. When Blue came out to check on him, he was bare-chested to protect his shirt from the oil and banging a wrench on the motor.

"How the hell can you see what you're doing in this light?" Blue asked, watching Tinker work in a series of shadowy flashes.

"It's got a short or something. I tried to fix it but I don't know shit about electricity."

"Want something to eat?" Blue said, holding out a pan to his friend. "Nothing in the place but brownies which we should be thankful are not sunflower seeds."

88 |

They polished off the half pan of brownies while talking about things that brought them back home for a minute.

"Know what we should do some night, Tinker? Phone the Legion back home. We'll get a bag of wine and a bag of quarters and get drunk and go to a pay phone and phone the Legion. A Saturday night, eh? We'll talk to the guys and listen to the Seaside Cowboys in the background. I bet you ten to one they're playing "Candy Kisses" when we call. That's the great thing about us being together out here, Tink. When we talk about home we see the same pictures, smell the same air. We'll tell them back home that we're playing in a club out here. The Aquarius Club. Playing rock noise and eating acid for breakfast. I'm going in before I go blind," Blue said, pointing to the light.

"Did anybody see the strobe light?" a hippie was asking the population in general as Blue walked into the kitchen. "It was in there before but I don't know what happened to it."

Blue would have asked him what a strobe was but his thoughts were drifting elsewhere so he simply shrugged and opened the fridge door, looking for food. There was nothing there but another pan of brownies and a quart of milk which he was helping himself to when Nathan came into the kitchen, holding a girl's hand and introducing him to Sherry. Behind Sherry and Nathan, though, came a far more startling apparition.

"Blue, meet Lee. Lee, Blue," Peter? said, introducing them.

Peter? and Lee were also holding hands, but the significant difference for Blue was that Lee, effeminate or not, was definitely a guy. Lee released his hand from Peter?'s clasp to grasp Blue's hand.

"So you're the living proof of Peter?'s pet theory. I haven't seen him this happy since the first night I said I would go out with him."

Chewing on a mouthful of brownie, Blue only nodded in response, but had a mild choking reaction that escalated to strangulation when Peter? asked if Tinker and Blue were lovers.

Blue spent so much time spitting brownies into the sink in order to be able to vehemently deny the charge that he barely remembered the question when he was finished.

"Don't be offended, Blue," Peter? said mildly. "Just curious about the two of you living together."

"Hell, we're from Cape Breton," Blue said. "There's none of that business goes on back there. Almost everybody's Catholic, you know."

"Oh, dear, spare me from the Catholics," Lee sighed. "Obsessively heterosexual males can be so close-minded," he remarked to Peter? as the two of them walked toward the stereo room, leaving Blue, Nathan and Sherry in the kitchen.

"We're not, you know," Blue told the remaining two and having reasserted himself against any possible rumours about him and Blue, walked out of the apartment into the pulsating light of back yard.

"Better get that shirt back on, Tinker, old buddy, 'cause have I got a story for you," he warned as he came down the back steps into a scene that disoriented him. Motor parts were spread around the yard and Tinker was sitting in the driver's seat of Peter?'s van, which was on the ground several feet from the vehicle.

"What did you take the seat out for?" Blue asked.

"I've been sitting here for the last ... oh, infinity ... asking myself that very same question. I know I knew what I was doing when I did it, but I forget. Blue, do you think those brownies might have been poisoned? I don't feel right. I don't feel bad, but I don't feel right."

Blue remembered why he had come out to see Tinker and told him.

"I hope you cracked him on the head," Tinker said, snapping his right fist into his left hand for emphasis.

"Holy shit, Tinker, it didn't even occur to me. That's the trouble with parties with no booze. You lose your sense of reason. A few beer at a party back home and that guy'd still be spitting out teeth. Well, I think I would of punched him, but he's with Peter?, and I liked Peter? before I knew about him. I can't see myself punching him now. He's practically a friend. Tinker, old buddy, there might be worst things happening to us than food poisoning. We might be turning into a couple of friggin' pacifists."

But Tinker had long ago disappeared, working at the far side of the van and when he came back he was carrying the front passenger seat which he put down beside the first one and offered it to Blue. The two of them sat in silence in the flashing strobe imagining the front seat of the Plymouth as it sped down the highway toward home.

"Gas," Tinker said after an unmeasured lapse of time. "The van was out of gas. That's all that was wrong with it. Found that out when I went to empty it so I wouldn't wind up blowing myself up like Charlie did. But ... I needed the practice," he said, sweeping his hand to take in the yard filled with automotive parts.

18

The Aquarius Café had never booked an act before, depending instead on the spontaneous appearance of hopeful amateurs, but the exception to the rule took place on an October night when the café filled with Berkeley professors, musicians and writers from across the city, reviewers from fringe and establishment publications and a random sampling of San Francisco's counter culture population.

Five weeks after the party at Peter?'s, Nathan brought a copy of *Rolling Stone* magazine to the street corner where Blue and Tinker performed. In the magazine, Blue saw his own startled picture under the headline: "Blue Antivoice – the ultimate musical revolution?" The article, written under the byline Peter?, argued that the paradigms of music needed to be shattered and recreated before the Great Revolution could find its true spirit, its true song. No revolution could succeed without articulating through music a sense of its soul. "The only true history of a people is the history of their music," Peter? wrote.

> "The shattering of establishment music has begun with the arrival in San Francisco of Blue Antivoice, a Canadian whose musical roots reach back to the Highlands of Scotland, and whose voice at first reminds the listener of badly tuned bagpipes. But as one listens closely, the singer's voice takes on the energy of exploding glass, the sound of a brick being thrown through the Establishment's concept of music. It is a sound which can only be described as Pre-Primitive. Blue Antivoice's lyrics are rich in man-as-crustacean metaphors, a soul encased in the shell of a creature that resonates to the earliest stages of evolution. One hears within that sound the agony of becoming, the genius of discord, a genius of insights, observations and wit which Blue Antivoice modestly attributed to his imaginary mentor, The Other Fellow."

The article mentioned John the Baptist's heralding of the Son of Man, managed to weave Peter?'s theory of Plato's *Republic* throughout the piece until Blue's presence wavered in the reader's imagination like fire-shaped shadows on the wall of a cave. Blue recognized his photograph as the one taken in Peter?'s apartment during the party.

"You know what would be really great?" he asked Tinker as he passed him the article to read. "If this story was in the *Bulletin* back home. That would be really something. Who do you know reads this rag?"

"That's pretty good," Tinker said, looking up from the magazine. "He calls you John the Baptist in it."

"That's only second best, Tinker. Why get your head cut off when you can be crucified?"

"What does that mean?"

"Haven't the faintest idea, but I'm going to try it on Peter?. Bet he thinks it's really deep."

The rewards of stardom came quickly to Blue. Along with the magazine, Nathan delivered a message from the manager of the Aquarius Café offering Blue fifty bucks to play there on Friday night.

"Fifty bucks and I still get to pass the hat, tell him that."

"Great," Nathan said. "I can see next's month's headline already. 'Singer holds out for thirty-two cents!' Look, Blue, don't fool around with this thing because of money. Not yet. Peter? is turning you into an idea which means people are going to discuss you, and to do that they have to listen to your music. That's a dream, man. Greater composers than Bach and Beethoven have probably starved to death because nobody wrote about them in *Rolling Stone*, or whatever passed for it."

"We got this guy back home, eh? Farmer, a horse trader," Blue said to Nathan. "He says if you can't buy it or sell it, it doesn't exist. Well, the way we're going to work this thing is get Tinker to be the opening act. That'll get us a few more bucks. A few jobs like this and a little luck and we'll be home for Christmas. Or on the Grand Ole Opry stage."

Tinker opened the evening, chording on Blue's guitar while Gerry contributed some violin comfort to his songs. Both singer and musician were favourably applauded and substantially rewarded when the hat was passed around the largest crowd ever to seek access to the Aquarius Café. While they warmed up the audience for the evening's headline entertainer, Peter? introduced Blue to Dr. Herman Silver, a professor of Psychedelic Psychology at Berkeley. It was Dr. Silver, Peter? explained, who first inspired him to explore the possibility that the laws of music as practised for several thousand years were in fact not laws at all but a behavioural pattern being endlessly repeated throughout time. "Our creative expectations condition us to produce within established rules," the professor interjected.

"And," Peter? re-interjected, his finger punctuating the air, "the Big Clue, if you will, is the correlation between music and mathematics. How can anything that can be plotted on a graph, that can be as precise and predictable as two plus two equals four, be considered truly creative? We need to break out of this bubble of pseudo-creative behaviour patterns that mankind has mistaken as reality for four millennium and turn on to the true reality beyond it. Do you follow me?"

Tinker pulled up a chair and joined the coven of revolutionaries, watching Blue's face while he listened to Peter?. Back in Cape Breton, they had often been in barns and houses where the conversation suddenly turned to Gaelic to convey information too sensitive for young ears. It left Tinker wondering what secrets he was never going to know because they were locked up inside a language he would never learn to speak. It left the unilingual behind to nod or smile stupidly in the flood of foreign inflections. Tinker found Blue a joy to watch during these moments because Blue didn't pretend to understand – he thought he did understand. That conviction turned him into a furrow of brows and a concentrated squint filled with tics and knowing nods to the speaker, much as he was doing now. He appeared to hang on to every word that Peter? and Doc Silver, as Blue was already calling him, had to say about the reality of another consciousness. Once, he turned to Tinker with a wink that asked, *Do you think I'm going to get away with it?*

"Blue, what does he mean by this 'another reality' business? Help me catch up to this conversation," Tinker asked Blue while they all sat at the table, his question oozing with curiosity.

"Well, I better get up there before they start a riot here," Blue said, sliding his chair back and reaching for his guitar and wiggling out of Tinker's trap. "Doc there can tell you while I'm tuning up."

"You have a wonderful voice, conventionally speaking," Doc Silver said to Tinker. "You could probably earn a living with it singing establishment songs."

"If I can't find a garage to hire me soon I might have to," Tinker replied.

"What your friend is involved in, if Peter? is right, is the cutting edge of a new reality. I teach Psychedelic Psychology which examines historical patterns of behaviour. One of our most common clichés, 'history repeats itself,' is a basic clue that not only do individuals adopt patterns of behaviour that inhibit their true self-expression, but that whole peoples, whole cultures, the whole species for that matter, do as well. From the Trojan War to the Vietnam War, the patterns haven't changed one iota, nor has the music.

"There is the martial music of the oppressors and the protest music of the oppressed, but the reality is that they are one and the same. The oppressed just want to change places with the oppressor so that they can play the martial music. In between those two forms, of course, there is all the sentimental music that has been developed over the centuries – classical and popular – love and loss music that lulls us into believing that it reflects our finer selves. The truth is that even more than religion, music is the opiate of the people because we believe it is our finest expression of beauty. What I propose, and Peter? here is my most faithful disciple of the thought, is that the subliminal message that music has transmitted throughout the ages is one of violence and suppression. To prevent history from continuing to repeat itself we have to stop the music, so to speak, and take new bearings on reality and begin from that point to find our way toward a fully enlightened society. That's what Psychedelic Psychology is about."

"Do you have to take acid then?" Tinker asked.

"While I do admit to using LSD myself for valuable research purposes, I don't recommend it to my students beyond experimental use because it is not the answer, only a glimpse of the answer. True reality, I believe, can't be artificially induced in a people. It has to become a universal consciousness, an awareness transmitted around the globe and throughout future generations through the only creative vehicle capably of sustaining that reality. Music!" Doc Silver said emphatically. "Music!"

"I kind of see what you're getting at, I guess," Tinker said. "It's a little like this guy back home that I used to work for, Charlie. Charlie is working on an invention that he says is going to revolutionize the world. It's still top secret, though, so don't ask me what it is."

"Not 'revolutionize,' Tinker," Peter? said, turning to Doc Silver for approval to continue. "There is no revolution involved because to revolt is to imply violence. We try to avoid words that associate our search for true music with the conventional and violent patterns of establishment music. What we are searching for is best described as The Great Growth. We grow through the walls of the music currently confining us, crushing our best aspirations."

"And 'The Red Lobster' does this?" Tinker asked doubtfully.

"Blue's music is best considered as a signpost along the way to the new reality," Peter? explained. "It doesn't necessarily anticipate what the music of the future will be, but Blue, particularly his voice, brings the establishment music to a crashing conclusion. I can only describe it as a hopeful satire of the whole spectrum of music, the end of what has been and the beginning of what will be."

19

The conversation was silenced when Blue, ready to perform, welcomed everybody to the Aquarius Café.

"*Ciad mille failte*, as we say in Cape Breton. That's Gaelic for a hundred thousand welcomes. My buddy Tinker, the guy you just heard, and me, we came out to 'Frisco because we heard about the gold rush, but we missed it by about a hundred years so we're singing for our supper these days. I'm just going to sing a few things for you, most of which is a song called 'The Red Lobster' which I've been working on for quite a while. When it's done it's going to have a hundred verses and the chorus after every one of them. I wrote two verses just this week, making it sixty-three finished. So just sit back, relax and enjoy yourself while I sing it for you."

Blue began picking the musical introduction on the guitar and looked up at the audience again.

"We got this fellow back home, eh, Farmer, a horse trader whose idea of Holy Communion is lobster. One time he told me that his dream was to wake up one morning and see a herd of lobsters pulling a flat car of beer into his yard and then committing suicide by jumping into vats of boiling water. If they were land creatures he'd probably be raising them for a living. So I'd like to dedicate this song, what there is of it so far, to my old friend, Farmer."

> Your beauty traps me
> like a lobster in a pot
> and I turn red
> when the water gets hot
> ....

Blue's voice, filled with dangerously sharp fragments of broken notes and the shattered remains of a melody, crashed through the candle-lit café as the newly discovered singer performed for an audience whose curiosity was quickly turning to opinion. The gallery of expressions ranged from suppressed giggles to shock to fingers-in-the-ears to head-shaking disbelief to the intense, nodding approval of those who heard what Peter? told them they would hear. No one was unaffected by Blue's work.

By the tenth verse, seduced as usual by the power of his own material, Blue had slipped into a trance out of which the volcano of sound spewed forth while his strumming arm cranked down on the guitar where two strings had already joined the spirit of his voice by snapping in two. The audience, hypnotized or paralyzed by the irrepressible onslaught, was pinned to its seats the way former San Francisco residents had been pinned to the floors of their homes by the roofs of their houses during the quake of '06. And with forty-four more verses to go, Blue was only a small piece of the way into "The Red Lobster," growing louder and more confident as it progressed. Only Tinker had an inkling of what was to come if the song continued on without interruption, which it didn't.

It was during the thirty-third verse, as Blue's voice reached up in an effort to assault higher octaves and bring renewed vigour to his epic work, that the screaming started, along with a sudden shuffling of tables and chairs and the frantic movements of people in panic. The external discord became so pronounced that it disrupted the reverie of Blue's internal one, drawing the singer to the surface of his song to see where his unexpected competition was coming from. It was at the moment, with his eyes barely able to adjust to the candle-lit darkness, that Blue saw people leaping up from their tipping-over tables, and saw, at the last moment, the reason for their terror. The huge, black bulk leapt from the darkness and hurled itself at Blue whose scream, the audience noted, was surprisingly in tune.

The maddened intruder hit Blue with the impact of a football tackle, tipping the singer and his stool to the floor and pinning him there. Fangs bared, the beast lunged at Blue's throat and wiped his face with a long swipe of its tongue.

"Barney!" Blue shouted once he realized that his throat hadn't been ripped out and that it was saliva, not blood, on his face. Throwing his arms around the German shepherd's neck, he buried his face in the dog's fur. "Barney! My old buddy Barney!" he yelled, the words muffled by the dog's neck. Next came the realization that if Barney was here in the Aquarius Café smothering him with dog kisses then—

"Hi, Blue. Are you surprised? We read about you in *Rolling Stone* and then saw the poster for tonight's show. Barney, let Blue up."

While Blue gazed up at the silhouette, back-lit by an aura of candle light, standing over him, he could hear Tinker's voice reassuring everyone that the dog was not rabid, just an old friend of the family who dropped by to say hello.

—

For a variety of reasons, most of the audience chose the unexpected intermission provided by Barney to tiptoe out of the Aquarius Café, leaving in their wake Tinker and Blue, the hippies from Colorado and their friends from the street. Two tables were shoved together and Tinker and Blue introduced Karma, Kathy and (without a great deal of enthusiasm from Blue) Capricorn to Peter?, Doc Silver, Gerry and Nathan.

Looking around him, Blue was really beginning to enjoy his fate among what he had begun to call the gentiles, to whom he brought word of Cape Breton. Tinker was lost to him already, he and Kathy carrying on a shy courtship of glances and blushes. Blue felt no such certainty. Karma was with Capricorn again. The jealousy of it kept Blue off balance about where he belonged in this picture. That he belonged was a given, but he deeply dreaded the thought that some cosmic prankster had written another one of those awful songs where he winds up as the best friend. No more demoralizing a role can befall a fellow, Blue always thought, than to be trusted by a girl. It was one of the world's more effective forms of castration, but that fear was only a distant ripple in the joy Blue felt about this night, which belonged so strongly to him that he didn't even try to control it, just let it happen. Together, he and Tinker told Karma about how Blue rose from the cracked concrete sidewalk to become a story in *Rolling Stone* and the first star ever featured at the Aquarius Café, which never pays anybody to appear, anybody, that is, but Blue and his Pre-primitive sound. The best part was that he could see she was really interested, and tried to interpret what that meant. And when Tinker and Blue, assisted by Peter? and Nathan, had filled in the missing months, it was Karma and Kathy and Capricorn's turn to catch up.

Taking Barney with them, they explained, Capricorn, Kathy and Karma had driven the van down the mountain to get supplies. Actually, Capricorn said, they ran out of gas on their way down the mountain and had to coast all the way to town. On their way back to the commune, they found themselves following a strange convoy of police cars, squad and ghost. When the traffic turned up the mountain trail leading to the Human Rainbow Commune Capricorn simply drove past and continued along the main road. After a few minutes, they returned, concealing the van and sat in it, watching and waiting. It was more than two hours before the cars descended, Tulip and Cory seated side by side in the back seat of the first squad car. The rest of the commune population was carried away, one or two to a car like princesses in a small-town summer parade. When the police were out of sight they drove their van up the mountain.

"The place was a shambles," Capricorn told them. "Furniture tipped over and ripped apart. Holes broken through the walls. Clothes thrown around. They were looking for drugs, of course, but found nothing. A few seeds and twigs, but nothing to justify arresting everyone in Colorado. But you could tell that they had a good time. They enjoyed destroying the commune. You could feel that sort of sick pleasure people get out of destroying things. It's what's most attractive about war, I suppose.

"What they didn't get was our crop of grass, thanks to Cory's foresight. We were always cautious about a cop raid so we never kept much smoke on hand. We weren't into pushing it, anyway, just personal use. Cory made a small paddock around where we planted it, but never let the horses in there, of course. But the moment he heard the police cars arriving, he took the horses from the pasture and opened the gate to the paddock. By the time the cops finished wrecking the buildings and began looking elsewhere the horses had already taken care of the grass."

"We had to stay there for three days," Karma said, continuing where Capricorn left off. "The horses couldn't do anything but stand under a tree, staring at sunsets and sunrises like animal Buddhas. We couldn't move them for days, then Kathy and I walked them down to the farmer who sold them to us and asked him to look after them until we got back. Then we drove here."

"Well," Blue stated firmly, "we got to get Cory and Tulip out of jail. It's not fair locking a girl up like that. You must miss her something awful, Cap, old buddy. God meant you two to be together. I could see that way back in Colorado. Ask Tinker if I didn't say that! So let's bail her out. I got fifty bucks right here in my pocket that should cover it. There's no way you two should be apart."

"She's out," Capricorn said. "She and Cory were the last to be let go. The FBI kept them a week, but they really had nothing to charge them with. It was me they were looking for. There's a federal agent, Bud Wise, who is obsessed with me, but we won't go into that. The important thing is that Tulip is back at our pad, and Cory—"

"Tulip's free! Wow! That's the best news I've heard since I left Cape Breton. You hear the man, Tinker? Tulip's free!"

"There's a God, Tinker! There's a God and my mother's got Him lassoed inside her rosary and He works just for her, doing nothing but looking after her bouncing baby boy Blue."

"You think that's what your mother's been praying for, Blue? For you to move in with a hippie in San Francisco? Dare you to phone her and tell her that her prayers have been answered," Tinker nodded with feigned innocence.

"The Lord works in mysterious ways, as the other fellow says, Tink. Take my mother's prayers, for example. Did I ever tell you about the time I shot the flaming arrow through Sandy

Malcolm's parlour window? They got the fire out before it did much more than scorch the couch in the parlour. It was an accident anyway. I was trying to shoot the arrow into his coal shed but the wind must of took it or something because it takes this weird curve toward the house and goes through the open window and sticks in the couch. My bad luck was that Sandy Malcolm's mother was lying on the couch and she was like two hundred years old and what does she do but goes and takes a stroke. You'd of thought I shot her through the heart the way Sandy Malcolm went on after the fire department got the fire out and the doctor got his mother to the hospital. I was about eight, I guess, but Sandy Malcolm was swearing to my mother that I was born to hang by the neck until I was dead; I could see it in my mother's face that she was scared he might be right. She took after me with Dad's pit belt that night, and then hung this rosary around my neck," Blue said, fingering the rosary. "I guess she figures as long as I'm wearing the rosary nobody will loop a noose around it. It's worked so far."

Tinker and Blue were in their hotel room gathering their belongings. Blue told Karma and Kathy they would load up the Plymouth in the evening and move into the Human Rainbow Commune, San Francisco branch, first thing in the morning.

"I don't get it, Blue. Why didn't we just pack up and get out of here tonight? They asked us to move in, for Christ's sake! When you said, 'in the morning,' like you were going to think about it first or something, I pretty near punched you. What if they change their minds tonight?"

"Tinker, I had to buy us a little time. We're moving into a hippie commune. I know that. You know that. But what both of us know, too, is that these hippies eat like birds, and I don't mean carrion crows, to quote the other fellow. We need to have signals, like if I say, 'Let's go hunting, Tinker,' then you know that we are going after some meat that comes from that delicious animal called the hamburg. If we work out a few codes like that, then we'll be able to talk to each other in a crowded room without telling anybody else anything."

Tinker walked over to the window and looked down into the parking lot at the back of the hotel. The shape of the rusty Plymouth was a ghostly presence in the unlit alley. Behind him, Blue picked up his guitar, flicking notes into the silence that had fallen in the room, the fragments of music revealing a glimpse of Blue that Tinker saw far too seldom. He believed that Blue was neither a poet nor a songwriter but a mellow, bluesy musician. He never brought it up anymore because Blue never heard him when Tinker used to try to encourage him.

"Blue," Tinker said, turning around to look at his friend propped against the pillows of his bed, strumming his guitar, "I wish we had gone there tonight. I don't like having time to think about stuff like this. It makes me scared. Christ, it makes me lonely. Explain that to me if you can. I'm about to move in with a girl I think I love and it makes me lonely and scared. Do you ever get scared, Blue?"

For a moment, he thought Blue hadn't heard him. He never glanced up at Tinker's confession or question, never missed a note of the piece he was quietly exploring.

"Sometimes," he said finally, watching his fingers work the strings as if they mattered more than what he was saying, "but the way I look at it, Tinker, loneliness and fear are like a couple of nuns at a high school dance, grim chaperons there to make sure we don't have a good time while we're alive. We have to say to hell with them or we'd be still back in Cape Breton wishing we had gone to San Francisco."

20

"Know what these hippie pads remind me of, Tinker? Those McDonald hamburger joints we were eating at all the way out here. Every one exactly the same. Same beaded curtains, same incense, same posters, same music blasting from the record player. Looks just like Peter?'s place and every other we've been in since we got here."

Blue was lying on a mattress which was on the floor of the room he had just moved into with Karma. He stroked Barney lying on the floor beside him and studied the walls and ceiling. Tinker's eyes toured the room, as well. The walls were papered with posters celebrating rock music and criticizing war, posters of seaside sunsets complete with quotes from "Desiderata" or Kahlil Gibran, and psychedelic posters that gave Blue a headache. The posters occupied three walls but the fourth puzzled Blue. Karma had clearly begun blocking out a painting, using all of the 16-foot-wide, 12-foot-high plaster wall. Its early stages didn't make a lot of sense to him.

"Know what I think, Tink?" he said to his friend who had dropped in from the room next door. "I think we're at the beginning of a brand new story. 'Once upon a time' time, to quote the other fellow. With a little luck we'll live happily ever after, old buddy."

"Or wind up in jail, Blue. I've been thinking about the fact that the cops are looking for these people. I know Kathy and Karma wouldn't do anything wrong but who knows why Capricorn is on the run. What happens if we get caught with them?"

"I've been thinking about that, too, Tinker, and our best bet is the 'dumb Canadians' routine. You know, we're just a couple of nice guys who fell in among thieves, to quote the other fella. One of the best things Farmer ever showed me was the weasel path. Farmer says that no matter what situation a guy gets in, even if it's a good one, he'd better figure out what he'll do if something goes wrong. Even a good situation might turn out to have a husband in it, he says. If a guy can't find a noble way out, then he better find a way to weasel out of it. That's what he calls his weasel path. It's a good idea, Tinker. Says he learned it in the war where it came in real handy while he was trying to stay alive."

Tinker nodded.

"So how do you think you're going to like living like a married man?"

"It's awful real, Blue."

"What's real is relative," Peter? said, pushing the bead curtain aside, allowing Gerry and Nathan to enter the room ahead of him, then followed them carrying several newspapers. "So what awful reality awaits you, Tinker?"

"A job in a garage, I hope," Tinker said.

"I don't know about you getting a job in a garage, Tinker, but it looks like there might be a job in the music business for you, Blue," Peter? said flipping through the papers. "The *Herald* called you 'a cacophony of horrid sounds and meaningless words,' but that's the mainstream papers for you. The important point here, Blue, before you become upset, is that the paper bothered to mention your performance at all. People who don't trust this reviewer will want to hear you for themselves. *The Voice* is considerably more insightful.

> Blue Anti-voice has developed a sound that, while many were snickering and laughing behind raised hands, attracted, not unlike Saint Francis of Assisi, an audience of animals. A German shepherd from off the street wandered in at the sound of the music and proceeded to affectionately maul the musician. Such omens should not be dismissed lightly.

"But I've saved the best for last. The *Subterranean* reviewer, a close personal friend, I might add, has written that

> Blue Anti-voice has discovered a new dimension to music comparable to the discovery of the sub-atomic world in physics. Like quantum physics, that dimension's value and reality will be lost on most people, but its influences will affect our daily lives for eons to come.

"So is all this good or bad?" Blue wondered aloud.

"Good, Blue. Any note written about an artist is good, isn't that right, fellows?"

Gerry and Nathan agreed that they would consider killing to get that much press coverage from a single performance.

"How would you like to be on the cutting edge of a brand new sound," Peter? asked suddenly. "I've been thinking about it all night. You've got something special, man. You just need some musicians and a manager, a manager that knows the city, and musicians that are as uncontaminated by success as yourself. So, presto! as the magician says, we've come to offer you both."

Blue evaluated Peter?'s proposal, noting especially Peter?'s insight that Blue possessed something special. He could modestly blush at the observation, but not honestly deny it. He looked at the others. "What do you guys think?"

"I've been thinking about it, and I don't think I can play that bad," Gerry confessed sadly.

"Sure we can," Nathan said. "We'll just tune our instruments to Blue's voice then play it for real."

"Can I be part of this?" Tinker asked.

Gerry, Nathan and Peter? looked at him, their faces filled with the bad news. "Sorry, Tinker, but we've heard you. You couldn't sing a bad note if you tried. But there are lots of garages in 'Frisco," Peter? assured him. "What we need now is a name that will announce our arrival. Blue Anti-voice is too much of a portrayal of a single personality. We're a group now, a movement."

"What did that guy in the *Herald* call me? That word...."

"Cacophony?"

"Right. I like the sound of that. Ca-co-phon-y! How about Blue Cacophony?"

"Perfect!" Peter? said with the others nodding agreement.

"What does cacophony mean, anyway?" Blue asked.

"You can look it up later," Peter? replied. "What we need now is a place to practice."

"A secret place," Blue cautioned. "We don't want someone coming around and stealing our sound before we get it out there. In the meantime," he said to his band members, "Don't quit your day job, to quote the other fellow, but on the other hand be ready to join me on the stage of Ryman Hall. We are on our way, gentlemen."

"You know what the other fellow says, Tinker, love begins when she sinks into his arms and ends with her arms in the sink. Only trouble is, buddy, it's us with our arms in the sink."

Blue was fussily trying to fish dishes from the sudsy water in the kitchen sink without getting his hands wet. Tinker was drying whatever cups and plates Blue caught in the hot, greasy pool.

The rules of the Human Rainbow Commune (San Francisco branch) were simple enough. Capricorn had convened a meeting of the population to welcome Tinker and Blue to the commune and to inform them of the rules. There was no mention of what Blue called "our expulsion from Colorado."

Everyone contributed what they could financially, and each person was delegated a domestic chore each day; sweeping, scrubbing, shopping, laundry and whatever other jobs God had originally delegated to mothers to perform for their children. Tinker and Blue explained that the only household chore in which they were well-trained was hauling kindling and scuttles of coal from the shed in the back yard to the stove in the kitchen, a trade for which there was little demand at the centrally heated Human Rainbow Commune. They were now apprenticed to each other as this day's dish washers, tomorrow's grocery shoppers.

There were eleven people living in the three-story commune besides Tinker and Blue; Capricorn and Tulip, Karma and Kathy, and the rest were familiar faces with forgotten names from Colorado, but Blue missed one member from the Colorado location.

"Where's Cory?"

"Cory's gone political, man," Capricorn replied. "After they arrested him on the mountain and he found out what happened while he was hiding up there ... that's his own word, hiding ... when he found out about the trial in Chicago, and about Bobby Seale gagged and chained to his chair right there in the courtroom, well, Cory lost it. Not much political news reached us in Colorado. That's how we wanted it, an unpolluted new beginning. The commune tried to have no interest in any of what was happening down here, especially the war and the president. So the story of the Chicago Seven, well, we heard there was a trial but didn't chase the details, not what happened to those people in the courtroom. Even if I did know it all, I don't think I would have told the rest, even Cory, although he has a cultural stake in what happened there.

"What we were trying to do there – what we are still trying to do here – is transcend cultures, creeds and politics. That doesn't mean that none of us have political views. We all do because how can a person not have opinions, but they are just that, opinions. None of us are bound to someone else's opinion. We are not a political movement because we are not on a power quest; we are on a spiritual quest. We recognize that violence is wrong. The path of non-violence is the one thing common to everyone in this commune. It's not a religion we have here because that in itself is a power quest. We welcome all religions that teach that violence to each other and the planet is wrong.

"But the path you choose doesn't automatically transform itself into your destiny. That's what Cory discovered, that he isn't ready to live separate from what is happening to his people. He thought he could make an individual choice for himself, but a week in police custody and an overdose of newspapers and television broadcasts about political America taught him more about himself than he learned during eighteen months on a mountain top. That's what he told Tulip.

"Spiritually, it's not up to us to judge Cory for going militant in his rage. Destinies unfold at their own pace and Cory's right now has led him to join a cell of the Panthers."

"The Black Panthers?" Blue gasped. "You mean Cory's one of them now? When I heard what they did to that guy in Chicago it even made *me* mad. Reminded me of the story they tell back home about the strike at the coal mines when the police shot Bill Davis to death. Ever hear about that? It's a holiday we hold every year now for miners murdered by the police or the coal companies. Davis Day! Besides, most mine accidents are murders, you know, but you never hear of a coal company going to jail, just miners going to their graves. So we know where Cory's coming from, but the good news is he's still here and not in jail. Where?"

"I've run into him a few times, and last week he dropped in here to visit Tulip, but ideas are like continents, once they begin to drift apart an ocean opens up between them and it's hard to communicate across an ocean," Capricorn explained.

"Well, I'm sorry Cory's gone but I'm glad he's doing something he believes has to be done. I guess there's something Tinker and me should tell you before you sign us up for this path you're talking about. We're Catholics and we're Liberals."

"Oh?"

"Well, I'm not sure if the Catholic Church is non-violent or not. Tinker and I have been battered around by a few nuns in our day but who hasn't, and if the Pope tells us to go to war we have to go. And we were born Liberals, just like we were born Catholics. That's pretty well the way it works back home, you're either Catholic and Liberal or Tory and Protestant. There's exceptions, of course, but it generally breaks down that way and the Liberals really like it because Catholics have so many kids who grow up to vote like they're supposed to. So we belong to a church that's not afraid to throw a punch, as the other fellow says, and the Liberal Party, both of which we inherited from our fathers who would kick our arses all the way back to Cape Breton if we ever converted to something else, like becoming a Protestant or a Tory."

"Or becoming a hippie living in a commune in San Francisco learning how not to fight," Tinker added. "Okay, I understand this not fighting bit, but when is it all right to fight?"

"Never," Capricorn replied. "We practise non-violence with people, animals and insects."

"Yeah, I got that part when I was in Colorado. I think it's a great philosophy to have as long as nobody's bothering you, but what if somebody comes along and wants to steal your van? How do you stop him if you can't crack him in the jaw?"

Something like a smile threatened to twist Capricorn's serious mouth and he changed the subject. "I've been meaning to talk to you about the van, Tinker. It's been behaving badly since we got to the city and if you don't object, I'd like to make van maintenance one of your responsibilities."

"That's vantastic, Tink," Blue said. "Get it? Vantastic?"

21

Wondering what he had gotten himself into, Blue watched Karma blocking out the bare wall for her painting. When he asked what she planned to paint, she had replied that she was going to create a mural of her lives.

"Your lives?"

"Yes, in panels like a comic book page."

"You don't mean lives like you were once Napoleon or anything like that, do you?"

"No, Blue, of course not!"

"Whew! For a minute there I thought you were talking about reincar—"

"I was never Napoleon. I have no feel for his time at all and that must be because I wasn't here at the time, don't you think?"

"Whoa, whoa, whoa! Karma, for the love of Christ, hold her right there, girl! You're not serious about this?"

"I know what you mean. It used to scare me, too."

"It doesn't scare me!" Blue snapped. "I read all about that Budoo stuff, where you come back as an ant or a carrot or something. All those lives might make a good religion for cats but I'll take my chances with good old Catholicism myself."

"I'm surprised, Blue. It's such a good story I thought you'd like it, everybody being born over and over and over until each of us gets it right. That's the happiest ending I can imagine; everyone fated to fulfill themselves, and God just waiting for us to get there."

"There are stories and there are stories, and some stories should be banned in Boston, as the other fellow says. Explain to me where we go between lives, if you please? Do we just slip out during a heart attack and hang around with the angels just waiting for some chick to get knocked up in the back seat of a Chev so we can come back? I don't think that's what God's got in mind, girl. Why would you want to believe that?"

| 111

"Because if we've chosen the lives we're living then there's a point to everything, isn't there? And God's not to blame for anything, we are. Capricorn has this theory about a spiritual evolution. Maybe it takes millions of years for a soul to grow up. That's exciting, don't you think? I decided to believe it instead of horrible stories about Heaven and hell, spiritual winners and losers. With reincarnation, we've all chosen our crosses so they can't really be crosses, can they? So they must be something we need."

"Funny you should say that. We got this nun back home, eh...."

"Not Sister St. Farmer, I hope, Blue."

"No, Mother St. Agnes. She was our grade six teacher and one time she told us that if everybody in the world could put the crosses they had to bear in one big pile in the middle of a field, and then each one of us was allowed to go through the pile and choose whatever cross we wanted to carry instead of our own, well, Mother St. Agnes said that once we got a good look at the crosses everybody else had to bear, that we would just pick up our own again and be grateful. You know how sometimes somebody says something to you and it just sticks there like something you already knew, well, this story was something like that."

"So was my story," Karma said. "It just felt so perfectly true that I can't imagine believing anything else."

"I'll say this about dying in one place and getting born in another, Karma. I hope it's true, because if Tinker and I don't get some money together soon that may be the only way we'll ever see Cape Breton again."

Karma pulled a chair to the wall, stood on it and began sketching in the upper left-hand corner. The shape that began to emerge had little recognizable reality for Blue, resembling an ugly mask more than any person Karma might have been in her previous lives. While she worked he wondered if she meant to be drawing what she was drawing or if she was just really bad at it.

Karma stepped down and back a few feet to study the lines on the wall. Blue got up off the mattress and started to tip-toe from the room in case she might ask him....

"What do you think?"

Blue froze in mid-stride, his back to the drawing, then turned slowly, looking thoughtful. "Hmmmmm," he said, then repeated that profound observation again. "Well, it's—"

Karma covered his mouth with her hand.

"I'm not into violence, Blue, but if you tell me it's 'interesting' I'll tear your tongue out."

Her light-hearted warning slammed the lid shut on the only word Blue could come up with under this sudden pressure of needing to appreciate art. Without "interesting," he was as helpless as a parent trying to guess what his three-year-old expects him to see in the picture she has drawn for him.

"I like it a lot better than Tulip's stuff, I'll tell you that. I have an idea of what you're drawing, but Tulip's...." The statement could only be finished with a baffled shake of his head, recalling the wildly painted canvases hanging on the walls of the Human Rainbow Commune.

"I think Tulip's work is wonderful. Lots of people do, and the Warehouse Gallery is going to exhibit her work next week. I'm learning a lot from her paintings," Karma said, looking to the wall again, drawing Blue's reluctant attention back to the point he was hoping to avoid.

"It kind of reminds me of a face," Blue said, then gambled. "Maybe a Halloween mask?"

"Close," Karma said.

Blue sighed with relief.

"It's a Mayan ceremonial mask. This panel will be filled with Mayan impressions that I've had for as long as I can remember. I used to have dreams about the Mayans when I was just a little girl. Warm, sunny, primitive dreams – and I'd never even heard of Mayans at the time. I just knew about them."

Blue decided to be blunt about this. "What's a Mayan?"

"They live in Central America, Blue. They used to have this really great civilization but it got ruined, first by themselves, I think, and then by us. That's my earliest impression of a previous life. Once the colours go on I think you'll like it a lot."

"I'm sure I will," Blue replied, terrified already of the remaining panels on the unpainted wall.

22

"Tinker, you remember Silly Sadie?" Blue asked, wandering into Tinker and Kathy's room, but the subject froze on his tongue when he saw his friend look up at him over the pages of a book.

"What are you doing?" he asked.

Tinker shrugged apologetically, explaining that Kathy had given him the book to read.

"*The Electric Kool-Aid Acid Test*," Blue read, running his fingers along the title. "You got to be kidding. Who'd buy a book called something that? You better be careful there, buddy. I know you, remember? You read two books and the next thing you'll think you can write one."

"I'll leave that job to Kathy. What about Silly Sadie?" Tinker asked, slipping out from under a conversation he didn't want to have.

"Wouldn't you say she was just about the craziest person in town? Remember the time you dropped the fire cracker behind her and she chased you over street yelling, 'The Devil will piss on you yet, Tinker Dempsey.'

"Anyway, she was a weird sight, wasn't she, wandering around town with a pair of bloomers on her head and pink hair rollers sticking out of the legs holes and no teeth and muttering to herself and taking fits. They say the moon played her like a tide. Well, I must of told you what Farmer told me about her, huh."

"What was that?" Tinker asked on cue.

"About when she was young? Farmer's about her age and he said she was be-u-ti-ful. She really was something to look at and a guy can put up with a lot of weird stuff if he figures there's a pot of poontang at the end of the rainbow, Farmer said. She used to take fits even back then. Nobody minded much, though, because she was so pretty, but the older she got the uglier and crazier she got. Is Farmer ever glad now that she wouldn't have anything to do with him back then because he said she was pretty enough to marry.

"Think if something like that happened to you. Say, for instance, you married Kathy and her being a hippie and everything you can't tell what's just hippie talk and what's really her. Suppose sometime she started talking about, oh ... say, being Napoleon or something like that and you were so much in love with her you couldn't tell whether or not she was hatching into another Silly Sadie, what would you do?"

"This is about Karma, right?"

"Aw, Jesus, Tinker, she thinks she's Chinese. You know the way they have all these lives in their religion, well, she's one of those. Or all of those. Could be a phase, as the other fellow says, or it could lead straight to a straightjacket. I need a second opinion."

Offering the book in his hand as evidence, Tinker's thoughts shaped themselves into words.

"There's not a single book in this commune that you or I ever heard of in school, Blue. I know. I went through all the titles. The guys in this here book here make Silly Sadie look sane and they're all supposed to be geniuses, for Christ's sake. Capricorn says the real difference between the people in this book and the establishment isn't long hair or music. It's questions. People who ask questions that nobody wants to answer should jump in a bus, just like these guys, and drive as far away from society as they can get, according to Capricorn."

"Bet he wants to be the driver."

"I don't really care who's driving as long as I'm the mechanic. What have you got against him anyway? He treats us fair, doesn't he?"

"When somebody you don't know is treating you fair, you better wonder why, boy. That's the first lesson Farmer ever taught me. But what does that book have to do with Karma?"

"Remember when we picked her and Kathy up in Kansas? Well, if the bus in this book had picked the two of them up they would have been right at home in it, more at home than in the Plymouth. That's what I think. I don't think the people in this book and the people in this house would have to explain much to each other. Not like us. Every time we open our mouths somebody is asking us what we mean, and every time they say something to us we have to ask 'Huh?' I don't think crazy enters into it, Blue. We're just a long way from home."

Blue collapsed on a wooden chair beside the bed and his eyes wandered around the room, growing more and more interested in what he saw.

"That's a flower over there," he said, pointing to a watercolour thumb-tacked to the wall.

"Yeah," Tinker confirmed. "Kathy did that. She drew all of these things to go with a story she wrote."

"A flower in a jug," Blue went on, nodding his approval. "And that's a building on that wall over there, a whole street of buildings, and a dove perched on one of those peace signs everybody wears. You're lucky, Tinker. You don't have to guess at anything Kathy does. You should see Karma's paintings. But even her paintings are simple to get compared to Tulip's. Did you see hers? Looks like something Monk did in the DTs, but I guess you must need some kind of talent to live in this commune. Good thing we can sing. But you think Karma's okay?"

"I like her, but what difference does it make anyway, Blue? We're not going to live here forever. Besides, the way it stands right now, we're in a foreign country, broke, no jobs and not many places to crash unless you want to move back to the hotel. We're sort of trapped here, but it could be worse, couldn't it? We could actually be back at that hotel. So we make the peace sign, sing the right songs and we'll get along just fine. If we have to be trapped anywhere, here's as good a place as any. It's like we're prisoners of peace instead of prisoners of war."

"We're prisoners of a piece of something, Tinker old buddy, that's for sure," Blue said. "What bothers me, Tink, is that I can't see a minute beyond where we are right now. I used to be able to imagine every mile of the drive back home. That was the whole point of leaving home, for Christ's sake. Make some money and get the hell back where we belong, telling our stories until we're broke again.

"Now I can't see me without Karma no matter how many different ways I try to figure out how to get us out of here. I'm the guy who saw Danny Danny Dan's funeral, for Christ's sake. It shouldn't be any problem for me to imagine going home next summer, should it? But if Karma won't come I'm probably not going to go either. But if she does come— Christ, that's too scary to even think about. Farmer told me you had to be careful around women. Not get led by the brainless head, as the other feller says. I'm glad he's not here to see this. I went and drowned my first time in the water, Tink. I'm in love. So this is what sex is all about."

"So the mighty Blue is in love, is he?" Tinker teased his mangled friend.

"Keep 'er down there, Tinker," Blue warned, hushing him with hand gestures. "A rumour like that gets back to Karma and I'm done for. As it is, I'll probably be washing dishes here at the Human Rainbow Commune until I look like my grandfather. What I need is a record contract. Cross your fingers, buddy, because that's our ticket out of here."

The bead curtain pushed aside and Kathy walked into the room.

"Am I interrupting anything?"

"You live here, I don't," Blue replied, getting up from the chair. "I was just telling Tinker here how much I like your paintings. You should give up writing and start giving drawing lessons. I bet there's people right in this house who could use them."

"Thank you, Blue. But you don't have to leave just because I'm here."

"Have to go anyway. The band's having a rehearsal over at Peter?'s," explained Blue who always seemed to have an explanation for leaving Tinker's presence as soon as Kathy turned up.

"Are you playing at the party tonight?"

"Party?" Blue asked. "Who's having a party?"

"The commune. There's a notice on the bulletin board downstairs. Each member is allowed to invite three people. You could invite the band. It would be a chance to play for some new people."

"Did you know about this?" Blue directed the question to Tinker who shrugged his ignorance of the commune's social calendar. "I thought we were supposed to make these decisions together. If any of us have a suggestion everyone has to agree to it, right? But this idea belongs to his royal highness, I bet, so we don't have to be consulted at all. Just insulted. What we need here is a coop-de-thaw. I've got a good mind to invite everybody I see between here and Peter?'s," Blue added.

"Take my invitations over to Peter?'s with you," Tinker said to Blue as his friend was leaving the room. "You know everybody I know over there."

—

Blue Cacophony practised in the scrap of backyard at Peter?'s place, Blue singing the words of his songs while the rest of the band struggled to produce sounds to match the author's vocal renderings. Blue was patient with their efforts.

"With practice you'll get it down perfect," he assured them. "It's easier for me because I'm the guy who was inspired to write these songs. Gives me a head start."

Gerry opened his mouth and dropped his bow. "Nathan, can two people, say you and I, get caught on the same acid trip?" he asked.

Nathan replied with a sudden squeeze of his arm, releasing a crazed alley cat into the neighbourhood.

"Squeezed your bag a little too tight there, did you, Nathan?" Blue asked, picking at his guitar. "Occupational hazard, the other fellow says. Look, guys, I know it's not easy. That's because you book-learned your music. Nothing wrong with that, but I have to teach you something different. Bach can't help you here, but I can, and I'm going to make you guys a million bucks. Now, let's try a few more tunes before we call it a day. We'll want to be good at the party."

The practice was interrupted by Peter?'s arrival, clapping for silence. When silence did fall upon the neighbourhood from the stilled instruments, even Barney wandered from under the sound-deadening step where he waited for Blue.

"We've got our first gig, men. I talked to the woman who runs the Warehouse Gallery, the place where Tulip is showing her work, and we can play during the opening. She read about Blue in *Rolling Stone* but never got a chance to hear him. She said a lot of people are curious and that gave me an idea.

"What do you think of this? We begin telling the press that we refuse to record. That creates the impression that we've already had offers. And if we do get any offers we say no."

"Aw, Jesus, I don't know about that, Peter?" Blue argued.

"Blue, we have the vehicle now. Blue Cacophony isn't a band, it's a revolution. It's everything we ever dreamed about. We haven't even played anywhere yet and we're getting lots of press. Critics are debating Blue Cacophony's merits. A legend is hatching as we speak. Carpe diem!"

"Yeah, well, I was an altar boy, too, and to tell you the truth in plain English, I don't remember ever dreaming about a revolution. I just want to get a little gas money, and maybe a couple of million bucks besides, and records is where the money is."

"Capitalist garbage. There's no money in records, Blue. The record company gets ninety per cent and never pays taxes and you get ten per cent and it all goes in taxes. Then they tour you to death with nothing to do but take drugs and screw a different girl in a different hotel in a different city every night. Our legacy to the future will be a musical legend shrouded in silence, our absolute rejection of music as it has mutated over the ages."

"That's just fine, Peter?, but there's something to be said for drugs and screwing, you know. Especially screwing. If I can just get the gas money, I'll take the couple of million in trade."

"How do you fellows feel about this?" Peter? asked.

"I agree! No recordings, for Christ's sake," Gerry said. "Some of us might have a future. I'd hate to see a record of Blue Cacophony turn up some time down the road just when I might be getting somewhere with my music – the way an old porno movie haunts some big movie stars."

Nathan was gentler. "I think the legend idea is a good one, Blue. After all, we're suppose to be a street band. I didn't having touring in mind. And never in my wildest dreams did I plan on us recording. I'm curious as hell about what's going on here, but we have to draw the line somewhere."

"Do you guys hear what you're saying. This is our chance. Records are pictures of voices, for Christ's sake. I bet there was lots of great singers a hundred years ago that we don't know anything about because we never heard them, so we never heard about them. But I bet everybody from now until Doomsday is going to know who Elvis is. I'd kind of like my chance."

The vote was clear.

"Perhaps a rumour about not recording could get the record companies really interested, couldn't it, Barney? Who knows, they might even start bidding on us. That would change a few minds around here," Blue said as he and the dog walked back to the commune, following a different path than the one that brought them there. It was a brisk detour of four blocks that passed a small diner where the cook made his hamburger patties by hand instead of a meat-measuring cup, and the fried meat oozed with greasy juice. The cook, Blue and Barney were on a first name basis.

23

Blue Cacophony had played during the early stages of the commune's house party, the performance taking most of those who had been invited by surprise. The living room where the band played stayed empty except for a curious few who visited, listened and left the domestic auditorium to join the swelling crowd in the kitchen. Blue Cacophony's music, Peter? reminded the band members, wasn't for everyone. Not yet, anyway. Only one fan was present throughout the group's performance, sitting on a legless couch, his hands tapping their odd sense of timing on his thighs while Blue Cacophony cut across the tradition of music like a chainsaw across a stand of pulp.

"When I heard you guys at the café," the fan told Blue as the group was packing up its instruments to join the party, "it didn't make any sense. But I took a hit of acid tonight and wow, man, you were really great!"

The silence that had fallen upon the living room helped ease the congestion in the kitchen. Tinker and Blue formed a huddle in one corner of the room, watching the party unfold into clusters of meaningful chatter while the stereo screamed socially conscious lyrics in electric rhythms. San Francisco parties were nothing like those that had shaped their experience back home. Neither Tinker nor Blue knew how to find their way into them. It made them homesick.

Blue reached out and grabbed a long-haired stranger who passed too close to their section of wall, mumbling indistinguishable lyrics to himself.

"I was just reminding Tinker here of the party they had for us the night before we left Cape Breton. It was up at Port Ban. You should see this place. A neat little cove that you have to climb down a hundred feet to get to, with a great waterfall to wash off a hangover in the morning. No cops can get within a mile of the place without being seen.

"Must've been a hundred people there that night, and a trainload of booze. I'm not kidding about the trainload, either. That's how the liquor gets to our town, by train. It has to come that way. Only way to keep the town from sobering up, as the other fellow says...."

"I gotta go to the bathroom, man," Blue's audience apologized, backing away.

Blue turned to Tinker to continue his story when a commotion in the kitchen distracted them both. Moving casually to explore it, they saw people milling around someone in army fatigues, but someone not spit-polished and precise enough to be an enlisted man. It was army surplus all the way up to the black tam. In the middle of a welcoming embrace from Capricorn, the newcomer in camouflage caught sight of Blue.

"How's my favourite redneck?"

"Hell, Cory, you can't even see my neck anymore," Blue said, grabbing a fistful of the hair that hung to his shoulders now. "Got a band, too. Blue Cacophony. Were you reading about us?"

"Got yourself a one-armed fiddler and a music philosopher for a manager. Why couldn't you just burn your guitar like everybody else? When I heard you had a band I said that horse trader he told me about must have been his father. I'm coming around to hear you sometime. But the last time I saw you, you were driving down a Colorado mountain getting as far away from us as you could."

"The Lord moves in mysterious ways, as the other fellow says," Blue answered. "Cappi here told me you joined the Panthers," he said, jerking his thumb in the direction of Capricorn. "What the hell happened up there, Cory?"

"The FBI came, busted us, took Tulip and me in. Kept us for a while and then let us go, but I came out of their office through a different door than I went in. I couldn't hang on to all that peace and love shit, knowing what I know." The last remark was directed at Capricorn, testing his attitude. Capricorn's shrug was judgement free.

"What were you doing when the FBI came, Cory?" Blue asked.

"I was over by the horses."

"What were you doing there?"

"I was just standing there scratching the mare's forehead and staring at the mountains, thinking about nothing. That was the best part of being up there, thinking about nothing."

"So how many cops were there?" Blue probed.

"Three cars and a van."

"What'd you think when you saw them?"

"I'll tell you this, you're asking more questions than them."

"Just trying to get the story, Cory. When I met you, we were standing with the horses, remember? Since then the commune's been raided by the FBI and the cops, you and Tulip and the rest were arrested, the whole commune was burned down, they kept the two of you for a few days before they let you go, and now you're a Black Panther and you'll probably never see another horse again as long as you live. Sounds like a hell of a story. What were you thinking when you saw the cops? The story, man."

"The first thing I did was walk the horses in the paddock so they could munch the grass, then started watching the raid. Then for a fraction of a second I actually thought it was a movie. Four brand-new police cars roaring into the commune on that rut of a road and our people running from one building to another like they were going to get away from it. Somebody even screamed. I thought about running to the woods. I was far enough away from the action to do it. Shit, I've been in the back seat of a police car more times than I can remember but I've never gone running scared through a forest. So I stuck with the devil I knew, scratching the mare's forehead, waiting for it to end. I guess I knew way down that it had to end sometime, the commune that is. We're just not allowed to get away from it, man. The Man just won't let us!

"Then I got scared, really scared. There was a dozen cops in flacks, armed to fight a real enemy. Then it struck me that these cops *really* thought we were dangerous. It's a joke down here in the city where there's usually somebody watching the pigs, but it was no joke up there. They had us cornered and if they fired every bullet they owned into us, no one would have ever known.

They really are at war with us, Blue," Cory said, pausing a moment to re-imagine it. "That's about it, I guess."

"About it! Christ, Cory, the cops haven't even captured you yet. How'd that happen?"

"When things began to get still around the cabins one of the cops looked my way and saw me and the horses. Then they came at me, five of them coming in a slow semi-circle, aiming their guns and walking like they were crossing a minefield, sighting me down the barrels. Strange thing was I stopped being scared. They made me lay in the grass and one of them searched me while the other four rested their barrels all over me, one on my head, one on my neck, one on my kidneys and one on my balls. They weren't very happy that I didn't have a gun. Then they pushed me over with the rest.

"They wanted Capricorn. Especially that creep, Wise. They had to settle for Tulip and me. Tulip because she's his woman and me because I was black."

Tulip let out a small chuckle that turned the kitchen's attention to her.

"When Bud Wise was questioning all of us he kept asking us why we had a nigger up there. A couple of the cops said they'd probably know what Cory was doing up there if they took off his pants. Then Wise turned to Cory and asked him if he was a Black Panther.

"'I am now,' Cory told him, and that's when they arrested all of us. Wrecked the place first, though, looking for evidence. Couldn't find guns or drugs."

"Couldn't see the forest for the trees, you mean," Cory reminded Tulip. "They sniffed every pot in the place looking for drugs, even held a conference over a bag of oregano. They never noticed the field I led the horses into, and the horses getting hungrier and hungrier. The more they ate, the hungrier they got. These guys are standing around us with guns, talking tough about drugs, and Tulip and I look at each other and get giddy. I could see her shoulders shaking and she was looking at the ground and I knew that if she looked up at me again we weren't going to get out of there alive because the only way we'd have been able to stop laughing is if somebody shot us. Then everybody else caught on and started laughing."

"The cops thought they had it figured out then. I heard one of them tell another that we were on drugs and had to be watched very carefully," Tulip remembered. "When they didn't find any, they took whatever they could, food they didn't recognize, books to prove we were subversives, anything that looked suspicious to them."

"Then they put us in different cars and took us to the station," Cory added, "The feds were using the state police office down in the town. I didn't laugh much after that."

"So when did they burn the commune?" Blue asked.

"A couple of days afterwards, wasn't it?" Cory said, turning to Capricorn for confirmation. "They made it impossible to go back."

"Not impossible," Capricorn corrected. "Just difficult."

"So I don't get it. You and Tulip spent time in jail because they wanted Cappi the Con here. Who's this Wise character?"

"Some other time," Capricorn said.

"But why did you join the Black Panthers?" Tinker asked.

"Those cops gave me a good education," Cory explained. "In Colorado I was pretending colour didn't matter. Even after they murdered King, I still tried to do it his way, follow his path of non-violence, but they straightened me out about that. And they let me know who they feared most of all because they kept asking me did I know Stokley, did I know Eldridge?"

"Who're they?" Blue asked.

"Stokley Carmichael? Eldridge Cleaver?"

Blue reflected for a moment.

"Cleaver. Wasn't he the guy on *Leave it to Beaver*?"

An uncomfortable quiet settled over the kitchen as Cory glared at Blue, his expression slowly changing to amusement.

"He means it," Cory said to the rest, throwing his arm around Blue's shoulder and laughing. "The dude really means it. Listen Blue, this place you come from ... what's it called again?"

"Cape Breton."

"Right. How did you get here from there? Spaceship?"

Cory's story got lost after that. The party shifted to other centres of attention, but Cory and Blue hovered at the edge, leaning side by side on the kitchen counter, each nursing a beer, listening to the music from the network of speakers that Capricorn had installed and the murmur under it. Blue's thoughts were mulling over a conversation Karma and Cory had had in their bedroom when Karma took Cory there to see the progress to date on her mural of lives. The three of them passed through the rattle of beads and the moment Cory looked at the wall he said, "Mayan. Were you Mayan?"

His question led to a long discussion between Cory and Karma about karma and cultures and the evolution of the soul. The figures in the first panel were just about finished, and while they talked Blue wondered who he would be living with in the next panel. He was still guessing at it back in the kitchen when Cory spoke.

"What did you mean before when you said I may never see another horse again?"

"We got this guy back home, eh, Farmer ... I told you about him. Well, he told me that he's never seen anybody go back to horses. He's been trading them all his life and he noticed that once people give up their horses they never go back. First, it's a truck and then it's a tractor and then the barn becomes a garage and pretty soon there's not even any room in it for horses. Those horses the farmers didn't want anymore Farmer began selling to the Americans. 'From working horse to rocking horse,' was what Farmer used to say. Horses that lost their job on the farm were becoming toys for Cape Breton's summer people, see. But he'd never seen anyone, farmer or American, who went back to buying horses once they gave them up. I guess that's what I was thinking about when I said that to you.

"Actually, Cory, it was me Farmer was talking about when he told me this, which was after I told him about this trip Tinker and I were going on. He said he was sorry to hear about it because he was training me to be a horse trader, see, and when I told him I wanted to do some travelling he figures I'm never coming back.

'Oh, you'll come back home,'he said, 'but you won't come back to the horses'."

"Will you?" Cory asked him.

"I used to think so, but the way I had it worked out then isn't the way it's working out. I don't know now whether Farmer is right or not, but I'm right about you, aren't I, Cory?"

"Probably. When I think about the future I don't see any horses in it. Not the horses, not the commune, not Capricorn."

"Not that mustang of yours? How'd he get you to go up there anyway? A girl? Drugs? What?"

"No, man, his vision. There's nothing wrong with Capricorn except maybe he's on the wrong planet. He's not on mine, that's for sure, and there's no place for me on his. Right now, I'm where I should have been from the beginning, and where I belong right now. Eventually, we all wind up where we belong, I suppose."

"I hope you're right," Blue replied, "because I know where we belong, Tinker and me, and it's on the other side of the world. You belong in that uniform and we belong in Cape Breton."

24

Tinker had drifted away while Blue and Cory were talking, he and Kathy slipping into the solitude of their room where Kathy opened her palm and presented two small pieces of paper to him. Tinker took one and examined it while Kathy placed the other one under her tongue.

It had been a curiosity stirring in him ever since he had seen people "dropping acid" and experiencing what Blue described as "visitations from the Little Flower."

"Those drugs are just a shortcut to the DTs, Tinker," Blue told him whenever they had watched people on the street or in the commune reaching out to touch or stroke the empty air in front of them, or just Wow!-ing over the colour or sound or shape of something as ordinary as a stone on the street or a weed growing through a crack in the sidewalk. "You can get away with that shit here in San Francisco but if they tried to pull that off back home they'd be delivered straight to the Little Flower."

"You two are always doing that," Kathy complained to Tinker, "talking to each other in telegrams. Blue says 'the Little Flower' and you start to laugh and it's like a whole conversation has taken place with just three words but nobody else is included. You do it all the time."

"Okay, I'll explain. The Little Flower is this place in Sydney where guys on the booze are sent to dry out," Tinker explained.

"You send your drunks to Australia?"

"No, Sydney back home. I can't believe you never heard of it. It's the biggest city on the island. All its businesses even advertise on television. Everybody from home goes there to shop for Christmas, but whenever we say Sydney, everybody asks, 'Australia?' Blue always said Americans don't learn about anything but themselves in school and he's beginning to sound right.

"Anyway, the Little Flower is this place where they take in drunks to dry them out, which is about the time they go in the DTs. So when Blue says that people on drugs are taking the shortcut to the Little Flower he means they don't get to enjoy a few months on the booze first. They just take a little pill and start seeing things, and seeing things is your passport to the Little Flower. Have you ever taken any of that stuff?"

Kathy, said that she had, a couple of times, and found it expanding, although her explanation of exactly what it was that expanded was lost on Tinker. But his curiosity had been fanned by the book he was reading.

He had told Blue about these people on the bus in the book and the way they took LSD, "like a Catholic taking Communion, Blue."

"Sounds like a Black Mass to me," Blue said. "Or a bunch of Holy Rollers. We got to stick with the booze, buddy. That's our culture. Just ask the other fellow. If God had wanted us to do drugs he wouldn't of turned that water into wine, would he? He'd of turned it into a barrelful of LSD."

Tinker didn't tell Blue about the plans he and Kathy made.

Tinker's second thoughts about taking LSD were crushed by the fact that Kathy had already took hers, ruining any chance he might have of talking them out of it. He put it under his tongue and sucked terrifyingly, tracing the chemical's absorption into his blood, counted to ten and concluded that nothing was happening.

"I'm not feeling anything. I don't think it's going to work. You know, drugs never really have any effect on me. Not even aspirin. If I have a headache and take an aspirin nothing happens. There's a certain percentage of the population that doesn't react to drugs, you know. Any doctor will tell you that. I think I'm one of those. Nothing's going on. Maybe I'll try it again some other time."

"It takes longer than thirty seconds to work, Tinker. Don't worry. It will happen."

"Who's worried? I was just worried there that it wasn't going to work. I think it will be great if it does. But it could happen, couldn't it, that sometimes it just doesn't work? Well, if that happens to me then we'll just have to try some other time, okay? But if it does work ... ah ... does everybody do stupid things like talking to God or taking off their clothes and walking outside, you know that kind of thing?"

"I've never seen anybody taking their clothes off and walking outside, Tinker," Kathy assured him.

"Oh, God, I hope I'm not the first! I don't mean I want to take my clothes off, Kathy. I mean that drugs make you crazy, right? You must have dreamed about not having any clothes on in church or someplace. Think of having that happen to you and not being able to wake up. But don't worry, I'm not going to take my clothes off.... I'm not going to take my clothes off.... I'm not going to take my clothes off.... No matter what happens I am not going to take my clothes off.... I will not take my clothes off.... I will—"

"What are you mumbling about, Tinker?"

25

Silently chanting his mantra, waiting for the naked madness to strike him, Tinker talked to God about mini miracles, like not letting the acid work, like protecting him from the Devil if the drugs did work, and offering to take the pledge for life. "No drugs ever again if this cup can be passed from me. Please God, don't let it work. Please God, don't let me take my clothes off...."

Tinker's prayerful pleadings continued until the walls started to breathe, or, he quickly reminded himself, until they *looked* like they had started to breathe, seeming to expand and contract like a chest wall, like an iron lung. He killed off the hallucination by reminding himself that the room was candlelit, that he had seen the same effect when the power failed in his own home during winter storms and lantern light flickering on the wind-pounded wall made the house appear to be breathing. He turned his attention to the lone candle and studied its flame which was so still it could have been painted on the top of the candle, but the walls, when he looked at them, continued to breathe. His winter storm theory collapsed and he became vividly aware that the house was alive; it had swallowed them all.

"We've got to get out of here," he whispered to Kathy, uncrossing his legs to stand and run from the building. When he stood he screamed and leapt onto the mattress, gripping his feet and warning Kathy not to touch the floor.

"It's full of electric currents. We're trapped here. We can't get out and the house is going to swallow us, me, you, Blue, Karma, the band, the music, your writings, everything is going to be swallowed. We're being eaten alive," he said in a voice reaching panic.

Kathy came to him on the mattress, soothing him with a calm voice, reaching to take his feet in her hands.

"Tinker, you sat with your legs crossed for too long. Your feet fell asleep, that's all. The house is not alive. We're not being swallowed. Just relax and listen to the music and let it happen,

| 131

but don't let it scare you. I won't let anything happen to you, I promise."

Tinker watched the walls. They were still breathing, but Kathy's assurance was stronger than the inhaling and exhaling around him. He began to relax, listening to the music. He found it funny that he had to stop and listen for it since the music was everywhere, wild rock rhythms spilling down on them from the ceiling like an invisible rain.

"Why is music invisible?" Tinker asked Kathy, but the question created its own answer for Tinker. Music wasn't invisible. Kathy, as he looked at her, was transforming herself into music. A vapour of soft notes surrounded her and began replacing her physical presence with a gently constructed harmony.

"You're made of music," he told her excitedly. "I can see you and you're made of music. If I could read music I could read you, I could sing you!"

"That sounds better than being eaten alive by a house, Tinker. Do you want to stay here where it's quiet or go join the party? We'll do what's most comfortable for you. Stay here?"

Tinker could barely discern Kathy's features through the veil of music encompassing her, and he could feel the notes from the stereo pattering off his head and exposed arms. He wanted to walk into it, walk into the forest of dense music that he knew waited in the common room beyond the bedroom.

"Hold on to me," he said, reaching for Kathy's hand, letting himself be led into the strobe-lit action of the party.

The music was raining so thick he could barely move through it toward the corner where Kathy was leading him, a safe place to sit and watch. The music smelled of things familiar, sandalwood and cigarettes and marijuana, and it broke over them like a storm, pounding and pushing with its two-fisted bass, and soaring and diving like a family of screeching eagles, but the wildness of the music remained leashed to a harmony that kept it from flying apart into a violent cascade of brutal sound.

Tinker sat on a pillow in the corner, huddled close to Kathy, studying the impressions that flowed toward him through the music. Everyone in the common room was made of music, he realized, as he detected each presence through the atmosphere of music that encased them. Some were wonderfully complete in their personal melody, and some were sadly fractured and poorly composed in the essence of their music. It seemed as if everyone's soul had slipped outside for Tinker to see, making him wonder about himself.

He looked down at his arm and it was barely there because it was encased in a musical haze, and the song of it grew inside and began sounding itself through him. Unheard through the torrent of music from the stereo he began to hum the tune of himself, an air so pleasing that he knew he would remember it for as long as he lived. He felt happy to be composed of music that made him feel like singing, because looking around the room he could see that more than a few people at the party would not be happy to encounter the truth in the music of which they were composed. Some people were enveloped in their music, some were shrouded in it.

A motion of music swaying near the stereo caught his attention, and Tinker recognized it as belonging to Capricorn. He was surprised that he recognized Capricorn through the music, but it was music that couldn't belong to anyone else. What surrounded him was powerful and uncomplicated, a music focused on a single, simple, uncluttered theme.

"Capricorn means exactly what he says," Tinker whispered to Kathy. "I'll have to tell Blue. He won't like to hear that."

Tinker's eyes moved around the room trying to find Blue, unable to anticipate what kind of music sang the essence of his friend. When he located Blue it was through the rectangular door of the kitchen, leaning on the counter beside Cory. In the harsh electric light under which the two of them stood, Tinker's perception of the music within people faded. There was no aura of any kind surrounding the people in the kitchen, just their stark physical presence. Watching from his place on the cushion beside Kathy, Tinker grew curious.

"Who's that standing beside Blue?"

"That's Cory. You were talking to him earlier, Tinker."

"I know Cory, Kathy. I mean standing on the other side of Blue."

"There's no one on the other side of Blue."

"Yes there is, and I know him from somewhere," Tinker said just as the unidentified figure turned toward the doorway and beckoned Tinker with a finger. Tinker was slow to rise from the comfort of Kathy's company but curious about the stranger who had the dress and manner of someone from home. Blue was paying the guy no attention at all as he and Cory leaned beside each other on the counter, no longer talking, just gawking through the doorway at the swirl of the party.

"There's only Blue and Cory out there," Kathy stressed as Tinker started to rise.

"And that other fellow," Tinker said, stopping suddenly. Recognition exploded across his face. "That's who it is! It's the Other Fellow! So help me God, Kathy, it's the Other Fellow!"

He released himself from Kathy's grip and walked slowly toward the kitchen, the way he would approach someone whose name he was trying to remember as they were about to meet on the street. The awareness of music evaporated as the Other Fellow's presence grew more solid and confident. He smiled at Tinker and nodded, the expression on the Other Fellow's face reminding Tinker of the nun who taught them in grade nine. But he resembled Farmer, too, but a Farmer with a beard not unlike Christ's. The face seemed always familiar but forever changing. The Other Fellow, Tinker realized, had been conjured into being by all the borrowed, stolen and original sayings that fired Blue's imagination and shaped his opinions.

I think I'm seeing a figment of Blue's imagination, Tinker concluded, at the same time trying to protect his sanity by reminding himself that his mind was, temporarily, he hoped, stranded on the foreign shore of a phantom island inhabited by people composed of music, and by the Other Fellow, who bore a striking resemblance to the whole town he grew up in.

"How's she goin', bye?" the Other Fellow asked in an exaggerated accent from back home.

"Not bad," Tinker replied.

"What's not bad?" Blue asked.

"Me," Tinker answered.

"You? You what?" Blue asked.

"Me. I'm not bad," Tinker replied.

"So who's asking?" Blue wondered.

"The Other Fellow," Tinker said, nodding toward Blue's left.

Blue glanced over his shoulder at an empty space beside him, shrugged and said to Cory, "Looks like my buddy's had ten too many beers. Geared to the gills, as the other fellow says."

"I never said that," the Other Fellow complained to Tinker who relayed the message.

"The Other Fellow never said that."

"Never said what?"

"Geared to the gills. He always says 'geared to the ears.' You're always doing that to the Other Fellow, making him say what you want instead of repeating what he really said."

"Who told you that?"

"The Other Fellow," Tinker said, turning to listen to what else the Other Fellow had to say. "If you don't start quoting him right, the Other Fellow's going to take off and find somebody else to travel with."

"Are you planning to frig off on me? Is that what you mean?" Blue asked, lost and confused by Tinker's rambling.

"I'm not going anywhere on you, Blue," Tinker promised. "But the Other Fellow could use a little more respect. That's all I'm saying."

"Frig the other fellow and the ship he rode in on, as the other fellow says...."

"What I said was 'the horse you rode in on.' You'd think a horseman like Blue would get that much right at least, wouldn't you?" the Other Fellow sighed hopelessly to Tinker.

"...because what I want to know is whether or not you and the Plymouth are planning to take a trip without me?"

"I think Tinker has already taken a trip without you, Blue," Cory said, assessing Tinker's determination to hold a conversation with the kitchen sink into which Blue was flicking his cigarette ashes.

"What do you ... mean?" Blue asked, comprehension arriving with his question. "Aw, Jesus, Tinker. Don't tell me you're doing drugs. Not the acid, man. Not the acid!"

"What did you call me?" Tinker asked. "Man! That's what you called me, not 'boy,' or 'bye' as the other fellow would say." Tinker turned to wink at the Other Fellow who had suddenly disappeared, just a thin vapour of him hovering around Blue, as if he had been reabsorbed.

"This isn't funny, Tinker. This is serious business. You're scrambling your brains, boy. It's going to be just great if I have take you home in a straight-jacket and sit you in the tavern and feed you beer through a straw for the rest of your life while you carrying on conversations with imaginary men. If you're going to have imaginary conversations, for Christ's sake, have them with women. That's how you practice on women, by pretending to talk to them. But you're hallucinating. The Other Fellow, for the love of God! Please, Tinker. Throw it up or something. And promise me right now that you'll never do this again."

"Blue wants me to take the pledge," Tinker said, dropping to his knees. "Father Blue, bye, I swear on the sacred heart of Jesus, his mother, father and all the rest of them saints and sinners that I will not take another hit of acid until I get a note from my mother saying it's okay. Okay?"

Then Tinker collapsed on the floor in belly-bursting laughter while Blue gave him a worried look.

Kathy came into the kitchen and talked Tinker back onto his feet. Cory cautioned Blue to be quiet, hushing a burst of angry blame that had begun to erupt from him toward Kathy. Blue held his peace as Tinker and Kathy started to leave the kitchen. Tinker turned in the doorway, solemn and sad-looking, and addressed Blue's judgementally knitted brows.

"Now listen to me, Blue. I know you're pissed off and all that, but listen to me because this is important, really important, so listen to me, old buddy, old pal! If I talk to the Other Fellow or the kitchen sink or Jesus Christ or anything like that again tonight, I want you to pray for me, okay, buddy? Pray for me! But what's really important, are you listening to me, Blue, what's really important is that if I start to take my clothes off you have my permission to shoot me."

26

Blue was curled up behind Karma on their mattress the following morning. Having slipped away from the party to spend most of the night finishing her Mayan existence, Karma was now planning the next panel in her mural. Blue's thoughts drifted and swirled like cigarette smoke but kept coming back to the party and the fact that Tinker had taken drugs.

He had heard Tinker earlier in the kitchen making tea and toast, knowing it was him because it wasn't the hushed sound of a hippie making herbal tea. It was the sound of someone steeping a pot of real tea, humming a jig, and Blue knew he was the only one in the commune who could name that tune. It would have been the perfect time to try to talk some sense into Tinker about using drugs, but the comfort of being curled up behind Karma, stroking his hopeful way toward a post-party private celebration of their convenient nakedness, left Tinker and his drug problems in the kitchen by themselves. There was all afternoon to preach to him, Blue concluded, his hand sliding its slow way toward Karma's breast.

"The next panel will be from a life in India. Sometimes it feels Hindu and sometimes it feels Buddhist. Maybe I spent two very different lives there, one of each. That's possible. I'll have to know before I start."

"Haven't you ever been a Catholic?" Blue asked, his hand retreating from her breast as from a live coal gripped in the depths of hell.

"I believe so. I have very strong feelings about being a nun in the Middle Ages."

"There you go!" Blue said, sitting up. "That just proves it. You're wrong about this reincarnation business. If you'd been a Catholic nun in the Middle Ages you wouldn't be a hippie in the ... whatever age this is. You'd be in Heaven. There's no way a nun or a priest is going to live a whole life for God and not get into Heaven. Everybody knows that."

"Every Catholic, maybe," Karma said, "but there are some other spiritual ideas in the world, Blue. Do you really think that just because you are a Catholic you are going to Heaven and I'm not?"

"Not me, necessarily," Blue admitted, unable to take his eyes from her breasts that became exposed when she turned to talk to him. "But a nun, for God's sake! She has to go to Heaven. She goes to Mass and Communion every day, lives in a convent where she has no chance at all to commit a sin, or even think of one, I bet, and she teaches little children all about God. Where do you think I learned so much? So if you were a nun in another life, Karma, you wouldn't be here. Unless, of course, you were the most awful nun who ever lived, and you're not, Mother Saint Sebastian is, just ask Tinker. He'll back me up on that one. One time she broke a guy's nose with her pointer."

"And will she go to Heaven, Blue?" Karma asked, teasing her hand along his thigh as she did.

"Maybe a day in Purgatory first. Aw, don't do that when we're talking about God, Karma," Blue said, weakly pushing at her hand, then letting it go. "I got a better idea. Let's not talk about God."

"But I want to," Karma smiled. "I want to know what you think, Blue. I want to know how you feel."

"You're feeling how I feel right now," Blue moaned.

"Okay then, I want to know what you believe. Everyone always asks 'What do you think?' or 'What do you feel?' but nobody ever really asks 'What do you believe?' Except Capricorn. He makes me really think about what I believe," Karma said, removing her teasing hand, becoming more serious.

"Oh, yeah. And where were the two of you when Caprihorney asked you that?"

"Blue, you are a jealous, possessive monster and I think Barney should have bit you the moment you came into my life, but he didn't. I just wish you'd spend as much time thinking about me and you as you do thinking about me and other people. Do you, Blue? Do you ever think about us?"

"Of course I do. What do you mean, anyway? How can I not think about you. You're right here with no clothes on, for Christ's sake. I even think about that when you're not here. What are you looking at me like that for?"

Karma got up from the mattress, pulled on her painting smock and sat on her meditation pillow staring at the panel she would paint next.

Blue watched through the wall of silence that Karma had drawn like a blind between them. He heard the sound of the door closing, Tinker leaving the house.

—

Tinker walked aimlessly through the streets of San Francisco, needing to be away from the commune, needing something to do, something to fix, something to put right. Afternoons of tinkering with the Plymouth and the van in the backyard of the commune had been empty acts of disassembling and reassembling vehicle parts, although there had been some disturbing benefits to his daily routine. Practising over and over began revealing to him the role of cogs and plugs and belts and chokes, the finely tuned difference between one setting and another. He had begun *hearing* the motors, always adjusting them now for a sound that told him the car or the van not only ran well, but that it *felt* good. Charlie had taught him a lot, Tinker acknowledged, and because of it he felt a sense of betrayal to his mentor to suddenly discover that he may not have learned as much as he thought about motors in Charlie's Guesso Station.

He needed a job. It had been hinted at during the weekly council of commune members that not everyone was contributing enough to meet the needs of the commune. Tinker realized that the general direction of this complaint was toward Blue and him. Blue and the band spent so much time practising that there was little street revenue being produced, and Tinker hated street singing so much that without Blue pushing him he no longer did it, choosing instead to go out walking alone, where he passed small greasy spoons advertising for dishwashers and knew that eventually he would have to walk into one. It was the kind of job that didn't require a lot information about social insurance numbers and citizenship. He paused often in front of garages where mechanics in grease-stained coveralls worked at the internal organs of a car, but those opportunities were beyond him, or his connections.

Capricorn had told him that a lot of the civic crap about citizenship and green cards could be overlooked if Tinker could just meet someone who operated a small shop, who needed a hand and who would pay in cash. Bureaucracies, with their psychotic need to document everyone's existence, Capricorn told Tinker, were the grinding stones of civilizations, that every civilization had eventually been ground to dust by its own bureaucracies.

"Ignore their games. It's a big city and somewhere in it there is a place for you and your skills, Tinker," Capricorn assured him. "Believe it and be patient."

Capricorn spoke the same kind of clichés as mothers, priests and teachers but coming from Capricorn, words like "Believe it and be patient" didn't have the same trite tone. "The next thing you know, he'll be asking you to stick your finger in his side," Blue remarked when Tinker told him that Capricorn sounded like he really believed what he said.

An image from the previous night flashed through his mind as he thought about Capricorn's words, an image of Capricorn composed of music, of everyone composed of music, of his own music. He tried to recall the song of himself he had hummed when he had looked down at his own hand and found its flesh replaced by strands of music which he recognized as himself, believing he would remember it forever, like the back of his own hand or the colour of his own eyes, but it was gone now, vanished, like the Other Fellow, who suddenly flashed through his thoughts and faded away so fast that Tinker laughed.

Sitting in the doorway of an empty building, examining a montage of memories surfacing from his acid trip, Tinker tried not to think about Blue who had a tendency to turn into a priest when his own commandments were broken. He rehearsed his defence while watching the activity around a construction site at the intersection. Disrupted intersections were everywhere along the busiest streets, and people walked over steel-covered holes in the sidewalk or were redirected to pedestrian detours made from sheets of plywood. He had noticed them often since their arrival without giving them any thought until now.

Watching two men in white hard hats talking at the site, one in a business suit, the other in coveralls with muckers, which miners named their steel-toed rubber boots, on his feet, Tinker realized what these sights meant: a subway. Under his feet this very minute men were tunnelling their way beneath the city, mucking, drilling, loading, blasting.

He had never been underground but his father had, and his grandfather and most of the men back home. His father still worked in the town's last coal mine, but many of the others who lost their jobs had left for the hard rock mines of northern Ontario and the tunnels that needed to be blasted through mountains or under cities all over North America. And then they came home with their stories, and through them Tinker and Blue and the boys they hung around with all came to know the dampness and the darkness and the tragedies of the mines, and their wild, drunken romance. Their geography included Sudbury, Timmons, Thompson, Blind River, Elliot Lake, names more familiar to them than the capital cities of the ten provinces. Perhaps none of those young eavesdroppers would ever get to Regina but a lot of them expected to go to Sudbury. That was where Tinker and Blue would be this minute if they had not decided on San Francisco instead.

An impulse propelled Tinker to his feet and he walked toward the two men.

"Excuse me, are you guys working on this subway?"

The two men turned toward the interruption.

"I was just wondering if you knew if anybody from Cape Breton is working here."

"What are you talking about?" the man in the suit asked, not hiding his impatience.

"I was just wondering if anybody from Cape Breton is working here," Blue explained. "Guys from back home work all over the world on jobs like this and I was just wondering, that's all."

"Canadians," the man in the muckers explained to the other, then turned to Tinker. "Not that I know of and, in my experience, if there were any here we'd be aware of it. I worked with crews from that place, an island isn't it, up north a couple of times. Good miners." The last two words were directed toward the man in the suit.

"What were their names?" Tinker asked.

The man in the muckers looked at Tinker again, puzzled. "I don't remember, really. One was called Angus, there was another named—"

"You don't remember his last name? Or his nickname?"

"Look, son, we're busy here. What is it you want? Are you a miner?"

"No, but my father is," Tinker replied proudly. "I'm a mechanic myself."

"Really," the man in the muckers said with more interest. "Have you ever worked on underground equipment?"

"No, but I'd like to learn," Tinker said.

The man in the muckers pulled a stained notebook from his pocket explaining to the man in the suit as he did so that they needed mechanics underground. He wrote down an address, ripped the page from the pad and passed it to Tinker.

"Go to this address and ask to see Hank. He'll look after hiring you. And get that hair cut. You can't work around dangerous machines looking like a girl. You could get scalped down there. Or gang-banged."

27

Blue came back from band practice and found Karma still working on her India panel. She didn't acknowledge his entry into the room although he knew she must be aware of him. He took out his guitar, sat on the bed and began strumming, humming "The Red Lobster" air, distractedly toying with the sixty-ninth verse.

"That's a nice-looking litter of puppies," he said, tossing the comment to her as an ice-breaker.

"It's not a litter of puppies. It's a tiger and her cubs."

"I'd of gotten that in a few more guesses, I think. I can see what you mean. They're tigers alright. And being in India of course they'd be. You weren't a lion tamer, by any chance? Or a tiger trainer, I mean."

"This is the starving tiger and her cubs that the Buddha fed himself to out of compassion during the lifetime when he was Mahasattva. It was a wonderful thing to do, don't you think?"

"Fed himself to? How do you mean 'fed himself to'?"

"He allowed a hungry and sick tiger to eat him so she could get her strength back and feed her young. He sacrificed himself, just like Christ."

"Whoa! That's going a bit far, don't you think? Just like Christ? Jesus Christ didn't lay down his life for a bunch of dumb animals. He did it for me. And you. Everybody. Your Buddha's got a screw loose, if you ask me. You know what those tigers grew up to eat? Christians, that's what."

"Those were lions, I believe. If you think your life is more important that any other life then what I believe does sound stupid, I suppose. Do you think I'm stupid, Blue?" Karma turned to lock his eyes with the question, a tease of a smile on her lips.

Trapped me, Blue thought, scrambling for a weasel path that would leave the relationship no more wounded than it already was.

| 143

"No, I don't think you're stupid, but I think you could use some horse sense, though. You watch the next time you see a horse coming to a river that it wants to cross. You'll see him stretch his chin along the surface. Some people think it's to drink and some say it's to test the temperature, but what he's really doing is measuring how deep it is by using the fine hairs under his lip. Farmer told me that those hairs are so sensitive they work like sonar. That way the horse knows what he's getting into. I could use a few of those hairs myself, I think," Blue said, scratching his hairless chin. "Might teach me when to keep my mouth shut.

"Look, Karma, I don't care what the Buddha did with his body so I sure as hell don't want to get in more trouble with you because of him. About what I said this morning, about you being naked, remember? That wasn't what I meant by what I said. Some of the things I feel sound really, really stupid when I try to say them."

"I've noticed," Karma said.

"I don't mean about you being naked. I mean about you being not there. Like when I have dreams where I wake up and you're not there and you're not coming back so when I really wake up I need to prove you're still there. Sometimes, when Farmer and I would go to pick up a horse, eh, an old minker, say, that people had owned since it was a colt, well, when we'd be trucking it away the woman would be crying, sometimes even the man would have to walk away as if we couldn't guess what he was doing. I could never understand it, you know, but sometimes if I think about you not being here I get this image from being with Farmer. I'm even writing a song about it," Blue said, picking up his guitar. "The chorus goes like this."

> You're gone and I'm alone with
> nothing to do but drink
> And feel sorry for old horses
> and ladies dressed in mink

A knock on the door casing interrupted Blue's song.

"Can we come in, Blue? I got something to tell you," Tinker said, pushing aside the strings of beads, holding them to let Kathy go ahead of him.

"You joined the frigging army!" Blue said, staring at Tinker's hair.

"Oh, Tinker, you didn't," Karma said, alarmed.

"No, I got a job," Tinker said, explaining the events of the morning including the haircut which Kathy had supplied with a pair of scissors and a great deal of sadness.

"The pay is great and I get to work with diesel mechanics and big equipment and everything."

"What about your social insurance number?"

"When I went to the office there was a form belonging to someone else who's been hired and I memorized the numbers and then just changed the last three around."

"I can't believe nobody from home knows about this job," Blue said. "A tunnel right here in San Francisco. Big money, I bet. You know, Tinker, if we call the Legion back home and tell whoever's there to spread the word I bet we could have a hundred guys out here next week," Blue said excited, unaware of the uncertainty in the glance that passed between Karma and Kathy. "You could probably get them on at the tunnel, eh, Tink? We could put them up here at the commune until they found a place. Or at the hotel. They'd fit right in there, some of them, anyway."

"I better put in my first day before we start hiring other people," Tinker said. "But I was thinking that I could put a word in for you first chance I got."

"That might not be such a good idea there, Tinker. I ... uh ... my fingers, right? Hate to lose my fingers underground and not be able to play the guitar. Besides, with the band there's just not going to be time for working underground. We artists can't be too careful but you go right ahead, but looking at that haircut, know what it does? Makes me homesick as hell. That's just what you looked like when we were crossing the causeway on our way out here. Same ears and everything.

"Do you girls know what's going on back home right now?" Blue asked Karma and Kathy. "Colours. You'd love the fall colours. The mountains turn all red and gold. People drive all the way from these here United States just to take pictures of it. It's really something, isn't it, Tink? If we were there right now we could go walking up one of the mountains and you two could stop wherever you wanted and just paint pictures and write poems and Tinker and me could spend the day picking off rabbits. Some days, it's nothing to get ten—"

"What do you mean picking off rabbits?" Kathy asked.

"With the .22. There's nothing like it, huh, Tink? Go walking in the woods when the colours are changing, the sunlight streaming through the leaves in these great streaks like the rays you see coming from Jesus in holy pictures, and carrying the gun and watching for rabbits. Then we could take them home, you girls could skin them and stew them up for supper. Or make pies out of them."

"You could kill ten rabbits in a day?" Kathy said. "How could you? They're so cute."

"So if I shot ten rats would you feel the same way?" Blue asked.

"To kill ten of anything ... to kill *anything* seems so cruel. And it's so much bad karma," Kathy said with a shiver.

"A hippie we picked up one time told us the same thing, that we'd have bad karma from eating so much meat, remember, Blue?" Tinker recalled.

"Yeah, and know what I learned since then?" Blue said. "I learned that I like my Karma bad," forcing a smile out of everyone in the room.

28

Blue, Gerry and Nathan had partially earned their gig at the Warehouse Gallery by helping to move Tulip's huge canvases from the commune where they were hung on walls, stored in the basement and, in one instance, required the removal of a wall. Gerry, acting as foreman, directed with his one arm while Blue and Nathan cut the plaster and tried to release what everyone agreed was Tulip's masterpiece. Only Blue's opinion dissented, pointing out that Tulip's real mastery was wine-making, recalling and recounting for those who had not been there the evenings they spent in the Colorado Rockies sipping wine.

"That wine went down a lot smoother than this chalk," Blue said, hacking up a white cloud of plaster as he stepped back and lit a cigarette.

"This isn't going to work," Capricorn said entering the room, seeing the way despite their efforts to free the plaster from the wall, it was crumbling, threatening the painting itself. "There has to be another way."

"There is," Blue volunteered. "Why don't we go to the paint store, buy a bunch of cans, go to the Warehouse and squirt it all over a wall? Say it was this one? Who's going to know the difference? Bet Tulip herself wouldn't know."

"Your appreciation of art is astounding, Blue," Capricorn said. "And look at the three of you, so covered in plaster that I bet I could pass anyone of you off as Michelangelo's David at the show tonight."

"What David would that be?" Blue asked as Nathan slapped him on the shoulder to draw him back to the problem at hand.

"Just somebody Capricorn met over in Italy, Blue."

Capricorn's solution met with resistence from Blue who didn't think it was such a great idea to remove a whole wall.

"Just tear out the wall in the room behind it—"

"That's our bedroom," Blue reminded him.

"We can put something else there," Capricorn said.

"What do you mean, something else? Karma and I pay good rent for that room."

"Yes, she does," Capricorn conceded. "I mean something else like another wall, not another room. If we tear the plaster off the other side of this wall, then we can cut the studs and lift this whole wall away with Tulip's work intact."

"If Tinker was here he'd come up with a better solution," Blue muttered, but the work of art had to be at the show before Tinker got off his shift in the tunnel.

Peter?, who had taken several of Tulip's paintings to the gallery in the commune van, returned and began helping with the dismantling of the wall. Blue watched more than he helped as part of his room was being torn down to get at the studs. Shaking his head, he wandered into the common room hoping to see the painting crumble from the pounding hammers and prying bars. Capricorn was sitting alone on the legless couch studying the wall. Blue plunked himself down beside him and did the same.

"It's a marvellous creation," Capricorn acknowledged. "I'm going to miss it."

Blue looked at the smeared wall, unable to find a face or a flower, not a single recognizable moment or event, only the childish display of coloured oils that they were working hard to rescue. He kept his silence until he had examined the wall to exhaustion.

"Listen, Cap, can I ask you a serious question?"

"Sure."

"Are you pulling my leg? I mean are you really going to miss this thing? I've seen a lot of Tulip's stuff and it all looks like this wall, only smaller. I know quite a bit about art, took it from primary to grade seven, including abstract art. The nun would get us to run our pencil around the paper every which way, then colour in the shapes that got made. Even then none of it got to look this bad. I mean I like Tulip, eh. Makes great wine and everything, but I'm not so sure she's the next Norman Rockwell. Tell me what you're going to miss about this wall."

"Tulip's sense of harmony," Capricorn explained. "It's in all her work, but this is her masterpiece, her first real masterpiece. There isn't a form or colour that's out of balance with any other aspect of the painting. If you could stop judging it, Blue, and just sit with one of Tulip's paintings I think you'd find yourself relaxing, almost meditating. It has the same effect as listening to peaceful music. Tulip's paintings tap into the fundamental truth that the underlying nature of the Universe is harmony, not violence."

"Well, there's where I'd have to disagree with you, Cap. This painting looks pretty violent to me. It's like Tulip took everything she ever saw and put it in a Mixmaster. And if that's what she meant to do, then I don't have to look very far to see that she's right, people running around killing people, dropping bombs, burning them alive. We even crucified God, for Christ's sake! So when you say harmony is the nature of the Universe, well, that's saying a lot but it doesn't mean anything, just like this painting. People may say they believe in harmony and all that but when you come right down to it we don't. Not the way we act, anyway."

"But the point Tulip is making is that harmony isn't a human value," Capricorn explained. "It exists in and of itself and everything else exists because of it. Whether we look at an atom or the whole Universe, the relationship of everything to everything, protons to neutrons, planets to planets, depends on balance and harmony. Violence isn't natural, not even in humans. Blue, do you realize that less than one percent of the people in the world are at war or killing each other at this moment. The other ninety-nine per cent are just trying to get by, and most of them would just like to get along with everybody else. But that one per cent is like a drop of poison in a glass of clear water, distorting our perception of human nature out of all proportion. That's where we need to begin, Blue, trying to transform that one per cent. Tulip's paintings don't leave out that one percent, they absorb it into the natural harmony. She glimpses things then recreates them on canvas."

Blue pondered the painting.

"If she's trying to say what you say she's trying to say then why doesn't she just say it? I live in a three-dimensional world here, buddy. I like my chairs to look like chairs if you know what I mean. So when artists go ahead and draw a chair that looks like a plop of cow shit then I begin to wonder, boy. You can say what you want about harmony but I'm the musician here, remember.

"Look, we got this guy back home, eh, Henry Bruce. Well, he's an artist. Used to be a few years ahead of us in school but everybody in town knew he could draw. When he drew a bird, boy, it practically flew off the page right there in front of you. Then he goes to art college. Ears and eyes start turning up in the weirdest places. And it just gets wilder and wilder the longer he's there, but I haven't told you anything yet. It was like he was becoming a hippie before he knew hippies were coming.

"The last few summers he's been holding parties out at his place. He's got this farm in the country, hayfields and trees and mountains, all this beautiful stuff and all he wants to do is put eyes in the middle of people's foreheads. He'd invite a few of us out there and supply us all with booze, eh, and food, lots of food. There'd be baloney and cheese and grapes, and beans on the stove and stuff like that. Tinker and I've been going almost every time Henry has one of his parties.

"What he does is get us all as drunk as we can get and then he wants us to eat ourselves sick along with it. He's got this old barn that's falling down. He's been tearing it down actually, board by board. People really go in for barn board nowadays. All the tourist places sell barn boards, but they don't sell Henry's barn boards, let me tell you.

"What Henry Bruce does with his barn boards is saw them into foot-long pieces and get us to throw up on them. I mean just get drunk and vomit on the boards. Then he puts those boards in the oven and dries them out. He'd have a dozen boards going at some parties. Then he examines the results, the way the vomit forms or something. Who knows? Anyway he'd pick his favourites, okay, and shellacs them, coat them with shellac and then you know what he does? Sends them to a gallery in New

York and they get up to five hundred bucks apiece for some of them. And that kind of says it for me, Capi. Vomit! Everybody's selling horses, as the other fellow says.

"You know we're going to have to carry this friggin' wall all the way to the gallery, don't you? It won't fit in the van."

29

Blue smoked a cigarette on the sidewalk in front of the Warehouse Gallery. The exhibit was up, Blue Cacophony's gear was set up, and people were beginning to filter in for the opening. After a few minutes he spotted Tinker who had gone home from the tunnel, showered and was now arriving for the show. They leaned against the building trading pieces of their day, Tinker describing for Blue a mucking machine he had been working on underground while Blue relayed the details of arranging the art show.

"Let me ask you this, Tinker. You know that wall between the common room and Karma's and my room, the one Tulip painted? Well, if you had to move that wall, say, a couple of miles, how would you go about doing it?"

"The wall! Of course! I went back to the house for a shower and I knew something was different. It just felt roomier somehow. I thought it was because the place was empty, everybody being down here, but now that you mention it the wall was missing. You mean it's in here?" Tinker said, nodding his head toward the warehouse.

"Yeah. If you had to move it what would you do?"

Tinker thought about it for a moment. "I think you'd have to tear down the wall behind it then cut the studs and laths, otherwise the plaster would crumble all to hell. How did you do it?"

"That's pretty well the same idea I had," Blue said with a shrug, pushing off the building and walking toward the door.

Inside, the warehouse walls were hung with Tulip's collection, while in the middle of the floor stood Blue's bedroom wall. A small card stapled to the end of it said the title was *Harmony*. People who had received invitations, street handouts or read about the opening in the underground press were arriving in larger numbers. A collapsable table was covered with wine and cheese. Blue tested the wine, unimpressed.

"Tulip would of done better to make her own instead of buying this Naptha Valley shit."

"I think it's the Napa Valley, Blue," Tinker said, pouring himself a glass.

"Whatever. Tastes like naptha to me. What do you think of this stuff, Tinker?"

"It's okay. Leaves my mouth a little dry—"

"No, I mean Tulip's stuff. I had a talk with Capi this afternoon about it. He really likes it so that should put you on your guard, buddy. I told him about Henry Bruce and his abstract barn boards, but he still thinks Tulip's paintings mean something. Harmony, he said. 'They're filled with harmony.' How can you know that when there's nothing there to recognize? That's what I'd like to know."

"I can't say I don't like them, Blue. I guess I never really thought about them before. Remember when the art nun used to make us—"

"I was talking about that just this afternoon. So it's not like we're ignorant about abstract art or anything, huh. We know what we like."

"I guess I'd have to say I like them, Blue."

"Now why do we have to say that, Tink? Besides the fact that we like Tulip so we're not going to say that we don't like them. That would be like telling your own mother she can't cook. I suppose that's part of it, too. Tulip's no spring chicken, is she? She's got to be at least thirty. You'd think by now she'd be able to draw as well as colour."

Kathy and Karma, holding Barney by the collar, joined them at the food table, taking a glass of wine, a nibble of cheese.

"It's overwhelming to see Tulip's work gathered together like this," Karma commented, scanning the walls as she spoke, confirming her remark to herself. "We're witnessing something important tonight."

"You bet," Blue assured her. "Blue Cacophony's debut."

"That too, Blue, but look around. Tulip's work is affecting a lot of people here."

"Yeah, the ones on drugs.... Just kidding," holding up his hands to ward off the dual glares of Kathy and Karma, then he pointed across the hall to where Peter? was tacking No-Recording-Devices-of-Any-Kind posters in the wall spaces between Tulip's paintings. Behind him, the gallery owner removed them. They argued. They compromised. Peter? took down his posters and nailed them to the outside of the gallery.

"This no-recording gimmick of Peter?'s is just about the worst idea I ever heard," Blue mused. "I got to change their minds about that. There's a big opportunity drifting by here and we're just watching it float away. A musician without an album is like a ... like a ... like a parent without a child. If we recorded I bet they'd sell like crazy, at least in the Co-op back home, eh, Tinker?"

Peter? walked toward them and signalled Blue with a head gesture to get ready. The exhibit was filling up. There weren't many people Blue didn't already know by sight or by name. They were from the neighbourhood, from the crossroads of Haight-Ashbury which, it occurred to Blue had been turned into a small town by the people living there. All over the city, neighbourhoods had their own population and their own character and their own characters. Nobody lives in the city, Blue thought, just in a corner of it. He and Tinker had picked up a lot of knowledge about a few of the city's streets, felt as at home in their neighbourhood now as it was possible to feel without actually being back home. That's how everybody survives these places, Blue realized, by carving huge cities into small, manageable neighbourhoods. He stored that thought for a future song.

Except for a few unfamiliar faces, it was the people from the neighbourhood here to see Tulip's work, to hear Blue Cacophony's debut. It was a neighbourhood that happened to be the capital city of hippiedom, famous all over the world for reasons weird to some, wonderful to others, but a neighbourhood nonetheless, a small town inside a big city, Jonah inside the whale just trying to survive. The people from the neighbourhood were filling up the gallery the way people home would fill up a dance hall to hear the music of a Cape Breton fiddler. Everything around him, the people, the paintings, was suddenly familiar. Standing with his guitar, waiting for Nathan and Gerry to get ready for the performance, Blue located Tinker and Karma and Kathy standing together watching him, waiting. They nodded to each other with an intimacy that they shared with no one else in the gallery.

The drone of Nathan's pipes spiralled like thick smoke from his instrument, joined a moment later by an agonizing note from Gerry's violin, signalling the introduction of Blue's voice rising from his throat like a wounded crow. People turned toward them, some staring, some listening, a few moving toward the band to stand front and centre and sway with closed eyes to a rhythm most others had difficulty identifying.

Unexpectedly, a half-maddened chorus of moans and whines ricocheted through the gallery as Barney, unable to find any place to hide, panned Blue Cacophony's debut. What caught everyone's attention, however, was not the unkindness implicit in Barney's review but the atonal harmony of these two enemies, artist and critic raising voices in some discordant choir. Barney's canine complaint complemented Blue Cacophony's music with a fullness that turned everyone's ear, voluntarily or involuntarily, toward the music. It was a duet that was not lost on Peter? who immediately began coaxing Barney closer to the band, dragging him forward by the collar, fitting together a puzzle of misshapen pieces: young musicians, dog, instruments and revolutionary theory, re-forming his philosophy of music to accommodate Barney's appearance in it.

Blue Cacophony played through its forty-minute gig, unloading Blue's lyrics in a shatter of sound and German shepherd that confirmed for Peter? the conviction that his discovery of Blue – his creation of Blue Cacophony – was the thin edge of a wedge meant to rupture old standards, challenge human aural perception, a sound in the wilderness announcing the destruction of the martial man, the birth of a new music to which mankind could march toward the new Republic. Blue, less philosophical at the moment, caught Peter?'s eye with an eyeroll of his own. Peter? responded with a reassuring thumbs-up, ignoring the obvious plea to get the dog off the small stage where Blue Cacophony was being upstaged. With the relentless accompaniment of Barney, Blue Cacophony finished its set by providing the audience with a teasing sample of Blue's work-in-progress, "The Red Lobster" which, Blue announced, was only seventeen verses away from completion.

—

While Blue, Gerry and Nathan were putting away the equipment, Peter? spoke to a cluster of reporters representing the spectrum of newspapers who probed him about the band, its sound, purpose and newest member.

"Oh, yes, Barney's been practising with the band for months," Peter? replied. "He's a part of it. Even has his own agent which happens to be me. What I believe is that for music to grow through the atrophied state that it has been caught in for the past several thousand years, new elements have to be explored. I'm sure you are aware that man is not the only creature that sings, but he has not opened his music up to the possibilities that exist all around him. He often copies other creatures' sounds, but rarely has he invited other creatures to gather around the campfire and share their songs. That is what Blue has done with Barney, invited him to join the band, to contribute, for we must never lose sight – although I fear most people lost sight of it in the dim dawn of early time – that music is not man's monopoly. All creatures sing to the Universe, and every creature, no matter how small or insignificant, is in greater harmony with the Universe than the most enlightened, the most talented, the most brilliant of men. Blue Cacophony is striving, through Blue's genius, to restore to us our fundamental reality. We are witnessing a music that belongs to the Universe, is in harmony with the Universe in a way no other music has ever been. I predict—"

Blue half listened to Peter? trot out his favourite theories and expound upon them. Any question directed at Peter? by a reporter or a friend was a challenge to him to explain the meaning of life. Blue wondered if Peter? shouldn't wear a sign around his neck warning reporters and other innocents that a philosopher resided within. *Ask questions at your own risk.* Putting away his guitar, Blue noticed one weary reporter break free and wander toward the band.

"As a musician, I wonder if you would give me a few words on the exhibit? How does a musician who works in sound perceive abstract art which, it could be argued, could be duplicated by a child?"

"A few words?" Blue said. "Guess that's why you're asking me and not Peter?. But look, buddy, I spent a lot of time studying these paintings and I have to tell you that no child did them. An old woman did. Well, older anyway. Tulip. I saw you talking to her. Now you take that wall over there. Do you know what was on the other side of that wall? My bedroom. Would I have donated it to this show if it wasn't a masterpiece? There isn't a form or colour that is out of place with any other aspect of the painting. Watching it for me is like meditating. Tulip gets in touch with the underlying truth of the Universe here. It's all about harmony. I'd like to think that some of that harmony is in our own music. That's Blue Cacophony. You ask Peter? and he'll tell you how to spell cacophony."

While the reporter made notes, a small cluster of people had drawn around the interview, Karma with a much quieter Barney, Kathy and Tinker, Capricorn and Tulip.

"Thank you, Blue," Tulip said. "I wasn't even aware you noticed my paintings. My wine, yes, but not my paintings. If I leave a couple of bottles in your room will they bribe you into saying more nice things about my work?" she teased. To which Capricorn added a cryptic question of his own. "Blue, tell me, is there a difference between a horse trader and horse thief?"

"Let me ask you about your music, Mr. Blue. Is the dog a gimmick you'll be using regularly?" asked the reporter.

"Talent doesn't need gimmicks, to quote the other fellow. As for Barney, well, some people seem to think that after tonight he should be in the band and some people think those people should be shot, but I left my gun home. The band will be meeting tomorrow to discuss Barney's future."

"Then I can report that the dog is not a band member? Once the word gets out, a lot of people will be flocking to your next gig to see the singing mutt. This is your chance to nip that rumour in the bud because I think my associates over there have already decided that the dog's the story. Who knows how many people will pay money to hear a rock-and-roll dog singing with Blue Cacophony. If you don't want that to happen, could you give me a denial before people are misled into spending their money?"

"Hundreds, eh? Well, like I said, the band will be meeting tomorrow to discuss it and I suppose once Peter? gets through arguing his case Barney will be the lead singer and have his own set of drums. How much you figure people would pay to hear a dog sing? They pay an awful lot to hear Bob Dylan, don't they? Could be Blue Cacophony's going to the dogs, as the other fellow says."

"A last question. Why have you decided against recording?"

"Well, not everybody in the band is in favour of not making a record, but what I was a saying when I suggested it was that the best legends are the ones we don't know anything about, like the angels at Bethlehem when Jesus was born. We know there was a whole host full of angels up in the sky singing 'Silent Night,' right? No one disputes that because it's right there in the Bible, but they never made a record, so all we can do is imagine how beautiful it must have sounded. Unheard music is the sweetest, as the other fellow says.

"We got a saying back home, eh. A horse that's not for sale is worth a lot more than one that is."

"I don't follow you," the reporter said.

"I'm not Jesus Christ so you don't have to follow me, now do you? Unless you want to hear Blue Cacophony's music, that is, because it's not for sale. And you can quote me *and* the other fellow on that."

30

Blue sat on the mattress, guitar in his lap, watching Karma at work on another panel, his thoughts drifting in a slow rhythm to the lazy swirl of incense that reminded him of High Mass. Where one of the walls had been, their ration of privacy was now defined by a canvas curtain. Blue sipped a beer and steered his thoughts away from the plan fermenting in his belly. Instead, he let snatches of sentences from the newspapers swim through his mind, caught them, let them go, then beckoned them back for encores. Some reviews, of course, he would never allow to survive in his ocean of memory, but other were confused or flattering or enthusiastic enough to merit his repeated appreciation.

Tulip's exhibit, to the commune's surprise, was applauded left, right and centre by the critics, one or two of whom, Capricorn pointed out with amusement, had stolen Blue's insights concerning the nature of Tulip's harmony and made them their own. Blue called them weasels for not crediting to him his own quotes. Tulip had mixed emotions about the unanimity of appreciation which applauded her work, missing, she said, "the right-wing fascist reactionary reflexes" that normally counter-attack abstract art, drawing dull parallels between the artist's work and the proverbial four-year-old child turned loose in a paint pit. "The establishment wants to hang me on their walls," she said. "Whose victory is that, I wonder?"

Blue Cacophony inspired a wider spectrum of opinions, ranging from "a night noise" to "more performance than music ... not unlike listening to an abstract train crash," to "a sound on the cutting edge, nay, the razor's edge, of an exciting new music era." With few exceptions, the critics were reluctant to dismiss Blue Cacophony on the basis of relevancy, musical ability or even on the subject of dog-as-musical-instrument. Most publications avoided the trap of trying to assess the musical merits of Blue Cacophony by concentrating on the story – not the group's music, but its refusal to record.

Once Blue had told the first reporter that there would be no recordings of his songs, he then fell wholeheartedly into the spirit of the idea, going to every one of the music and art critics present, supporting and reinforcing Peter?'s position. Blue Cacophony would not sign with any record label regardless of the offers being made, Blue informed them, while eluding efforts to pin him down to exactly what offers had been made.

Impressed by Blue's anti-establishment convictions, the *Rolling Stone* critic wrote that "The singer/song-writer of Blue Cacophony is a disciple of non-commercialism and so, if for no other reason, this band deserves both support and encouragement...."

"They called me a disciple in this paper, Tinker," Blue pointed out. "Remind me to send a copy to the old lady. She'll think her baby boy still has a chance to become a priest."

"I don't think that's the kind of disciple they mean," Tinker said, but Blue was already rambling on toward other subjects with Gerry and Nathan who sat with him around the kitchen table, reading the reviews and passing them along while they waited for Peter? to turn up for his share of the limelight.

Peter? did arrive, carrying an armful of the same newspapers, and with the news that Blue Cacophony had two more gigs, clubs willing to pay them, or at least divvy up the cover charge.

"But I've been thinking about it," Peter? said, "and the thing that would make Blue Cacophony perfectly committed to its art would be the band's refusal to take any money for its performances. That coupled with a refusal to record—"

"Aw, Jesus, Mary and Joseph, Peter?, where do you get these friggin' ideas? If anything should be committed around here it's you," Blue argued. "Play for nothing! We've been so busy practising that we're not making a dime on the street anymore, and Capricorn is giving me funny looks like I'm not buying my share of sunflower seeds around here or something. It's one thing not to record, and it's another thing to hire a dog as my backup singer, but when it comes to no money, it's one thing too far, as the other fellow says. How about the rest of you guys?"

"I'm with you all the way about not recording," Gerry said to Peter?, "and I hate to disillusion you, but I need some money."

Nathan expressed similar capitalist aspirations, pointing out that he and Gerry and Blue used to do pretty well for themselves on the street. "We each had our own corner of the world out there. We pooled our talents with you and Blue to see where this road goes, but we have to eat along the way."

Peter?, recognizing that his modern Republic had suffered a slight setback, did not push the issue, telling them that one performance site, The Buddha Tree, would guarantee one hundred dollars for the night, and at the place where it all began, the Aquarius Café, the band would get a dollar a head.

"Blue Cacophony's first world tour has begun," Blue cheered, not bothering to note that the two gigs were three blocks apart.

—

Blue picked up the book that Karma had begun reading to him after she had given up trying to get him to read it himself. There wasn't a lot he could find to argue against in Kahlil Gibran's world, except that he wasn't Catholic, not even Christian. This book was probably on the Vatican's list of things Catholics couldn't read, along with *Fanny Hill*. Tinker, he noticed, was reading all the time now, working and reading. Still, Blue was careful not to be too critical of Gibran in case he might have been Karma's brother in an earlier life. Or cellmate in an asylum somewhere.

The last thought made him chuckle.

"What's so funny?" Karma asked.

"Oh, I was just thinking about something crazy," Blue replied, and scrambling to escape further interrogation he opened the book to a random page.

"Listen to this. 'Would that you could live on the fragrance of the earth, and like an air plant be sustained by light. But since you must kill to eat, and rob the newly born of its mother's milk to quench your thirst, let it then be an act of worship.' So he's saying here that we have to eat meat, right, but it's okay as long as we say grace before and after meals. So how come you won't go for a burger with me?"

"You know I don't eat flesh, Blue. I can't make you or anybody else stop if you don't want to. It's something you have to discover for yourself, but when you think about the thousands and thousands of animals who have to die in order for you to live your life, doesn't it make you sad?"

"Aw, well, if you're going to think like that every time you sit down to eat, you're going to ruin a lot of good meals, girl. But I don't get it. You're saying it's not okay to eat meat, but it's not a sin if we do. That doesn't make sense. It's either right or it's wrong, right? It's a sin or it isn't. It's not a Commandment, so even if it's a sin, it's probably a venial one. Even Jesus ate meat, didn't he? Didn't he? So would that be a sin in your book?"

"Blue, there is only one sin in what you call my book, and that's our failure to love."

"Listen, lady, I can commit a dozen sins before breakfast, and that's not including the thoughts that go through my head.

If you only know of one sin in the whole world, then we live in different worlds. So is that sin of yours eating meat?"

"No, Blue, it's what I said. It's our failure to love. If people loved each other, then we wouldn't hurt each other."

"So murder's not a sin, or stealing or sex or anything like that? Is that what you're saying?"

"They're just the symptoms of our failure to love, don't you see? If we loved each other we couldn't do the things we do. You told me once about the time you and Farmer dyed an old horse's eyebrows and then sold it back to the same person you bought it from, telling him it was a much younger horse, and sold it for a lot more than it was worth, remember. Well, suppose you had bought that horse from Tinker, would you have cheated him like that?"

"Hell, no. Tinker's my best friend. I'm not going to trick him."

"Because you love him, right?"

"Well, I wouldn't go around using words like that about a guy, but he's my best friend. I wouldn't trick him, or cheat him, if that's what you mean."

"If that man you bought the horse from was your father, would you have dyed it and sold it back?"

"And get my arse kicked up around my ears? Of course not!"

"Because you love your father, right?"

"Yeah, but that's not why I wouldn't do it. He'd kick the supreme shit out of me, Karma. I mean it."

"Would you sell that horse to me, Blue?"

"No," Blue said evenly. "But you're saying if I loved everybody in the world I wouldn't cheat anyone. How can I love everybody? I don't even know most of them."

"But if you thought of everybody as your best friend, if you saw them as people you love, then you couldn't cheat them, could you? You can only cheat the people you don't love, so you see, Blue, the sin isn't cheating or any of the other awful things we do to each other, it's our failure to love people. That's all that Jesus or Buddha or any great spiritual leader has had to say to us, isn't it, to love one another."

"If it's that simple, Karma, how come it takes ten years to become a priest? Even ministers have to study for years just to be Protestants. Because the Bible is that thick, that's why, and it's too confusing for just anybody to read. I tried to, and there's a lot more in it than those three little words. People have spent their whole lives studying exactly what Jesus really meant when he said 'love one another,' you know. And here you are, a girl, for Christ's sake, with all the answers. Just love everybody. Do you love everybody, Karma? Could you love Hitler? Answer me that! Could you love Hitler, huh?"

"I wonder what would have happened if somebody did, Blue?"

"Oh, there's no talking to you, girl," Blue said tersely, standing up, starting to leave the room.

"Don't be angry with me, Blue. I'm just trying to understand who I am, and I can't know that without knowing what I believe, can I?"

"How come everybody is so big on understanding themselves, and finding themselves?" Blue asked, turning back toward Karma. "That's what this is about, isn't it? Finding yourself? I don't even know what that means, Karma, or maybe I'm just lucky, because I know who I am. It's the things that tell me who I am that are important to me. One of those things is home. I know I talk about it too much for some people around here. I see Capricorn and other people rolling their eyes when I talk about it, so I know that I talk about it too much, but I'd rather bore them than forget where I come from. And I know who I come from, Karma. I can tell you six sets of grandparents down both sides of family all the way back to Scotland. Some of them looked like me, and some of them acted like me, and if you looked at my birth certificate and theirs, you'd find the same name over and over. I've been to school, just like you.

"I had to read the stories in my English books, but know what, none of them were any better than the stories the old man would tell about his old man, or about working in the mines, or even Farmer talking about why things are the way they are. And I believe what they believed. I was baptized in the exact same church as my two grandfathers, for God's sake. Besides, just because I tell stories about the nuns and priests doesn't mean that I don't love the Church. I do. That's where I know God, and when you start this business about meditation and one sin and all that crap, I have to remind myself about false prophets. Even this book is called *The Prophet*, for that matter. It's full of stuff to get a guy thinking. There's nothing wrong with thinking, but there's wrong thinking, as the other fellow says. It's not easy to hang on to everything I know when everybody else is different. Even Tinker's changing, everything's changing, and it scar— bothers me. I don't want to lose what matters most, and that's home." Blue paused, trying to be finished. "And you," he added apologetically.

"Blue, I don't want to take any of that away from you, and most of all I don't want to take me from you. But when you ask questions, there's only one way I can answer, and those answers always upset you. I can't say what you want to hear, but I love you, Blue. I want us to find a way not to hurt each other."

"When you say that, do you mean you love just me, or do you mean you love me like in *love one another*, as the other fellow says?" Blue's voice edging back from an angry precipice.

31

When Blue came into the kitchen, Tinker was at the table reading another book. Blue ran a glass of water for himself and stared at the cover, trying to identify the white block on the spine.

"It's Audel's encyclopaedia of mechanics," Tinker explained, holding the book up for Blue to examine closer. "Casey, this mechanic I'm working with, tells me I got good instincts about machines but he says I got the technique of a hog butcher. He's showing me things that Charlie forgot to mention, and he told me about these books that can teach you a lot about machines and fixing them, so I joined the library on my way home—"

"Joined the library!"

"Yeah! I just walked in there and nobody batted an eye, so I signed up and signed out this book. It's about everything I like, and you won't believe this but it knows a lot more about the Plymouth than I do. I'll let you borrow it after I'm finished."

"Tinker," Blue said, sitting himself across from his friend, "do you ever wonder what's happening to us? I mean, here we are stranded in 'Frisco until we get enough dough to go home. That's not really our fault, and you got a job and I got the band so I figure we should be home for Christmas. Know what would be really great? To be crossing the causeway on Christmas Eve. Not tell anybody, just come home on Christmas Eve with a carload of gifts that'll make the old lady cry. You know how soft she is, but I digress, as the other fellow says.

"But we're not home, Tinker. Which is my point. We're sitting in a purple and green kitchen full of nothing to eat, with somebody called the Gratefully Dead on the stereo instead of Scottie Fitzgerald on the radio, talking about library books. This is going to be a funny story someday but I'm not laughing right now. I feel like I'm getting squeezed. You know how when you're in a stall and a horse leans all its weight against you, squeezing the breath right out of you, well, that what's it's like here, except

| 165

that it feels like everything I know is getting squeezed out of me. I know how to punch a horse back off me when that happens, but I don't know how to get out from under this, Tinker."

"You'd know how to get out from under it if you were talking about Capricorn. You'd just punch him like a horse. So it must be Karma. Again."

"What do you need to go to a library for, Tinker? You read me like a book. Yup, it's her again. I'm glad God made women so beautiful but I wish he hadn't made them so damn smart. Listen to this. There's only one sin in the whole world. Did you know that? Only one sin. The priests, the nuns, even the Pope got it all wrong with their mortal sins and venial sins because there is only one sin in the whole world, and it's not even sex. It's something called ... THE FAILURE TO LOVE," Blue said, dropping his voice to the bottom of his larynx. "I won't try to explain it, but it's a heresy. I'm in love with a friggin' pagan, Tinker. What do you think about my idea for Christmas?"

"I like the idea, Blue, but I don't like what happens when I think it through. Christmas itself would be great, but then all that's left is February, and you have to love home a lot to want to be there in February. As the old man used to say, everywhere else in the world February is the shortest month but in Cape Breton it goes on forever. Think about it, Blue. The Big Ice, cold wind, frozen water pipes, snow storms to be shovelled away, your fingers and your toes curled up inside your gloves and boots trying to stay warm but they can't, and your ears stinging red, standing on John Beaton's Corner cursing the goddamned cold. When I think of home, it's always summer and that's when I'd like to go back. Besides, I like the tunnel. I feel a lot closer to home down there than I would freezing in my own bedroom next February. And Blue, I'm not interested in running away from Kathy."

"I never ran away from anything in my life, you know that, so don't accuse me of it," Blue snapped. "I was just thinking that it would be nice for us to go home for Christmas, that's all. I didn't know you didn't like home."

"I didn't say I didn't like it. I just don't see the point in going home for the winter when I hate the winter, but you sound an awful lot like somebody who wants to run home to Mommy just because your girlfriend won't baby you."

Blue's fist flashed across the table and Tinker jerked away from the surprise attack, tipping his chair, crashing to the floor. The table up-ended on top of him, and Blue dove into the mess of friend and furniture, swinging wildly. They rolled around, punching and kicking at whatever they thought was each other, cursing and grunting until the kitchen filled with the membership of the Human Rainbow Commune who wrestled them apart.

Blue and Tinker stood at opposite sides of the kitchen, glaring, panting angrily, but making no effort to shake off the people who held them apart. The others in the kitchen kept a confused silence until Karma lifted a cloth to wipe a trickle of blood from Blue's lip. He pushed her hand aside and ran from the room. A moment later, the front door slammed.

It was after midnight when Blue returned to the commune. He wavered in the doorway of the common room, then took a staggering step toward Tinker and Kathy's door when Karma intercepted him and guided him into their room, easing him onto the mattress.

"Gotta talk to Tinker," he mumbled.

"Tinker's asleep. He has to work in the morning. You better sleep, too, Blue. There'll be a lot to talk about in the morning."

"Tinker's not asleep. I know my buddy. He's not asleep. Get him for me."

"Let him be, Blue. If you need to talk to someone, talk to me tonight. What do you want to talk about?"

"Winter. Have you ever been in Cape Breton in the wintertime, Karma? You should see it. The ice come down from the North Pole. People call it the Big Ice, and it covers up the whole ocean. It looks as calm as anything, but when you walk out on it you can feel the ocean rising and falling under it, all those waves trying to break, but can't. It feels like something being smothered and struggling under a pillow. And there are seals everywhere, big ones and little ones as cute as kittens. They get lost, you know. Seals get lost really fast, especially if the wind jams the ice up tight. Then they can't find a way into the water so they go looking for an opening. They might follow the river then and wind up inland. Once, eh, this guy back home that works at the Legion, well, he heard a knock on the door and when he answered it here was this seal barking like crazy. But the bartender wouldn't let him in. Said the seal didn't have any ID. He didn't care that the Legion had the approval of a seal, as the other fellow says.

"Another guy found one in his porch and beat it to death with a hockey stick. And the snowplows are always picking off seals that get caught on the roads. Most of them, though, people capture in garbage cans and take them back to the ocean, but it's not easy. A scared seal is a dangerous thing. When it's lost and doesn't know what's happening to it, even if you're trying to help it, it doesn't know that, does it? How can it? Like that guy in the porch. He didn't kill the seal because he wanted to. He scared the shit out of it and it scared the shit out of him and both of them had nowhere to go so he grabbed the hockey stick and ... two minutes for slashing, to quote the other fellow again."

Blue paused.

"But Karma, if you could come down with me onto the Big Ice in February, it has to be February, at night, with a full moon, and just go out on the ice far enough to feel it moving under us, it's so still all you can hear is the rifle crack of ice shifting once in awhile, and maybe a seal barking, but mostly nothing at all, just silence and this strange snow-bright moonlight that lets you see all the way to Prince Edward Island. It's really beautiful. It is."

"I know," Tinker said, barely visible behind the beaded doorway. He pushed the beads aside and came into the room.

"My old buddy Tinker." Blue stared up at him. "Told you he wasn't sleeping. So do you want me to say my act of contrition or what?"

Tinker made a sign of the cross over Blue's head and Blue stuck out his hand. "Shake on her, buddy," he said, gripping Tinker's hand and hanging on to it for a moment. "My toes get just as cold as yours, you know, but there's things to remember and there's things to forget."

"...as the other fellow says," Karma and Tinker chimed in together.

32

The Commune Council gathered around the table in the kitchen to discuss an agenda that included the violence of the previous night, new developments at the commune in Colorado, and the contribution each member was making toward the food and financial needs of the San Francisco site.

Blue, nursing a hangover, had been coaxed by Karma to get up and join the discussion since his and Tinker's future with the Human Rainbow Commune was once again being called into question, as it had been in Colorado. He groped his way to the bathroom and, returning with cold water dripping from his face and hair, told Karma that Henry Bruce, "this artist I was telling you about would of gotten a thousand dollars in New York for what I just threw up in there." Karma guided him out to the kitchen.

"There was an incident here last night that contradicts every value we have," Capricorn said. "Two members of this commune had a violent confrontation—"

"Who were they? Point them out and I'll kill them," Blue interrupted.

"Blue, don't do this," Karma pleaded.

"It's not a joke, Blue. You haven't the faintest idea of what we consider important. If it wasn't for Karma, you wouldn't have anything to do with the commune, and we'd all be a lot happier. We're not playing a game here. We're trying to do something creative with our lives, not destructive. You can call it naive, childish, foolish, whatever you like...."

"All of the above, as the other fellow says."

"...we've all been called it before. Where we're going, or even what's to become of each of us we don't know, but at this moment, here, now, we believe in something worth living for, and we believe in each other, and we're trying hard not to succumb to violent solutions. What happened here last night is unacceptable. What has to be decided this morning is just how acceptable or unacceptable yours and Tinker's behaviour is to the rest of the Council, and the rest of the commune. Can you explain what happened, or why we shouldn't expel you?"

"Because what happened last night wasn't violence," Blue said, looking around the table. "It was just a friggin' fist fight. Tinker's my best friend, for Christ's sake. It's not like it hasn't happened before. Maybe it's still bothering you but it's just another story to us now," he explained. "Look," he continued, "if you're going to talk about throwing somebody out, you better know that Tinker didn't start the fight, I did."

"Well, it's not how we solve problems here," Capricorn said. "There are more humane ways of dealing with conflicts than physical violence."

"Is there now! And how well does that work, huh? Tinker and I had a problem and now we don't, but me and you, Capi, we've had a problem ever since we met, right? Maybe if we had of stepped outside the first time we realized we didn't like each other, at least we'd know where we stand now instead of sniping at each other like a couple of old women. So much for your civilized way of dealing with it, which I think is just another way of saying that you'd like to get rid of Tinker and me and this is your big chance, but it's not fair to Tinker and if you think Tinker should of turned the other cheek, then you can kiss my other cheeks, buddy! That's all I got to say."

Watching Capricorn take a deep breath, Blue silently started to count ... one, two, three.... At the stroke of ten, Capricorn began to talk and Blue knew that commune leader had been counting down his anger, trying to control it. Blue flashed him a quick wink and smile, the remnants of his hangover vanishing as Capricorn's ears reddened with suppressed rage. "Gotcha, you bastard," Blue whispered to himself.

"This meeting isn't about getting rid of you or anyone, Blue, it's about getting rid of violence as a concept. Everybody in this commune was taught in school and even in the movies to celebrate a violent history. Our country, yours too, I suppose, has made heroes of men who have committed genocide. We don't even allow ourselves to see that there is really no difference between what the Germans did to the Jews and what this continent has done to the Indians, or what it is doing to the Vietnamese right now. Some of us want to find another way of living, another way of seeing, another way of being.

"We understand anger, we know rage, and we believe it's the greatest waste of energy on the planet. We've come to accept the basic truth that violence is not natural. The point of our commune here, and will be when we are able to go back to Colorado, is to create a society in which we have nothing to fear from one another."

To Blue, who could see Capricorn visibly cooling down, the speech sounded as much a recitation and reminder to the speaker as a sermon to himself.

"I think most people in this commune," Capricorn continued, "see and accept the fact of why you and Tinker are here, and we believe Karma and Kathy's influence will probably be more creative on you than yours will be destructive to them. The Commune Council has the choice of calling for a vote on your banishment by all the membership, or issuing a warning directly to you. Does anyone have any objection to a warning instead of a commune vote?" When no one replied, Capricorn went on. "We'll forget what happened here yesterday, but there mustn't be an occurrence of it ever again, Blue. Can you agree to that?"

"No problem, buddy," Blue said, making an open-handed gesture. "Tinker and I don't get into it more than once or twice a year anyway and the next time it happens, you won't even know it happened," Blue promised, but under his cocky assurance to Capricorn he felt a surprising wave of relief that his fate had not been put to the vote.

"The next subject is Colorado," Capricorn said, moving the meeting along. "For some unexplained reason the FBI have gone back to the commune a number of times since Tulip and Cory were released. People from the commune who have gone back to check it out learned from the townspeople that the FBI have been crawling all over the place. They've ransacked anything they hadn't already destroyed, and have been removing things from the site like the water pumps, even the old compressor."

"Maybe they think we had a laboratory up there," Tulip offered. "The two things they were most interested in when they interrogated us were drugs and Capricorn. Special agent Bud Wise is convinced that we were supplying the whole world with LSD, that it was part of Capricorn's plot to destroy democracy in the United States, although they didn't even see Cory let the horses munch the marijuana right under their noses. Maybe they're looking for chemical residue in the pumps to prove we were manufacturing it. Wise is certainly going to do whatever he can to manufacture a case against Capricorn."

Tulip's speculation fuelled Blue's curiosity again.

"What makes you so important, anyway?" he asked Capricorn. "Every time the subject of police comes up around here, so does your name."

"They're afraid of the message Capricorn is spreading," Tulip explained. "Study your history and you'll find Capricorn crucified all the way through it for offering alternatives. Peace, real peace, is the most frightening thing in the world to people with power. And peace is what we're reaching for here, all of us. The establishment exists on the exploitation of the masses. When individuals break loose from the masses to think for themselves, the establishment becomes scared, and frightened politicians and police forces are the most dangerous people in the world. They can't believe that Capricorn has no personal power ambitions. From their Wall Street fortresses peace is a plot."

"Well, pardon me for living on Wall Street, wherever it is," Blue said, "but when you're talking about crucifixions and peace and stuff like that in the same breath as Capi here, I have to think about things like the anti-Christ and—"

Karma placed her hand on Blue's arm, and when he turned to her she drew him in with her eyes. "Let it go for now, Blue. We can all talk about it some other time." Blue slowly opened his hands, releasing the subject like a caught bird while giving Capricorn a look that said the subject would come back again.

Capricorn went on to tell the Council that until they knew what the FBI's interest in the Colorado commune was, and until the heat of that interest died down, the commune would continue to operate from its San Francisco quarters. Everyone was instructed to keep commune activity at its current low, underground profile.

"Since we are not, despite the FBI's conviction to the contrary, manufacturing or selling drugs, we do have some financial problems," Capricorn went on. "Almost everybody is contributing what they can, earning it selling flowers, face painting, making jewellery. Tulip made a major contribution after her art show. But food and rent for two houses here in San Francisco plus other expenses like Tulip and Cory's legal fees, are mounting up. Some people haven't made much of a donation to our communal needs, at all. Particularly you and Tinker, Blue."

"Tinker will get his first cheque next week and take care of both of us," Blue said, "and I'm working on some ideas."

"The commune shares what it can, Blue. If one of us can't contribute for whatever reason then no demands will ever be made on that person. But we can't tolerate someone among us not making any effort at all to contribute. Tinker will pay his way now that he is working, I'm sure of that. But you're also working, but contributing nothing."

"You guys know the weird trip Peter? is on. He's kept the band so busy practising that there hasn't been any time to get out on the street and hustle a few bucks with my talent. He doesn't want us to record. Hell, he's even asked us to play for nothing, but nobody should play for nothing. We got this guy back home, eh—"

"Farmer," Capricorn interjected.

"Farmer doesn't play the fiddle," Blue replied, wondering how Capricorn had reached that conclusion. "John Joe on the Mountain does, though. He can jig a pretty damn good tune. Anyway, he lives up on a mountain way back of Skye Glen, this little place down the road a ways from Mabou.

"One day, Farmer and Monk and myself were bringing this horse up to John Joe's. Farmer is driving along, swigging from a bottle of Monk's shine and he's pretty hammered.

"Anyway, we get to John Joe's and unload the horse and go into the house. John Joe pays Farmer and we're sitting around talking back and forth like this when Monk spots the fiddle hanging on the wall in the kitchen.

"'How 'bout a tune, John Joe,' Monk says to him, and John Joe says to him, 'I'd love to play for you gentlemen but every tune I ever learned on the fiddle I learned drunk, and I can't for the life of me remember them sober.' You see what John Joe was getting at, eh? Farmer didn't bring the bottle into the house, so Monk sent me out to the truck for it. It was wonderful to hear how a few drinks of Monk's shine restored John Joe's musical memory."

"There's a point to this, I assume," Capricorn said.

"Of course there's a point to it. The point is that unless you are singing in the church choir you shouldn't sing for nothing. John Joe understood that, but Peter? doesn't. He's got this idea that the band should become a legend by not recording."

"We've read about it. We've also read that you've decided that it's a good idea, as well," Capricorn added.

"You know what the other fellow says, don't you? Don't believe everything you read. And Farmer, this guy we got back home, says if a preacher is preaching temperance to the people coming in the front door of the church, you can bet he's bootlegging his own booze out the back door of the church. Now what I'm going to say can't leave this table, promise?" When everyone nodded agreement, Blue went on. "Capi, I wandered around the commune here trying to figure out just how you wired the whole house so that music comes out of everything including the toilet bowl. She's a neat job, I'll give you that."

When Capricorn acknowledged the compliment, Blue went on. "A guy who knows so much about wires and stuff must know something about recording music."

"I worked for a small record company for a while," Capricorn said.

"Good. I'm glad to hear that because a small one is more important than a big one. In a small record company you probably had to do a lot of things, eh? With a small company you'd learn a lot about everything, am I right?"

"Right."

"Well, here's what I'm thinking. Everybody knows now that Blue Cacophony isn't ever going to record. There's been a lot of publicity about that. One guy from a radio station told me it was too bad that his 'larger listening audience,' as he called them, was never going to have a chance to hear the band. I bet there's a lot of people who would like to listen to us day and night like the Beatles instead of just when Peter? finds us a gig. Since people can't buy our music by walking through the front door of a music store, don't you think they should be able to buy them at the back door?"

"You're talking about pirating your own music," Capricorn said as lights of understanding began to blink on in the faces around the table. "You're dead serious, aren't you?" he added, while the silence of the others assessed Blue.

"Yup! So are you too holy to listen to the rest of my plan or what?"

"We'll listen if the rest agree," Capricorn said, counting the affirmative nods like ballots. Everyone agreed to listen. "Go on."

"The way I got her figured, people want what they can't have. If mothers wouldn't let their kids have carrots the kids'd be stealing them all the time and be a lot healthier. So now that everybody knows that they can't have Blue Cacophony's music, they'll want it. They call it the law of supply and demand, and laws are made to be obeyed, as the other fellow says, so I'm simply obeying them.

"Now all you have to do, Capi, is figure out how to record the band, find a way to make the records, organize the people in the commune to sell them without letting Peter?, Nathan or Gerry know, and I'll take care of the rest."

"And just what would 'the rest' be, Blue?"

"All the other stuff. Do you think we can do it?"

Capricorn let the challenge roll across his mind, then spoke. "We can do it, but why would we?"

"For the money, of course. I worked that part out, too. The commune gets twenty per cent. Peter? gets twenty per cent. Nathan gets twenty. So does Gerry. Barney and I get the rest."

"Do you see a problem here, Blue?" Capricorn quizzed him. "Like how do you cut the band in and out at the same time?"

"They're good musicians but they haven't got any common sense at all, so it's a good thing I do. They don't need to know about the money until they need it, right? Really need it, I mean. Until then we'll just keep it for them."

"Oh, I see," Capricorn said, his voice rising sarcastically. "You'll look after it for them. I thought there was an angle we were missing."

"Not me. You. You'll take care of it for all of us, Capi. We could be talking about hundreds of dollars here, and I know thyself, as the other fellow says. The way I am, I can't be trusted with money, even my own. The last time Tinker and me had a fight like we did yesterday was last June at the race track back home. We split on the quinella, eh, and it came in and paid fifty-four dollars. Tinker told me to collect it because he had to go pump gas at Charlie's Guesso. So I cashed the ticket, and then I got this really good feeling about the exactor and put the whole works on a longshot combination, eh. Going to surprise Tinker, you see. Well, I surprised him all right. The two smelts came in just the way I picked them, but I didn't pick them to come in seventh and eighth.

"So when Tinker came to me to collect his money that evening I had to tell him I lost his twenty-six bucks. He called me a bastard for losing his money because he was going to buy dingle balls for the Plymouth, then he punched me in the face, so I kicked him in the balls and away we went. So the point is that I'm honest. I won't steal a guy's money if he knows I got it. But I might get ideas he won't like very much, like long-shots at the race track. So that's why you're going to look after the money for all us, Capi."

"Not afraid I'll keep it all myself, Blue?"

"Now that would tell me the truth about you in a hurry, wouldn't it, about whether or not you're more Judas than Jesus there, Capi, old buddy? So are you in or what?"

Capricorn turned his attention to the rest of the table. "Blue is offering us an interesting ethical adventure here, don't you think? Common sense tells me to stay as far away from it as possible. It's clearly rooted in the concepts of greed and ego and for that reason alone the commune should walk away from it, but it's so insanely charming I doubt if I can resist. How do the rest of you feel?"

The decision to have the Human Rainbow Commune venture into the record producing business was unanimous.

33

Tinker was bent over the fender of the Plymouth. Beside him, a crescent wrench held open an encyclopaedia, its pages tattooed with greasy thumb prints. Disassembling the innards of a vehicle in order to apply new knowledge gleaned from library books and his job, re-ignited Tinker's passion for things mechanical. Peter?'s van, the commune's van and the Plymouth which Tinker now considered his fleet, were all healthier than they had been for years. The difference was noticeable to everyone driving or riding in them.

Blue, watching Tinker from the window of his and Karma's bedroom, noticed the difference more profoundly than the others, who felt the difference only in the vehicles. Blue saw the difference in Tinker. He missed the reckless confidence with which Tinker used to pound out a dull, rhythmic thud on the engine with a ballpeen hammer, or feverishly tore at wires and filters. The methodical approach that Tinker now used, removing parts and holding them as references while he leafed through the encyclopaedias, or his newly acquired habit of listening to the engine like a doctor listening to a heartbeat, had Blue concerned for his friend. While he watched Tinker bend to read from the book, Karma came and stood beside him at the window.

"It's in his people, you know," Blue explained.

"What's in whose people?" Karma asked, raising her eyebrows to another of what she now called out-of-the-Blue remarks.

"Reading. It's in his people. They were all like that. Every time you'd go into his house, you'd catch his mother reading something. They say his old man even carries a book in his lunch can. Tinker told me that when he was a little kid, his mother used to read to him every night. When he started school, they used to be on him all the time about reading on his own, but he was stubborn. Funny, isn't it, how he got away with not reading all the time he was with them, then the minute he gets free of them, the first thing he does is pick up a book. The genes will out, as the other fellow says."

"What is it with you and reading, Blue? You treat it like it's something evil. It's not like you can't read and it's not as if you're stupid. It's like, I don't know, like you're scared of books or something."

"I'm not scared of books," Blue snapped. "I just don't have time for them. There's lots more important things in the world, you know, and better places to learn about the world than in books which are just somebody else's opinion anyway.

"Sometimes when Farmer gets a horse that's broken down, he takes it to this guy's farm – a sound horse is worth money but an unsound horse is just dog food, as the other fellow says.

"Lauchie Dan is just an average Joe except that he knows how to heal horses. He'll check the horse for Farmer and if it's really old, or really lame and he can't do anything for it, he'll say so. Farmer calls him the last honest man on the planet. Anyway, this one time, Farmer took this young gelding up there for Lauchie Dan to check over. So while Lauchie Dan was running his hands over the horse Farmer was telling him that the farmer who used to own the horse had the vet in to look at it. The vet told him that the horse had stifles and tendon problems and that he would never be any good for work, so the guy sold it to Farmer for next to nothing. But Farmer thought it was a shame that a horse so young was worth so little, 'so I wanted your opinion,' Farmer told Lauchie Dan.

"Lauchie Dan never even glanced up from checking the horse all the time Farmer was talking to him, but when Farmer finished, all Lauchie Dan said in this accent that he has was, 'Dos vets, dey don't know naughting, dey just learned it from a buk.'

"Well, that pretty well said it for me, Karma, girl. 'Dey just learned it from a buk,' because a month later, once Lauchie Dan had worked on him, that gelding was as sound as the day it was born and the vet's book-learning had nothing to do with it. And a fifty-buck deal turned into seven hundred bucks when Farmer sold that gelding.

"Everybody back home is always saying get an education, it's the only way to get ahead in the world. Then the next day they're all complaining that all the people with an education leave the island and never come back. So who wants to never come back? Not me."

"Some educated people must come back, Blue. There are teachers and doctors and lawyers, aren't there?"

"Exceptions to the rule, says the other fellow," Blue replied. "And now Tinker's into the books."

"With Tinker working every day, and you playing or practising so many nights, the two of you don't get to see much of each other, do you?" Karma said.

"Weird, huh. Here's me and my best buddy sleeping next door to each other in the same house, and hardly ever seeing one another anymore. Do you suppose he notices that?"

"Of course, he does, Blue. It's just that sometimes circumstances get in people's way. Nobody means anything by it. It just happens. Capricorn told me once that most of our relationships with other people are circumstantial, that once the circumstances change, the relationship no longer exists. But the real friendships are those that don't depend on circumstances, just on each other."

Blue, watching Tinker from the window, dwelled upon his own knowledge of what Karma said.

"My father tells these stories about when he was young and working the mines up north, or factories in Toronto, eh, and it was always with other guys from home. Same as Tinker and me, I guess. They travelled together, worked together, got drunk together and all that stuff, and then most of them eventually came home and settled down, but you hardly ever see them talking to each other.

"There was this one guy, Alex John, that my father went away with. The old man told more stories about the two of them when they were on the road than an accountant can count. But then they came back and lived in the same town ever since and I don't think I ever saw them do more than wave to each other. Then Alex John got killed in a car crash and the old man went to his wake, but didn't even take time off work to go to his funeral. He just said that the stories about him and Alex John were from a long time ago and far away. It's like they had nothing in common when they came back home, like they didn't even know each other anymore.

"But then there's this other guy from home, Andrew. He lives in Manitoba. Doesn't get home except maybe every five years. He's the old man's best friend. Andrew comes in the house and they're into the stories right away like they were just picking up where they left off yesterday. Is that what you mean?"

"I believe so, Blue."

"And you say it was Capricorn who told you that? I wonder where he got the idea from?"

"Probably stole it from some old book, Blue," Karma said.

"Know what we should do, Karma? Go down there and visit Tinker."

—

"Hey, Tinker," Blue called out from the back step where he stood with Karma, taking a deep breath of cool, early December air. "Know what this weather reminds me of? Your mother's chicken frico and rabbit pies. Karma and me were just talking about her, and the first thing I thought off was her frico."

Tinker lifted his head from under the hood. "What were you talking about my mother for?"

"The way she reads, and the way you took after her," Blue answered, pointing to the open book on the fender. Then he turned to Karma, telling her more about Tinker's mother as they walked down the steps and toward the Plymouth.

"Tinker's mother is French, you know—"

"Acadian," Tinker corrected.

"Whatever," Blue continued. "Anyway, Tinker's mother cooks these really great things. What would you call her chicken frico, Tinker, soup or stew?"

"Frico," Tinker said, settling his elbows on the fender to wait while the visitors approached.

"The French back home are stubborn like that. They'd even rather speak French than English," Blue explained. "Anyway, her frico is like stew or soup, but the best thing of all is her rabbit pie. In the fall, if Tinker and me get a couple of rabbits, we bring them to her and she makes rabbit pie for us. You'd love ... well, maybe you wouldn't, but most people would love it. I'd give my eye teeth for a piece right now, wouldn't you, Tink?"

Tinker sniffed the air with closed eyes, as if he could smell what Blue described.

"Remember the time—" Blue asked, and before he could get any further, Tinker laughed, pulling his thoughts from under the engine hood to the story at hand.

"The rabbit in the snare?" Tinker asked, and getting a confirming nod from Blue, went on. "One time Blue and I were hunting rabbits ... we got a couple that day, I remember ... and we were coming through the woods kind of quiet in case we see any more. And we do, only this one's caught around the neck in a snare. Snares really piss Blue and I off. They're cruel as hell. Some people might not even check their snares after they set them, so a rabbit strangles in it and then just rots.

"The rabbit is still in a coma, so Blue gives me the dead rabbits and his gun to carry and loosens the snare and takes off his jacket and wraps the rabbit up in it. We figure if we can get it home maybe we can save it, have it for a pet or something. So we start making our way back to town.

"There's this place in the woods up behind the race track where lots of people go to drink. We come out of the woods at just that spot and we see this old guy passed out, snoring a cord of wood a minute. Blue whispers to me that maybe the old guy's caught in a snare, too, and we start to laugh, but when Blue see the guy's big hat – he was wearing one of those salt-and-pepper hats ten times too big for him – he gets an idea and tiptoes up beside him, takes the rabbit out of his jacket and puts it under the hat, then he sneaks back to where I am in the woods and tells me that we're going to show the old guy some magic.

"Blue says what we'll do is walk out of the woods making all kinds of noise to wake the old guy up and then Blue will tell him that he knows magic, and then he'll pull the rabbit out of the man's hat. But before we could get ready to play our trick we hear this scream and go running to where the old guy is, and there he is chasing his hat around the clearing. He'd leap for it and the hat would leap away and the old guy would land on his face and get up and try it again.

"Well, Blue and I took to laughing so hard that we fell down, and finally the hat leapt off into the woods and the old guy just sat there trying to shake what he thought was the DTs from out of his head.

"Once the rabbit took off into the woods and I realized it was okay, I asked Blue if he wanted to go hunt it, but Blue said, 'Ah, let it go'."

"It was getting dark," Blue explained to Karma.

The laughter brought Kathy from the house, curious about the carry-on in the back yard, and when she asked about it, Tinker promised he would tell her the story later.

"Where you come from, does everybody drink?" Karma asked Tinker and Blue. "Every time you tell a story, somebody is drinking too much in it, it seems."

"No," Blue assured her. "Not everybody drinks. Hardly any of the nuns do, huh, Tink?" sending the two of them off into laughter again. Then taking Karma's question more seriously, Blue added, "Not everybody drinks a lot, but a lot of the stories happen when people drink. We got this guy back home who lives next door to me, eh. He never had a drink in his life. Not so much as a taste of beer. That's all everybody ever says about him, that he's never had a drink in his life. He's kind of famous for it, but that's all anybody has to say about him. Now you take some of the other people we know, Farmer or Monk. They've tasted the devil, as the other fellow says, and their hell, in our humour, wouldn't you say, Tinker?"

Tinker looked across at Blue leaning on the opposite fender, wondering what he might add.

"It's kind of like that novel you gave me to read," Tinker said, directing his explanation to Kathy. "You know when you're reading it that there's a whole town there, but the story is about just a few of the people. If nobody in the story gets sick, then the story doesn't need a doctor, and if there are no children in it, the story doesn't need a school, but that doesn't mean the rest of the people don't exist. Just because the story's not about them doesn't mean they don't have stories of their own."

"But don't you ever talk about anything else?" Kathy asked. "Even to each other?"

"Not in mixed company," Blue said, winking at Tinker.

"I'm serious," Kathy said. "I know more about your home town than I do about my own, and I've never even been there. Putting the two of you together is like watching two magnets pulling toward each other, except that it's Cape Breton that you're pulled toward."

"The way my old man explains us," Tinker replied, "is that everybody back home, the Irish, the Acadians, the Scotch, all have the same story – homeless people thrown out of their own countries by the frigging British, but they all washed up on the same shore, Cape Breton, see. And the old man says that an island is the easiest kind of land in the world to love, so they all just loved the island for being there to catch them when they were floating across the ocean.

"The old man's Irish, see, and they had a potato famine in Ireland so his father's father had to leave Ireland and come to Cape Breton. My mother's people, the Acadians, got thrown out of Nova Scotia by the British. Most of them were shipped to Louisiana during the expulsion of the Acadians, but some of them sneaked away before they could be expelled and came up to Cape Breton. And, of course, the Scots had their own problems, as they never tire of telling us. So just about everybody on the island comes from a lost home, and according to the old man they remember those homes with sad songs and funny stories, He says there are two things about Cape Breton that we're born knowing, that it's home, and that we'll probably have to leave it someday.

"I didn't tell you about this before, Blue, because I didn't know where to fit it in, but this was the conversation the old man had with me the night before we left. I think maybe he was worried that I might not come back, so he wanted me to know why Cape Bretoners go around acting like they're God's chosen people."

"Yup, we do, don't we," Blue said, "and does that ever piss those mainlanders in Nova Scotia off, eh, because they know in the bottom of their hearts that we are."

34

Tinker and Blue sat in the back booth of the greasy restaurant waiting for the waitress to bring their orders. During the conversation in the backyard of the Human Rainbow Commune, Blue had begun hinting to Tinker that a good cup of Cape Breton tea was what they both needed. Tinker picked up on the code word they had agreed upon at the hotel before moving into the commune, that when one of them said he wanted tea, it meant "T" as in T-bone steak or some other part of a red-blooded animal. Tinker agreed that a cup of tea would be nice if they could find a restaurant that served it right, then weakly extended the invitation to Karma and Kathy.

Karma declined on the grounds that Tinker and Blue put milk in their tea, to which Kathy added, "And ketchup on it." Barney joined them instead, and was now curled up under the table, waiting for the manna to fall from the culinary Heaven above.

"When Kathy said that about ketchup," Tinker said, "did you think she broke our secret code?"

"No way, man," Blue assured him. "They'd never let us go hunting hamburgers. Did you see Karma's face when you were talking about the rabbits? It was just a lucky guess, that was all, trying to trick us into telling them the truth."

"Why would they try to trick us unless they suspected the truth?" Tinker wondered.

"Women's intuition," Blue explained. "You see, Tink, what you got to understand about women is that they have this extra instinct that warns them about men. God gave it to them so that mothers could use it to sense if something is wrong with their children, but some of them misuse it to sniff around and find out what their men are up to, not their children, and that's not really fair, like using snares to hunt rabbits."

The waitress placed the plates in front of them, hamburgers with the works, french fries swimming in a grey pool of gravy, a couple of Pepsis.

"Hmmmm! Real food," Blue said, inhaling the heat rising from dish, waiting for Tinker to finish squeezing ketchup onto his order. He flicked a gravy-sodden fry under the table and listened to the snap as Barney snagged it. "So how are things in the pit, buddy?"

"I like it, Blue. Casey, the chief mechanic, is really great to work with. If he's working on something and I'm helping him, he explains everything he's doing. If he tells me to go get a wing nut, he'll tell me exactly why he needs it and where it will go, and why it needs to be there. He doesn't treat people like flunkies. If you don't know something, he teaches it to you. When I finish working with him, I'll be able to go to any mine or tunnel in the world.

"And he's as strong as a bull, Blue. I bet he could straighten a horseshoe with his bare hands. So tell me how the record business is going."

Blue chewed on a bite of hamburger, swallowed, and washed it down with a swig of Pepsi.

"Capi and me are working on it. He's practically living in the basement, for God's sake. Have you been down there since he started? There's enough wires down there to electrocute half the city.

"He's rigging up a microphone for me to wear. First he tried it on Barney, but most of the sound that came out of it was Barney scratching at it like a giant flea. So what we're going to do is fit it up to me, but getting the sound even is the big problem, he says. If I'm the only one wearing the mic then it's me you hear the most. I told him that that's okay with me, but you know what a stickler he is for democracy.

"Anyway, looking at all that wire lying around, it reminded me of the time when I was eleven or twelve and Burton's store used to pay seven cents a pound for copper. Remember when the Power Commission had that storehouse below the tracks? Nothing in it but big rolls of copper wire, all of them coated with insulation and most of them so heavy I had to drag them, five or six rolls I guess, down to the field above the beach and build a bonfire to throw them in. Burn the insulation off them, you see. Then when they had cooled down I pounded the wire as tight as I could, got a wheelbarrow and took the whole works up to Burton's. Twenty-five bucks' worth, my greatest crime.

"Anyway, I tell this story to Capi and he chuckles, saying that it reminded him of something that happened in high school. He went to school in New York City, but we knew that much, right? Anyway, I guess he was always a wizard with electrical stuff, which makes him the right guy for the job he's doing for me.

"He says he was 'competitively motivated at the time,' to quote the man directly, although it's the kind of thing the other fellow will say someday, don't you think? He wanted to be first in everything he did, but there was this exam he was worried about. The guy teaching the subject, who is the vice-principal of the school, to boot, doesn't like Capi one bit, and Capi thinks that just maybe the guy is small enough to flunk him just to keep him from getting a scholarship at the end of the year. So to protect himself, Capi stays in the school after it closed one afternoon and breaks into the vice principal's office, looking for the exam questions, but he can't find hide nor hair of them. So what he does then is wire the office, hoping to overhear the vice-principal discussing the exam questions. It was a long shot, Capi said, but it was his last shot at keeping this guy from flunking him. Then he sets up the earphones in an empty closet in the boys' locker room. He knows what time the teacher has a free period, so Capi sneaks to the closet at that same time to listen.

"What happens is that the teacher is not discussing exam questions at all, but talking dirty to his secretary, and Capi hears the whole thing. The two of them are talking real rot to each other, he says, while they are obviously taking off their clothes, and then obviously doing it.

"What Capi doesn't know is that when he wired the office he somehow, he still doesn't know how, connected his wiretap to the intercom so the whole school hears everything that's going on in the vice principal's office. Capi hears people pounding at the vice principal's door, and the vice principal and his secretary being caught red-handed. The secretary got fired and the principal got suspended, then transferred to the worst school in the city. Someone else gave the exam and Capi passed with flying colours.

"After he tells me all this, Tinker, and he's laughing out loud while he's telling me, he says that the story wasn't nearly as funny when it was happening as it was re-telling it, and I said to him, 'You're getting the idea.'

"But getting back to your question, Capi says that we'll make recordings of a bunch of gigs and pick the clearest pieces for the album. We should have it out by Christmas or New Year's, but we have to be careful not to let any of the guys in the band go down into our basement."

35

Blue whacked his elbow against the side of the van on the off chance that it would startle Capricorn, who was working inside, into jumping up and banging his head on the metal roof. Then he slid the door open and climbed inside.

Capricorn, seated on a wooden box, was mounting a reel-to-reel recorder on a shelf he had installed in the van. "We'll park the van behind your gig tonight," he explained to Blue, "and hide a couple of mics inside and record the show. Three or four gigs should give us more than enough material to edit for an album."

Getting Blue to hold a bolt firm with a screwdriver, Capricorn screwed on a nut from underneath, bolting down one side of the recorder, then repeating it on the other side of the shelf. Capricorn tested the firmness of the installed machine, took a couple of the wires hanging from it, lifted the lid of the box he had been sitting on, and revealed a dozen connected batteries. Attaching the wires to terminals, he turned on the recorder and the reels began to roll.

"There's enough juice to run the machine for four or five hours," Capricorn explained, turning the recorder off.

"So how do you sneak the mics into the club?" Blue asked, pointing to the coils on the floor.

Capricorn moved to the front of the van, sat behind the wheel, turned the key and lurched away, tumbling Blue around until he eventually made his way to the passenger seat. "We're going to do that right now," Capricorn informed him.

"We?"

"It's going to take two of us to do this."

"But it shouldn't be me. I got to call a rehearsal. Tinker's the guy you want. He's really good at this."

"Breaking and entering? Tinker's good at it?"

"Well, he hasn't actually done all that much of it, but he learns quick."

"I think we can handle it ourselves," Capricorn said, bringing the subject to a close unless Blue wanted to leap from the moving van, which he briefly considered before settling into the fact that he was on his way to a life of crime and probably life on Alcatraz.

"What are you going to do with your share of the money?" Blue asked as Capricorn drove them through the streets of the city.

"I'd like to see the commune move back to Colorado as soon as the heat's off the place. Hopefully that will happen before California slips into the sea. If there's any cash in this zany scheme it will help us get set up there again."

"They say that, eh, that she's going to disappear into the ocean. Well, Tinker and me'll be back home by then, I hope. The last thing we need is to be part of the next Atlantis."

"You think there was an Atlantis?" Capricorn asked with unmasked surprise.

"Well, it's a good story, and besides, Farmer and me found out that Cape Breton's part of that story."

"Blue, you aren't going to tell me that Atlantis sunk in the Mediterranean and surfaced in North America as Cape Breton Island, are you?"

"No. Why would I tell you that? Atlantis sank in the Atlantic Ocean, the way I hear it, and it still hasn't surfaced that I know of, but that's a pretty good theory you have there, Cape Breton as Atlantis. I'll have to work that into a song. But there's a weird story to how I found out about Atlantis."

"There's no chance I'm not going to hear that story, is there?" Capricorn mused.

"If you don't want to hear it—"

"I'm all ears, Blue."

"Farmer — I told you about him, the horse trader — we brought a couple of Clydes to these hippies who were living up back of Brook Village.

"That was funny the way Farmer changed his mind about hippies. We'd see them hitchhiking on the road and Farmer'd be swinging the truck at them like he was going to run them over or something and they'd be jumping in the ditches, and he'd be calling them fruits and commies and all that stuff. Then one day this hippie comes up to him in town and says he looking for a team of Clydesdales to work the farm they bought in Brook Village. He explains to Farmer that the people living on the farm, a bunch of hippie brothers from Connecticut, 'weren't into machines, man,' well, you know the way you guys talk, Capi, and so they wanted work horses.

"All of a sudden, Farmer realizes that there might be more business in these hippies than in the all truck-and-tractor farmers who have been slowly putting him out of business. So Farmer finds a team he can buy cheap and sells it to them for a bushel of American dollars.

"Anyway, we're putting these horses in the barn and the hippie is telling about how much he loves Cape Breton and how the earth speaks to him and all that. Later, Farmer said to me that if we smoked as much of the earth as those hippies did, it'd speak to us, too. Then the hippie tells us that the reason he and his brothers came to Cape Breton was because he read in a book that Cape Breton was one of the seven spiritual centres of the world. Some prophet in a coma told him that, he said."

"Edgar Cayce?" Capricorn asked.

"Who?"

"Was the prophet's name Edgar Cayce? There was an American mystic named Edgar Cayce who people called the Sleeping Prophet."

"That's it! I don't remember the name, but it was a sleeping prophet, that's for sure. What did I say? He was in a coma. Close. Anyway, this hippie is telling us about how Cape Breton is this spiritual centre and Farmer is saying he's not surprised because the island has been spitting out priests and nuns and ministers at the rate of two or three a family for two hundred years, so it must be spiritual, and all the time he's winking at me.

"Then the hippie begins telling us about the lost continent of Atlantis, and how in a previous life he used to live there. I wonder if he knew Karma? Anyway, it was kind of a paradise until it got screwed up, he said. That's what life's all about, the hippie told us, recreating Atlantis.

"By this time, Farmer can hardly keep a straight face, but while the hippie is telling us this he's holding the money for the horses in his hand so Farmer is nodding his agreement and not taking his eyes or his mind off the money.

"By the time we get out of there and down the road, Farmer can hardly keep the truck out of the ditch we're laughing so hard. Still, after that Farmer never saw a hippie he didn't pick up and give a ride to, and try to sell him a horse, of course."

"So do you believe this story, Blue?" Capricorn asked as he pulled the van into an alley behind Club Peace & Love, the venue for Blue Cacophony's gig that night.

"Well, I didn't at first, not when the hippie was telling us, but then when Cape Breton got in the picture, being the spiritual centre of the Universe and all, it began to make sense."

"I thought you said Cape Breton was one of seven spiritual centre of the world? Now it's *the* spiritual centre of the Universe?" Capricorn asked.

"You're right on both accounts, Capi, but this place looks like it's not open yet," Blue noted as the van pulled to a stop.

"It isn't. That's why we're here. You're going through the window and coming around to open the door. Then we set up."

36

"So I said to Capi, 'Look, the only way we're going to be able to wire this place is by breaking in,' so I got him to drive us over there this afternoon and I came through a window out back, opened the door and let Capi do his thing. He has three mics hidden in here ... but here comes Peter? so let's change the subject."

Blue was sitting with Karma, Kathy and Tinker at a table in Club Peace & Love waiting for the rest of the band to turn up. Peter? approached alone.

"So how's it hanging, Peter??" Blue asked, reaching for a subject that would move the conversation far from the plans hatched at the Human Rainbow Commune.

"Is that a serious enquiry, Blue?" Peter? asked, puckering his lips to blow Blue a teasing kiss, taking pleasure in watching Blue begin to squirm.

"Aw, it's just something guys say to each other. It doesn't mean anything, does it, Tinker? We say it to each other all the time, eh, Tink? Everybody does. I bet even the Pope says it."

"Don't worry, Blue, I won't break up with Lee just because you're showing a little interest." Before Blue could respond, Peter? made a sudden shift to the serious and sat down.

"We have to be careful, Blue," he confided. "The papers are making a bit of news out of Blue Cacophony's refusal to record. Nothing big, just little mentions here and there, but these things have a way of growing. We may start feeling some capitalist pressure to jump through the money hoops just because there's a pile of it waiting on the other side. It's the big temptation, Blue, and it's coming. I can feel it. Most opportunities aren't! Did you know that Blue, that most opportunities aren't really opportunities at all? They're really just tests to see if you have the courage to turn them down and go on looking for the truth. That's what Blue Cacophony is doing, looking for the truth, and to get there we have to stay pure, Blue. I'm depending on you to keep the other guys from getting greedy about easy money."

"You can depend on me to do the right thing, Peter?, you know that, old buddy. You got more principals than all the schools in the country...."

"You mean principles?"

"That's what I said."

"A school has princip-a-l-s, a person has princi-p-l-e-s," corrected Peter?.

"Whatever, but you got all these principles, eh, and I've got mine, which is just one, Peter?, and that principle is this, look after your buddies. So I'm going to take care nothing happens to you. You're the guy with the brains, and in the land of the stupid, the guy with the brains is the smart one, to quote the other fellow, so I think you'll find out about that truth business of yours with or without selling a million records."

"I appreciate your faith in me, Blue, it is reassuring to know that a fellow intellect—"

"Don't take this wrong or anything, Peter?, but it isn't you I have faith in. It's God. You're free to ask all kinds of questions as long as you don't ask the ones that piss God off, but I'm a Catholic, so my questions are all behind me, eh."

"I don't follow that train of thought," Peter? said.

"I mean there's only so much thinking I can do before I run up against a wall in matters of faith. I mean I have faith, but sometimes I come across questions that threaten to pole vault me right out of the Church if I'm not careful. That's the thing about being Catholic, question the Church and you question God. You Protestants don't have to worry about that, but you're probably just kindling for the Big Fire anyway. But not us Catholics. We were born in the faith, as the other fellow says."

"Do you believe this?" Peter? asked with an amazed shake of his head.

"Have to. I'm Catholic. But what I mean when I say I don't have faith in you, Peter?, is that I have faith in God, and it could be that God has different plans for me than you do, so if ... just 'if' now ... I have to make a choice, I have to chose the one I have the most faith in, right? You can understand that, can't you?"

Peter? nodded agreement. "We both want the same thing, Blue, that's our karma."

"Your karma, my Karma, maybe my old buddy, Farma. I'm going to write that down, but can I change the subject here, Peter?? It's about Barney," Blue said, nudging the dog that slept at his feet. "Does he have to be in the band? Not that I have anything against him. Heck, next to Karma, I'm his best buddy. I just don't know about singing with him."

Peter? gave heavy-browed consideration to Blue's question before answering. "I think he has to be in the band, Blue. After all, it was you who told the papers that he would be, and the dog is why half the people will be here tonight, all that publicity. From my perspective, I see the union up on stage of you and Barney, man and dog – nature's great companions – as the first step toward a time when the lamb shall lay down with the lion, the Great Peace. Though we are travellers along the same spiritual highway, Blue, I realize that we don't always see the same horizon, so it might be of significance for you to know that 51.042 per cent of all the acts that appear on *The Ed Sullivan Show* include a human and an animal. Of that figure, 62.943 per cent of the animals are dogs."

"I didn't say I wouldn't sing with Barney, did I, Peter?? I was just wondering, you know. Where'd you learn so much about Ed Sullivan, anyway?"

"I did my own research one Sunday night when I had nothing better to do than watch that sad parade of talent prostituting itself on television. It was last Sunday night, in fact, and I kept those records because that kind of trivial data appeals to certain people."

"I know what you mean," Blue agreed. "For example, there's not a whole lot of people in the world who know that your arsehole has to vibrate ninety times a second before your farts can make a noise. I don't know what that means in the grand scheme of things, but you gotta admire anybody who can count that fast."

"I got a weird gig Monday morning," Nathan told Blue and Gerry as they packed up their gear and carted it out to the van, under Peter?'s supervision. "I was playing down at my corner, trying to pick up a few bucks on the side, and a woman came up and asked me to play for a funeral. She said her husband was in the army during the war, and died yesterday. He wanted a piper at his funeral, she said. I told her she probably wanted somebody from the American Legion for that gig, but she says, 'No, the bastard kept me a prisoner of war for twenty-three years. A goddamned Communist hippie playing the pipes at his funeral will go a long way toward making the whole experience worth it.' Offered me a hundred bucks so I said I'll be there."

"You mean you know where's there's a wake?" Blue asked. "Hey, Tinker, this woman Nathan knows, her husband died. There's a wake." The information brought Tinker across the floor to join the musicians. "Want to go?" Blue asked.

"You can't go to the wake," Nathan said. "You don't even know the guy."

"Sure we can go," Blue argued. "What's stopping us? Respect for the dead. That's what they teach you where I come from. Respect for the dead. One time, eh, when I was in grade six, that was before Tinker caught up to me in school, well this guy died who used to be janitor of the school. Well this morning the nun tells us Old Malcolm is dead. She told us to get our jackets on, made us get in ranks of two by two, and marched us through the snow all the way to the janitor's house. We all went in and looked at him. He didn't look like he was enjoying it very much. Suit and tie, as the other fellow says. A man should be buried with his boots on, and if those boots are a mop and a broom, what the hell, bury them with him. Anyway, the whole parade of us looked at him, then we got down on our knees and said the rosary. And we stole about a dozen plates of cookies and stuff out of the dead guy's kitchen on our way back to school. What that taught us, eh, because the nun said that's what it taught us, was respect for the dead.

"Now this guy who died fought in the friggin' war, didn't he? What more do you need to know about a man than that. He fought in a friggin' war! On our side, to boot! I say we go down there tomorrow. Nothing wrong with praying for a man's soul."

"You're morbid, man," Gerry said.

37

The following evening, Blue and Tinker walked solemnly into the funeral home where, according to the information posted on the wall, the remains of William Joseph Rubble were available for viewing between the hours of seven and nine p.m.

"That's the problem I have with these funeral homes," Blue said. "They keep worse hours than the liquor store, the one back home, anyway. You barely have time to get comfortable at a wake and the undertaker is ushering you out and closing the door."

—

Tinker and Blue had talked long into the night about the wake, and brought the subject up the following morning, carrying it into the afternoon. From Nathan they had found out where the funeral home was, and from the obituary in the newspaper they found out the times for viewing the remains. The Last Passage Funeral Home was open to the public from 2:00-4:00 in the afternoon, and from 7:00-9:00 in the evening.

"The evening's when we want to go," Blue advised. "That's when things start to liven up, right, Tinker?"

Recruiting mourners for the evening visit presented Tinker and Blue with a few problems, most of them rooted in the fact that nobody else wanted to go. Most members of the commune, and the entire band along with its manager, had difficulty appreciating the social opportunity that had presented itself in the unfortunate death of a man no one had ever heard of, and whose wife had hired a hippie piper as a mean-spirited trick on him.

"What is it about this man's death that appeals to you?" Peter? asked Tinker and Blue.

"Each man's death diminishes me, as the other fellow says," Blue replied.

"Donne." Peter? stated.

"No, I'm not done, the dead guy is done," Blue answered. "It's just that there's some things you don't get around to thinking about, you know, because they don't require any thinking. Like respect for the dead. A guy dies, you go to the wake. What's to think about?"

"I've never been to a wake," Karma said.

"I went to my grandmother's funeral, but I was too small to go to her wake," Kathy added, pooling her experience with Karma's.

"I buried a friend once," Capricorn told the table. "He died of cancer. His cancer was caused by living next door to a factory that spewed out poison. His own father went on working in that fucking place although his son was dying and so were half the children around there. When he died, the factory gave his father three days off with pay. Compassionate leave, they call it. That factory is gone now, burned down, but my friend is still dead."

"My arm—" Gerry started, then suddenly withdrew.

"Your arm what?" Blue asked, and the others let his question float in the sea of their silence while they allowed Gerry time to continue, or room to withdraw.

"I hated the violin. Every week my parents drove me to my lessons, made me play, made me practice, and made my plans for me. I was going to be a great violinist. Like you can *make* anybody be great. A person is great, or he's not, and I knew I was never going to be what they wanted me to be. One night, when they were driving me to practice, a drunk truck driver hit our car. I still don't remember anything about it, but when I woke up my arm was gone at the shoulder. So were my father and mother. Dead. I didn't go to their wake, or to their funeral. I was still in the hospital. All that came out of the accident uninjured, the doctor said when he told me about my parents, was my violin. My first thought was that I had a good excuse for never playing it again. That's a terrible thing to think of when your parents are dead and your arm's been cremated, isn't it? But do you know what my second thought was? How much I wanted to play it. I cried and cried and everyone thought I was crying for my parents but I was crying for my violin.

"At rehab, they had people fitting me for a new arm, but I told them I didn't want a new arm. What was the good of an arm that can't push a bow? One woman there who designed prostheses really tried to help me. It was her who designed my bow, but I guess that's not really about wakes, is it? Sorry about that."

"No," Blue corrected him. "This is exactly what happens at wakes, Ger. People remember stories about other wakes."

"I've never known anyone who died," Nathan said. "In fact, when I play at the funeral on Monday, that'll be the first time I was ever near one."

"You guys don't hold wakes anyway, do you?" Blue said to Nathan. "Don't you plant your people before sundown or something?"

"Our burial rites are different than yours, yes," Nathan replied, "but what music do I play for this guy's funeral?"

"We'll come up with something. Maybe I could write something and the whole band could perform it at the funeral," a suggestion unanimously voted down. There was also a motion to vote down accompanying Tinker and Blue to the wake at all.

"I can understand people going to wakes in a small town where everyone knows each other," Tulip said, "but this is San Francisco and wakes happen every day that we don't know anything about, or care about for that matter. It seems silly to me to go to a stranger's wake. I for one am not going."

"You're wrong about this being a city, Tulip," Blue said. "I used to think it was a city, too, but now, after a few months, Barney and I walk the same streets every day, nod to the same people, talk to the same people, eat in the same place. So do all of you if you think about it. A city is just a bunch of small towns. We live in one here in the district. Tinker works in a different small town, right?"

Tinker nodded his agreement. "Yeah. When I first went into the tunnel, I didn't know anybody. I would eat my lunch in a corner by myself until the rest of the crew invited me to eat with them and talk about things, and pretty soon there's lots to talk about. I met guys in the tunnel who worked with guys from back home. One of them even invited me and Blue to his daughter's wedding next spring. If I wasn't living here, eh, I'd probably be living with those guys wherever they hang out; that'd be a small town, too. Blue's right, about that, and he's right about the wake. The dead guy's not a stranger. Nathan met his widow and she asked him to come, and we're friends of Nathan's so it's the same as an invitation.

"I'll tell you this. Back home, eh, the older the dead person is, or the less you knew him, the better the wake. You never went to your grandmother's wake, Kathy, but I went to mine and I didn't have a lot of fun so you didn't miss much, but the other ones that Blue and me went to were great."

—

Blue walked directly to the coffin and crossed himself while Tinker stood a polite few feet behind, waiting his own solemn moment with the deceased. Blue studied Mr. Rubble's powder-and-rouge face and recognized him for a boozer. Death couldn't hide that fact, not with a nose like that. Other than that, he didn't look like anybody Blue knew, but death changes a person. At almost every wake he ever went to, the remains barely resembled themselves, mostly because it was the first time he ever saw most of them in a suit and tie. That was probably true for Mr. Rubble, too. He barely resembles himself, so it's no wonder I don't recognize him, Blue thought.

Saying an "Our Father," three "Hail Marys" and a "Glory Be," Blue crossed himself again and took stock of the funeral room.

It was a small room, smelling like cheap perfume over an unwashed armpit. A woman, darkly dressed, was seated near the coffin. No one else was present. Blue walked toward her.

"Death's a bastard, to quote the other fellow," he whispered, leaning to clasp her hand in consolation. His words of comfort brought her head up as quickly as Blue's dropped toward her, the clunk of skulls emitting a hollow echo through the room.

"Who are you?" she asked, rubbing her forehead.

"Blue. I'm a friend of Nathan, the piper you hired. When I heard about your husband being in the army, well, I'm from Canada, eh, and we got this guy back home, Farmer, who used to be in the army, too. Who knows, they might even of known one another over in Italy or Germany or in some tavern somewhere. I'll have to ask Farmer about him when I get home. He'd remember a name like Rubble. And he'd of come to the funeral. So I came for Farmer, for all the soldiers who couldn't get here," the last words drawing Blue's attention to a chamber empty of anything but a bored-looking widow, himself and Tinker. Examining the wife more closely, he concluded that her husband didn't drink alone.

"You didn't know my husband?"

"Not in so many words, Missus."

"Then I don't understand why you are here. Are you some kind of pervert or something?"

The blast of her breath in Blue's face informed him that not much time had passed between the widow and her last whiskey. "Oh, no, we're not weirdos, Ma'am. We do this all the time back home. It's called respect for the dead. Help the family through their suffering, if you know what I mean. Some people need a priest to do that for them when a man dies, and other people need a wee taste of the devil, as the other fellow says," Blue said, patting a bulge in his belt.

"The devil?" the widow asked, growing alarmed.

"Missis, now don't take offence, but it's an old custom where I come from to offer the husband or wife of the dearly deceased a small glass of something to help them through their sorrow."

Tinker, who had finished his moment with Mr. Rubble, stepped up beside Blue and offered his hand in sympathy. "It's something we do back home, Ma'am. Blue doesn't mean any offence."

"Are you offering me alcohol?" the woman asked, primming in her chair.

"Only if it will help you through this terrible moment, Ma'am."

"Exactly what kind of alcohol would you be offering?"

"I got rum and Tinker here has lemon gin," Blue interjected.

"I prefer whiskey when I do indulge," the widow confided, "but I won't turn down your generosity. I suppose a small drink would help. Gin would do nicely."

"Is that a kitchen or a closet over there?" Tinker asked, taking the bottle from Blue's belt and adding it to his own. Discovering that it was a kitchenette, he went to fix the drinks, leaving Blue to console the widow.

"That's my buddy, Tinker, going to get you a drink. Awfully small, these funeral homes, aren't they?" Blue observed as he took a seat beside the widow. .

"There's bigger. There's even bigger rooms in this funeral home," Mrs. Rubble said, "but so's the cost of the funeral but— Look, just who are you?" the widow asked sharply, only to be interrupted by Tinker's sudden presence, offering her one of the three coffee mugs he carried. "Oh, thank you," she said, reaching to relieve him of one-third of his cargo, then turned back to Blue. "I still don't understand why you're here," she said more softly.

"Well, it's like this, Missus. Tinker and me got lonesome when we heard about your husband's wake. I guess you do it different in the city, but back where we come from, a wake's a guy's last chance to be alive. People always get sentimental and begin telling stories. Like maybe his brother tells one about him, and then a buddy of his, then someone else. Before long, the first thing you know if you're sitting there listening, is that you get a pretty good look at the guy even if you barely knew him. Tinker and me are old pros at wakes."

"You want me to tell you some stories about that bastard?" Mrs. Rubble asked, nodding toward the casket then draining her cup and passing it back to Tinker. "Refill that for me and I'll give you a wake to remember." Tinker took her glass and hurried off to the kitchenette, winking his assurance to Blue that this was going to work out okay.

"So how did you meet?" Blue asked.

"Oh, he was going off to war. You know young girls. They think a donkey looks good if he's wearing a uniform. Well, part of him was like a donkey, but you boys are too young for me to go into that. Anyway, the way it was during the war, we were cheering our boys on, not like those girls today, spitting on those poor soldiers. So he was going overseas and he only had a few days leave and we danced and we drank and laughed and sang and we sobered up married the morning he had to ship out. I never saw him again until after the war."

Tinker returned with the refilled mugs. Each of them took a reflective sip, gazing at the coffin. Only a bulb of nose was visible from where they sat.

"So he came back from the war," Blue prompted.

"It's one thing to send a man off to war. It's quite another to welcome him back. If he'd been killed I'd have probably gone on loving him forever, but I wound up living with him forever. At least it seems that long. I can't believe the bastard's dead, but he must be or else the smell of this liquor would have him rising up out of that coffin like Dracula."

"'Finnegan's Wake'," Blue nodded to Tinker.

"Who's that, dear?" Mrs. Rubble asked.

"'Finnegan's Wake.' It's this Irish song about a guy named Jim Finnegan who everybody thinks is dead but then at his wake this fight breaks out and some of the liquor splashes over Jim and—"

"The liquor splashes over Jim," Tinker sang, picking the song up from that point in Blue's narration. "My God, see how he rises/—"

"Well, for the love of God," Mrs. Rubble laughed, "drink up before any of this stuff splashes over my husband. God couldn't be that cruel, could he?"

"How about another splash for yourself," Blue said, taking the cup from her hand and passing it to Tinker. "How's the gin holding up, buddy? You're sure you wouldn't like some rum?" he asked Mrs. Rubble.

"I wouldn't touch rum unless it was the last drink in the bar. Ask me again when the gin is gone, dearie."

Tinker left for the kitchenette, his walk more deliberately navigational, like a sailor aboard ship. Mrs. Rubble watched him go. "He's a nice boy," she said.

"One of the best. So what was he like when he came home from the war?" Blue probed.

"He was a big useless prick, dearie, that's what he was, a big useless prick. As big and useless as his own prick was after he came back. Useless. The hardest work he ever did was finding me greasy spoon jobs. Do you know how hard one woman has to work to keep two people drunk? Damn hard! That's how hard. Where is that boy with the bottle?"

"Probably gone to the bathroom. I wouldn't say it in front of him, Tinker has his pride," Blue explained, "but he doesn't have a lot of capacity, to quote the other fellow. Usually he just drinks, throws up and passes out."

"If he's going to throw up you know where to point him," she instructed Blue, pointing at the coffin.

"Do you know what's really, really, really stupid? I was sitting here before you boys came in, thinking how much I'm going to miss him. I went to bed every night praying the bastard would die in his sleep and when he did finally choke on his own vomit, the first thing I thought of was how much I was going to miss him and, God damn it, I still feel that way," she admitted, tears welling up.

"We got this guy in the band I play in, Gerry, he felt the same way about his arm, but he learned to play the fiddle with his teeth so I don't think he even misses his arm, unless maybe he wants to pick that side of his nose. What you're feeling is called phantom pain. Losing your husband like that, it's just like losing an arm, and if you lose an arm, even if it's not much of an arm, you miss it."

Tinker returned with the fingers and a thumb of one hand wound through the ears of three cups while with his other hand he carried the guitar he had retrieved from the Plymouth in the parking lot. "Nothing sadder than a woman with a crying jag," he said to Blue when he saw Mrs. Rubble's tears, and offered her a cup.

Blue took his cup and relieved Tinker of the guitar, setting it at his feet, instructing Tinker to remind him to ask Gerry about phantom pain. They fell into another respectful silence for the length of time it took to empty their cups and have Tinker weave his way to the kitchenette for refills and return.

"Did your husband have a favourite song?" Blue asked, "'Cause Tinker here has a voice that'd make a nun fall in love."

"The only song he ever listened to in his life was 'Prisoner of War'," Mrs. Rubble remembered. "He'd get teary as a child when he heard that one."

"So do I," Blue answered, picking up his guitar, hitting the opening chords. Without hesitation, Tinker began.

Oh, the war ships had landed and I went ashore
For fighting was over for me evermore
For the enemy they found me
And took me a prisoner of war so they say
But the good Lord and his mercy was with me one day—

Suddenly Blue banged a note of discord from his guitar, startling the others into opening their eyes.

"You scared the living Jesus out of me there for a moment, buddy. I thought you were Christopher Lee," Blue told the sombre-looking undertaker in a tuxedo who stood in the doorway looking appalled. "Doesn't he look just like Christopher Lee in a Dracula movie there, Tinker? What's the matter, buddy, you look like you just saw a ghost. Bet you saw a few of them in your time."

"What! Are! You! Doing!?" the man hissed.

"We're friends of the family. Just helping the lady through a tough time. Oh, you mean the guitar. Normally we'd be playing that in the kitchen back home, but that kitchen you got back there isn't big enough for a decent pisser. Why don't you have a little snort and join us," Blue invited.

"This is no way to behave in a funeral home. If you boys don't leave this minute I'll call the police and have you removed," the undertaker whispered hoarsely. "We have another wake in this building and your noise is upsetting the family. Now leave!"

"These are my friends, and if you're throwing them out, then you'll have to throw me out, as well," Mrs. Rubble replied. "How would that look in the papers? That a funeral home threw out the widow of one of its customers?"

"Then stop this music," the undertaker ordered. "The doors close in fifteen minutes, and I want all of you to be on the other side of them when they do. Show a little respect for the dead, please."

"You think we got no respect for the dead?" Blue asked. "Look, buddy, Tinker here and me got more respect for the dead than we do for the living. I've never punched a dead man but I've punched a living one—"

Tinker held out a hand to restrain Blue's threat to go toe-to-toe with the undertaker over the touchy subject of respect for the dead.

"Take her easy, there, buddy," he told Blue. Then, turning to the undertaker, he said, "We'll be gone before you know it. If it will make you happy we won't even stop in to say hello at the other wake, although that'd be the polite thing to do."

As silently as he had appeared, the undertaker withdrew, leaving Mr. Rubble's three mourners to say their farewells.

"Know what I'd like to do, Mrs. Rubble? Take Mr. Rubble and put him in the back seat of the Plymouth and bring him home and have a real wake. That's what I'd like to do, but Christopher Lee would probably have the cops chasing us all the way to Canada," Blue decided.

"Give me those cups so we can empty those bottles and get out of here," Tinker said, collecting the cups.

"It's a damn shame that we can't have a little music for my man," Mrs. Rubble mourned. "He wasn't really so bad, you know. Only when he drank. Trouble was the bastard drank all the time."

"I think we should give him a song," Blue said, reaching for the cup Tinker offered.

"Do you know 'The Old Rugged Cross'?" Mrs. Rubble asked.

Tinker and Blue exchanged uneasy glances.

"I'm sorry, Ma'am, but that's a Protestant hymn. We wouldn't be allowed to know that one even if we did," Blue said. "But Tinker does a great job of 'Ave Maria.' Monk, this guy we know back home who saw the Virgin Mary, told Tinker that the Holy Mother told him that the best version she ever heard of that hymn was when Tinker sang."

"Monk didn't say that," Tinker corrected. "He said he thought she probably liked the way I sang that hymn."

"Like you said, Tinker, Monk *thought* she would of liked the way you sing 'Ave Maria.' All I'm doing is improving on Monk's thought for him. Don't be modest, man. Your voice is a gift from God, as the other fellow says, and since Mr. Rubble here is obviously not a Catholic we can't go blaspheming that gift by singing 'Ave Maria' at a Protestant wake. The Lord might turn your tongue to a pillar of salt. So what can we sing?"

The three of them pondered the contents of their cups while sipping inspiration from them, an inspiration that manifested itself to Blue first.

"Here's one the three of us can join in," Blue said. "You and me will join in the chorus, Missus Rubble. If you don't know it, you'll pick it up first time around. Take her away, Tinker, old buddy," Blue instructed, striking the opening chords on the guitar. Tinker tipped back his cup, drank, and began.

Look at the coffin
With golden handles
Isn't it grand, boys,
To be bloody well dead

"Here's the chorus," Blue informed Mrs. Rubble.

Let's not have a sniffle
Let's have a bloody good cry
And always remember
The longer you live
The sooner you'll bloody well die

Look at the widow
Bloody fine female
Isn't it grand boys
To be bloody well dead

Let's not have a sniffle
Let's have a bloody good cry
And always remember—

The black-clad undertaker loomed in front of them, imposing silence with his speechless presence.

"Well, I guess it's time we were getting along there, Tinker, old buddy," Blue said, putting down his guitar. "Can we drive you anywhere, Missus?"

"Yes, home would be nice," Mrs. Rubble replied, rising and walking to the coffin to stare at her husband's remains while the undertaker shrank back to stand at the door like an usher, waiting for the mourners to leave the premises. After a quiet moment, Mrs. Rubble held her cup over her dead husband and watched a few droplets of gin trickle out, land on his forehead and run down to his ear.

"Nothing!" she shrugged. "He's finished, not Finnegan," and walked out the door flanked by Tinker and Blue.

From the parking lot, they followed Mrs. Rubble's instructions until she told them to stop the car in front of a rundown apartment building where they let her out, both giving her a hug of comfort, then got back in the car.

"Will you be at the funeral tomorrow?" she asked as Tinker started up the Plymouth again.

"Sorry, Mrs. Rubble, but I'll be working," Tinker apologized.

"And I'll be sick," Blue groaned, his head already resting on the dash.

38

A spring-warm sun burned off a week of November damp and fog, filling Golden Gate Park with eager Sunday sun-worshippers. Barney rested on the brown grass, Karma and Blue using him as a pillow as they lay side by side. Blue plinked at the guitar lying across his chest, and studied the groupings of park people, quipping to Karma that it looked like a shopping mall of protests.

The hippies seemed to think that since they were in the park on a day that drew so many strolling civilians away from their normal routines, they had an obligation to turn the lazy flat-on-your-back-basking-in-the-sunshine day into something meaningful. One circle of flower children smoked marijuana in open defiance. On another slope, a colourfully clad group followed their choir leader's fingers like a bouncing ball, chanting "No More War!" Another group of freakily dressed boys and girls proudly proclaimed their sexual orientation. In a silent circle another group, holding posters of Martin Luther King and Bobby Kennedy, held an ongoing candlelight vigil for the murdered leaders.

The protests were listlessly inoffensive, increasing the tolerance of people passing by, and besides, there was plenty of commerce to distract people from confronting the country's social problems as presented by its runaway children. These people could not understand why these youngsters would choose to smoke dope when there was a much more socially acceptable addiction available to them: alcohol. They could not grasp why children who were raised on the heroic Hollywood deeds of John Wayne would suddenly turn on "The Duke" and challenge the patriotic intelligence of the White House and Pentagon. They could not understand why queers would want to advertise their sickness on street corners and demand the acceptance of society when their own families, the bedrock of that very society, probably threw them out of the house for talking back.

What the public in the park could understand, however, and upon which it hitched its hope for the future of this lost generation, was the greedy hustle of commerce among these strangely clad entrepreneurs. The flower child selling bouquets stolen from the city's gardens and greenhouses they could appreciate. That was just good old American know-how at work for the good old American dollar. The hippies exhibiting trays of jewellery or leather-works were also understandable. Maybe no passer-by would want to wear earrings made of fish skins or foreskins, but they could understand the economics of it. The guy selling lids of grass or the girl selling hits of acid were reprehensible, of course, but they still had a chance of growing up, of maturing in the business world, becoming the Joe Kennedys of the future, America's dynasties of tomorrow. They just had to break through the penny ante existence of being street-corner pushers and become the wealthy importers of contraband. Even the street singers with their begging caps on the ground in front of them were in business, some of them probably already destined to read their own names written the lights of Las Vegas's nightclub life. The heart of America took comfort in knowing that amid all the idealistic chatter of its children, the genetic urge to make money was already manifesting itself, and that instinct would save America from its dreams.

With Karma reading to him from Kahlil Gibran, Blue's mind drifted towards the great epic of his own life. He strummed while in his head he hummed the chorus of "The Red Lobster," hoping that by repeating it over and over the momentum would fling him forward toward the eighty-first verse. As the words began to form from a swirl of uncertain images within him, Blue brought them to his lips, testing them softly, letting most of them escape. He kept the spontaneous phrase "a spider's web." Inside each lobster trap there is a web of netting that lures and locks the lobster inside. Blue let that remembered knowledge spin itself out inside of him.

Already, Capricorn had recorded four sessions of Blue Cacophony performances and, according to Blue's understanding, was currently extracting from that mother lode the band's greatest gems. Capricorn called it editing, to which Blue replied, "If I wanted an editor I'd write a book," but terms and titles aside, Blue Cacophony was only a few technical hurdles away from the covert distribution of its first album, and Blue was already plotting the content of their second release, the complete recording of "The Red Lobster." But first, the song needed to be finished.

Karma's voice beside him, while he avoided the pagan words of her book, was soothing to Blue, and slowly from the chaos that coaxes the soul to creativity, images and rhythms and rhymes began to emerge. Blue turned them over in his mind, discarding the failures and polishing the survivors into poetry. Finally, with his head still resting on Barney's back and the blue hat tipped across his forehead, shading the sunlight, Blue gave the new verse its first run-through, not unaware that, as he began to sing, Barney's mad harmony fell in beside his own.

The net in the trap
Is like the spider's web
Cold as a heart
In January or Feb-
Ruary, oh I get wary

When you're around
Set the trap
Watch me drown

Red lobster, red lobster
Don't you dare sob, sir
'Cause love is you and love is her
You're the meat. She's the but-tur.

"Hey, I recognize you. You're the singer with Blue Cacophony," spoke a voice Blue couldn't place. He lifted the rim of his cap to see a hippie wearing a fifteenth-century-era plume hat standing over him. Blue greeted him back, explaining that he was writing a work-in-progress.

"Oh, are you with Blue Cacophony, too?" the hippie asked. "I recognize the dog from the gig you had at Ellis Dee's. So how's it going, man?" the hippie asked, taking a seat in the grass beside Blue and Karma. "I'm Columbus."

"Blue. This is Karma. You anything to Christopher Columbus?"

"Could be. I'm out to discover America, too, so it might be genetic."

"What have you found so far?"

"Not much. The buffalo are gone. How about your own discoveries?"

"To tell you the truth, Cabot's my man," Blue confided.

"Cabot?"

"John Cabot? You must of heard of him. He discovered Cape Breton. Columbus discovered the New World but Cabot discovered the real world, as the other fellow says."

"Can't say our ships have crossed," Columbus replied, getting up. "So this Cabot gentleman, where would I find him?"

"Just go northeast about four thousand miles, you'll come to a causeway with an island on the other side of it. Cross that, it'll cost you a buck and a half, and ask someone to point you to the Cabot Trail. He lives along there, just ask anybody."

"Thanks, man, and your dog's great for the band." Columbus said, then taking his bearings and setting his sails, he wandered away to the northeast.

Karma rolled onto her stomach to look down into Blue's face, putting her book away. "John Cabot doesn't live on the Cabot Trail, does he?"

"Not right on it, no. He has this little place just off the highway...."

"Blue, what if he tries to go there? The poor boy is obviously suffering delusions. Maybe he took too many drugs. Maybe he hurt his head," Karma scolded.

"And maybe he's Christopher Columbus. You more than anybody should give the guy the benefit of the doubt. I recognize what you're putting in the latest panel on your mural. That's the Tower of London where the Brits kept the men they were going to decapitate."

"And the women. Ann Boleyn. Mary Queen of Scots."

"Aw, Karma, I hate it when you do this, you know."

"Well, that's beside the point, anyway, which is that you may have sent that poor boy on a four-thousand-mile trip."

"Pilgrimage, I'd call it. He'll forget about it the first time he stops to take leak, but even if he doesn't, I sent him to the safest place I know. What more can a brother's keeper do? So which one is it?"

"Which one what?"

"Ann Boleyn or Mary Queen of Scots? Which one is it?"

"I thought the subject of my previous lives frightened you," Karma teased.

"I wouldn't say frightened, Karma. It's not like you're a Vincent Price movie or something, but it's weird. What if you were Ann Boleyn and I was John the Baptist? We wouldn't be able to do anything but look at each other from our respective platters and go to Heaven for never having committed the mortal sin that is the most fun of them all, but what fun would that be? It's a lot simpler being Catholic. Some night I'm going to baptize you in your sleep. But of course, before I wake you..." Blue winked.

39

Tinker sat beside Capricorn in the basement of the Human Rainbow Commune and watched him spin wheels of tape, catch snippets of sound and splice them to other snippets of sound, melding the seams into each other like wax. He was fascinated by the process but wondered why Capricorn had asked him down to the basement. Tinker hadn't been playing any active role in the production of Blue Cacophony's bootleg album.

"I was listening to something here," Capricorn began at last, the tape responding to his hand on the switches, running back and forth between spools as he assembled the results he wanted. "I'm afraid Blue's music doesn't do much for me, well, nothing, actually, so I don't pay much attention to it beyond trying to make it reasonably presentable. But something caught my ear here and I want you to listen to it."

Capricorn started the tape and the high-speed train crash that was Blue's voice filled the basement, accompanied by Barney's baying and an agony of fiddle and bagpipes. Tinker recognized the words of one of Blue's newest creations, "Failure To Love," the verses running into a chorus to which Tinker silently mouthed the words. "We can't blame our lives on the stars up above/When we know we are guilty of the failure to love." Both of them listened to the entire offering, then Capricorn turned off the tape recorder.

"What do you think?" he asked Tinker.

"Between the two of us, it's the first one of Blue's songs that I might actually like to sing, but if I did, he'd take my interest in one song for an interest in learning them all. Blue's my best friend and all that, and the best way to keep it that way is for Blue to think his songs are beyond my ability."

"Are they?" Capricorn asked.

"What do you mean?"

"I've heard you sing. You've got a good voice, a very good voice, but I've heard you do things with it, too. When you sing

'Delilah,' your voice becomes Tom Jones's. The same for Jagger. Could you do Blue?"

"Sing like Blue?" Tinker asked, mystified.

"Look, this is a good song," Capricorn explained. "It has Karma's influence all over it because these thoughts come from an open mind – not Blue's. It may even be an important song for some people, but it's not going to get a hearing in this condition. What I was wondering is, can you sing like Blue and still hold a tune?"

"What have you got up your sleeve, Cap?" Tinker inquired.

"If we could record you doing a listenable version of Blue's voice, I could replace Blue with you, but keep the Blue Cacophony sound. It will actually make an interesting contrast, the song sung in tune to discordant accompaniment. But it still has to be able to fool a lot of people, including Blue and Gerry and Nathan, so they think it happened by accident on stage. Tinker, there are people who will respond to these lyrics, but not to this arrangement," he said pointing to the silent recorder.

"So you're going to pass me off as Blue on this album," Tinker said.

"Just on the one song that's worthy of your voice."

"Well, like you say, Cap, that song may have Karma's influence all over it, but your idea has Blue's influence all over it. That must scare the shit out of you, man. Let's do it!"

—

Blue glumly studied the sandwich in front of him and gave a shake of his head to Barney who was curled up under the table waiting for the ample morsels that Blue always allowed to fall from his plate when they went out dining together. Dining together with Karma, however, severely altered the menu from which they ordered. Hay sandwiches, Blue thought, lifting it to his mouth and taking a bite of sandwich so gritty with unrefined grains that it reminded him of swallowing beach sand. They were sitting in a vegetarian café a long way from the greasy spoon that was Blue and Barney's choice.

"Like it?" Karma inquired. Blue, who usually enjoyed banter as the best part of any meal, chewed faster, trying to get to a place in the process where he could talk as well as chew.

"It's not a matter of liking or not liking, Karma," he answered eventually. "It's, well, it's a lot of work for very little taste."

"You're suppose to enjoy it, Blue. Take your time and enjoy it. If you think about every bite you are eating, if you savour it, or appreciate as a gift the very fact that you have something to eat when so many don't, then you can't help but be grateful and enjoy it. The food we eat, like the air we breathe, is what keeps us healthy and alive, although both the food and the air most people eat and breathe may be killing us now instead of sustaining us. Besides, if you clean your plate, you won't get constipated," she said, half teasing, half ordering him to take another bite.

"Now there's a thought to help me digest this, just think about what it will look like coming out. Wonderful. When do you get anything done, girl? All this thinking about what you're doing, even when you're eating or going to the toilet, doesn't give you time to think about the future, does it?"

"Some lives are wasted by living in the past, some lives are wasted by living in the future. The present is the only place we can be alive. At least that's what the other fellow told me," Karma said taking a bite.

"Who? Tinker? Oh, I get it, you're teasing me. Well, here's what I think about thinking about what I'm eating. This hay here—"

"Alfalfa sprouts. The least you can do is tell your digestive system what to prepare for before you start to eat."

"Okay, these alfalfa sprouts and the rest of the stuff in here, cucumbers and whatever, my stomach will sort all that out, take a long time to chew. If I take a bite and begin thinking about what I'm chewing here, it tells me a lot more about being a cow than being a man. You chew and you chew and eventually you find yourself looking around bored as a cow in a field watching a train passing by while it's chewing and chewing and chewing. After awhile, the cow gives up chewing and swallows the alfalfa and stores it in her cud, and later on, when she's more hungry than she is bored, she pulls it back up and chews some more. That doesn't happen to a guy eating burgers and fries, or a whole bunch of other human food. Now, when I'm eating a burger, my mind's not on the burger, it's on writing new songs or a way to make some money or what it will be like when I get back home. If the world turns out the way you want it to, then we're all going to be put out to pasture chewing our cuds and thinking about how wonderful the hay is and not even planning for tomorrow. Then along comes the Russians and they put barbed wire on the pasture fence and we're all Communists." Blue snapped another bite of his sandwich.

"I find it funny, Blue, that you seem to know cows so well and would still rather eat them than watch them."

"Like I told you before, if you think about what you're eating all the fun goes out of it. A hamburger doesn't remember that it used to be a cow so why should I remind it?"

They chewed on in silence while Barney grew impatient under the table. Then Blue swallowed and began talking again.

"Instead of sitting here thinking, 'Hey, God, thanks for the hay,' I was thinking about the past. Now I know you're not suppose to do that according to your religion."

"It's not my religion, Blue. It's a way of trying to be at one with the Universe."

"If my mother knew I was living with a girl who would rather be at one with the Universe than a good Catholic, she'd have a cow."

"And you'd probably eat it," Karma said. "Okay, tell me what you were thinking about in your past."

"The recent past really, and the near future, all the eating sins, right? I was thinking about Columbus, wondering if we could find him?"

"We wouldn't know where to begin looking."

"We'd look around Cape Breton when we get home next summer. That was the other thing I was thinking, Karma. Me and you, Tinker and Kathy in the Plymouth heading for the east coast. We'll have some bucks socked away by then, and be crossing the causeway in time for the July first picnic."

"You mean July fourth," Karma corrected.

"You Americans! You think the whole world revolves around your history. Well, for your information, July first is the national holiday of Cape Breton. Anyway, that's what kicks off summer, and anybody who spends a winter in Cape Breton deserves the summer, as the other fellow says."

"You're not spending the winter in Cape Breton, Blue."

"Well, the other fellow's other fellow says, anybody who has to spend a whole winter away from Cape Breton deserves to spend the summer there. So what do you think, you, me, Tinker and Kathy, the Three Musketeers, headed for home?"

"Maybe, but it's time right now for you and me to head home," Karma said, picking up the bill. "I'll pay for this."

"You bet you'll pay for it. I could of bought six bales of hay back home for what they're charging for that one sandwich I ate, so when we get there next summer, I'll treat you to a jumbo pack," Blue said, and picking up his guitar in one hand and taking Karma's hand in the other they began walking home, Barney chaperoning.

40

"What do you think about Blue's idea?" Tinker asked Kathy, tapping around the engine of the Plymouth with a wrench. Blue's suggestion that Karma go home with him the following summer had expanded to include Tinker, Kathy, the Plymouth and half of San Francisco.

Kathy, sitting on the roof of the Plymouth, her feet over the windshield, was painting the elevated hood while Tinker tinkered under it. Under her brush, an orange and black butterfly slowly spread its wings. Eventually, they would droop down over the fenders. It wasn't Tinker's first choice for decorating his car. Tinker thought that something along the line of King of the Road would best reflect the miles his beloved car and he had travelled. Blue, on the other hand, inspired by Karma's past life in the Tower of London, proposed that they paint the severed head of Mary Queen of Scots on the roof of the car, letting rivers of blood flow in rich red paint down over the rest of the car body. In the end, they settled for the Monarch butterfly that Kathy and Karma proposed because both girls refused to put their talents to work depicting royally crowned hoboes or severed heads.

"I would like to go, Tinker, but I don't want to leave the commune."

"We'll come back," Tinker promised. "Just for the summer, Kath. The way it is with us, see, is that we have to go home for the summer. I know a hundred, two hundred, people from my hometown alone who are all over the place working right now, but come next June or July, they'll begin collecting their backtime, packing their bags and heading for home. The same is true for everywhere else on the island. I bet next summer half the cars crossing the causeway will be filled with people coming home. Cape Bretoners and summer are like that, like Arabs and Mecca. We just have to go home. It'll be the first time for Blue and I. We've never got to go home yet and they say that returning to the island for the first time after you've gone away is the

| 219

best feeling in the world. And if you come with me, you'll learn something about the rest of the world."

Kathy slid down from the roof of the car to stand beside Tinker while he explored the Plymouth engine with new expertise gleaned from his experience in the tunnel.

"I want to go to Canada, Tinker. I want to go there very much. You and Blue are always teasing us about being dumb Americans who don't know anything about anywhere else in the world – and sometimes I think you're not teasing at all, that you mean it. Well, maybe we don't know where the capital of Canada is, or what city it is, but we do know something more important about Canada. That it's there. I'm female. I'm not going to get drafted. But I know lots of boys who have been. A few of them went to Canada instead of into the army, but even those who decided to be drafted, who are in Vietnam right now, thought about it, Tinker. Canada gave them a choice. I don't know if you understand what that means. If Canada refused to take our draft dodgers, then they would either be in prison or in Vietnam. Maybe they'd be dead. Instead, they're free. They can't come home, but they're free.

"I don't know anything about Canada, but I know what it means to people like me, and I want to go there. I want to go there with you, but I'm scared. You're not the only person in the world with a home, you know. This is my home. The commune and the things it's trying to do is my home. I'm afraid that if I go to Canada with you, to Cape Breton with you, we won't come back. You'll have me skinning rabbits or something for the rest of my life," she said, lightening her tone.

"No rabbit-skinning, I promise, but how about this idea? We go home and start our own commune. Monk, this old guy I know, lives on this overgrown farm where he makes moonshine. You and me, Karma and Blue could move in with him and he could teach us his trade. And Monk's just as holy as Capricorn. We could call it the Hangover Heaven Commune or something, and save the world from there. Or how about The Pot of Golden Glo at the End of the Human Rainbow Commune?"

"You sound just like Blue," Kathy told him.

You have no idea how much I sound like Blue, Tinker thought, tempted to tell her about the recording, but instinctively felt it needed to be kept not so much from Kathy as to himself. "We got all winter to think about next summer and what we're going to do," he said.

"What about staying here, Tinker, or going back to Colorado when it's safe?" Kathy, expecting no answer, left the question hanging in the air and walked around the car to climb over the trunk and across the roof, repositioning herself in front of the elevated hood, picking up her brush again.

Under the hood, Tinker was a still-life-with-wrench, paralyzed by Kathy's question. By suggesting that he not go home, she had conceived the inconceivable.

—

The Plymouth, travelling back toward San Francisco, looked very unlike the car that departed from Cape Breton. Kathy's butterfly on the hood had been joined by other works of art; on the trunk, Karma's paint had converted the mock wheel rim into a peace sign composed of interlinking doves, and Tulip had decorated the four doors with an abstract mural which, Blue told her, looked exactly like a work "by Henry Bruce, this artist we got back home." He didn't mention Henry Bruce's medium. On the roof, in lieu of Mary Queen of Scots's head, a calligraphic "Peace & Love" transmitted the message of the times to any low flying aircraft or UFOs.

With the wind whipping through his rolled-down window, it occurred to Blue for the forty-fifth time since the weekend began that they had broken the bonds of urbanization and were now in a world where ocean and landscape replaced skyscrapers and subways. "Look at that, Tinker, we're right in the middle of miles and miles of nowhere, just like home."

"This reminds you of home?" Karma asked, studying the way the continent sheered off in steep cliffs to a rocky shoreline hammered by the pounding surf of the Pacific Ocean. "Does Cape Breton look like this?"

"What makes it remind me of home, Karma, is how much it's not like home. Know what I mean?"

"Probably not," Karma said. "It reminds you of home because it doesn't remind you of home? Is there another way to explain that mystery, oh, Master and Wise One, a way that a simple-minded girl like myself can grasp?" she asked, placing her hands together and bowing slightly Buddhist-like before a spiritual master.

"It's like when you see a woman who doesn't look anything like your mother so you say, 'She doesn't look anything like my mother,' and just by thinking she doesn't look anything like your mother, you're reminded of your mother. Well, that's why this place reminds me of home, because it's not like home at all. Isn't that right, Tinker?" Blue asked, leaning ahead from the back seat, where he and Karma and Barney were sitting, to solicit confirmation of his logic by speaking into Tinker's ear against the roar of wind.

Tinker shrugged, his thoughts closer to the landscape around him than the one he had grown up in. Going to Big Sur had been his idea, the seeds of the trip planted by one of the books Kathy had given him to read, and in reading it, he realized that Big Sur was part of their geographic neighbourhood. He had never been anywhere that people wrote about. In school, all the stories and poems in the English books were from England or the United States or other places far from Cape Breton. Home was a good place to live, he had concluded, but not a great place to write about.

It took very little to talk Kathy and Karma into taking the trip, but when Tinker told Blue he wanted to go to a place called Big Sur because a guy had written a book by that name, Blue borrowed the novel. He returned it to Tinker's room an hour later, throwing it on the bed and informing Tinker that the guy didn't even know how to punctuate "and if you meet him up there, tell him Sur is spelled s-i-r." When Tinker mentioned that his pay cheque was going to pay for the weekend away, however, Blue made certain that Blue Cacophony was gig-free, since neither him nor Barney would be available.

The weekend had been a literary and literal washout.

By the time they discovered that Big Sur was south of San Francisco they were cold and wet and in Oregon arguing whether it was Tinker, who had read the book, or Blue, who had read the map, who was to blame. Both lacked the innate wonder that Karma and Kathy expressed over finding themselves amid mountains ranges and mile-high trees, noticing instead only the stinging needles of rain riding in at an angle on a bitter wind. "I guess it's November all over the world," Blue observed while fighting a mild war with Karma over fair and equal shares of a sleeping bag that was too small to hold them both, but large enough to cover them, Barney between them like a nun at a high school dance.

They spend two days among monster trees that attracted rain clouds the way metal rods on barn roofs attract lightning, and slept two nights in the Plymouth after being turned down at two motels. Eating hamburgers from a tray hanging on the window of the car was the best part of the whole trip, according to Blue, Tinker and Barney. Tinker and Blue had enough tact to apologize for the pleasure they took in not having a choice. Barney didn't. Karma and Kathy nibbled at lettuce and cheese melted on their "hold the meat" hamburger buns and delivered to the car for the same price as a cheeseburger.

It was when they turned the car around to bring the sad adventure to an end that Tinker and Blue stopped sniping at one another about their navigational problems, realizing simultaneously that they had been heading north, heading home. Although the car zipped toward San Francisco, their imaginations were still driving a phantom Plymouth in the opposite direction.

"You see what this road was telling us, Tinker? We didn't get lost. No, buddy, we were on the right road all along, just like the smelts making their way back to the Big River after being gone from Cape Breton all winter. I don't care what the other fellow, says, you *can* go home again, and the next time we drive up this road there won't be any turning around, I'll tell you that. Vancouver, then east to the Canso Causeway. Big Sur's got nothing to do with us, that's why we never got there. Hell, if the five of us had any sense we'd still be travelling north, right Barney, old buddy," Blue asked, scratching the dog's ears and wrestling him around the back seat.

"Do you believe there are no wrong roads?" Karma asked, her question generally directed at Blue, but inviting the participation of all. "If you were standing at a crossroads in the middle of nowhere, which way would you walk?"

"Didn't you think this was a wrong road?" Tinker asked, pointing to the highway that had led them away from their destination. "We couldn't find a place to sleep, we barely found a place to eat, and we've been wet all weekend."

"You make it sound like Joseph and Mary in Bethlehem. Good thing you girls weren't pregnant," Blue said.

"But what Karma is asking is, do all those things make it the wrong road?" Kathy said, drawing them back to the question. "If I was standing at a crossroads, I would blindfold myself and twirl around until I lost all sense of direction, then I would start walking in the direction I'd be facing when I stopped. What about you, Tinker?"

"That's easy," Blue said. "He'd just follow you down that same road."

"Are you saying I don't have a mind of my own?" Tinker asked, a mild edge to his voice.

"No, you have a mind of your own, but what I'm saying is that that's not necessarily what does a guy's thinking for him." The remark brought a nasty glare from Kathy, a head-shake of disbelief from Karma and, in the rearview mirror, Tinker's eyes flared with anger. Sensing that he was taking the conversation down a wrong and unwelcome road, Blue began extricating himself from the mire of his own words. "I don't mean anything dirty, that's just your own minds at work, so see, I'm saying you have your own mind, after all, Tinker, but what I really meant is all these books you're reading, they're changing your mind faster than I can argue with you. You read a book and it changes your mind. You read another one and it changes your mind again. So I guess it takes Karma's question right back to where we are, right? On the wrong road. Myself, I'd say we're not on the wrong road, just travelling in the wrong direction."

"Then let Tinker answer the question," Karma said.

"I guess I like the road less travelled by, like the poem says," Tinker said.

"There's a perfect example of what I mean," Blue countered. "When did you start reading poetry?"

"In grade nine, remember. That's where I know that poem from. I've heard you quote it yourself, except when you did it was the other fellow who said it, not Robert Frost. So I suppose I would look at all the paths to see which one had the fewest people using it then go down that one to see where it took me. That's exactly how we got out here to San Francisco, Blue, by picking a road nobody else we knew was on. What about yourself, Karma?"

"That's an easy one," Blue said. "She'd just send three of her lives down the other roads and take the one that was left," his remark ignored by the rest."

"It wouldn't matter to me," Karma answered. "Oh, I might pick a road that was lined with buttercups, or choose another one because it was going into the sunset, or it's opposite because it was going into the sunrise, or one that goes up into the mountains. Eventually, they would all bring me to the same place, myself."

"All roads lead to Karma, as the other fellow says," Blue quipped, restless in the tension. When no one said anything, he broke the silence by asking if anyone was going to ask him what road he would choose. Their attention turned toward him although the question itself remained unasked.

"Well, I'll tell you this much, it wouldn't take me to Big Sur, no siree. If I was standing in the middle of a crossroads the first thing I'd do is build a store or a tavern and make tons of money off all the people who would be standing there scratching their heads, wondering which way to go, then I'd pick the road heading for Cape—"

"Jesus, what's this fool up to?" Tinker muttered, watching in his rear view mirror. Behind them, a half-ton truck was weaving recklessly through the traffic, which had grown increasingly heavy the closer they got to San Francisco.

Blue glanced out the back window, saw the truck, and said, "You can take him, Tinker." Both girls leaned toward Tinker, intercepting Blue's challenge. "Please don't," they pleaded, and Tinker stopped toying with the idea, deciding to let the truck pass without creating a karmatic link that, if he understood Kathy and Karma's theology, would cause the car and the truck to tangle in traffic over and over until the world ran out of roads and eternity ran out of time. He eased off the gas, and watched the truck's reflection approach in the rearview mirror.

Once the truck had pulled beside them, it seemed to stall there, pacing itself to the Plymouth. When Tinker looked across, a greasy head and tattooed arms leaned out the passenger window shouting words snatched away by the eighty-mile-an-hour wind. It was Blue, from the back seat, who caught them as they whipped past ... "fuckin' hippie fags...." Bent on countering the insult, Blue pulled himself half way through his window, leaning out to utter a few choice opinions of his own, but before he could, one of the tattooed arms with a bottle of beer in its grasp suddenly pulled back and fired.

Tinker didn't see the action taking place beside him until the bottle shattered across his windshield, washing it in a foam of beer. Trying to keep the Plymouth from drifting into the traffic, he fumbled frantically to find the wiper knob. Over-compensating, he pulled the car too far to the right, felt it buck against the guardrail with a screech of peeling paint that brought screams from inside the car. The Plymouth bounced off the rail and spun onto the road.

Blue, frozen in the backseat window, saw what Tinker could not, the half-ton pulling away from them in a squeal of rubber, the chorus of blasting horns behind them, and the on-coming traffic beginning to react as the Plymouth started spinning through a slow-motion moment that converged upon the path of a transfer truck. Brakes squealed all around them like slaughterhouse pigs as the Plymouth sped blindly toward the truck and

Blue closed his eyes, only to open them an uneventful moment later to discover that in an incomprehensible and forgiving choreography, the two vehicles had been released from the apparent fate of their violent ballet, allowed to miss each other and escape.

Charmed, the Plymouth spun across the highway, and Tinker, finding the wipers, cleared the windshield in time to see a wall of rock in front of them. He cranked the steering wheel hard to his right, pulling the Plymouth around so that it slammed against the wall sideways, and skittered along it until they were jolted to a halt against a culvert. Blue, when Tinker had turned the car away from the head-on collision with the wall, was sucked back inside the Plymouth by the force of the shifting direction, his head volleying hard against the door frame.

A silent stillness filled the Plymouth as the passengers took quiet inventory of themselves, listening and slowly flexing for signs of aches or breaks.

"Everybody all right?" Tinker asked at last, just as the first faces began to appear in the windshield, other drivers tentatively exploring the interior for blood and death. Barney, with a whine, leapt past Blue through the window and onto the road.

"I think so," Kathy answered, her voice an unfamiliar pitch.

"Nothing broken," Blue replied, feeling his head fill with pain.

"Karma?" Tinker asked.

"Karma, girl," Blue said, giving her arm a soft shake, getting no response. "Karma?" he called louder. "Karma!"

The doors of the Plymouth opened and people began helping the passengers out, but Blue resisted, clinging to Karma, insisting that she answer, getting only terrifying silence in response.

A state trooper was suddenly in front of Tinker, asking questions to which he could barely reply, aware only of the rising panic in Blue's voice as he called to Karma. Kathy tried to climb into the back seat. Restraining arms forced her to sit and wait for the ambulance for which the trooper had already radioed.

Blue fought against efforts to pull him from the car until a woman leaned in the window on Karma's side of the car, dropping an Indian-pattern blanket over her un-responding body. "Keep her warm against shock," the woman explained, adding, "I'm a nurse. Let me see if there's anything I can do."

Blue released Karma from his hold, backing off, recognizing that the woman was offering more to Karma than he could. Slowly, he allowed himself to be drawn from the car while the nurse replaced him, her fingers reaching for a pulse in Karma's throat.

"You okay, buddy?" Tinker asked Blue who now stood ashen in front of him. "This Mountie here called for an ambulance."

"State trooper," the policeman corrected him. "Are you all from Canada?"

Before Tinker could explain, Blue's survival reflexes took over. "No. Tinker and me are. We just came down from Vancouver. We picked these girls up hitchhiking. They're Americans though, I know that. Isn't that right, Kathy?" he asked, including her in their story. Kathy nodded, indifferent, intent on the nurse who was now hunched over Karma in the back seat like a lifeguard over a drowning victim. An increasingly loud siren announced the ambulance's approach.

"I have no pulse," the nurse told the attendants as they reached the Plymouth. The two white-clad men replaced the nurse, carefully removed Karma from the back seat and placed her on a stretcher, working over her even as they wheeled towards their flashing vehicle. Blue went running after them, leaping into the ambulance with the stretcher, leaving Tinker and Kathy to deal with the trooper.

"Are you family?" one of the attendants asked.

"Her husband," Blue replied. "How is she? Help her, for the love of God, help her!"

"Sit back and let us do our work," one attendant said, bending over Karma while the other one steered the ambulance back onto the highway, yelling to the police officer that they were going to Sausalito General. On the radio, he contacted the hospital. "No vital signs," Blue heard, and softly sank back against the side of the ambulance and removed the rosary from around his neck.

"I believe in God...."

41

"I think I did it," Blue told Tinker and Kathy in the lobby of the hospital.

"Did what?" Kathy asked.

"Brought Karma back to life. I think I did it."

"You think you did what!" Kathy shouted angrily while Tinker arched his eyebrows. "You're a sick person, Blue, a really sick person."

"I'm just telling you what happened. You can ask the doctors if you want. They took her in here from the ambulance. DOA, they said, Dead on Arrival is what that means, but they just kept working on her in the emergency room. And I just kept praying. All of a sudden, there's all this activity inside the emergency room and then this doctor comes out and tells me that Karma is alive, that it looks like she's going to be okay, but they're going to keep her here overnight for observation. She got a bad blow on the head and they want to be sure there's no concussion. The doctor thinks she must of hit her head on the post between the doors or something.

"When he was telling me this, I was still saying my rosary. I held it up and showed it to him. He said sometimes things happen that doctors can't answer."

"So you're taking the credit for Karma's recovery," Kathy said testily.

"I'm just telling you what happened, that's all. You can believe whatever you like, and so can I, and I don't believe I ever prayed like that in my life. I know I didn't. It was so deep it wasn't even prayer. It was just me and God, talking. It was really something, and when the doctor told me she was alive, I just ... I can't even explain it."

"You're not thinking of going into the business or anything like that, are you, Blue?" Tinker asked.

"Raising people from the dead, you mean. No way, man. That's a job for the apostles and the priests, to quote the other fellow. But I know something now that I didn't know before. Praying is hard work, man. I'd hate to have to do it too often."

The three of them walked out into the parking lot. Blue planned to remain at the hospital, close to Karma whom none of them had yet seen because she had been sedated and was under orders to have an undisturbed rest. The plan was for Tinker and Kathy to return the following day with the commune van to pick up Karma and Blue.

"The Plymouth looks kind of DOA itself," Blue noted as they approached Tinker's car, where Barney – who had returned to the scene of the accident once the fuss had settled down – sat erect in the back seat. Its sides were badly caved in from the encounters with the guardrail and rock wall, and the grill was crumpled from its sudden stop against the culvert, its alignment more than slightly askew.

"It's still running, though. I got it this far," Tinker said hopefully as Blue reached in to scratch the dog and assure him that Karma was okay. "It'll get us home and then we'll see. Maybe you could say a rosary for it."

—

A few days later, Peter?, shrieking, swept into the common room of the Human Rainbow Commune, attracting the timid curiosity of the residents. Doors opened slowly, people tiptoeing toward the action, watching Peter? whirl like a wounded animal before finally collapsing into a legless armchair, his tirade wilting into the merest whimper as his head sank into unhappy hands, tears leaking between his fingers.

"You get hit by a truck or break up with Lee or what?" Blue asked.

Capricorn's efforts to examine him only resulted in having his exploring hand impatiently batted away from Peter?'s forehead. Finally, deep-breathing himself into a semblance of order, Peter? began uttering a broken brand of English. "Hear?" he asked. "Did you ... you know ... hear? The radio! Did you hear?"

"Hear what?" asked the Greek chorus of the commune.

"The radio! We're ruined, Blue, ruined!"

"Back up there and take another crack at her," Blue advised. "Now do as the other fellow says and start from the beginning, Peter?, and, here, let me help you.... Once upon a time...." Blue began, his index finger informing Peter? that that was his cue to pick up the story from that point.

"Our plans! Remember our plans, Blue?" Peter? moaned. "Blue Cacophony was going to remain pure, was going to establish the soundtrack of man's next evolutionary leap, his intellectual giant step, then fade into the mythology of music with no trace left behind except its own legend? Remember how much we wanted that, all of us, you, Gerry, Nathan and myself, wanted to keep our music from being recorded for mass commercial consumption? Remember that, Blue?"

"I remember, Peter?" Blue said, sneaking a guilty peek at the others. "And we never will, old buddy, we never will."

"Too late! Too late!" then dropping from the high drama of his performance, Peter? told them what had happened.

"On my way over here to visit Karma – how is the poor girl? – waiting for a light to change, this freak walked up to the van and asked me, 'Hey, man, wanna buy any grass, hash, acid, Blue Cacophony records?' I thought he was indulging too much in his own wares, and the light changed before I could pursue his maddened statement. But it was the radio ... I'm listening to Janis one minute and trying to beat time to Blue Cacophony the next. It took a moment to register, but when it did, Blue, the whole world changed just like that," Peter? said, snapping his fingers.

"Did you hear me, Blue? Blue Cacophony on the radio! We've been sold out, my friend. The deejay played a Blue Cacophony number, then says it's from the underground recording. Somewhere in this city some bastard is counting his thirty pieces of silver."

"We'll find that bastard, Peter?, don't you worry about that, and when we do, we'll ... we'll ...we'll ... well, we'll think of something then to do to him. But it was on the radio, you said. You heard Blue Cacophony on the radio? Me? Singing? On the radio?" Blue asked, making excited turn-on-the-radio signals to the others with a hand held behind his back. "What song? How'd I sound?"

"Who cares?"

"Well, I do, Peter?. If somebody went through all that trouble to get our sound out there, I hope it's worth his while. I'm not saying it's not wrong, Peter?, but you ride the horse you're given, as the other fella says. It doesn't have to be the end of the world, you know," Blue offered in consolation.

"Ah, but that's just the point," Peter? replied sadly. "It is *not* the end of the world. But it was supposed to be, this pathetic world we live in anyway," making a global gesture with his hands. "Now we're just an evolutionary dead end. Or a revolutionary dead end, if you can tolerate bad puns at a horrible moment like this. History's full of grand ideas that have been melted down and moulded into golden calves, and Blue Cacophony's just part of the herd now, Blue, nothing special at all."

"Maybe whoever did it just couldn't keep it to himself," Blue said. "Maybe he thought this world right here needs us more than the next one does. You never know what a fellow's thinking when he does something like that. Maybe someday we'll look back on this and drink a toast to him. It could happen, you know."

"No, it couldn't. Something's gone, Blue. It's difficult to explain if you can't feel it yourself, but something is gone. Maybe this is how cynics are born."

"Don't waste your time trying to wear the cynic's cloak, Peter? You're a rock, man. Peter? the Rock. You're the believer. Did you ever notice that people hardly ever ask each other what they believe? People ask each other how they feel or what they think, but not what they believe. Karma and me had a talk about this very thing once. Peter?, my boy, no matter how many bastards are around you, and that's a lot more than you might imagine, you're not interested in believing in anything but your fellow man. It's your unfortunate fate to care. Hell, you're such a believer, I bet I could sell you a lame horse every day if I wanted to."

"Don't put my beliefs on your pedestal, Blue. Don't assume to know me so well," Peter? said, rising from the chair. "I'm going out to find Nathan and Gerry. Do you want to be with me when I break the news?"

"I should be, I know, Peter?, but we're just about to have a meeting here. Some important commune stuff just came up, you know."

"Your commune business is none of my business so I'll go find them. Try not to take it too hard, Blue," Peter? said, walking like the father of a dead child to the door, leaving in his wake the now broken silence of Blue Cacophony.

"What's thirty pieces of silver worth these days?" Blue wondered aloud with an uninspired smile when the door closed behind Peter?. "Will somebody turn on the radio, for the love of God?"

42

There was something familiar about the abstract design on the cover of *Failure To Love*, the Blue Cacophony members agreed, although none of them could quite put a finger on it. "Well, I wouldn't have it hanging on my wall, if I had a wall," Blue said, walking along the edge of an admission that no one picked up on. Having joined the rest of the band at Peter?'s, he brought with him several copies of the album which, he explained, he had wrestled from a street pusher, describing the bloody fight that had ensued. "But when I heard the cop sirens I had to run before I could make him tell me where he got them."

Instead of resorting to violence, Peter? proposed that they call in the police, an idea Nathan and Gerry agreed with, but Blue opposed.

"We can't do that," he reasoned. "If we do, Tinker and me'll be deported and the commune people, especially Capricorn, will go to jail. Besides, it's not like we're a legal band, paying taxes and all that. Capricorn says we could have the IRS all over us for tax evasion, same as Al Capone. Hell, they could re-open Alcatraz just for the four of us here. The last thing we need is the cops, believe me."

Blue's reasoning altered the band's strategy for dealing with the bootleg album. Instead, they would each use their resources to track down the illegal operation, and kill it. Nathan and Gerry were frantic to capture the master recording and burn it at the stake, then hunt down every existing copy of *Failure To Love*, and smash them to fading fragments of a horrible memory in their musical careers.

—

Blue squatted beside the radio on the bedroom window sill, tirelessly twirling the dial back and forth across the amber station numbers, scanning the San Francisco skies for the sound of his song. It was a labour that paid off fairly frequently. "Failure To

Love," aided by the bootleg romance surrounding the recording, had caught the attention of a few of the city's deejays, and the air play created interest in the record. Commune members smuggled copies from the boxes in the basement to the distributors on the street. Explaining the series of blinds and double-blinds that he had set up to prevent the record from being traced back to the commune, Capricorn assured Blue that they were above suspicion in the pirating Blue Cacophony's music.

While San Francisco's radio stations squacked and squealed under Blue's unrelenting search for the squack and squeal of "Failure To Love," which he never failed to recognize, it was not the song's success that occupied his mind, but Karma's exceptional quiet. She was intensely working on another of her past-life panels, one that reminded Blue of Russia.

The morning after the accident, Blue, who had spent the night stretched across three chairs in the waiting room, was allowed in to see Karma. She lay in the bed, and when Blue spoke her name, she turned her attention slowly towards him, as if reluctant to leave her thoughts, and smiled.

"Just because Tinker and me said we enjoy a good wake every once in awhile, you didn't have to go trying to oblige us, you know. For a while there, the doctors thought you were a goner. How are you feeling?"

"Fine, Blue. Is everyone else all right?"

"Yup, except for Tinker. He's not injured, just heartbroken because the Plymouth's pretty well totalled. Kathy didn't get a scratch. Barney bailed out the open window with a bark and a howl, and I got out alive myself, although I don't know how. I saw what was suppose to happen to us, and it didn't. It's like guys in the war who stand in the middle of sixteen million bullets and never get a scratch. If I live to be fifty, I'll never figure out how we didn't get creamed by a transfer truck. But we didn't. Fate foiled, as the other fellow says. Kathy and Tinker'll be coming to get us later in the van if the doctor lets you go home."

· Later that day, with a word of caution and a warning to get lots of rest, the doctor who attended Karma allowed her to be released. Tinker and Kathy picked them up at the hospital, and drove them back to the commune in the van. Shortly after they had returned, Blue polled the residents, casually wondering if they noticed anything different about Karma. The answers generally agreed that she was normal ... "for Karma." Blue couldn't explain his worry that Karma wasn't the same after the accident as she was before it.

"She's not all that much fun anymore," Blue confided in Tinker. "She just wants to meditate and paint. We talk and all that, but I don't know, Tinker, it's like too much of her came back from the dead or something."

The tuner slipped past a familiar sound and Blue eased it back, picking up the lyrics of his song. Turning up the volume, he sang along, adding the original fractures to the recording that Capricorn's electronic skill and Tinker's voice had repaired. Karma put down her brush and turned to listen.

"How does it feel to hear your work on the radio?" she asked when the song ended.

"Pretty good, but they're really your words, aren't they, 'the failure to love' and all that? Maybe I should say we both wrote it instead of feeling like I stole the idea from you."

"Why, Blue? When you tell stories about Farmer and the people you know, you're not stealing them, are you? You're just repeating them. And if you hear a song you like and learn to sing it, does that mean you stole the song? This is no different. You heard me say something and you took it and turned it into a song that thousands of people are hearing, and it'' not my idea, really. It's been around for a long, long time. It's just that I think it's more than an idea. I believe it's true. Maybe someone who hears your song will believe it's true, too. Songs and poems are the oldest way in the world for ideas and stories to travel. As your other fellow might have said, minstrels were about the very first newspapers."

"I almost forgot. We're back in the newspapers again, Karma. Peter? brought some clippings around today. I can't say they all said nice things about the album, but Peter? says there's no such thing as bad publicity, but he really hates it, though. I guess I didn't really know how serious he was about this not recording business. He still wants the band to stay together, but it's not the same for him. When I think of what he wanted, I feel bad, but when I hear "Failure To Love" on the radio, I know what I wanted. Two people running in opposite directions can't get to the same place...."

"...as the other fellow says," Karma interjected. "No they can't, Blue."

Karma's remark hung in a silence Blue was reluctant to explore. Instead, he turned his attention to the new panel. "Is that a Russian or what?"

"A Tartar, actually. I have strong impressions about having been a child in that culture a long time ago. If I'm right, then I never grew up. I died very young."

"Your soul is kind of a song of its own, eh, travelling around the world like one of those ideas you were just talking about, India, Russia, England, all those places. So do you think a soul like yours is looking for the right place to be born or the right place to die? Because getting off the planet is what it's all about for you, right?"

"Something like that," Karma said, picking up her brush and turning back to the panel. "And what's it all about for you, Blue?"

"Staying within screaming distance of a priest when my number comes up, then once he splashes me with the sacrament of Extreme Unction it's straight to Heaven for me. You should try being a Catholic, Karma. It's a lot easier. But until that day comes for me, in about a hundred years time, I hope, I have a career to think about. The album is getting us lots of work. Peter? said we even have an inquiry from the Fillmore. Stick with me, girl, and you'll be eating your sunflower seeds off gold plates with silver forks."

43

All through December, Christmas bore down on Tinker and Blue like a runaway train, each day being one boxcar longer and heavier than the previous, with carols on the radio, store windows dressed with the season's scenes and sales, and the appearance of more and more charity Santas on the city's street corners. Being away from home was no longer a lark but a torment, one that enhanced their sentimentality, increased their beer binges, and drove them into each other's crying jags in the sullen belief that no one in all of San Francisco was able to appreciate the sad fate to which they had been sentenced but themselves. Feeding each other a steady diet of memories, they composed daydreams in which they took a train across Canada to Cape Breton where they caught the local bus on Christmas Eve which would take them home.

"It's the best bus in the world," Blue reminded Tinker. "It picks up more hitchhikers than passengers, and it delivers you right to your door if it's raining or snowing. Greyhound won't do that for you."

Talk of the bus made Tinker more mournful than ever. "If we had the Plymouth we wouldn't have to make up stories about trains and buses and planes and hitchhiking," he sighed to Blue, remembering the mangled condition of his car following the accident. It had been parked out back of the commune until the night it disappeared.

Blue explained to Tinker that San Francisco had an abandoned vehicle policy, where the city paid wreckers to tow old cars away. They were taken to a salvage yard, stripped of anything valuable, and crushed into a cube of metal to be melted down and used again.

"They must of seen the Plymouth and thought it was a write-off. Who knows, maybe someday you'll buy a new car and feel all warm whenever you touch the front fender, and that's because it used to be the Plymouth's front fender," Blue comforted Tinker.

"Rein-CAR-nated, Blue?"

"You never know. If my KAR-ma can do it, maybe your CAR can, too, buddy."

—

On Christmas Eve homesickness reached its peak with both of them. There were no formal plans to celebrate the holiday at the commune, nor any to impede its celebration. The season's decorating took an independent path. Someone had strung the six-foot corn plant with blinking lights. Someone else set out an array of candles that flickered around a miniature Bethlehem scene on top of the stereo. A wreath hung on the door. But for Tinker and Blue, none of it was real because none of it was home.

They had gone shopping, wandering through stores, buying gifts for everyone at the commune. Their most delightful discovery was that there were stores where for a quarter more a woman would gift-wrap their purchases, adding ribbons and bows. "The only thing they'll wrap for you in the Co-op back home is the meat," Blue told the woman while watching her turn the boxes over, every corner as crisp and sharp as a hospital bed. "Merry Christmas now," they said in parting, carrying their shopping bags out of the store, stomachs grumbling with the sudden awareness that, unescorted by vegetarians, they were free to go to any restaurant they wanted. They walked into the first tavern they could find, ordered beer and burgers, and indulged each other's blue Christmas.

"I'll be home for Christmas
Please have some snow
And lots of Golden Glo

'Cause I'll be home for Christmas," Blue sang, lifting his beer to Tinker. "Merry Christmas, buddy!" It was the first toast of a whole loaf as they talked themselves into deeper depths of homesickness and despair with the arrival of each fresh beer. They toasted each other, the commune, each and every person from back home who came up in their conversations or stories, and the baby Jesus, whose birthday they were celebrating.

The burgers they had for lunch had already been digested when they noticed that it was now time for supper, ordering more burgers. "We should of taken Barney with us. He'd of had a hell of a Christmas in here," Blue moaned. They kept checking the clock, discovering, each time they did, that they just had time for one more beer.

Noting that it was almost too late to go home and face Karma and Kathy whom they were committed to taking out for a Christmas Eve dinner in a restaurant less bloody-minded than the one they currently occupied, Blue brought up the idea of delaying their return even longer by taking in midnight Mass.

"If we tell them that we were in a tavern all day, they'll get as grumpy as wives, but if we can go home and tell them we were at Mass, well, what can they say?" Blue reasoned. Tinker could find no flaw in that reasoning.

An inquiry of the bartender told them that they would find a Catholic church five or six blocks away. Carrying their shopping bags, they set off on unsteady steps seeking spiritual sanctuary.

"Just like home," Blue said when they stepped inside the church, both of them inhaling deeply of the incense, noting the racks of flickering candles dedicated to the Mother of God, the manger scene in the corner of the church, the plaster saints holding vigil from a hundred nooks and crannies in the walls. Tinker elbowed Blue as they genuflected beside a pew, directing Blue's attention with a nod of his head to the lineup outside the confessionals where lights above the doors indicated that four priests were hearing confessions.

"What do you think?" Tinker whispered.

"I guess we have to. We haven't been to confession since we left home. We don't really have to go until Easter. According to the other fellow, Heaven's waiting for us as long as we make our Easter Duties, but now that we're face to face with it, I guess it would be nice to be able to go to Communion tonight, and considering the nature of our current lives, we're in no state to just walk up to the altar there, stick out our tongues and say Amen."

The two of them stepped into the shortest line, then into cubicles on either side of the same priest, waiting in the dark for the small hatch door to slide back, making the priest's silhouette vaguely visible through a thin dark fabric while a sinner confided his or her venial and mortal mishaps. Blue was busy rehearsing his litany of sins when a sound, as familiar in San Francisco as it was in Cape Breton, caused him to catch his breath, the sound of the priest pushing back the wooden panel. It was Blue's turn, a chore that was never easy. But never in his whole life, had he had to say what he was about to say:

"Bless me, Father, for I have sinned. It has been more than ... six ... months ... since my last confession." He waited for the priest to begin an investigation of the circumstances that would keep a Catholic boy away from the sacraments for half a year; a list of sins so severe that he feared confessing them, sins that included living with a non-Catholic, luring her every night, or at least every night he could, into the sin of sex, knowing that he was inflicting upon her mortal soul an eternity of damnation because Karma not being Catholic she didn't have the great escape of confession enjoyed by Catholics. He began to regret his presence here, to fear it, to sweat.

"*Sí?*" asked the priest.

"Huh?" asked Blue.

"*No hablo inglés,*" said the priest.

"Sorry, Father, but my Latin's pretty weak," Blue answered, then with a deep breath he began to confide the depths and despairs of his soul, finishing with the fact that as early as a few hours ago he had lied about his age to a bartender who sold them beer, lots of beer, "but I don't feel drunk." He managed to get it all out without interruption, although a number of times the holy father had tried to interject. But Blue, once on a roll, was not about to allow himself to be interrogated if he could help it. He ended with a fervent Act of Contrition, asking God's blessing for having sinned against Him, promising never to repeat any of them again.

"That's all, Father," Blue finished up.

"*No hablo inglés. Tiene que encontrar otro cura.*"

"What's that, Father? Three 'Hail Marys' and 'Three Our Fathers'? I can do that, thank you very much." He left the confessional, giving Tinker's door a happy rap with his knuckles as he walked past. Tinker eventually came out scratching his head and knelt beside Blue. Bowing their heads, they prayed together.

After Mass, outside the church at 1 a.m., they waved at the rare passing taxi with no success. They started walking toward home, hoping that eventually a cab would pull up. As they walked, Tinker studied the urban geography around him, finally declaring, "This is around where Mrs. Rubble lives, Blue," a fact that opened their Christmas hearts to the lonely widow, who was an additional excuse to delay their return to the commune where they envisioned Karma and Kathy waiting with the patience of snipers for their return.

Certain that they had the right neighbourhood, they scanned the tenant names of one apartment building after another until Tinker pointed to Mrs. Rubble's name. Her husband's name had been scratched off with a pencil. They pushed on the buzzer to no avail, and finally decided to stand out on the street screaming, "Merry Christmas, Mrs. Rubble," a greeting that seemed to have aroused a large number of Mrs. Rubbles of both sexes, all yelling for them to go home. Finally, a timid voice ventured down from a night window, asking, "Who wants me?"

"It's us, Mrs. Rubble. Tinker and Blue. Remember your husband's wake? We brought you a gift," Blue said, lifting two bottles from one of their shopping bags, allowing them to clink together with an unmistakable sound.

"Come on up, boys."

Mrs. Rubble was obviously trying to make the best of her first widowed Christmas. Her small, near-slum apartment was immaculately clean. A tiny tree, not a foot tall, stood on the television, glittering under the weight of more than one box of tinsel, four blinking lights and a half dozen miniature plastic snowballs. Her table was covered with a Christmas tablecloth, virgin white except along the dust lines where it had been folded and put away year after year.

Mrs. Rubble herself was also dressed in the Christmas spirit, her hair having recently returned from the hairdresser's where it was newly fluffed, the grey that Blue remembered having vanished under a mahogany tint. Her best dress, a red velour, was stretched around her, trying to contain the noticeable difference in Mrs. Rubble since those slimmer days when she had purchased it. Christmas carols spilled quietly from the radio. On the end table beside the chair in which she obviously had been sitting, was an open box of chocolates and a tall glass of something inebriating. Mrs. Rubble was celebrating Christmas.

"Maybe she wasn't calling out our names when she was sitting here tonight, but I don't think my own mother would be more happy to see us," Tinker whispered to Blue when Mrs. Rubble went to the kitchen for glasses.

"You really didn't have to bring me anything," Mrs. Rubble said on returning, and placing the glasses on the table she began looking through the shopping bags with a possessive assurance that here was a Santa Claus. Tinker and Blue looked at one another and, discovering each other's cowardice, shrugged, letting Mrs. Rubble oooh! and aaah! over Capricorn's sandals, Tulip's tubes of paints, the various trinkets and baubles that were bought with others in mind. Her loudest gasp was spared for the sparkling gold chain and cross that Blue had purchased for Karma. Her second loudest utterance was for Kathy's silk shawl. She wrapped herself in it, then, bending her neck, asked Blue to close the clasp of her necklace.

Sitting around the living room, Tinker and Blue quickly overcame the sobering lull that had been midnight Mass and soon the three of them were toasting each other with more joy than on their previous social encounter. After a few drinks served by Mrs. Rubble, her manners wore out and it was every man for himself. It was then, going into the kitchen to get his own drink for the first time, that Blue saw the turkey on the counter.

"That friggin' thing is bigger than some of the horses me and Farmer used to truck around," he said.

"Oh, some social workers or something brought that around. I can hardly lift it and it won't fit in my tiny oven. I suppose some poor family with ten kids is trying to share a little bit of a bird while I have that monstrosity. There's enough meat there to feed an army."

"How about if they were an army of pacifists, Mrs. Rubble? There's enough meat there to feed half the vegetarians in San Francisco and we know exactly where they are, don't we, Tink?"

—

With Blue carrying the turkey and Tinker dragging along their two shopping bags, now filled with potatoes, carrots, onions and half the ingredients from Mrs. Rubble's cupboard, the three of them stood out on the street waiting for a taxi. "I bet this is why Joseph and Mary had to take a donkey," Blue observed, looking down the quiet street. Finally, a taxi pulled up. They climbed inside, wished the cabbie a merry Christmas, and gave him the address.

44

"Fire!"

Capricorn's voice roared its alarm through the Human Rainbow Commune, waking the few residents who hadn't already been lured from their bedrooms by a familiar, yet foreign, smoky odour that had awakened them in the early morning hours.

"There's no fire here, buddy," Blue corrected Capricorn while addressing his remarks to the group of curious onlookers who clustered in the kitchen doorway. "Merry Christmas."

"Merry Christmas," Tinker chimed, throwing his greetings over his shoulder while he continued the busy employment that kept his back to the crowd and his hands in the sink.

"Merry Christmas," added Mrs. Rubble, standing up with a creaking back-stretch from her inspection of the oven.

Capricorn returned their greetings with a distracted nod while looking around the kitchen, his open hands asking a speechless question.

"We're cooking you Christmas dinner," Blue explained, lifting his beer in a toast to the project, then setting it down beside several empties that explained the festive glow in his eyes.

"What kind of a dinner?" Capricorn inquired, staring at the stove.

"Turkey with the works, as the other fellow says," Blue answered, pointing to Tinker who was peeling vegetables at the sink. "We're going to put out a spread that'll make your mouth water. Our gift to you."

"Blue, I know it slips your mind, but this is a vegetarian commune."

"I know that, Capi, but this is Christmas! Christmas without turkey is like … is like … turkey without stuffing, and I'm even making my mother's own stuffing. I watched her do it a few times, and it isn't all that hard, bread and empty the cupboard as near as I could tell. But let's make a few introductions here. Mrs. Rubble, this is everybody. Everybody, this is Mrs. Rubble."

"It's just not the same when you don't have to fight over the legs, is it, Tinker?" Blue observed from his self-promotion to the head of the table, carving knife in hand. "Sure I can't interest any of you in a slab of breast? Turkey's hardly meat at all, more like an evolved vegetable."

"So that's what today's fashionable carnivore is devouring," Capricorn said, pointing to the platter where Blue was trying to chop off a leg for Tinker, his swinging hand rising higher each time the turkey successfully fended off the amputation. Finally, he struck the gladiator's blow that allowed him to raise the leg high over his head, a Roman arena champion displaying his enemy's heart, and say, "Hey, Tink, catch."

Once the vegetarians had come to terms with the turkey in their oven, the idea of Christmas dinner acquired a cheerful appeal. A communal competition of ideas and recipes erupted, along with a theological dialogue on the ethics of gravy. By the time they found their way to the table only Karma and Capricorn had resisted Mrs. Rubble's gravy ladle, but there were just three for turkey, and Barney brooding under the table.

With dinner set on Mrs. Rubble's Christmas tablecloth, Blue halted the proceedings, ordered everyone to stand, and began singing "Happy birthday to you, happy birthday to you, happy birthday, dear Jesus, happy birthday to you..." his carving knife conducting the others to join him, after which he drove it into the chest of the golden turkey. "Let's eat!" The table became a murmur of memories.

The chatter led Mrs. Rubble and Tulip to discover that they grew up a generation and a few blocks apart in Lowell, Massachusetts. They began mining each other's memories. Blue insisted that Tinker tell the one about the Christmas his Grandmere died, a story that led Capricorn to wonder if, besides themselves, there were any other living Cape Bretoners "since the national hobby back there appears to be burying each other."

The talking took them through dinner and into a fruit salad dessert hurriedly made by Kathy and Karma. Clearing off the table, Blue took the turkey into the kitchen, carved away huge chunks of it, added some gravy and put it down in a corner where he knew Barney would discover it long before Karma would. He scratched Barney behind the ears as the dog devoured his Christmas dinner.

"Blue," Karma said, standing behind him.

"I dropped it, Karma, and Barney ran in before I could pick it up and you should never try to take food away from a dog unless you don't need your hand," Blue explained, drawing Karma's attention to the fact that her vegetarian dog was lapping the last of the gravy from the plate. She held out a small package to him, Christmas wrapped.

Blue took the gift, his eyes resentfully finding the gold chain and cross around Mrs. Rubble's neck. Opening the package silently, his mind scrambled for an excuse. Inside, he found a silver ring in the lobster claw shape of Cape Breton Island, a fragment of turquoise inset on the western coast to indicate his hometown. She had commissioned it from one of the silversmiths in the district.

"Karma, I ... my ... your ... gift..." he said, slipping the ring on his wedding finger, finding it a perfect fit. His stammering excuse was rescued by a sudden disturbance in the living room and Tinker's voice wishing Cory a merry Christmas.

"It's Cory, Karma. Let's wish him a merry Christmas," Blue said, guiding Karma out of the tight corner he found himself in.

Cory, in black beret and fatigues, was a long way from Colorado where Blue first saw him, beads and headband, among the horses. They passed around the handshakes and hugs, offered him a Christmas dinner which he accepted, but adding, "I don't bring good news, man. That FBI agent, special agent Bud Wise picked me up again yesterday. Lots of questions about Colorado."

"He'll never stop hunting Capricorn," Tulip said.

"No. That's the strange thing. It's Tinker he was asking about," Cory said. "It's Tinker they're looking for."

"Me? The FBI are looking for me?" Tinker said with disbelief.

"You, man. He picked me up yesterday, grilled me for a few hours and let me go. Told him I didn't know anything. I waited until today to come over, making sure there was no tail on me."

"But why?" Capricorn asked.

"Some wild idea that an illegal alien named Tinker was inventing something. He asked me over and over what kind of research was going on up there. He's crazy, man, crazy, but then again he's with the FBI and so insanity is prerequisite, right," Cory said.

"What do they mean 'illegal alien'?" Blue said, recovering from the shock of Cory's news. "Tinker's not Mexican, he's Canadian."

"An illegal alien is anyone who is in this country illegally," Capricorn explained. "You fit the description."

"No we don't, we're Canadian—"

"We're fucked, that's what we are, Blue. At least, I am. What did he say about inventing, Cory?"

"Something subversive to undermine the American energy industry, Tinker, but they didn't go into details so I don't know what he meant. In fact I'm not sure he knew what they meant."

"I do," Kathy said, tears rising with her words. "It's my fault. When you told me in Colorado that you were planning to invent an oxygen engine, I thought it was a wonderful thing to do. With an oxygen engine we can stop poisoning the planet with fossil fuels. I wrote about it in my journal. They took my journals away along with everything else when they raided the commune, including Cory and Tulip. I'm sorry, Tinker, but I never thought—"

Tinker's touch assured her there was no blame, but his mind swirled around the wild, unwakable dream that he was ... "wanted by the FBI. I'm wanted by the fucking FBI. Blue, what are we going to do?"

"We can be in Vancouver by tomorrow night, and home for New Year's Eve, Tinker."

"But they'll be watching the bus stations. You've seen the movies. You know how they are. When the FBI has you in its sights they got you, man. I'm fucked."

"We won't need a bus, buddy," Blue said.

"Whatever we're going to do, we have to decide quickly," Capricorn said. "The FBI looking for you brings them close to me. If they picked up Cory, they'll be looking for Tulip next."

"So there's your choices, Tinker. Cell mates with Capi in Alcatraz or buddies with me back home. What's to decide here? We drop the FBI a postcard from Calgary and they stop looking for you and the heat's off Capi here."

"I got to think about this," Tinker said, getting up, taking Kathy by the hand and leading her toward their room.

"Oh, shit," Blue groaned.

—

While Tinker and Kathy were in conference, Blue tried to forget the fact that it was Kathy to whom Tinker was talking the situation over with and not him. When Peter?, Gerry and Nathan arrived at the commune, Blue threw himself into assisting Mrs. Rubble and Tulip, who expanded the dinner preparations of a Christmas plate for Cory to include their most recent guests. Soon they were sitting at the table again, the band members being filled with turkey and filled in on Tinker's unexpected notoriety. Their appetites for turkey soon turned the Human Rainbow Commune back into a vegetarian stronghold – no scrap of meat to be found.

When Tinker and Kathy returned, Tinker announced that he didn't want to leave San Francisco, not his job nor Kathy who was not prepared to leave the city with him. "I'm learning a lot in the tunnel. I'm learning a lot period. They never caught you, Cap, maybe they won't catch me. I'll just have to lay low for a while."

"And where are you going to lay low?" Blue asked. "The FBI knows you're some kind of a hippie. They'll go through here like the SS, arresting everybody. You know where the best place to lay low is, Tinker. You may not like winter in Cape Breton, but it's not prison."

"I know a place," Mrs. Rubble offered. "I don't have a spare room but I do have a day bed, and I don't know a single FBI agent so there's no reason for them to go looking for you at my apartment, is there?"

"It could do for a while," Tinker said thoughtfully, noting that Mrs. Rubble's apartment was within walking distance of work. "It will give me some time to think about what I really want."

Peter?'s efforts to find out more about the oxygen engine were ignored by Tinker who had more important things on his mind, but the implications of Tinker's invention were as self-evident to him as Blue's music.

"No wonder they're looking for you, man. You're talking about an energy source that's as natural as breathing. It won't just salvage the planet from our inhuman greed, it makes that source of energy available to everyone. The ultimate democracy, I always believed, is reflected in the potential of solar energy. No one owns the sun, man. Like God, to use a metaphor I don't believe in myself, it belongs to us all. So does the oxygen we breathe. Economic dynasties will topple with the development of your engine. Maybe even governments. No wonder the FBI wants you, and I'm willing to bet they don't want you alive. The powers-that-be want the massive contents behind that modest cranium of yours to stop functioning, and if it takes a bullet to do that, then so be it. The FBI is not without its executionary resources."

The others weren't paying a lot of attention to Peter?'s rambling exploration of Tinker's pending invention until the suggestion that Tinker would not be taken alive.

"We better get moving," Blue said. "Tinker, pack! I'll drive Tinker and Mrs. Rubble over with the van. None of you know where she lives, so you can't give my buddy up, not even to save your little pinky fingernails. Come on, let's go, everybody move! We gotta get Public Enemy Number One out of here."

After a flurried moment to pack, the whole population followed Tinker and Blue down the stairs into the backyard where a stunned Tinker stopped the parade.

"What's up, buddy? You look like you've seen Danny Danny Dan's ghost," Blue said.

Tinker's forefinger pointed weakly toward the tan and brown vehicle parked beside the commune van.

"Oh, you mean the Plymouth," Blue said. "Didn't I tell you about that? I guess not. Gerry knew this guy, eh, does body work. He came by one day when you were at work and took it. Not a bad job, except that new coat of paint kind of ruined Kathy's butterfly and the other paintings. It was supposed to be your Merry Christmas gift, but this Christmas is not very merry, as the other fellow says."

Tinker approached the Plymouth, reaching out with a timid hand, as if afraid it would disappear under his touch. It didn't. He walked around it, looked inside, opened the driver's door, turned the keys in the ignition and the engine leapt to life. Letting it idle, he walked to the front of the car, opened the hood and studied its vibrating engine.

"Tinker, I don't think this is the time to be thinking about taking it apart," Blue said.

Tinker lowered the hood, took his suitcase from Blue, put it in the back seat, then opened the passenger door for Mrs. Rubble, hugged Kathy, and sat behind the wheel. Blue leaned in the open window.

"It's like I said, buddy, by tomorrow night we can be in Vancouver, both of us." Tinker shook his head wordlessly. "Think about it because there's worse things than being in jail, buddy. If we stay here, we'll have to stop calling you Tinker and start calling you Aloysius."

Tinker shifted into reverse, backing the Plymouth out of the yard, finding his voice as he did so. "I'll call you later, Kath. Blue, thanks, buddy. Next summer. We'll drive home next summer."

45

"Blue, wake up, you're having a bad dream."

Blue's eyes flew open, saw Karma leaning across the bed shaking his shoulder, searched the room to get additional bearings, then closed in momentary relief. He felt his rapid heart, and, sitting up on the side of the bed, slowed down his gasping breath.

"A nightmare, a god-awful nightmare. It was next summer and Tinker and I were driving across the Canso Causeway on our way home. The causeway's only a mile long but we kept driving and driving and driving and we couldn't get to the end of it. Then we could see that the island was sinking, going down inch by inch into the ocean. Tinker was driving faster and faster trying to get there but we couldn't reach it. First, the coastline started disappearing into the water, then the forests, then the mountains and then it was just gone. When we got to the end of the causeway, Cape Breton wasn't there anymore, nothing but bubbles, as if something alive was drowning down there. Tinker and I just looked at each other, talking without talking the way it works sometimes, and got back in the car and Tinker started to drive off the end of the world and if you hadn't woke me up the two of us would of drowned. You know what the other fellow says about dying in your dreams, don't you? If you die in a dream you'll die in your sleep, although I don't how they know that."

Blue looked around the room again, grateful for the three-dimensional facts of bed and chair and three walls and the tarpaulin that sheltered their privacy ever since Tulip's exhibit, and for the reality of Karma's hand on his shoulder.

"I've seen ghosts, Karma, and I've seen lots of dead people laid out in their parlours, but I've never seen anything that frightened me like that nightmare of Cape Breton drowning ...

except that time I thought you were dead, of course ... watching it drown and knowing there's no place to go home to...."

There was a dim glimmer of January dawn outside their window, and Karma's suggestion that they go for a walk sent a shiver through Blue, but he consented without resistance. Dressing quietly and warmly, they were outside a few moments later, walking wordless blocks together, Karma's hand in Blue's, both hands shoved deep into his jacket pocket.

"Are you homesick, Blue?" Karma eventually asked, then answered her own question. "That's a foolish question, isn't it? You're always homesick."

"Worst disease on the island. I know people who get homesick and they never left Cape Breton once in their lives. Some of us die of lung cancer and some of us die of heart attacks, but homesickness gets us all," Blue said, filing the new thought away as possible material for Blue Cacophony's next album.

Spotting an "open" sign in a window across the street, Blue thought he could smell the coffee, and guided Karma through the non-existent traffic into what had once been the sunporch of a house, now converted into a narrow diner, divided by a long counter, stools on one side, grill on the other, two booths at the back. The Chinese owner greeted them with a nodding smile and placed two plastic menus in front of them.

Karma decided quickly on black coffee and a roll, but Blue lingered over the menu which promised eggs afloat on a sea of bacon fat, the bacon itself, slabs of butter sinking into hot toast, and home-fries heavily salted and wallowing in ketchup. But reading the beverage list, he held up his hand to stop the owner-waiter, chief chef and bottle-washer, from pouring coffee into his cup, ordering tea and toast instead.

Waiting for his order, Blue lit a cigarette, opening the door for Karma to remind him of his earlier words, that some people in Cape Breton die of lung cancer.

"It's not the cigarettes that do it, it's the coal mines, black lung. Most of the miners I know smoked all their lives but the ones who are dying are dying from black lung. Cigarettes get a bad rap, if you ask me. We had this guy back home, eh, used to smoke a couple of packs a day. He got emphysema and the doctor made him quit smoking. He choked to death in his own bed because he couldn't get the stuff in his lungs up. When he was smoking all the time, he was always coughing and hacking and that was helping his chest, see, and when he stopped smoking he was dead in a few days. Ask Tinker, he'll tell you the same story."

"Then why doesn't Tinker smoke?"

"He thinks it'll give him cancer," Blue muttered as the man behind the counter set the toast and tea before Blue. Blue studied the tea, looked at the man's receding back, looked at Karma who caught his mystified eyes.

"What's wrong?" she asked.

Blue's animated hands made up for his speechless tongue, pointing and questioning all at once, directing her attention to the tiny pot and porcelain thimble that had been placed in front of him.

"Your tea?" Karma asked. "What's wrong with it?"

"You don't see anything wrong with this picture?" Karma shook her head. Blue picked the lid off the pot, glanced inside, then lowered the lid again. "It's green," he whispered. "I asked for tea, not pee."

"It's Chinese tea, Blue, and it's very good. Taste it."

Blue poured a little into the earless cup and took a timid sip. "Not bad, I guess, but it's not King Cole. Excuse me, could I get a little milk here, please?"

The waiter brought him a glass of milk and looked aghast as Blue tried to pour a little from the glass into the cup, an operation that caused most of the milk to trickle down the side of the glass, forming a white puddle on the counter while the milk that did find its way into the tea turned it chalky.

"No good," the owner said. "No good to do that. Make tea bad," and taking another tiny cup from the shelf he poured from the pot and sipped and savoured and sipped some more. "Proper way," he said. "In China, tea very important. Many ceremonies for tea. Tea to sleep, tea to wake, tea for hunger, tea for aroma, very important. No milk. Never milk."

"Back where I come from tea's very important, too, buddy," Blue explained. "We don't have a lot of ceremonies, but tea's a religion with us, even have our own 'teaology,' as the other fellow says, which really means people get together over a cup to gossip. Now, I don't drink a lot of the stuff myself, but this morning, feeling a little homesick, I saw tea on your menu and thought, tea and toast. When I was a kid, eh, the old lady used to make us toast and tea every night before bed. Weak tea, mind you, because we were kids, but we'd dunk our toast in the tea and eat it. When I saw your little cup here," Tinker said, holding it up, then holding a slice of toast over it to demonstrate that impossibility of dunking, "I knew it wasn't going to cure my homesickness."

The owner tried to follow Blue's words, glancing helplessly at Karma from time to time for translation assistance.

"See this," Blue said, pointing to his cup of milky tea, "this is weak tea. What I'd do, eh, I'd get rid of these lawn clippings you have in here and get yourself some King Cole tea bags, then you've got yourself a real cup of tea. I'd recommend you put a couple of bags in a good sized pot and let it steep for seven minutes. There's people who'll give you an argument on that, people who'll say a five-minute steep is perfect, and some who'll tell you that you have to boil the tea all afternoon before it's fit to drink. Steep it right, though, and when you pour it into the milk in the cup, it will turn caramel coloured and you're holding a taste of back home in your hands."

"No milk," said the owner, "in China never milk. Ruin tea."

"We've been making tea in Cape Breton for a couple of hundred years, so I think I know what I'm talking about."

"Tea in China five thousand years," the owner said, expanding the fingers, one finger for each millennium.

"Slow learners, arntcha?" Blue laughed, then diplomatically poured his milky tea back into the glass and poured himself a fresh cup from the pot. "Like the other fellow says, when in Rome do as the Chinese."

"You drink. I come back," the owner said, disappearing through a doorway.

"Blue, be careful you don't insult the man," Karma said.

"I'm not insulting him. I'm trying to teach him something about tea. We got this restaurant back home that happens to be owned by a Chinese family too. Order tea in there and you get King Cole. Some restaurants might give you Red Rose, but any real restaurant in Cape Breton would serve you King Cole. I'm just telling this guy that there's more than one way to fill a cup, to quote the other fellow."

"Well, don't forget that he's trying to tell you the same thing, Blue," Karma said as the owner returned carrying a clay bowl that contained a tiny teapot surrounded by more miniature cups. He placed it in front of them and Karma and Blue saw immediately that the elegantly decorated porcelain was not his standard restaurant dishware.

"Excuse me," Blue interrupted, "but my friend here, Karma ... I'm Blue, by the way ... is afraid I'm insulting you. If I am, I'm sorry. It's just that we do things different back home."

"No insult," the owner replied, introducing himself as Mr. Lo. Taking a couple of handfuls of Oolong tea from a package, he put it in the pot, then filled it from a boiling kettle he took from the grill area. He poured the water over the cups that were in the bowl, washing and seasoning them, he explained. Then placing the teapot back in the bowl, he filled it with more boiling water, letting it overflow somewhat, put the lid back on and poured more water over the cover. He took the cups out of the bowl and set them lip to lip on the counter, took up the pot of tea, which Blue felt had hardly had time to steep, twenty seconds at most, and began filling the cups. He filled the cups by passing the teapot over them, unconcerned with spilling liquid. Then he gestured for each of them to pick up a cup.

Following his lead, they held the tea under their noses, inhaling its aroma, then sipped it, finding it pleasant to the taste. He continued to fill the cups until Blue lost count of them, estimating that he had sipped eight or ten tiny cups, noting that if they had all been poured into one of his mother's tea cups, it would have been perhaps half filled.

Before each pouring, Mr. Lo took the teapot out of the water in the bowl where it was being kept hot, and ran the bottom of the pot around the rim of the bowl a few times.

"If host ring the bowl from right to left," he said, explaining a cultural subtlety, "the guest welcome to stay long time. If host ring pot round bowl from left to right, guest should leave soon."

Blue noticed that Mr. Lo was ringing the bowl right to left.

When they had finished the Oolong, Mr. Lo prepared another pot of tea, explaining the Oolong was for drinking at any time, but the next one had special qualities. According to Mr. Lo, the tea, which Blue tasted and enjoyed more than the Oolong, was a tea that was known for its flavour, but should only be taken after meals.

"When finish, some people use to wash faces. Good for complexion. Old men dry tea leaves after using and make pillows for sleeping, believe it better for health than feather or down," Lo added.

"Back home, we use the leaves for reading the future," Blue replied, examining the fine pattern of powdery leaves in his little cup. "What I see here, Mr. Lo, is me and you, a couple of lost souls adrift in San Francisco with a lot in common. Who would of thought that China and Cape Breton drink the same medicine? We might not have a different kind of tea for every occasion, because King Cole is a tea for all seasons, to quote the other fellow. You should hear my old lady. If she gets excited winning at bingo, her heart flutters until she has a cup of tea, and even if a neighbour comes in and tells her the doctor said the neighbour only has six months to live, the first thing the old lady'll say is, 'You need a cup of tea, dear' as if it was a cure."

Throughout the cultural exchange, Blue managed to eat his toast, and by the time they had been served sixteen or twenty cups of tea by Mr. Lo, Blue and Karma were ready to leave. There was no bill.

Out on the street, Blue asked Karma to wait a moment while he ran back inside.

"Excuse me, Mr. Lo, but on your menu here, you have bacon and eggs and hamburgers and stuff. Do you fry them up the normal way or do you do something healthy or Chinese to it?" Mr. Lo pointed to the grill. "Well, in that case, I'm sure to come back but when I do, I'll bring my own tea bag."

46

"He's just like a Cape Bretoner, all he can talk about is 'back home,' in China," Blue explained to Tinker a few days later, giving Mr. Lo, who was busy at his grill, his seal of approval.

Although the commune had decided that Tinker's moving out made it unnecessary to abandon their current quarters for new ones, Blue felt it was in Tinker's interests to change all their former patterns, including the greasy spoon that they and Barney used to frequent. Blue had been back to Mr. Lo's to test various aspects of the menu and decided that it was the natural choice for their change of culinary address.

Blue also agreed that the best thing for Tinker to do since he was staying in San Francisco was to keep on working in the subway tunnel, but for different reasons than Tinker's.

"If anybody at the commune gets picked up by the FBI, and they put us on a lie detector and ask where you are, we can just say you've gone underground but we don't know exactly where and it will register as the truth because you are underground but none of us ever knows exactly where, right?"

It was the first time they had seen each other since Blue's dream, and as Blue introduced Tinker to the new eatery, he explained in conspiratorial tones that besides great food, Mr. Lo's restaurant could serve as a rendezvous point. "If you call me or I call you and one of us thinks the FBI's wiretapping the phone, one of us will tell the other one of us that we don't want to see you and that you better *lay low, mister*, which will really mean I'll meet you at Mr. Lo's. Nobody knows it's here except Karma, and she's only been here once."

Noticing Tinker idly scanning the menu after they had placed their orders, Blue felt he should warn his friend.

"I know you don't drink it, but when you see tea on that menu don't let it make you homesick. I won't go into it, but take my word, you don't want tea.

"So how's it going, Baby Face? Remember who I'm talking about? Baby Face Nelson. One of the greatest gangsters of all time. Baby Face Nelson *Gillis*, to be exact. Father from Margaree, just down the road from home. Could probably find out he's a cousin of my own if I took the time to look it up, which might not be a bad idea. There's probably still places where being Baby Face Nelson's forty-fifth cousin carries some weight. Hell, I can't believe I got a buddy on the run. Think I haven't been trying to get that idea and my guitar together for a singalong? So tell me, how's life as a genuine criminal?"

Tinker put down the menu, squinting into the question. After an organizing pause he told Blue that it didn't seem real enough to keep him awake at night or anything like that, "... but there's times when I go cold as a frozen codfish just thinking about it, being arrested and jailed and all that. What I miss, though, Blue, is not being part of the commune anymore. What if Kathy gives up on me? We talked a bit about getting our own apartment, but she doesn't want to leave the commune, which, to be honest, is fine with me because Mrs. Rubble packs a pretty good lunch can. Pretty good meals, too, especially when she gets to the cooking before she gets to the cooking wine, but I don't want to lose Kathy over this silly engine idea of Charlie's. I don't want to go to jail either, but running away home's not the answer. I don't know what is."

"Be glad you have a home to run to if you need one," Blue cautioned, "because I had this nightmare that you and I were driving across the causeway and when we got to the other end, there it was, gone, as the other fellow says. Maybe it's telling us that if we don't go back soon, it will sink right out of our minds or hearts or something. It was just so friggin' ... friggin' lonely standing out there on the end of the causeway looking down into the ocean. By the way, you owe Karma your life for waking me up before we both drowned."

Mr. Lo placed three plates on the counter in front of them, two hamburgers with the works and one medium rare meat patty which Blue picked up and took out to the sidewalk where Barney lay, head on his paws, dreaming of just such a gesture. First, though, he asked Barney for a chorus, the dog taking his cue quickly, sounding a sudden howl through the neighbourhood.

Blue had come to accept that his backup singer was one of Blue Cacophony's positive attractions, and had begun to use their walks about the city as practice time, his voice encouraging Barney's agonizing harmony, not always to the pleasure of passers-by. Occasionally, there was gushing recognition.

"We're pretty well the regular band at Ellis Dee's now. Too bad you couldn't drop in to hear to us, Tink, but the FBI probably has it under surveillance."

"If I want to hear music, I guess I'll have to go anywhere Blue Cacophony's not playing. Besides, I'm getting sick of hearing your voice on the radio."

Blue, smiling at Tinker's acknowledgement of the success of "Failure To Love," quipped, "Didn't think I had it in me, did you, Tink? Didn't think that some day you'd turn on the radio and say to yourself, 'There's my best friend singing his hit song.' Know what I did last week? Sent a copy to CJFX in Antigonish. I know all they play on that station are fiddlers and Hank Snow, but wouldn't it be great if some morning on Gus MacKinnon's program he decided to play 'Failure To Love'? Think of my mother making the old man his breakfast and the next thing she hears is her bouncing baby boy's voice all the way from San Fran-frigging-cisco into her kitchen. We've accomplished a lot in a short time, Tinker, me with a hit record and you wanted by the FBI. Never in our wildest dreams, eh, buddy?"

"Hopefully it will all blow over in a couple of weeks," Tinker said.

47

Any hope that his notoriety would soon blow over and the FBI would move on to bigger and better criminals vanished on a February afternoon when Tinker, on his way home from work, glimpsed a headline of the cover of *The Subterranean* at a sidewalk newsstand: "Energy inventor sought in FBI manhunt." Buying a copy more furtively than he ever purchased *Playboy*, Tinker carried it under his jacket until he got to Mrs. Rubble's. Dropping his lunch can on the kitchen table he pulled out the paper, opening it to the article as he walked into the living room, and read the byline.

"Peter?" he muttered. The article heralded the arrival of a messiah whose pending invention would topple the military-industrial complex with the most democratic of notions, an economy sustained by oxygen instead of fossil fuel.

> Once the economy of Mankind begins to be powered by the oxygen engine, the very substance that sustains life itself,

that economy will become as organic as the cardio-vascular system. The greed that inspires us to rob the graves of ancient forests to fire the engines of capitalism will dissipate, and the nature of Mankind's bartering will become more benign because the economy, like our very lives, will depend on not polluting that environment. The more dependent we become on not polluting the environment, the more conscious we will become of our environment, making us more appreciative of it and each other. A species positively self-aware threatens the multinational plot to turn us all into fodder for the Dow Jones average.

Understandably, the FBI, the flunky arm of an Establishment which thrives on exploiting the masses, has launched a nation-wide manhunt for the renegade genius who goes by the alias of Tinker. This reporter has had the pleasure of sitting at the feet of this great teacher, listening hypnotically to his vision of the world as it will be AOE (After the Oxygen Engine). The place he describes conjures visions of an island paradise shimmering just out of reach, a mere causeway away for those of us who are prepared to believe in this Utopia, a place so clear in his mind that one is almost tempted to believe that he was born there, a child of Atlantis....

"I'm going to kill that guy," Tinker said, trying to evoke enough anger to overwhelm the sickening sensation in his stomach.
"What's that, dear?" Mrs. Rubble called from the kitchen.
"I said I'm going to drive over and see Kathy."
"Is that safe?"
"If I'm going to be gunned down, I'm going to be gunned down," Tinker called as he walked out the door, hoping he was joking.

—

Blue, leafing his way to the entertainment section of the *San Francisco Herald* in search of his name, paused over a headline, yelled to Capricorn who came into the kitchen and began reading over Blue's shoulder.

Agent Confirms FBI Seeking Fugitive Inventor

FBI sources confirmed yesterday that they are searching for a fugitive who uses the alias "Tinker."

"Some papers are trying to sell this guy as some kind of folk hero," FBI agent Bud Wise told the Herald. "But he's a Commie through and through. We are very anxious to apprehend him before he begins a campaign of terror throughout the United States of America."

Wise said that "Tinker" has been linked to the Human Rainbow Commune, led by a cult figure known as "Capricorn," who is wanted, Wise told reporters, in connection with the bombing of a New York factory. Both Capricorn and Tinker eluded capture during an FBI raid on the commune's Colorado hideout where written documentation was obtained that there is a plot to undermine the safety of the American way, Wise said. In addition, FBI agents have questioned members of the militant Black Panthers regarding "Tinker's" whereabouts.

"There appears to be a conspiracy of militant Communist organizations converging around this 'Tinker' character," Wise warned when questioned yesterday while leaving the Fucdepor Petroleum Building. Wise said that his presence at the building was to warn Fucdepor officials that there may be a plot to explode refineries owned by the powerful oil company. Wise denied that his visit was the result of reports that "Tinker" was inventing an oxygen engine that threatens the future of fossil fuel corporations.

"This is a dangerous criminal who threatens the peace and security of great American institutions like Fucdepor," Wise said. "The public's help is required in apprehending him, but no one should try to be a hero. We have reason to believe that this 'Tinker' is dangerous."

The FBI agent said the public could expect an artist's sketch of "Tinker" in the near future.

"Alcatraz awaits, as the other fellow says," Blue quipped to Capricorn who was still hovering over his shoulder, re-reading the article.

While the commune council gathered round the kitchen table to discuss the media attention being directed toward them, Tinker was parked across the street watching the house, waiting to attract the attention of someone who could carry a message to Kathy. He spent his time assembling what little he knew about being "on the run."

Escape to Canada was an option that lay at the bottom of his knowledge like a concrete foundation. If everything else went wrong, he and Blue and the Plymouth could make a run for the border and the safety beyond. Knowing that a "weasel path," as Blue called it, was available to him, along with Kathy's refusal to travel to Canada, gave him the courage to stay in San Francisco. His current circumstances, he felt, were the best he could hope for. Mrs. Rubble, happy with his company and his appetite for her cooking, wasn't going to betray him. At work, he was Al Dempsey, short-haired mechanic's assistant whom no one had ever heard called Tinker. There were no pictures, no fingerprints, no previous criminal record. Besides, the FBI was searching for a hippie in the Haight-Ashbury area, and Tinker's description no longer filled that look, or fitted that address. As long as his contacts with Kathy and Blue were carefully arranged, there was little chance that FBI agents would locate him.

"It's time to go into mercury mode," Capricorn told the commune council, explaining to Blue that among the properties of mercury was its ability, when touched, to fragment into a dozen silvery pieces scattering away from the finger – in this case the long arm of the law – to re-form when the threat was withdrawn. It was clear that the commune's location, while still undiscovered by the FBI, was widely known in the district and it was only a matter of time before someone sold them out to Wise to escape a drug bust.

"Any suggestions?" Capricorn asked, his question bringing a flurry of responses. Each commune member could find his or her own pad, keep little contact with each other except through the most trusted of methods, scribbling messages amid the graffiti on the washroom walls of Aquarius Café. Karma was apprehensive about the group splitting up, possibly becoming lost to each other.

"Maybe we should do what Tinker is doing, hide in plain sight," she said. "There are houses for rent right across the street. If we could get someone like Peter? to rent one of them for us, we could just move over there one piece of furniture at a time. That way, we could keep a watch on this house."

"And an eye on whoever might be watching this house," Capricorn added, liking the suggestion. "I think I can help us there," he said, passing a sketch around the table. It was a portrait of a middle-aged man with a large boozer's nose, small, mean eyes and a cruel twist to his mouth. "This is a drawing Tulip did from my information. The face you are looking at is my memory of FBI Special Agent Bud Wise. Watch for it squinting over the top of a newspaper, from behind the wheel of a parked car, from a shadowy doorway. He's picked up our ... well, my scent again. We've been just missing each other for years, but his lies about Tinker increases the pressure on us. He's scaring the hell out of the city to try to flush the two of us out. Wise is our biggest problem."

Blue studied the sketch. "Thine enemy is my enemy, as the other feller says; if this creep is out to get Tinker, then I'm out to get him."

"I have as much at stake here as anyone, but I've learned from personal experience that revenge is a spiritually unhappy act," Capricorn warned Blue. "We have no desire to get caught, but we're not going to jeopardize the commune's karma with acts of revenge."

"Revenge? I wouldn't think of it because vengeance is mine, sayeth the other fellow," Blue said, thumb jerking Heavenward. "No, Capi, my friend, I'm not thinking about revenge, I'm thinking about Monk, this guy we got back home. Monk used to be a hell of a boozer, one of the best until he saw the Blessed Virgin Mary and she took the taste for liquor right away from him.

"Anyway, this other guy we got back home, Farmer, was telling me about the time a bunch of them were on the booze at Monk's house for a few days. This was when Monk still had what the other fellow calls his discriminating taste. There were cases of empties piling up in the porch from all the drinking they were doing. When one of them would go to sleep, of course, the other guys would steal his booze. The big mystery, though, was that when Monk went to sleep they could never find his booze. They'd look under the bed where he was sleeping, and in the fridge and even in the flush tank of the toilet but they couldn't find it. Whenever Monk woke up, though, a couple of minutes later, he'd be sipping away at his own liquor. Later, after the Virgin Mary straightened him out, he told Farmer that what he was doing was putting his booze out in the porch with all the empties, hiding it in plain sight as Karma just said. Nobody looking at all those bottles would guess one of them was full," Blue finished with firm nod of his head at the ingeniousness of it all.

"There's a point to this story, or is it just comic relief?" Capricorn asked.

"Oh yeah, right! I almost forgot. There is a point I was trying to make and this sketch here is it. In the newspaper, the FBI guy said that they would be putting out an artist's sketch of Tinker soon, probably putting it up in all the post offices. Well, we got a lot of artists of our own right here, right, and what if we made our own sketches of Tinker and took them to a friendly printer and got our own FBI posters made? What I was thinking was that if we made maybe ten different sketches of Tinker, bearded, bald, white, black, Chinese, all kinds of different faces, then we could take them around to the post offices ourselves and put a different sketch in each post office. That way, we could confuse the hell out of the police. When they get their own sketch of Tinker, wherever they're going to get it I don't know, it would look like just another empty bottle among all the other empty bottles."

Kathy, liking Blue's idea, expanded on it, suggesting that they not make up faces but go out in the street, she and Karma and Tulip, and begin sketching real faces so that when they did put the posters up, other people would recognize them and the FBI and the police would be running all over the city arresting the wrong Tinkers.

—

When Kathy, Karma and Tulip came out of the Human Rainbow Commune, San Francisco branch, each carrying a sketch pad, they spoke together briefly on the sidewalk and then went their separate ways. Kathy walked past the Plymouth and once she had gone a block beyond his parking spot, Tinker checked the rearview mirror for any nondescript cars that might be pulling out to follow her, checked, too, the nearby doorways for lurking strangers, and the sidewalk for unfamiliar hippie faces that might be narcs or undercover agents.

Satisfied that Kathy was not being tailed, Tinker eased the Plymouth away from the curb and began his own surveillance. When she turned the corner at the intersection, he drove the car past her, pulled over to the curb and waited. Kathy walked past, forcing Tinker to make a meek toot with the Plymouth's horn which caught her attention and brought her into the vehicle.

"I didn't recognize it without the rust," Kathy apologized as the Plymouth pulled away, then told him about the commune council's meeting, the decision to move across the street, and the plans for Tinker's wanted poster.

"I'm sorry about all the trouble my journal is causing you, Tinker, you and Capricorn, because police are looking harder for him now, too. What can I do to make it better?"

"Nothing," Tinker assured her. "They took what you wrote and made it mean what they wanted it to mean, the same way people screw around with the Bible. It's not your fault so there's nothing you can do besides what you're doing with the posters."

"If you are only staying here because of me, Tinker, then I could go to Canada with you. You would be safe there," Kathy offered.

Tinker braked the car suddenly as if Kathy's offer was a child standing in the middle of the street. "You'd do that? Come with me even though you don't want to?"

"You know that it's not that I don't want to go, Tinker, it's that I don't want to leave here."

"Then we won't leave until we have to," Tinker replied, "because I don't want to leave, either. We've been through this before, kind of, but it's a lot easier to stay when your reason's a real person," he said, giving her hand a passionate squeeze. "If we drive around for a while, Mrs. Rubble will be going to bingo and we'll have the place to ourselves for a couple of hours."

To kill that time, Kathy suggested they drive to the wharf, find a place with tables beside a window where they could sip on soft drinks while she sketched preliminary studies for the wanted poster.

48

"Our first home," Blue said, looking around the empty room with a sad shake of his head. In his arms he held a box stuffed with odds and ends that he had accumulated in San Francisco.

A call to Peter? had set off a snappy chain reaction that, within a few hours, resulted in Nathan and Gerry renting the house across the street, examining it, putting down the first month's rent and damage deposit and taking immediate possession from an eager landlord who cared nothing for references or aliases. Under cover of darkness, the move began, each commune member slipping out the back door to circumnavigate the neighbourhood, approaching their new quarters from its back door, avoiding crossing the street between the two abodes where the move might be observed by FBI agents or potential informants. Even walking several blocks carrying couches, beds, tables and chairs seemed a less risky means of discovery than loading the van, which transported little besides the remaining boxes of *Failure To Love*.

"What about the wall?" Blue asked Karma, who explained that Capricorn said the damage deposit they left would cover part of the cost, and they would mail the landlord more money to cover the additional cost of replacing the wall.

"Not Tulip's wall, yours," Blue said, nodding toward the six past lives and three blank panels that decorated it.

"I suppose the next people who come to live here will just paint over it," Karma replied.

"We have to take it with us," Blue declared.

"We can't take out another wall, Blue, and besides, what would we do then, tear down a wall in the new place to put this one up?"

"I don't understand how it doesn't bother you. When I was leaving home last summer, standing there looking around my bedroom, knowing the minute I left my sister would be moving

| 269

herself and all her Beatles stuff into it and that it would never be mine again, I had a lump in my throat, and there was nothing on the walls to cry about except the Sacred Heart of Jesus and my autographed picture of Johnny Bower. But you've spent almost our whole lives together painting this wall and now you're just going to walk away from it like it cheap wallpaper."

They stood side by side enjoying Karma's lives for the last time: the Mayan mask, the Buddha feeding himself to the tiger's cubs, the medieval nun, the Tartar child, an African slave who drowned when the transport ship sank, and a mother of six children who lived an uneventful life in England except for burying children during the Black Plague.

"You sure got around, didn't you?" Blue said. "But I still think it's not fair to have to leave them behind."

"I left those lives behind, Blue. Why should it be any harder to leave the paintings? I'm glad I painted them, and I still have three more to do, but I'll do them across the street."

"But they're good paintings, Karm. I bet you could sell them if you wanted to, make a few bucks."

"That just takes us back to tearing the wall out which I am not going to do, Blue, so let's just take what we can carry and move into our new home."

—

Blue felt his way along the unfamiliar wall, trying to a find the hall light switch that was the key to finding his way to the bathroom his memory had misplaced. Sweeping his hand along the wrinkled wallpaper, he froze, suddenly aware that a figure loomed before him, its silhouette framed in the window, caught in a stream of street light. Hairs undisturbed since Danny Danny Dan's funeral now stood at full attention, and his hand came off the wall to make its way through the sign of the cross, slowly, so as not to attract the interest of the restless spirit.

"Is that you, Blue?"

"Who wants to know?" Blue asked, his voice an octave above where he intended it to be. Realizing it was Capricorn to who this question was squeaked, Blue regretted it even more.

"The ghost of Christmas Past," Capricorn answered, never taking his eyes from the window. "Don't turn on the light."

"What's out there?" Blue asked, materializing in the window light beside Capricorn, looking down on the still street.

"A raid. Karma's idea to move here got us out of there just in time."

"I don't see anything," Blue said, staring out on the quiet, dim street.

"See that grey Chev, the black van, those two people loitering in the doorway over there?" Capricorn pointed out. "This thing is going to happen tonight, man."

They watched the motionless street in silence until Blue whispered, "This reminds me of looking at one of those still life paintings artists do, you know, vegetables. Why do they do that, do you suppose? A world full of nude women and they paint vegetables. Good thing they're not songwriters, they'd starve waiting for somebody to sit still long enough to listen to the 'Ballad of the Onion and the Potato.' What do you think's going to happen here?"

Before Capricorn could respond, the van emptied itself of a half dozen darkly dressed agents, and the driver of the Chev, wearing a fedora, leapt from his vehicle to lead the assault on the empty house. Bursting through the door, the group rushed inside. Flashlights moved from window to window, floor to floor. Lights went on in the house and shadowy shapes moved from room to room. Less than ten minutes later, the agents filtered out of the house, shrugging to each other. The fedora came out last, stood on the street looking both ways as if expecting to see the former occupants fleeing up or down the street, then slammed his right fist into the side of a van.

"The fedora," Capricorn told Blue, "that's Wise."

"Too bad he wouldn't come in here alone," Blue whispered back. "I'd pull that hat down over his eyes and kick his arse up around his ears. Hell, the commune must be getting to me. I didn't say anything about breaking his neck or killing him, did I? Just a little arsekickin'. That arsehole wants to put my best friend in jail and here's me talking about shooting a boot at him instead of shooting him. I'm turning into a frigging hippie."

"What would the other fellow say about that, Blue?" Capricorn asked while they watched the men get into the van and drive away. Soon only Bud Wise stood alone on the street watching the the taillights disappear. Then, with all witnesses now gone, he gingerly pulled his right hand from his suit coat pocket, carrying it to his mouth with his left hand where he tried to kiss it better. The motherly gesture seemed to fail because the FBI agent then cradled the hand and walked around in obvious pain, before getting into the grey Chev and driving away.

"In his report, Tinker or myself will be responsible for that hand," Capricorn announced. "You can bet that we are now wanted for assaulting a federal agent."

"Well, if I can remember where the bathroom is, I'm going to use it," Blue announced, "then I'm going to make myself a cup of tea and think about this. Care for a cup?"

They sat at opposite ends of the kitchen table, sipping in a semi-rhythm, the only common gesture they shared while their thoughts wandered through the night in search of some sense to what was happening, had happened, was going to happen. It was Capricorn who broke the silence, asking Blue if he could talk Tinker into going back to Canada.

"It's not going to stop. Men like Wise don't give up. They're determined to the point of stupidity. His type will starve to death before they'll stop hunting long enough to enjoy a meal or do anything else remotely related to the act of being alive. It's the military mind. You find people like him in all uniforms; soldiers, cops, bike gangs.

"With the formation of armies, we human beings learned to discipline our savagery and turned it into something far more lethal than it was ever meant to be. And Wise is about as mindless as that mentality comes."

"I don't agree with you about armies there, Capi. If it wasn't for armies, we'd all be Nazis now. Think about the Second World War, but what I'm thinking about right now is you and this Wise guy. I think you and him have more history than me and my grandfather, and it's not about bugging a teacher's office in high school, either. Bombs? Factories? Big league, as the other fellow says. Well?"

"I told you I had a friend who died, poisoned by the very factory his father worked in. What would you have done if it was Tinker? So I made a small bomb. A small explosion followed by a big fire. It was something I didn't take time to think about, because I didn't care at the time what happened to me. I was just pissed off, man, so I left big elephant tracks to lead the police back to me. For a reason I still don't know, the factory had a contract making some gadget to fit a gadget that was going into some military weapon so the feds made it their crime. Wise picked me up for questioning. From the start it was clear the guy hated me and was going slaughter me. I knew it and I was terrified. I was only a kid, a stupid kid, but a very scared one.

"When he stormed out of his office to get the paperwork started, there was nothing to think about. I just got up and walked out. I suppose that's the first commandment of law enforcement, never leave a suspect unattended, so I can only imagine Wise's face when he came back to the office, or the dressing down he got when he lost his prisoner.

"I haven't seen him since, but I've sensed him and smelled him a dozen times. I've become his very own one-man FBI project, but this is as tight as the noose has ever been."

"Karma was trying to explain karma to me, the way lives criss-cross all over time. We're in one hell of a tangle now. Your karma has become Tinker's karma, and everybody that touches either one of you winds up in it like a fly in molasses," Blue said, lighting a cigarette.

"Can I have one of those? Thanks," Capricorn said, exhaling a puff of smoke. He took the cigarette out of his mouth and studied it. "I'd hate to start this habit again."

"So why are you playing with it?" Blue wondered aloud. "Tired of being the good guy? Want to get back to the real world? Thinking about killing yourself? We got this guy back home, Monk, I was talking about him earlier. Reminds me of you a little bit. Just a little, though, but like you, he's trying to live different from everything he knows about himself. Only difference between you is that you don't claim to have seen the Virgin Mary. You just claim to be God."

"You believe that, don't you, but do you know what I'm scared of, Blue? That you might be right, that we're making it all up, that we're all really horse traders at heart. But in the end it's not about God, you know. It's about us, about being human. Paradise depends on us. Whether or not we ever lost it, Eden, I mean, doesn't matter. What does matter is that we can dream of it, conceive of it, ache for it. All that's missing is the will to discover it, or re-discover it, depending on what you believe, but that will come. Sometime."

"Actually, Capi, you remind me *a lot* of Monk, but there's no point trying to convert me. I'm already converted. I'm the Catholic here, remember, but let's get back to what you're saying about Tinker, about getting him out of here."

"There's no point to him dragging this out any more than he has to, Blue. Get him out of here."

"You let Kathy go and I'll talk to Tinker."

"Let Kathy go?"

"Yeah, let her go. She's under you spell, you know. Tinker would of been long gone if she'd of gone with him, but she wouldn't leave the commune to go to Cape Breton. Tell me that's not somebody under a spell?"

"Blue, Kathy's not my prisoner, but if what you say is true, I'll ask her to leave with Tinker. She doesn't need the commune to be who she is and maybe it would be a good thing for her if she did leave."

"Wouldn't hurt you any either, would it, Capi, to have Tinker run to Canada so you can feel the pressure come off you, but this time we're both pulling in the same direction, to quote the other fellow, so I'll talk to Tinker, but you know, when you're Public Enemy Number One it's not easy to just walk away from all that. I know from experience. 'Failure To Love' is going to be Number One by the end of the month, Peter? tells me, although he says he doesn't care. Wise words from a guy who can't take his eyes off the charts, don't you think? Reminds me of this guy back home, used to be a boxer, pretty good one I heard, until his brain got shook loose, so he's kind of punchy, but one time he says to me, talking about boxing, of course, 'Got my name in *Ring Magazine* once, page eight, column four. Didn't mean nuthin' to me.' I think of him every time Peter? tells me he doesn't care about our song being on the hit parade, as if I'm not watching it go up the charts myself like it was a beautiful woman walking down the street."

"Know what I like about you, Blue? Your trust in your fellow man," Capricorn sighed.

"Thanks, buddy, but I couldn't hold a candle to you in that department. That's why you're handling my money."

49

"You all know what the other fellow says is wrong with the world, dontcha?" Blue shouted into the microphone. "All that's wrong with the world is our— hit it there, Gerry," he ordered, commanding the fiddler to begin the three-chord intro that Blue called an overture, "all that's wrong ... take it, Nathan ... all that's wrong..." he continued as the fiddle and bagpipes swelled around him, pushing his acoustic guitar to keep up, "all that's wrong with the world is ... THE FAILURE TO LOVE! and here we go with our version of that great piece of wisdom, and our biggest hit so far, 'The Failure To Love'."

—

While the Human Rainbow Commune was going underground, Blue Cacophony was rising to the surface of San Francisco's counter-culture consciousness. Blue, Peter? pointed out, was a fairly anonymous member of the commune, and Gerry and Nathan had no philosophical connection with it at all. Barney was an even more obscure member than Blue. And there was no police link between Blue and Tinker, either, so there was no reason why Blue Cacophony couldn't go on playing, especially since Peter? had managed to get the band a gig at the Fillmore.

"It looks like everybody in San Francisco came out to see us tonight," Blue informed the band members after peeking out at the packed hall just before the group was scheduled to go on.

"It might have something to do with the fact that the Grateful Dead is playing later," Nathan suggested.

"Maybe it does, maybe it doesn't, as the other fellow says," Blue countered, "but we won't be opening for the Grateful Dead forever."

"We aren't opening for them," Gerry corrected. "We're opening for the band that's opening for them."

"Once we're done with this crowd, they'll be opening for us. Mark my words," Blue promised. "I just wish the others could be here to see us."

—

The commune members were giving a wide berth to places where Wise was most certain to be monitoring, especially following the headline news that Tinker had been arrested. Actually, Tinker had been arrested twenty times in two days, and the FBI and the city police were facing a rash of lawsuits. The Chinese community, which provided three Tinkers to the dragnet, was screaming racism even louder than the Black community, which produced two Tinkers. None of the arrests, however, had fired up the local papers and sizzled along the national wire services like the arrest of Reginald Regent the III, president of Fucdepor Petroleum, who was apprehended by an overzealous traffic cop who recognized Regent's face from the wanted poster in a nearby post office and wrestled the irate corporate boss into the local precinct in handcuffs. The arrest resulted in a public apology from the mayor and a promise from the governor to investigate the entire San Francisco police department.

Tulip, who had spent two days sitting outside the Fucdepor Petroleum Tower catching passing glimpses of Reginald Regent the III among his squad of flunkies, called the poster her finest work.

The embarrassed police force turned its frustrated rage on every long-haired hippie in the city, a rage made manifest by a city-wide sweep that led to several hundred charges for marijuana possession. Capricorn, having anticipated the city police's failure to appreciate the commune's practical joke, made a suggestion that whispered itself across the city well ahead of the drug busts.

In courtroom appearance after courtroom appearance, everyone arrested for possession of marijuana suppressed a smile as lab report after lab report was read before the judge, confirming that each and every defendant was guilty of carrying upon his or her person a weight ounce of oregano. On the courtroom steps, dozens of dismissed cases sat down, rolled the returned evidence into tubes and lit them, blowing the spicy smoke into the purple faces of the police while countless press photographers stood by, ready to record any trigger-happy activity.

―

"So there you have it," Blue announced from the stage as the final notes of "Failure To Love" wheezed from Nathan's reeds. "But there's something I want you people to know about that song. That song was stolen, pirated, as the other fellow says, and records of it and several other Blue Cacaphony originals are being sold all over the city. You can walk up to almost anybody who sells grass or acid and buy yourself a copy of the *Failure To Love* album. That's illegal, you know, to be selling an unauthorized album. In business that's a mortal sin the same as sex is a mortal sin in religion. Funny thing about mortal sins, though. Mortal sins and people are like the North Pole and a magnet. That's what's been happening to 'Failure To Love.' So many people are buying it that there's almost none left. Short supplies make everything more valuable. I know. I took economics. So it's no wonder that you might be tempted to leave here and go out and buy that illegal album. Destined to be one of the rare ones, I guess, because I can tell you this, Blue Cacophony will never, never, never record that album ourselves. And there's just a few left. So when you leave here tonight, you're going to be tempted, brother, as the other fellow says. Resist! Well, try to resist anyway. And if you can't, then you might as well enjoy it. Now here's a song you won't find on any album," Blue said, fingering the strings of his guitar.

"You've all heard about Tinker by now, I suppose, the mad bomber that's driving the FBI crazy. The FBI keeps warning us to be careful of him, but I don't think anybody is scared of a guy who's not scared of the oil barons. If you have to pick sides in this fight between Tinker and the FBI, who are you going to root for? The FBI? That would be like rooting for Fucdepor Petroleum. Or are you going to root for the guy that's driving them both nuts? We might even have ourselves a real live hero here."

Blue strummed in accompaniment to his introduction of the song. "What I hear about this Tinker reminds me of this guy I know back home, eh, Aloysius Dempsey. His father was Irish and his mother was Acadian so he didn't have a very Highland Scottish way of looking at the world except for what I taught him, but ... but...."

Blue's train of thought became distracted by a figure he recognized in the crowd but it took him a moment to place her amid the swirling psychedelic patterns that roamed the concert hall. "Mrs. Rubble, is that you? You stick out here like a hippie in a bingo hall, but thanks for coming. Sorry there people just recognized an old friend, so where was I? Oh, yeah, Tink— Aloysius. I guess I was just trying to say what the other fellow said so much better, Aloysius is the kind of guy who sneaks off to the bathroom with a book of poems under his shirt hoping you'd think it was *Playboy*. You know you don't need to be afraid of a guy like that, don't you, and that's what I think of when I think of this Tinker guy, as someone you don't have to be afraid of, so I wrote a song. Hope you like it.

>   Ain't afraid of no oxygen bomb
>   Any more than a cheerleader's pom-pom
>   But what really makes my pee run free
>   Are Agents Orange and Wise-eeee
>
>   But Tinker's on the run
>   Ain't got no bomb ain't got no gun
>   Just wants to find some peeeeace
>   Won't you leave him alone, pleeeease....

As soon as Blue Cacophony was off stage, Blue passed his guitar to Peter? and raced for the door to try to catch up to Mrs. Rubble whom he had seen leaving as the crowd rose to its feet in applause and participation in the last chorus of "The Ballad of Tinker." Mrs. Rubble was leaving in the company of several other people who looked like concert freaks but whom Blue suspected were undercover narcs or FBI agents grown uncomfortable with the mood of the concert following his impassioned musical appeal on Tinker's behalf.

Out on the street, the pseudo-hippies gathered to discuss Blue Cacophony's effect on the crowd, mumbling apologies to Mrs. Rubble who hurried from their midst toward the bus stop where Blue caught up to her as she stepped aboard.

"It was nice of you to come," Blue said, dropping a bus fare into the slot. "I didn't think you liked rock and roll," he continued, taking a seat beside her. "How's Tinker doing?"

"I'd do just fine if you'd stop trying to tip the cops off to who I am," Mrs. Rubble muttered in a decidedly Cape Breton accent, causing Blue to take a closer look, and to burst out laughing.

"She dupes to conquer, as the other fellow says. I saw those cops back at the Fillmore being polite to you, but I guess if you can fool me...."

"Well, everybody was acting as if your playing at this Fillmore place was something big so I was saying it was too bad I couldn't come down and see you. The rest of the story is Kathy and Karma's idea, with lots of help from Mrs. Rubble, especially her closet. Do you know who was standing outside the door watching everybody going in? Wise! Recognized him from the newscasts. He was wearing a cast on his hand. I winked at him and I think he got all flattered. Held the door open for me and everything. If he catches me now, I might have to marry him," Tinker told Blue.

"Wise winked at you, thinking you were Mrs. Rubble? What a sicko! Mrs. Rubble's fifty if she's a day. What kind of pervert goes around winking at old women like her?" Blue asked, reaching up to pull the cord that signalled the next stop.

"Where are we going?"

"Just going to take my mother out for a bite to eat at my favourite Chinese restaurant. We'll call Karma and Kathy to meet us there."

50

The four of them sat in a booth, Tinker trying to stay in character as he told the real women with them about the concert.

"Blue Cacophony just did four or five songs. In the time they had, they could have done ten, at least, except Blue would rather talk than sing. But the crowd was up for it. The band even got a standing ovation for the song Blue wrote about me, but I have to tell you, buddy," Tinker said, addressing Blue, "you even had me wanting to go out and buy one of your albums with that sermon about temptation. Farmer'd be proud of you."

"Farmer'd be proud of you too, Tink! Most wanted man in the state of California! I thought you really were Mrs. Rubble. I didn't think you hippies knew anything about things like makeup and brassieres and stuff like that," Blue said to Karma and Kathy. "It reminds me of the time Farmer took the old mare to the beauty parlour. I must have told you about that. Anyway, Farmer bought this old mare from this guy back home...."

—

While Blue retold the story about dyeing an old horse's brow and mane and reselling the same horse to the same owner as a younger horse, Tinker drifted off to ponder more urgent matters. At the Fillmore concert, it became clear that the FBI were seriously hunting him. Tinker didn't wink at the FBI agent as coolly as he made Blue believe. When he had come face to face with Wise outside the Fillmore, Tinker went weak just as a flake of mascara slipped into his eye, causing him to blink madly for a moment. When he regained his focus, he realized that Wise was winking back at him, and on the strength and stupidity of that gesture, Tinker regained his courage and continued on into the concert.

When Blue Cacophony started to bring "The Ballad of Tinker" to a close, Blue began ad libbing the words until the whole place was a frenzy of people chanting,

> Special Agent Wise, go see a head-shrinker
> It's you who's crazy, not Tinker!

The chanting grew more and more angry until Tinker wanted to be away from the place, and a dozen poorly disguised cops shared the sentiment, helping the old lady through the shouting crowd and out into the street where, they told her, she would be safe. He hurried off to the bus stop where Blue caught up to him.

There was also the fact that Peter?, along with his hero-writing, was setting up a meeting with Doctor Silver from Berkeley who wanted to discuss the concept of the oxygen engine in greater detail, but the more people wanted to know about his and Charlie's invention the less Tinker remembered about it. It all seemed to be spinning out of control and there was no telling how it would end up.

"...So now, every time Farmer takes a horse there, John Alex turns the hose on it full blast just to make sure the horse's coat won't run like a red shirt in white laundry," Blue wound up with a chuckle. "So what are we going to order?"

While Kathy and Karma shopped in the menu's noodle department Blue and Tinker's carnivorous appetites were asserting themselves among the sweet-and-sour chicken balls. Covered with a thick crust of batter and swimming in a pool of red sauce, you'd hardly notice it was meat at all, Blue explained across the table. It was a good compromise, he thought, taking his proof from the fact that no one argued with him.

"I wish I had a picture of this," Blue said to the girls, a nod of his head indicating his seat-mate. "Of course, Wise would sooner have a picture of you holding your number up, buddy, and personally, I think we should be out of here before your number's up – return to our own planet, as the other fellow says."

"It's something we really have to think about now, Tinker," Kathy said as Mr. Lo left with their orders. "I'm getting scared because nobody seems to be looking for me. What I mean is that it's my journal that started all this trouble. They arrested Cory and Tulip at the commune. Then they came looking for Cory again to try to find out about Tinker after they read the journal, but they never asked him about me. I went to see him yesterday just to make sure, and Cory told me that my name never came up in all the questioning, which is strange considering that my name is on the cover of the journal. So now I wonder if they aren't saying anything about me because they're trying not to scare me away, hoping to find me, then follow me to you."

"You wouldn't believe the route she took just to get us here," Karma said. "I think we walked halfway to Los Angeles through a maze of alleys."

Silence fell over the table while they digested Kathy's theory and waited for their food.

"Makes sense to me, Tinker," Blue said, lifting his elbows from the table so Mr. Lo could set his chicken balls and rice in front of him. "You and Kathy should pack up and leave for home right now. If you do, then in a week's time, this will all be nothing but a story to tell people who won't believe a word of it. Stay here and the other island awaits you, my friend, and I don't mean Alki-Seltzer, I mean Alki-traz."

"You come with us, we'll leave right now," Tinker said sharply.

Blue glanced across the booth at Karma, sensing that it wasn't a trip she was ready to take with him right now. The tone of Tinker's challenge told Blue that Tinker was sure Karma wasn't going anywhere. For a silent moment, he assessed the options while Karma gazed off as if she had never heard the conversation that had taken place between the two friends.

"Checkmate, as the other fellow says," Blue finally said as he picked up his fork.

"Blue," Tinker said at last, "I appreciate what you mean, but this isn't about you and me. The FBI aren't looking for you, just me. I'll decide when it's time for me to leave, okay? But I don't think you should attract any more attention to yourself like you did tonight. This is my problem, not yours. If I need your help I'll ask for it. You know that, don't you? But if I have to be thinking about your safety along with my own, then—"

"Then Tinker will lose his focus, Blue, and that's when mistakes get made," Kathy said.

"Got you finishing his sentences for him, does he?" Blue asked sharply. "Maybe in a couple of weeks he won't have to say anything for himself because you'll be speaking for him."

"Back off, Blue," Tinker warned, pushing the brown wig toward the back of his head.

"A fight here would be really wonderful," Karma said. "Then Mr. Lo can call the police and the two of you can explain your differences to them just before they put you in jail or deport you. Grow up, the two of you.

"Blue, Tinker is right. This is his problem. Your job is to be there for him if he needs you, but until then we have our own life to live. And Tinker, don't push Blue away. He just cares, although he won't use those words for it. Now, let's all of us go home, and Blue and I will take the leftovers for Barney. So say goodnight to Kathy, Blue, and kiss Mrs. Rubble on the cheek and we can go home to bed."

51

One wall of their room in the relocated Human Rainbow Commune had been divided into three panels by Karma, and within the space of one of them, she explored her seventh memory. The life within it hadn't yet begun to emerge from the blue wash of sky and desert-brown landscape but Blue was already guessing a wagon train.

."I saw the movie," he teased. "You die in the desert, arrows sticking out of everywhere, and Audie Murphy rides up just in time to hear your last words, then he buries you under a pile of stones and the rest of the movie belongs to him, or so he thinks because what old Audie doesn't know is that ... dun duh dah ... you're coming baaaack."

"Blue, why do you suppose so many people believe in an afterlife as long it's anywhere else but here?"

"Because it's like the other fellow says, everybody's dying to get off this planet. I think it would be a rotten trick to find out you have to come back, although," he said, reaching out to touch her, "some things just might be worth coming back for."

"You're right, you know," Karma said, giving his hand a squeeze then returning it to the vicinity of himself, the message clear. "It is a wagon train. I'll know more about it when I have to think about the people I'm painting."

—

"Well, Barney, old buddy, if the other fellow had told me a year ago that I'd be in San Francisco tonight with a hit record and my best friend on the Most Wanted list, I'd of had him in detox fifteen minutes after he said it, but here we are one year later and whaddya know, the other fellow was right," Blue confided, one hand scratching Karma's dog behind the ear, the other raising a beer to his lips. He sat in front of a blank scribbler page at the kitchen table, Barney sitting up quietly behind him, absorbing

| 285

the affection. The rest of the commune was in bed, slumbering through the hours between midnight and dawn.

"Last March, I was still in school trying to get a handle on economics and find a girl who'd go all the way. You're not a Catholic, Barney boy, so you don't know the embarrassment of going into the confessional month after month to tell the priest about your dirty deeds and hearing him ask if you committed them with somebody else. And when you say no, he asks you if it was with yourself. Who else, if there wasn't anybody there but yourself. But the priests like to catch you *red handed*, as the other fellow says, make you admit what they already know. It's not like a guy wants to be bragging to a priest or anything, but if he hears you month after month telling him that you haven't been with a girl, he's going to start thinking you're a real loser or something. Well, I'll have something to tell him when I go home, won't I, Barney?

"When I go home. Four little words I'm going to write right here, When. I. Go. Home. Those words scare me, Barney, know why? I get this feeling in the pit of my stomach when I say them now that says maybe they're not true, that maybe ... there's been guys from back home who've gone away and never made it back, fell in love or got killed or something like that. I never planned to be one of them, but this frigging city is like quicksand, just sucks you into it. Look at Tinker, in love and wanted by the law. Those things would never of happened to him back home. If we never left, he'd still be at Charlie's Guesso whistling at the girls and talking about his oxygen engine. His invention would never get him in trouble in Cape Breton, and then someday he'd get lucky and knock some girl up and marry her and make little Tinkers. But now the FBI want him to make licence plates, and if he winds up doing that, then it'll all be my fault, buddy," Blue confessed to Barney as he went to the fridge for another beer then returned to his chair. He reached over to the chair across from him and retrieved his guitar.

"If I go home...roam...dome...gloam..." Blue hummed, strumming his way through potential rhymes.

"If Tinker goes to jail it's going to be my fault, Barney, because tonight he put it right to me, come with me and we'll go right now, and I hesitated, and it's like the other fellow says, he who hesitates is lost. Only it might not be me who's lost, but Tinker, because I won't be going to jail. I'll just be sending my best friend there. He made me choose, but he knew what I was going to choose when he asked me. He knew I was going to choose to stay with you and Karma and the band. Well, to hell with him, that's what I say. To hell with him," Blue repeated, lifting the fresh bottle to his lips.

I just want to go home
never more to roam....

"I hate that, home and roam together. Almost every time you hear a song with home in it, the writer rhymes it with roam. Of course, they're natural partners because one is the opposite of the other, you either stay home, or you roam. I roamed and look where it got me, as far from home as a man can walk on this frigging continent. It's just a matter of turning around and walking back, is that what you think, Barney? Not that simple, my boy. Too many pieces of me scattered around this city for me to cram them all back into a suitcase and just go back home. There's Tinker. What do I tell his mother when I go home without him? That I lost him somewhere along the way? And what would the band do without me and you harmonizing us right into fame? And Karma, God bless her, and I think that He has. I can't turn my back on her even to face homeward, so what we got to do, Barney, old buddy, is wait.

"It feels like spring here but it's only the first of March back home, and that means summer's a long way away yet. By June, if we hang in here, everybody will feel different, feel like being home for the summer. Tinker will hear the call to go home and we'll be just like two salmon coming back to the Margaree River to give birth to their young; Tinker and I'll be homeward bound. And Karma and Kathy, too, I hope, and me and you. I know you're Karma's dog, but sometimes you feel like mine, know what I mean?"

Blue thought about what he meant by his last remark as he drank deeply off his beer.

"What I mean is that I used to have a dog once, too. Cu we called him. Cu, you see, is the Gaelic word for dog. We Scots are good at that, calling a thing what it is. Back home, our town faces a broad cove on the Gulf of St. Lawrence, and to the north there's this big river, and to the south there's this little brook. Those three things pretty well make the borders for the town. Know what we call them? Broad Cove, The Big River and The Little Brook. That's what I mean, you call a thing what it is, so when it came to naming the puppy I had, I called him Cu, not that I had any Gaelic of my own, of course, but everybody grows up knowing a few words like *poch ma hon* which means kiss my arse and stuff like that, and *cu's* a pretty easy word to remember and just as easy to spell which doesn't happen often in Gaelic, so since Cu was a *cu*, I called him Cu.

"Cu was no German shepherd like you. The dogs back home don't pay a lot of attention to their nationalities. Like if this Scotch terrier was walking down street and saw a French poodle in heat, he's not going to spend a lot of time worry about race, creed or religion, as the other fellow says, he's just going to join the pack that's howling around her, and good luck to the children. So by the time I got a puppy, this kind of activity had been going on among the different dogs in our town for longer than I was alive, so the only thing you could be sure of about Cu was that he was a dog. 'What kind?' some people asked. Now if they were asking me what kind of person I was, well I could take them all the way back to Scotland and the Hebrides and recite my great-grandfathers for seven or eight generations, but I never held it against my dog that he didn't even know who his father was.

"Anyway, Cu was my best friend until Tinker came along, but you know, in some ways Cu was still my best friend because we used to do this a lot, this very thing. Some nights I'd have to stay up late studying, or just stay up after a dance and sit in the kitchen beside the coal stove and Cu would lay beside me and we'd listen to a hockey game if I could pick one up on the radio, or listen to WWVA in Wheeling, West Virginia, or we'd just talk. That's what this reminds me of, me and you reminding me of me and Cu, and me telling Cu my troubles, stuff I couldn't even tell Tinker, stuff not sinful enough to tell the priest, so I'd confess to Cu that I wish I could be a musician and have all these girls wanting to go out with me and make lots of money. When you get right down to it, the things I told my dog were much more important than anything I could tell my priest or my mother or my best friend. With a dog, you can be scared or lonely or sad, and they just look up at you with big brown eyes just the way you're doing now, and never say a word about it.

"Did I ever tell you what Farmer once said to me about Cu's eyes? Farmer was eating a sandwich with lots of meat in it and Cu just lay there looking up at him – not begging 'cause I taught him not to, just looking – and Farmer's trying to ignore him. Finally he tears off half the sandwich and throws it in front of Cu and says to me, 'If I had that dog's eyes I'd never have to buy another drink as long as I live.'

"So this whole thing is making me homesick, Barney, me and you in the kitchen talking like a couple of old friends, sharing a beer, trying to figure life out. Sometimes, just when I figure I got it figured out, along comes something new to smash my figuring all to hell, like Tinker tonight, and Karma, too. I thought I was trying to get us all safely out of the city and back home and what happens? I get my bluff called and I didn't even know I was bluffing. I thought I just wanted to go home.

I just want to go home
But Karma just wants to go ooohm....

52

Capricorn's arrest stunned the Human Rainbow Commune.

After Tulip and Cory had broken the news, the members sat around the council table, first in inarticulate silence, then trying to piece together what they had heard.

Cory explained that Special Agent Bud Wise had been picking up members of the Black Panthers, questioning them, accusing them of being connected the Human Rainbow Commune and the elusive Tinker, asking them if they had heard anything regarding the existence of an oxygen bomb.

"The brothers," Cory explained, "couldn't help but make half-hearted denials about a conspiracy between the Panthers and the commune to produce an oxygen bomb. Ah, man, we hardly ever get a honky FBI guy so scared. If he wants to believe in the oxygen bomb or the System or even Santa Claus, that's none of our business, is it? So the brothers kind of helped Wise hang on to that belief by not quite denying that Tinker and his bomb exist. Tinker doesn't really have a bomb, does he?"

The week before Easter, Cory told them, one of the Panthers, whom Cory called Chug, had been picked up and taken to Wise's office for questioning. In the middle of being grilled by Wise in his own office, another agent knocked on the door and said that Reginald Regent the III was on the phone. Wise told the guy he would take the call in the office next door, telling Chug to stay where he was until Wise got back. Chug recognized the name of Reginald Regent the III as being one of half the population of San Francisco who was arrested when the counterfeit Tinker posters hit the city's post offices, and the one person whose arrest made so many headlines that anyone not already buried for at least a week was aware of who he was. Chug saw the blinking light on the phone on Wise's desk and picked it up. Not good manners, but then again, it was the FBI that invented wire-tapping, Cory reminded the commune council.

"Old Reggie the III was raging at Wise that Fucdepor shareholders were becoming unnaturally interested in, and worried about the idea of an oxygen engine. 'That engine, if it works, will destroy this country's ecomomy as we know it, replacing it with some idealist's idea that everybody can generate their own power for a few pennies a day. Communism! Wise, you'd better find this fucking Tinker character and get rid of him.' Christ, he told Wise, if the oxygen bomb actually exists it couldn't do more damage than the reality of the oxygen engine. 'Bring those engine plans to me,' the president of Fucdepor Petroleum ordered.

Wise, clearly intimidated, stuttered and muttered and tried to explain that being an FBI agent there were certain rules he was required to follow, and getting rid of people, if he understood the petroleum president's message correctly, wasn't part of the bargain.

"You've already made your bargain with the Devil, Wise," Reginald Regent the III told him. "I make your rules now. But I can assure you that if this Tinker character is caught and shot while trying to escape or simply disappears, there will be no serious legal consequences. You're not my only pet cop, but if you don't turn him up by the end of the week, your own career with the Bureau is as dead as this Tinker is going to be, and your second career as my mole in the FBI dies along with it. I have every record of every bonus ever wired from this company to your account for every favour you've ever done for Fucdepor. Get the job done, and when it's done, you can begin thinking about retiring and taking on the role of head of security for Fucdepor." With that, Reginald Regent III slammed the phone in Wise's ear, and Chug slowly lowered the phone he was holding.

"Chug told me this after they released him. I had to get in touch with Tinker. I couldn't chance being followed here, so I wrote what I just told you in a note and left it at the Aquarius Café to be passed along to the first commune member who came in," Cory explained.

"And that was me," Tulip said, picking up the story.

Tulip had brought the note back to Capricorn. When he read it, he told Tulip that the conversation Chug overheard proved beyond a doubt that democracy was a facade behind which corporations like Fucdepor Petroleum hid and governed the country only in their own best interests. Anyone who gets in their way is expendable, he had informed Tulip.

"When I asked Capricorn if we should rush a message to Tinker, he said no. If there was any surveillance on the commune that we're not aware of, it could be Tinker's death warrant. Tinker's doing a fine job of hiding himself, Capricorn said, but there's something else we can do to help Tinker and every man, woman and child in the United States of America."

With that, Capricorn spent the night fashioning remote surveillance equipment from the accumulated inventory of the commune's recent recording venture. He then asked Tulip to help him load up the van. Early next morning, Good Friday, a holiday when the downtown business sector was tomb-quiet, Tulip and Capricorn drove to the sixty-story Fucdepor Center where the monster petroleum company kept penthouse offices that oversaw its international purchases of oil and governments around the world. He asked Tulip if she would wait in the van for him to come back. "If I walk out of the building, just wait and I'll come to you, but if I come out running, start the van and come for me," he instructed, and made his way toward the building.

One of the maintenance crew coming on shift didn't object to Capricorn standing behind him, whistling softly while he waited for the door to be opened so the two of them could get to work. The maintenance man even held the door open for him, since Capricorn was burdened down with an obviously heavy toolbox.

What would happen inside, according to Tulip, who listened through the night while Capricorn planned it all out aloud so he could listen to his own thoughts, and so Tulip could question them, was that Capricorn would find his way to the lockers where the staff coveralls and utility belts were stored. Then he would make his way to the penthouse suites and install eavesdroppers so he could listen to conversations from inside the van parked below. If Reginald Regent III could be taped making the kind of statements Chug had reported, and those tapes were turned over to the proper authorities, i.e., the underground papers and radios, it would go a long way toward taking the heat off Tinker, perhaps buy enough time for the truth about Tinker to get out, or better still, for people to forget about Tinker altogether.

Depending on the content of the tapes, they could also force the Senate or President to order an FBI investigation of Reginald Regent III, Fucdepor Petroleum and Special Agent Bud Wise.

Tulip, in her van, imagined Capricorn's progress up the elevator, picking the lock, prowling through the offices, placing his tiny microphones. The operation was going flawlessly until her visualization was interrupted by the very real arrival of a fleet of three limousines, pulling to a halt before the glass doors of the main entrance. Someone important seemed to emerge from every door the uniformed chauffeurs opened, each accompanied by two or three thick, dark thugs in sunglasses and black leather gloves. They made their way into the building, and from the way the rest deferred, and from her own memories of sketching him, Tulip knew that the first man going through the door was Reginald Regent III.

Immobilized, Tulip slipped into her head to try help Capricorn. There was no other hope for him. With no physical way to send a warning, she tried to subdue her panic by transmitting danger signals to Capricorn through spiritual vibrations. Remaining calm did not, unfortunately, stop the film of Capricorn's situation from un-spooling itself behind her eyes. She saw armed bodyguards rushing him, guns out, cornering him, waiting to be told by Reginald Regent III what to do. He all but ordered Agent Wise to have Tinker killed. Why not Capricorn?

The long, suspended moment of merely imagining Capricorn's danger was shattered by the siren-wailing arrival an FBI vehicle from which leapt a plainclothes agent. Although she couldn't see his face, Tulip knew that the man with his arm in a sling was Wise.

A long period of fear-filled time passed before the main doors re-opened and FBI Special Agent Bud Wise, assisted by the muscle-bound corps from Fucdepor, concealed Capricorn in their midst and led him to the car in which Wise had arrived. Surrounded like a fortress by the four corporate limos driven by the bodyguards, Wise's car moved away from the Fucdepor Centre.

Tulip started the engine and pulled away from the curb, following the convoy. It led her not to the FBI office building where most of the federal agency's business was carried out, and where she and Cory had been questioned, but to a different building several blocks away. Once she had watched Capricorn shoved inside that building by Wise and the petroleum company strongmen, she brought the news of Capricorn's arrest back to the Human Rainbow Commune, where a deep, fearful silence punctuated the end of her story.

53

By Good Friday night there was still no mention of Capricorn's arrest in the news. The commune members kept vigil at the windows, waiting for what many expected to be an inevitable FBI raid on the house. Throughout the night, they monitored all directions, relieving each other in shifts.

Blue and Karma, having finished a tour of duty, were back in their room, Karma losing herself in her painting, Blue strumming his guitar, toying with ideas for the ninety-sixth verse of "The Red Lobster."

"If they come tonight," Blue said finally, "I just want you to know that what I said one time about you being a nun, well, I didn't mean it the way it sounded, Karm. It's just that ever since the accident, it hasn't been the same with us. You've been, I don't know, far away or something, and we hardly ever, you know, do it any more or anything. Everything just seems to be changing so fast around here, with us, with me, I'm even the friggin' president now," having been the surprise choice by the commune members to fill in for Capricorn since his arrest – the other members figuring he was the person most likely to come up with a scheme to rescue their leader and his friend.

"I don't know what to tell you, Blue," Karma said, staying concentrated on her task, a small brush working character into the desert landscape. "But yes, you're right, something is changing. Maybe you're right about me being a nun. There's just so much confusion in me."

"You, confused!" Blue said. "Now there's a diagnosis I wouldn't of made. I thought you always knew exactly what you believed. Remember you told me once that if a person knows what he believes then he knows who he is? If you're confused, God help the rest of us."

"He probably will. Blue, what do you think will happen?"

"If, on the off chance that God doesn't help us, you mean? There's a few things I've been thinking over. Capricorn should of phoned a lawyer by now. We should of heard something. Maybe they were trying to beat some information out of him and they killed him instead. Don't look so shocked! You heard what Cory said. They want to kill Tinker, don't they? Boy, there was never any of this in Modern World Problems. Back when I was in high school, it was just us and the Commies, and we were the good guys. Now our own friggin' government is out to get us for just trying to sit around and talk about a better world. Your frigging government, I should say. I bet you'd never find the Mounties treating Canadians like criminals. Unless they were Commies, of course, but it's legal to be a communist in Canada. We call them NDPers.

"The other thing that could of happened is that they're just torturing Capricorn, keeping him alive to get information. But I can't figure out why Wise hasn't been calling the newspapers and the television people, getting his mug on the front page. It should be in the post office, I think.

"Or maybe because it's the Easter weekend, people aren't watching the news very much, and Wise is like one of those guys that goes around in a long overcoat, flashing his thing at little old ladies, or his little thing at old ladies, as the other fellow says. It's no fun doing it unless you have an audience, and Wise likes an audience, that much I know. I hope that's the only thing I have in common with that creep.

"If we get through the night, Karma, we have to talk about moving out of here in the morning, all of us, to a new place."

The Saturday morning newscasts made no mention of Capricorn's arrest, although Blue noted while turning the tuning dial up and down the amber panel of numbers, that two stations were playing "Failure To Love." There was no time to stop to listen.

Commune members were in various stages of sleep, some who were on the late shift watching for the FBI, deep in slumber, others groggily trying to snap themselves awake with coffee.

Blue said that he wanted everybody around the council table by noon. Then, accompanied by Barney, he left the commune.

"Hello, Mrs. Rubble. Is the man of the house around?" he asked into the pay phone.

"No, I'm afraid there's no man around this house," Mrs. Rubble replied.

"It's okay, Mrs. Rubble, it's Blue. Can I talk to your boarder?"

"I don't have a boarder anymore, Blue. The two of them left last night."

"And never came back?" Blue asked, panic rising.

"They won't be coming back. They moved."

"Where?"

"They didn't want me to ask, so I didn't, but I miss him something awful."

—

Blue and Barney walked the distance to Mr. Lo's, where Blue sat at the counter and ordered two hamburgers, one to go with no bun, and asked in a whisper Mr. Lo barely understood, if he had seen either of Blue's friends.

"Not since they were here with you," Mr. Lo replied, and their conversation fell to other topics that Blue distractedly engaged in until a cup of tea was set before him. Blue looked out from his fog of worry into Mr. Lo's smiling face.

"You look not so good. Drink this good tea. Remember, we be doing this for five thousand years."

Blue and Barney returned to the commune before noon, and Blue called the council meeting to order. Two subjects were on everyone's mind: what, if anything, they could do to help Capricorn, and whether or not they should move. Blue kept silent while others discussed the options open to them. Should they move all together to another residence like they did before? Should they split up and scatter around the city, using the Aquarius Café as an information and message drop? Should they stay put?

"I'm staying put," Blue announced as the discussion petered out without resolution. "There's no right or wrong way to do this. We're just groping in the dark, to quote the other fellow. I think everyone should make up his or her own mind about what they want to do or where they want to go. I've made up my mind. I'm staying."

"Why?" asked several voices at once.

"Because I'm pissed off, that's why! They made my best friend disappear. God knows what's happened to Capricorn. They've got us all shitting our pants every time we see a shadow, and that's what they want. It gives them big hard-ons to throw their weight around and beat people up or even kill them. So I'm staying put and I'm staying calm, because we need to find a way to help Capricorn. That's what you want me to do, isn't it, find a way? I know enough about selling horses to know that you don't lose your temper in the middle of making a deal. It'll just cost you money and maybe even a customer you could of sold another horse to later on. Just because I'm pissed off doesn't mean I'm stupid. If we stay calm we'll find a way."

Blue's passion made up everyone's mind. The members of the Human Rainbow Commune voted to the person to remain where they were. "We're all in the same boat, so we might as well sink or float together," Tulip noted. "I'm glad. Besides, I'm not worried about Capricorn betraying us or where we are, no matter what they do to him."

"Truth serum," Blue said. "He couldn't do much against that."

"Has anyone got any ideas?" Tulip asked.

"As long as nobody knows Capricorn has been captured, there's nothing anybody can do," Blue said. "What we have to do is make Wise show him to us so we can see he's all right, and the best way to do that is to tell the newspapers ourselves. We'll just call them and tell them and a reporter will talk to the FBI. They can't lie to the newspapers, can they? At least then people will be watching, following the news, so they'll have to treat Capricorn well. Once we know he's alright and where he is, we can plan how to help him."

"Well, Capricorn didn't rise up singing on Easter Sunday morning after all," Blue said to Karma as he turned the radio dial from one station to another. There was nothing on the news about Capricorn. Blue was afraid there wouldn't be. On Saturday afternoon, he went back to the phone booth with a pocketful of quarters and called every major radio station and newspaper in the phone book. Over the holiday weekend, there was barely anyone available, and barely any interest in the anonymous caller. News people who had drawn the short straw for the long weekend yawned questions back to Blue, who refused to give his name, and told him they would look into his claim that the FBI were holding Capricorn prisoner and withholding his right to call a lawyer. Obviously no one had called the FBI or the FBI had lied. The lack of news was eating away at Blue's stomach, aided by the fact that he had not heard from Tinker or Kathy since they left Mrs. Rubble's apartment.

"I have to go," Blue told Karma as he threw the bedclothes back and got up.

"Where are you going?"

"I haven't been to church since Christmas, and something tells me it might be a good idea to make my Easter Duties. The only thing that can guarantee a Catholic will go to hell is if he dies without making his Easter Duties, going to confession and communion. Miss that and that's the biggie when it comes to sins."

"I'm coming with you, Blue," Karma said, getting up as well.

A couple of hippies in a crowd of Easter bonnets, Blue thought after coming out of the confessional. He and Karma made their way down the aisle, looking for a pew that wasn't jammed with once-a-year families, most of whom frowned at the threat of intrusion from these two denim-clad dregs from Haight-Ashbury. Finally, Blue pushed his way into a pew, making room for the two of them, and knelt to say his penance before Mass began.

A decade of the rosary and three "Our Fathers," not bad for a guy who just confessed to being the head of a commune that was filled with all sorts of non-Catholic theories about how the world should be run. Finishing his penance, Blue remained kneeling.

God, he said in his head, yesterday, Tulip said we were all in the same boat, and I've been thinking ever since about that night Tinker and me stole Rory Dave's lobster boat to pull some of his traps and make some money selling our own live lobsters. First, the engine quit, then the sea started heaving us around, then Tinker and I started heaving our suppers over the side and nobody even knew we were out there. We made some pretty serious deals that night and we didn't drown. We didn't even get caught. You just washed us up near the Marsh wharf at dawn, and we walked home. The big question in town for a week was how did Rory Dave's boat get tied up way down there? We never told a soul.

I didn't keep all the promises I made that time, but God, I was only sixteen, just a kid. But I never forgot, and I'll never forget how it felt to crawl into my bed that morning, tired and warm and safe when I suppose I should of been dead or at least in jail. That was my dark night of the soul, to quote the other fellow, and ever since then I've known You were there, even when I didn't wear the halo I promised.

I'm not a kid any more, God, but I'm in just as much trouble. More! We all are, like Tulip said, in the same boat and people are hoping I can get them out of it. I wouldn't say this to just anybody, but You already know that I'm scared as hell— I mean heck, scared as heck, don't You? It's a different kind of a boat, but the fear's the same. At least this time, I'm in a state of grace which is more than I can say for that other time in the boat. I've been to confession, as You've heard, and Karma and me didn't even do it last night or anything. Actually, we haven't even done it for quite a while, which probably makes You happier than me, but I'll offer that up for Your help. I don't know what to do.

And God, Tinker's been gone for a couple of days and I haven't heard from him. I think he's safe, but the truth is no one's safe anymore, not really. I know Tinker promised You that night in Rory Dave's boat that he'd join the priesthood, but don't hold it against him now, please. Just get the two of us out of this, okay, and Capricorn and Karma and Kathy and Tulip and all the others at the commune. Thanks for Your time, God, and I'll probably be talking to You again. In fact, there's a pretty good chance of that. Oh, and Happy Easter. Amen.

"Let's walk to Mr. Lo's and get breakfast," Blue suggested after Mass. "You never know, maybe there's a message...."

There wasn't. They sat across from each other in what had become their own booth and waited for Mr. Lo to bring breakfast, bacon and eggs for Blue, unbuttered toast and jam for Karma, tea for both of them, Mr. Lo's choice since Blue had long since given up arguing that the restaurant should be offering King Cole on its menu.

"I'll tell you one thing for sure, Tinker put his last tank of Fucdepor gas in the Plymouth," Blue said, making small talk to drown out the noise in his head.

"Did they take the Plymouth?" Karma asked.

"That's a question I didn't ask Mrs. Rubble, but of course they did. Tinker might go somewhere without me, but he'd never go anywhere without the Plymouth."

"Would he go back to Canada without you?"

"No way! Maybe. I don't know. Nobody's ever wanted to kill Tinker before. Well, maybe this nun in grade nine. Kathy wanted him to go, said she'd go with him, and he's only one day's hard driving away from Canada, and that's not far when your life's at stake. There would of been a message, though, I know that."

"Unless there wasn't time," Karma said. "Would you be angry if he is gone?"

"No way! Maybe. I don't know. He should of told me. Wherever he is, he should of told me."

"Unless he couldn't."

"Unless he couldn't. When we get back to the commune, we're going to start watching the watchers, as the other fellow says. We're going to take shifts watching the task force's office, seeing who goes in, who comes out. See if we can figure out what they're up to. Maybe we'll see Capricorn or Tinker."

"Or Kathy," Karma said.

"Both our best friends gone just like that," Blue noted with a snap of his fingers. "Happy Easter," he said as Mr. Lo placed their food in front of them, then ordered a burger without the bun to go.

54

It wasn't the brightest idea I ever had, Blue told himself, as he sat in the shadowed doorway across the street from the FBI offices where Wise's task force was located. The drizzle made it hard for him to write in the surveillance scribbler in which they noted the comings and goings of the agents. They weren't sure how they would use the information, but they agreed some record should be kept.

The commune members were divided into shifts, two working together from the parked van during the day, from 8 a.m. to 8 p.m., and one person observing during the night shift. Blue was doing the first four-hour shift, eight-to-midnight, of the around-the-clock watch. Leadership, he decided, wasn't all it was cracked up to be.

Because it was late, and a holiday, there wasn't much activity around the door of the building, although God knew what was taking place behind its walls. The same grey Chev that Wise had been driving the night of the raid on the former commune house was in the parking lot beside the building. Blue tried to kill time by working on some songs, but discovered that whenever he was writing lyrics he sang them aloud, sometimes the same line over and over, and that wasn't such a great idea under the current circumstances. The rain reminded him of a story.

It was raining the night the Mounties arrested Monk for running a still. It was inevitable they were going to catch him sometime because no matter how carefully he hid his operation, he could not hide his reputation. The Mounties couldn't help but know who made the best moonshine on Cape Breton Island. Nobody turned Monk in, but nobody drinking Monk's booze would wake up blind in the morning, either. People respected his product, talked about it. Word gets around, so the Mounties had been watching for a long, long time, but Monk stayed invisible.

Then one night they walked in on him as he sat in a drizzle not much different that the one Blue was sitting in now. He was sitting around as casual as a man feeding wood to his kitchen stove, except that it was an open flame under a copper pot. He didn't put up any resistance.

The Mounties were red-faced when Monk went before the judge, and faced the evidence against him, a bottle filled with the contents of his still. It was strong stuff ... for tea. The judge had a good laugh over that and let Monk go.

Remembering, it reminded Blue of how Capricorn talked half the city of San Francisco into carrying around plastic bags of oregano, but the judges here didn't have the same sense of humour as the ones back home. Blue realized that the imaginary audience for this story he was telling about Monk was Capricorn, and wondered if he was inside the building. He didn't seem to be in any of the city's lockups. Between them, Cory and Peter? knew enough people in the jails to quickly learn that no one resembling Capricorn was in any place prisoners are normally kept. In case Capricorn was inside the FBI offices, Blue cast the telling of his story in that direction, a light-hearted jail story to pick up Capricorn's spirits.

What Monk did every time he walked out to his still, Blue continued telling Capricorn, was stop and make a cup of tea. He made it in a copper pot attached to coils of pipe that could have easily been mistaken for a still. By the time he got a fire lit and the water boiling in the vat, then added the tea, waited for it to steep and poured himself a cup, Monk figured that if the Mounties were following him, they would have made their move by now. So Monk would enjoy his tea, put the fire out and continue on his way to where he hid his still.

"You're the luckiest son of a bitch in the world," Farmer told Monk. "There must be something to that business of yours of putting a rosary in the still when you're running the shine."

In a few minutes, Blue would be getting relieved and he checked the scribbler to see his night's work.

9:15 - a guy went into the building.
10:16 - two guys come out of the building.
10:17 - one of the guys runs back into the building.
10:18 - the other guy is standing in front of the building.
10:26 - the first guy comes back out with a briefcase.
11:43 - a guy goes into the building.

55

Media silence concerning Capricorn's arrest carried over into Easter Monday, increasing to panic the level of alarm members of the Human Rainbow Commune felt for his safety. Blue could feel the failing expectations of those around him as minutes dragged into hours and hours into days. They had hoped Blue would come up with a plan that would free Capricorn, or at least verify that he was still alive and all right. The fact that newspapers and television stations had ignored his news leak left him frustrated and edgy with everyone.

"What am I supposed to do?" he asked Karma. "Go to the newspapers and write the story myself?" Hearing his own question, he picked up his guitar case, called Barney and left the commune for a rehearsal, a decision that did not rest easy with the rest of the commune's population who felt that Blue was escaping into an activity that could have waited until Capricorn came back.

—

"Peter??" Blue asked, as the band prepared for its rehearsal. "How well do you know that people at that paper you write for?"

"*The Subterranean*? Pretty well. Why?"

"I called every newspaper and television station in San Francisco telling them about Capricorn's arrest. None of them care."

"Of course they don't care, Blue. Fucdepor Petroleum or their subsidiaries probably own most of the mainstream media in this city, and people like Reginald Regent III sit on the boards of the others. If someone like Reggie Regent the Third puts the word out to ignore any rumours about Capricorn's arrest, then it will be ignored. To the establishment, freedom of the press means the freedom not to print any story that doesn't go well with morning coffee, or one that might upset the Masters of the State, as I call them."

Blue explained his rationale behind getting out the information that Capricorn had been arrested: first for his protection, and also to get the FBI to acknowledge that they had him in custody.

"You should have come to me earlier," Peter? told Blue, ignoring Blue's explanation that they had wanted to involve as few people as possible, especially with Reginald Regent the Turd throwing around words like "kill" and "disappear."

"*The Subterranean* is preparing to go to press this afternoon," Peter? continued. "Tomorrow is its distribution day. No one over there's going to be happy to hear from me at the last minute, but I'll see what I can do.

"But I need something from you, too, Blue. I've got this gig lined up for Saturday night. I know you have a lot on your mind but this could turn into something really big. Promise me you'll be there."

"It's a promise so long as there's nobody's wake I have to go to, or if I'm not in jail myself. Life must go on, as the other fellow says."

—

Karma's seventh life was finished when Blue entered the room later that afternoon. She wasn't there, so Blue had time to sit on a chair and study it. He had been right. It was a covered wagon. It had been making its way across the desert, and beyond that parched distance he could see hazy blue mountains, snow-capped, almost hear the cold streams of water leaking down the mountainside in trickles and rushes to feed the fertile foothills that rose gently before them. Those images were probably the last this family saw before thirst overtook them. The horses lay in brown heaps of death beside the weathered, torn wagon, and four people – a father, a mother holding an infant, and a young boy lying beside the father – were exposed to a sun whose only act of mercy was that it had finally taken the suffering away from this lost family.

Blue felt the conviction in Karma's painting, knew somewhere inside himself that this was more than a picture, that this was a painful portrait that had nothing to do with Audie Murphy. That Karma believed she was one of the victims she depicted wasn't the important thing, the tragedy was. Her other lives had not all been pleasant pictures but they had been filled with life. *The Covered Wagon*, as Blue found himself naming it, was not. Yet it was filled with a disturbing sense of peace at last.

Blue heard the beads of the door tinkling behind him and grew more alert. "What do you think?" Karma asked.

"Where's the arrows? These people should of been full of arrows, shouldn't they?"

"It wasn't Indians who killed them, Blue," Karma said quietly. "It was the heat. They died of thirst."

"Art buyers would pay a lot more for arrows sticking out of those bodies, I bet," Blue went on. "So where was your old buddy Buddha this time? When the lion was dying, he fed them the meat of his own bones, you told me. You'd think he'd of at least turned himself into a bucket of cold water for these people, especially with a baby with them. Which one are you?"

Karma didn't answer.

"Did you hear any more about Capricorn?" she asked. Blue told her about Peter? and his hope that the story would begin to come out on Tuesday, forcing the FBI to acknowledge that they had Capricorn. Peter? was going to talk to a couple of radio stations, as well, but wanted Blue to do the interviews since he had a high profile at the moment because of Blue Cacophony, and especially because of "Failure To Love."

"That worries me," Karma said. "It will draw so much attention to you. How do you feel about it?" she asked.

"I'd rather be in Philadelphia, as the other fellow says, but a man's got to do what a man's got to do, and I guess I got to go on the radio and tell people about Capricorn. It might help Tinker, too."

"I think about Kathy a lot," Karma confided.

"You think about her, but do you worry about her, too?"

"I try not to, Blue. Worrying is destructive to the person doing the worrying, and it doesn't resolve anything. When I find myself starting to worry, I paint or I meditate, or pray that she's okay."

"You keep doing that because if she's okay there's a good chance Tinker is, too. But that tells me something about your painting there. If you were painting that picture instead of worrying, then I think all those dead people laying around there are your worries about Kathy and Tinker, your fears for them and their unborn children, that's what I think."

Karma studied her own work thoughtfully from Blue's observations. "Maybe you're right. Maybe I am, but of all the people in the world, you're the last person I want to have to defend my life to."

"Well, you'll just have to do what you were talking about just now. When I'm bothering you, forget about me, and when I'm not bothering you, love me, and I'll do the same for you. Oh, yes, and it's a really, really good painting. Even without the arrows."

—

Despite challenging Karma on her claim that she did not worry, or at least tried not to worry, Blue experimented with loosening the lump of fear in his stomach by taking up his guitar and turning his thoughts to the ninety-sixth verse of "The Red Lobster," which he hadn't been able to get moving for some time now. Leaving Capricorn and Tinker to look after themselves for a while, he plunged his imagination into the cold water of the Gulf of St. Lawrence and swam around looking for images he could mould into lyrics for his epic undertaking.

After several efforts, resulting in numerous scratched-out lines on several scribbler pages, Blue began to find a direction he could follow, and following it to the end, he squiggled out the last almost illegible words before sitting back finally with his guitar to feel the verse flow along the instrument's strings to find its proper place in the sequence of romantic insights that comprised the slowly-completing-itself song:

> You're so pretty
> and such a fine talker

your words lure me
out of Davy Jones' locker
But I lie gasping
for air on dry land
It feels like
I'm going to be eaten
right out of your hand

Red lobster, red lobster
Don't you dare sob, sir,
'Cause love is you, and love is her
You're the meat. She's the but-tur

56

Blue could hardly believe that in the more than three hours he was lost in his own creativity there hadn't been a thought of Capricorn or Tinker or Kathy. He actually felt relaxed, in a tired kind of way, and brought his eyes up to study Karma's painting again. Maybe she was right, that there was nobody dead in that desert sand but her and her family a hundred ago or whenever it was. And maybe, he thought, recalling Tinker's and his crossing of the desert, that if they had met ghosts that night it wouldn't have been a war party of Indians at all, but a wagon train of dead people, Karma among them because they were fated to meet somewhere or sometime. He'd have to remember to tell her that.

Or maybe not.

He wanted to stay in their bedroom, ease himself into verse ninety-seven, but the day was growing dully toward evening and his shift in the doorway across from the FBI's offices. He went to the kitchen to make a sandwich to eat and one to take with him.

Tulip had the surveillance reports from the first shifts spread across the table, studying them. "I wonder if we shouldn't be trying to follow the agents who leave the office. Maybe they are going to where Capricorn is."

"Wise's car was there all day until I left at midnight," Blue said, looking at the reports. "It says here he left after one in the morning and came back before eight. The flies go where the honey is, to quote the other fella. I think Wise'd be where Capricorn is. We don't have enough people to follow everyone who comes and goes."

"Blue, I'm worried," Tulip confided, her admission bringing back the lump of worry that he had made disappear using Karma's technique.

"Nothing to be worried about, Tulip. We just watch the FBI office until they bring Capricorn out."

"Then what?"

"We'll follow them, for one thing, see where they take him, but you know what we really need? A camera. If we could take Capricorn's picture with Wise, that'd really prove we're right. We could give it to the papers, to Peter?'s friends' paper, at least. That's what we need, a camera." He was glad he had thought of a camera, although there wasn't a hell of a lot he knew about them: point, click and hope the FBI doesn't notice the flash? He'd have to talk to somebody who knew more than he did. Knowledge is not knowing something but knowing where to find it, according to the other fellow.

—

Blue left early for his shift, taking Barney with him, and taking a long detour by way of Mr. Lo's just in case. Nothing. No Tinker. No Kathy. No messages. Barney fared better, leaving the restaurant with a thick bone, compliments of Mr. Lo. "Looks like we both got something to gnaw on tonight," Blue told the dog.

Barney slowly chipped the bone down with his canine teeth while Blue, sitting beside him in the shadowed doorway, was having less success reducing the solid lump of fear that swelled inside him, sometimes choking off his ability to breathe, forcing him to take huge gulps of air.

By the time he had left the commune, Karma had already begun to block out her eighth life on their bedroom wall, and when she was involved in her work, she just disappeared. Blue's brief reprieve into "The Red Lobster" had passed, the fear growing through him again like a malignant tumour. When forced to discuss it publicly, as with Karma this afternoon, he referred to it as worrying, but it was fear, there was no doubt about that. Blue had felt fear before, the night lost in the boat for example, but it had formed and dissolved in a few dark hours. This fear was in its fourth day and getting stronger by the minute. To just sit and stare at the doorway across the street was maddening.

He was sure Capricorn was inside. Wise's car confirmed that for him. Tinker might be as well, because regardless of what Tulip said about Capricorn not betraying them, the FBI had techniques for extracting information like a dentist without novocaine. Sure, Capricorn might be able to suffer enough to protect the commune. It was his friggin' commune, wasn't it? And he loved Tulip. One thing the movies teach a guy is that men sometimes do heroic things for the women they love. But Tinker wasn't really part of the commune. He didn't even live there anymore. He had an establishment job in the tunnel. And Capricorn knew that he lived with Mrs. Rubble, although he didn't know where Mrs. Rubble lived. But it would take the FBI six minutes to find her if they wanted to. And Mrs. Rubble's husband fought for his country, so she'd have his pension. The FBI were no different than the politicians back home who went around to the old people at election time threatening to take their pensions away unless they voted for them. So maybe Tinker and Kathy never left Mrs. Rubble's at all. Maybe Capricorn gave up Tinker and Kathy for a promise from the FBI that they would leave the commune alone. It was a thought that Blue felt should make him mad, but he suspected that under torture he might give up the commune to protect Tinker. So maybe Wise came to Mrs. Rubble's door with his agents and took them away, telling Mrs. Rubble not to say a word or she would lose her pension. Old people believe in governments, Blue told himself, vaguely recalling his own fondness for all things patriotic.

And the reason why nobody knew about the arrests, Blue reasoned, was that Reginald Regent III wanted Tinker dead, but he also wanted Tinker's plans for the oxygen engine. Powerful people got what they always got, and that was whatever they wanted. Reginald Regent III got Tinker, and as a bonus, Capricorn was in the hands of his long-time enemy, Wise. Both Tinker and Capricorn were as good as dead, Blue decided, except for the plans. Reginald Regent III wanted Tinker's plans, and only two people on the planet knew the truth about those plans, Tinker and Blue. The plans didn't exist, but they would torture Tinker until he told them. Or until he died.

Imagining what Tinker and Capricorn were going through across the street worked the emotional alchemy of transmuting Blue's fear to anger – rage, really. He wanted to charge across the street and storm the FBI building. That anger told him a lot about the guys he'd seen in war movies who, when they were pinned down and helpless for hours and days by German gunfire, some of them, even the cowards who were cowering the deepest into the mud, would finally crack and charge from their foxholes into the machine guns or the artillery and get blown to bits. Once in a while, one of the soldiers, if he had a bigger part in the movie, might get a hand-grenade away, blow out the enemy position before he died. It always seemed so foolish before, watching them run toward their own deaths, but Blue was beginning to appreciate their frustration. Anything, anything at all would be better than sitting in a doorway scared to death and helpless.

Barney, sensing the disturbed stillness beside him, gave the bone a rest and instead rested his huge head on Blue's lap. Blue dug his fingers deep into the fur of Barney's thick neck and scratched, grateful for the company.

"Know what I saw once in a war movie, Barney? These guys were pinned down and they couldn't get out because the Germans were in a bunker and had them trapped. The Americans – it was always the Americans; see enough war movies and you'll be convinced they were there all alone – anyway, this American platoon had a dog, a German shepherd like yourself, for sniffing out mines and stuff. What they did in the end was strap explosives to his back and send him into the bunker. Blew the Germans from here to Kingdom come. The dog, too, of course, but in the end, they gave him a military funeral and he was decorated with medals and stuff. It was kind of sad, but it was kind of sick, too. I wouldn't ask you to do anything I ... wouldn't ... do."

—

Tulip arrived with the articles Blue had ordered while he kept his watch. From a nearby phone booth he had phoned the telephone booth at the corner of the street where the commune was located, letting it ring until someone passing by picked it up. Blue asked the unknown voice on the other end of the line to carry an emergency message to the address he gave him, asking someone to come to the booth for an urgent call. The strange voice on the other end of the phone told Blue that he would deliver the message, and left the phone hanging there for Blue to listen to the street noises while he waited. Tulip came a few minutes later, listened and shortly after arrived with Barney's harness, sunglasses and a walking stick that she had hurriedly painted white at Blue's request.

With his cane tick-tick-ticking along the concrete walk, Blue let Barney lead him past the FBI offices where Blue suddenly wrenched the harness, forcing the dog toward the door. Blindly feeling the glass, Blue eventually found the handle, opened the door and let Barney lead him inside where a uniformed security man behind an information desk asked what the visitor wanted. Looking away from the voice toward a plant in the corner in imitation of someone blind, Blue asked if this was the Crosby Building. Learning that it wasn't, Blue explained that his dog must have made a mistake although he'd always sniffed out the Crosby Molasses Company before.

"You don't happen to be eating biscuits and molasses?" Blue asked the security officer, who denied any such indulgence.

"I'm afraid I'll have to ask you to leave," the security guard said, coming around and reaching a hand out to guide Blue to the door only to jerk his hand back when Barney bared teeth capable of amputation.

"Easy, Barney," Blue told the dog. "Just lead me out of here so the man can get back to his biscuits and molasses."

"I'm not eating molasses. To tell you the truth, what you're describing sounds gross. Molasses is used for baking if I remember my mother's kitchen correctly."

"Not where I come from, sir," Blue said just as he managed to manoeuvre Barney into a position where he walked Blue into a marble pillar in the foyer. A noisy kick from Blue's boot to the base of the pillar, synchronized with his head seemingly striking the pillar, set off a dramatic sequence in which Blue first wavered backward, then sank slowly to his knees before collapsing into a heap on the floor. Barney licked his face.

"Are you alright, sir?" the security man asked Blue from a safe distance beyond the dog's teeth. "Do you want me to call an ambulance?"

Blue did not want an ambulance. To fend off professional assistance, he moaned, groaned, righted his askew glasses, began slapping the floor in a circular search for his cane, to which the security officer verbally guided him without ever exposing a hand to the seeing-eye dog. On his feet, Blue leaned against the information desk and went into his idea of someone feeling woozy. He asked for an aspirin and perhaps a glass of water if you would be so kind? The security guard waffled on the request, then decided that the quicker he got the pair of them out of there, the safer he was from the dog. Asking Blue to stay put, he rushed through a door.

Blue walked immediately toward the bank of elevators only to have one reach the ground floor just as he got there. He scurried back to the information desk and was gazing aimlessly around from behind his glasses when the elevator doors opened and two men got out. He almost stared when he saw Wise. From behind him, Blue heard the security officer returning, the glass being set on the counter, aspirin gripped in his hand. The activity attracted Wise's attention. He walked over to the desk. A low growl began in Barney's throat.

"Is there a problem here?" he asked.

"No sir," the security agent assured him. "This gentleman and his dog were looking for some molasses company's office and wandered in here by mistake. He had a slight accident."

"What's wrong with that dog?" Wise asked as the threatening tone increased. He looked at the dog, then studied Blue. "Do I know you from some place?"

"Can't tell, mister. I can't see you," Blue explained. Wise sifted quickly through his memory files for a place where these two fit, a blind hippie and a cross dog, but he was in a hurry.

"Get these two out of here," he ordered the security officer. "This is a secured area. No visitors who haven't already been cleared. You know that," and the FBI agent left the building, with the security guard asking Blue if wouldn't mind taking his dog and going.

"You mean you want my dog to take me and go, don't you?" Blue said.

—

"Capricorn's in there," Blue told those who were still awake when he got home. "We have to keep watching."

"You took a big chance trying that," Karma said. "What if you had been caught?"

"I know he pretty near recognized me there. He kept looking from me to Barney like he was trying to remember where he saw us before, but we didn't look much like the stars that were shining on the stage of the Fillmore that night, so he couldn't put it together, but even if he did, as soon as he reached for me Barney would have had his hand or his gun or something and I would of been out of there faster than a rabbit in a field of greyhounds."

"And what would have happened to Barney?" Karma asked.

"Barney would of got away, too, unless they shot him," then seeing the expression on Karma's face he changed his assumption to a joke, telling her he was only kidding. "We would both of gotten away, Karm. It's not like he was carrying a bagful of explosives on his back or anything like that, you know."

57

Blue stood beside the mesh gate through which the men tunnelling a route for the city's subway went to work. He had not gone to sleep after his attempt to get into the building where Wise was keeping Capricorn. Hours had been spent discussing with the others what he had done.

"What would you have done if you did get into the elevator?" Karma asked.

"Make it up from there," he answered, but he wasn't totally satisfied with the answer. The truth was he was pissed off and charged into the building without thinking his plan all the way through. What would he have done? Made for the third floor which had the most lights on at night, maybe? Maybe the blind guy could strike again. All he needed was a story to get him there, Blue thought as he watched the after-the-holiday faces approaching the tunnel entrance, looking for the one familiar face he knew, praying that it would be the next guy to come down the street with a lunch can under his arm. But Tinker never showed for that morning's shift. Blue waited well past any reasonable expectation that his friend was late, then found his way home to bed.

—

Peter? argued his story about Capricorn's arrest onto the front page of *The Subterranean*. It hit the newsstands in the early afternoon while Blue was still sleeping. Readers of the article got the facts without Peter?'s usual editorializing.

Using an unnamed source, he described the overheard conversation in which Fucdepor president, Reginald Regent III, had ordered FBI agent Bud Wise to take extreme measures in containing the so-called terrorist, Tinker. Capricorn, Peter? reported, entered Fucdepor Petroleum's office building on Good Friday morning to gather evidence that the oil giant had ordered the death of the mysterious inventor of the oxygen engine. During that break-in, several Fucdepor employees, including Reginald Regent III, arrived at work and caught Capricorn red-handed breaking into the president's office.

The FBI arrived on the scene a few moments later and Capricorn was taken from the building, placed in agent Wise's vehicle and driven away. He had not been seen or heard from since.

A spokesman for the FBI had denied that the series of events described in the article ever took place. No one at Fucdepor Petroleum would comment.

"Wake up, Blue," Peter? insisted for the Nth time, slapping him impatiently with a copy of *The Subterranean*. "You have a radio interview this afternoon." Blue struggled up from his plans to spend the day in a coma, groggily combed his hair, splashed water on his face and let Peter? lead him from the commune. Peter? nudged him awake when they got to the radio station.

—

"I have a special treat for everyone today," Vinyl Vinny told his listening audience. "In the studio this afternoon we have Blue, lead singer of Blue Cacophony and the man who penned the underground hit, 'Failure To Love.' But music is not Blue's main concern these days. Instead, he is worried about the fate of Capricorn, founder and guru of the Human Rainbow Commune, who has been reported missing and, according to this week's *Subterranean*, is being held incommunicado by the FBI. Have I got that right, Blue?"

"If you know the FBI are holding Capricorn in Communicado then you know more than I do," Blue said. "I don't even know where that is."

Vinyl Vinny experienced the first dead air of his deejaying career before he recovered. "Oh, I get it. A pun. In Communicado. Very good."

"Huh?" said Blue.

"Tell me, Blue, why are you concerned about the disappearance of Capricorn?"

"Because the FBI are holding Capricorn at one of their secret offices in San Francisco. We are positive of that. He's under arrest because the FBI have wanted him for a long time, but they're keeping him hidden because they want Tinker even more, and they think Capricorn can lead them to him. If they find Tinker, I'm afraid he's a dead man."

"But the FBI have denied the whole story, called it a figment of someone's imagination, an elaborate, unsubstantiated lie, to be exact," Vinyl Vinny said.

"Lie! What's FBI but FIB spelled almost backwards?" Blue argued back.

"Do you seriously believe that the FBI intend to kill this Tinker?"

"Look," Blue said, "if this was a movie, I'd walk out of it, the plot is so bad, but I can't do that. What's happening to these guys is scary. The FBI is controlled by the oil industry and who knows who else. Farmer, this horse trader I know back home, he was in the war, the real one, fighting the spread of Hitler, and he told me that you should never trust an officer unless he's leading you into battle, but if he's sending you, and you're willing to go, then, Farmer says, you're a sucker and that officer just sold you a sick horse, and Farmer should know because he's sold his share of sick horses in his day."

"And the moral of this story is..." Vinyl Vinny wondered aloud.

"That you shouldn't trust anybody who's got more power or money than you, because all he wants to do is keep that and get more. Some people get so much power and money they own the politicians and the police, and they get that power and money by selling trusting suckers like us sick horses. A guy like Capricorn, eh, and he'd be surprised to hear me say this, but a guy like Capricorn just wants everybody to have their own share of the world. Well, if everybody's going to have their own share, then somebody's got to give up a hell of a lot, don't you think? So what do you think they'd do to keep their share, and yours, and mine? Anything, that's what!

"This Tinker character everybody's talking about, and don't forget, they're just talking about him," Blue reminded listeners, "he's scared the daylights out of Fucdepor Petroleum. Did you ever see his oxygen engine? No! Did I? No! Did anyone? No! As far as we know, it's just talk, but they want to get rid of him for just talking about an engine that will make everybody's life better. If it is true, if this Tinker guy invents an oxygen engine, I'll tell you this much, he doesn't want to sell the rest of us a sick horse, he wants to share a healthy one with us. Well, maybe he'd like to make a few bucks off it, but Fucdepor would rather poison us to death with their oil fumes just to keep their greedy hands on a planet that belongs to every one of us...."

"So, Blue, you obviously believe that the FBI and the petroleum industry is involved in a conspiracy to make Capricorn and Tinker disappear."

"That's why we've come to you. The real radios and newspapers won't let us tell the truth, but you will. If you keep talking about this on the air somebody's going to have to say something about what's happening to Capricorn and Tinker, and I thank you for that, Vinny. Know what would be fine? We end this with you playing 'Failure To Love,' dedicated to those two martyrs."

—

It was raining when by the time Blue and Barney took up their position in the doorway across the street from where he believed Wise held Capricorn under arrest. There had been more FBI denials after the radio broadcast, denials strong enough to make even Blue believe them, if he didn't know better. Feeling a desperate lump in his throat, a hopelessness he tried to lose by burrowing his face into Barney's coat, Blue kept going through the no longer convincing motion of copying the activity across the street into the scribbler he kept folded and stuffed in his jacket pocket.

8:25 p.m. - a guy and girl went into the building.
8:43 p.m. - a different guy came out of the building.
9:16 p.m. - the same girl and guy come out of the building.
10:05 p.m. - a soldier went into the building.

58

"There's a soldier down here demanding to see you," the security guard said into the phone on his desk. "He says it's vitally important that he talk to you— Throw him out? I can't do that, sir! He's a Marine, he's wearing a 'Nam ribbon! He needs to see you, he says." The security guard hung up the phone and told the soldier that Wise would be down in a moment.

When the elevator arrived, Wise walked briskly toward the Marine who saluted him sharply. "Put that hand down, Corporal," Wise ordered. "You know better than to salute civilians."

"Normally I do, sir, but you are no ordinary civilian, sir, not if this story is true," the soldier said crisply, dropping a copy of *The Subterranean* on the information desk. Wise glanced at the headline, then brought his narrowing eyes back to the soldier, scrutinizing him.

"Is it true, sir? Do you have Capricorn under arrest?"

Wise detected an eagerness in the soldier's voice that delayed his automatic denial. "What would it matter to you if it was true?"

"Sir, my name is Jim Connelly, Corporal Jim Connelly. I don't know how much you know about this bastard who calls himself Capricorn, but I know him as Stephen Burns. He killed my father!"

Wise looked from the soldier to the security guard who was making a great pretence of not paying attention. "Come with me, Corporal, we'll discuss this in my office," the FBI agent said, leading the solider to the elevators.

"You say Capricorn murdered your father?" Wise said as the two of them settled into his office.

"I'd call it murder, sir, although the courts won't, but my father's dead and Capricorn's the reason."

"Tell me about it," Wise said, relaxing to listen to Corporal Connelly's tale.

| 321

"Sir, my father used to be the vice principal of one of the finest schools in New York City. He was a brilliant man with a great future in education. Your so-called Capricorn was a student at that school ... do you know this story?" the soldier asked, seeing a glint of recognition in Wise's eyes.

"I've been tracking Capricorn for a long time," Wise said, "gathering every piece of information I could about him to create a profile to help in his apprehension. It's been a while, but there was a story about a high school scandal—"

"That's the story, sir. I'm not saying my father was a saint, he and my mother didn't have the happiest marriage in the world, but I was just a child at the time, in the same school. Capricorn wired my father's office to the intercom and everyone in the school heard what took place between him and his secretary." Corporal Connelly stopped, taking an emotional gasp of air, clearly fending off a soldier's worst fear, his own tears. "Including me, sir, I recognized my father's voice over the intercom, but I was so young I didn't know what I was hearing. Everyone ... laughing, sir ... laughing at my father."

The Corporal walked to the window of the office and looked down into the dark, rain-stained street. Wise, a seasoned interrogator who knew when to keep his peace, waited. Eventually, Connelly returned to the chair he had been occupying.

"The result was that the school board transferred my father to another school, the worst in the city. He was an intellectual man, my father, brilliant. He could hold his own with anyone in an argument, but not in a fight, sir. Not in a fight, and in the school they sent him to, it was the only way anyone could survive, students and teachers. He turned into a frightened man who threw up every morning before he went to work. He lasted a couple of years, sir, in that school before he couldn't take it anymore. He killed himself late one August just before school was scheduled to open again. He begged for a transfer to a school he could handle. Any school, sir, rather than face those ruffians who made his life so miserable. And your Capricorn, he graduated at the top of his class. Does your research on him tell you that, that he ruined my father, killed him," Connelly shouted angrily, pounding his fist on the desk, "and they loaded him up with scholarships, made him the class valedictorian and sent him to Harvard University! Harvard, for fuck sakes! Harvard! What's wrong with this country, sir, I ask you, what has happened to our country?"

"I share your worries, son," Wise said consolingly. "At least you've chosen to do something about your country. You've joined the Marines, which means you didn't hide at home waiting for a draft notice to force you into service. You didn't run and hide in that Communist country to the north of us, that fucking Canada. There's the next place our soldiers should be going, if you ask me. No sir, Corporal, you enlisted and went overseas and you fought like a man. The evidence is on your chest and in your face. You're what America's all about, son."

"I swore when my father was kil— died, sir, that I would never allow myself to become as vulnerable as he was. He believed in the world of reason. He didn't know about the violence that exists even inside our own country. He didn't know how to survive it when he was thrown into it, and make no mistake, sir, it was Capricorn, not the so-called system, that threw my father to those wolves.

"When I finished school, I enlisted because I want to do two things with my life, contribute to my country and protect it. There is no better way to protect my country than learning the skills of a United States Marine, sir. So I enlisted. I've been tested under fire and I believe that I stood up to that test, sir. When my tour is up, I hope to go to university, sir, Harvard. I have the academic credentials, I believe, and if the best university in the country is going to train people like Capricorn to destroy it, it's only fair that it also educate those of us who are dedicated to protecting it. Then, sir, as a civilian, I intend to continue protecting my country as a member of the Federal Bureau of Investigation, if the bureau finds me acceptable, that is."

"There's no doubt about that, Corporal. If you ever require a personal recommendation, I would be more than happy to accommodate you."

"Thank you, sir. I don't know whether to be delighted or sad that the story in this newspaper isn't true. My reasons for wanting to join the FBI aren't without selfish motives. I dreamed from childhood of capturing Capricorn once I learned that he had become an outlaw, but when I read this headline I was so happy, I wasn't even sorry that it wasn't me. You'll pardon me, sir, for saying this, but until this afternoon, I had never heard the name Special Agent Bud Wise, but when I read it in association with Capricorn's capture, you became my personal hero. Just because the story's not true doesn't mean that I don't still respect you, sir. You're the only person who has kept after him when everyone else stopped looking, even after that bombing of the factory in New York. I'm sure that someday you will find him. If I don't first," Connelly said with a smile. "I was just hoping—" he said, rubbing his fingers forlornly across the headline that announced Capricorn's capture.

Wise and Connelly sat in their separate silences until it was bridged by Wise's decision to take the conversation between them one step further. "Could the agency rely on your discretion in a matter of national security, Corporal?" he asked.

"Absolutely, sir!"

"Very well, come with me," Wise said, leading the Marine through his office door, past the half dozen agents that were still in the office at that hour, all of whom were obviously members of a task force. Wise stopped with his hand on the knob of a door. "What I am about to show you, Corporal, must remain our shared secret. Is that clear?"

"Yes, sir," Corporal. Connelly said, a clearly confused expression in his face.

The door opened into a windowless office that had probably served as a storage area before it was requisitioned as an interrogation room. There was one desk and two metal chairs in the room. One of the chairs was located behind the desk which held a tape recorder, some empty cups, stationery and pens. The second chair contained a bearded figure whose battered head hung in fatigue. A set of handcuffs on either hand locked him to the metal rungs that supported the back of the chair. He lifted his head wearily and squinted into the light of the open door. The soldier froze in the doorway.

"Capricorn," he whispered so softly that Wise barely heard him. "You do have him," he continued in a clearer voice. "You got the bastard," and Connelly made a closed-fist move toward the prisoner before Wise grabbed his arm, holding him back.

"Easy, son, easy. Let me introduce you. Capricorn, or as you've known him, Stephen Burns," he said, walking over and slapping the cuffed prisoner across the face, "I'd like you to meet Jim Connelly, Corporal Jim Connelly of the United States Marine Corps. Does the name mean anything to you?" Wise asked in a teasing tone. "His father used to be one of your teachers, but something went sadly wrong with the unfortunate man's career when one of his students played a nasty joke. Corporal Connelly was in the school that day," Wise said, jerking Capricorn's head back by his badly matted hair, forcing the commune leader to look into the soldier's eyes through his own swollen eyes. "Corporal Connelly just got back from a tour of Vietnam, but you wouldn't know anything about that, would you, you fucking pacifist coward." He jerked Capricorn's head back even farther.

"I don't understand. Why haven't you told anyone?" Connelly asked Wise, never moving his hate-filled eyes from Capricorn's face. "After all the time you spent chasing him, I'd think you'd be parading him down Main Street America."

"There's a complication that we believe Capricorn can help us with, so it's not in the national interest to announce his capture at the moment."

"Has it got to do with this Tinker character that the newspaper article talks about?"

"You're quick, Corporal. The bureau is going to love having you in its ranks. We know there's a connection between Capricorn's organization and Tinker. The Panthers, too, but Capricorn is our best link. All we need to do is get him to tell us where we can find the fucker."

"What have you done to get that information, sir?" Corporal Connelly asked.

"As much as we can get away with. Sleep deprivation, no food, no water, some non-bruising physical interrogating, although you can see that some of the men interrogating him missed a few times, but none of it has produced much. He's a stubborn bastard, I'll give him that."

"No disrespect, sir," Connelly said, "but those don't sound like very convincing methods. The man's still got all ten fingernails, for fuck sake."

"If it was up to me, Corporal—"

"Of course, sir, I understand your restrictions, but do you understand that I don't have any?"

"Pardon?"

"I'm not an FBI agent, sir, I'm a Marine. Of course, the Marines don't teach their soldiers to torture the enemy. The mothers of America wouldn't like that. What the drill instructors do instead is give us soldiers very detailed information on the methods the enemy will use if they ever capture us. It's so detailed, in fact, sir, that a Marine could probably make any prisoner talk, if he had any prisoners, that is. The Marines only give us the information, you understand. They would be disappointed if we used it, naturally."

"Unfortunately, Corporal, I have the prisoner, not you. He's my responsibility," Wise pointed out.

"But I'm a distraught Marine just back from Vietnam, sir. I read about the capture of Capricorn, the man responsible for the death of my father. Between battle fatigue and my traumatic childhood, there's not a court martial in the land that would hold me responsible for charging in here, finding Capricorn, whom you were interrogating in the national interest, and getting information from him. If anyone ever finds out, that is, and I see no reason why they should. Not if Stephen Burns here just disappeared once we had the information you need."

Wise's doubts about what Corporal Connelly was proposing dissolved when he saw the wave of fear that washed across Capricorn's face as the soldier made his case. "I can't be here," Wise said.

"I could sure use a cup of coffee, sir. Not the trash they serve in the Marines, but a real cup of coffee, one that takes a good twenty minutes to brew. Could you get me one, sir? When you bring it back here, I guarantee you'll know where this Tinker is, and who he is."

Wise left the interrogation room rubbing his hands together in gratitude that there was finally about to be a break in the case. Giving a sick wink to the frightened Capricorn, he closed the door, looked at his watch and decided to treat himself to a long, comfortable shit.

"Are you crazy?" Capricorn asked as Tinker rushed behind his chair to examine the handcuffs. "How do you expect us to get out of here?"

Tinker pulled a package of small tools from an inside pocket and fiddled at the cuffs, telling Capricorn that if he could take an engine apart, "these things should fall to pieces in my hands." They did, and as Capricorn rubbed circulation through his wrists, Tinker told him how they would be leaving the building. Capricorn was standing behind the door when Wise re-entered the room. Before he could react to the empty chair, Capricorn and Tinker overpowered him, cuffing the agent with his own.

"Call the others in here," Tinker ordered, pushing his finger like a gun against the back of Wise's head. "No tricks," he ordered as he disarmed the FBI agent.

The six members of the task force filed into the interrogation room. By the time they realized that all was not well, it was too late. The soldier who had accompanied Wise into the room where Capricorn was being held opened his tunic, pulled out a canister and held it high over his head.

"Allow me to introduce myself, gentlemen. The name is Tinker, and this," he said, shaking the canister that looked as harmless as the fuel tank of a Coleman stove, "is an oxygen bomb. It doesn't need to go off. Whether it does or not is strictly up to you, because the fact is that I know that there are people who want me dead, and that this so-called task force plans to be my executioner, so it doesn't really matter if a couple of million people die with me."

The other agents, whom Capricorn took time to explain to Tinker weren't FBI at all but muscle men for Fucdepor Petroleum, understood that they were in a room with a mad bomber, a misunderstanding Wise had wisely allowed them to continue believing. They quickly disarmed themselves. Under the threatening shake of the oxygen bomb they allowed themselves to be tied together with their own neckties while Bud Wise gurgled from behind the gag of his own necktie.

Capricorn locked the room in which he had spent the past five days, and with Wise as their hostage, the three men left the building, Capricorn and Tinker flanking the agent to hide the cuffs as they passed the security agent, acknowledging him with nods of the head while he scratched his own, searching the log book for the signature of a dirty, matted-haired hippie who must have signed in. He shrugged, decided it must be an undercover agent.

—

Blue watched a cluster of people coming through the lobby of the building across the street and took out the surveillance scribbler to note his observation. At the same time, he heard a car start somewhere up the street. Barney's ears perked as a black car pulled quickly in front of the building and three people came through the door, rushing toward it. They may not have recognized the black car, but both Blue and Barney recognized the familiar tics and drones of Tinker's Plymouth, and the getaway driver behind the wheel.

While the three people coming from the building struggled to get into the car, both Blue and Barney raced from their shadowed doorway, Blue jerking open the passenger door behind the driver. He and Barney jammed themselves through the door and onto the seat. When he got as settled as the circumstances permitted, Blue saw Capricorn in the front seat. Sitting beside Blue in the back seat was FBI Special Agent Bud Wise and beyond him, a soldier who was busily working a pillowcase over the agent's head. Kathy peeled the car away from the curb with the fury of an Indy driver, and Blue began to laugh. By the time they pulled into the driveway behind the commune, his infectious laughter had tickled them all, all that is except for Wise.

"You know what the other fellow says about laughter, don't you?" Blue said, nudging Wise in the ribs as they guided him out of the car. "A joke can't laugh at itself. Is that why you're not laughing, Special Agent Wise?"

59

"It was Blue's idea," Tinker explained to the gathering around the commune's kitchen table, unaware that those were probably the kindest words he would ever utter. "He wanted to make some kind of Trojan Horse to get people into the building to get Capricorn out. Kathy and I started talking about it on a smaller scale and we came up with the idea about the soldier but we needed time to work it out and practice it, so we took off out of the city for the weekend."

"But Mrs. Rubble said you moved out of her apartment," Karma said.

"We told her that so she wouldn't worry about us, but we didn't want her to know what we were up to, either" Kathy explained. "We practised all we could. Tinker rehearsed his character and I practised driving the car."

"It was Kathy who came up with the idea of covering the Plymouth with black MACtack so they'd have the wrong description of the car," Tinker said, "then we were able to just peel it off when we got here and now there's a two-tone Plymouth parked out back. She also wrote my script, five of them to be exact. What I should say if Wise said this, and what I should say if Parks said that. We tried to anticipate everything."

"I had a good actor to work with," Kathy acknowledged, "but we had to wait until we could be sure that we had our story straight."

"Blue told us the story about Capricorn bugging the vice principal's office and about the secretary," Tinker said. "But because of the long weekend we had to wait until this morning to call the school in New York. Kathy pretended she was doing a research paper on changes in school administration over the past twenty years, and asked the secretary she spoke to for help. The secretary rhymed off the all principals and vice principals without even looking it up because she had worked for them all, and there weren't that many. A vice principal by the name of James Connelly had been at the school the year Capricorn graduated so we figured it was his office that Capricorn bugged."

"Did Connelly really commit suicide?" Tulip asked.

"Not as of four o'clock this afternoon," Tinker said. "We called three James Connellys in New York before we got the right one, and I pretended to be doing research on families, asking about his children. He has one son, Jim Junior, who is twenty-two, although he didn't want to talk about him much. My guess is he's not in the Marines. Maybe he's a hippie. Wouldn't that be a gas. But it gave us enough information to go ahead with our plan for late at night when the office building would be pretty empty, and it would be too late for Wise to check out Tinker's story."

"He wasn't about to check out Tinker's story," Capricorn said. "He was convinced. I don't know what Tinker told Wise before they came into the interrogation room, but in that room Tinker convinced me. If your oxygen engine doesn't work out, you should give acting a try."

"I'll bet he was good," Kathy said. "A natural."

"Sounds to me like all Tinker was doing was acting like a prick. Hell, he's been doing that all his life. So what did you think when you saw him?" Blue asked Capricorn.

"First thought I had was 'this is it, I'm a dead man.' I hadn't been allowed to sleep or drink or eat in I don't know how long. I was already having hallucinations and fighting hard to hold on to reality, so when I saw the soldier come in with Wise, heard what they were saying, I knew I was in serious trouble. It was surreal, man, here's this guy with a face and voice like Tinker's, but a hard, cruel edge to it that was frightening. I couldn't sort it out. I thought I was cracking up, but I was fighting to keep my mind. Finally, I convinced myself that it must be Tinker because it was the only hope I could find in all that madness, so I began trying to help him. He had been scaring hell out of me until that point, so I decided I may as well show it."

"That's what finally convinced Wise, I think," Tinker said. "I'm sure of it. Seeing Capricorn that scared was as close as he had come to getting his hands on me in five days, so he decided to leave me alone with Capricorn."

Capricorn looked into the empty soup bowl in front of him. "Just one more small bowl then let me sleep for a week."

"Hell, the way you attacked that first bowl, we could of filled it with meat and you wouldn't of noticed," Blue said.

—

People began drifting off to bed until only Tinker and Blue were left at the kitchen table. They shared an awkward silence during which Blue busied himself by making them a pot of tea, setting a cup for each of them, then sat across from his friend. Tinker was still in the uniform that he and Kathy had bought in a surplus store, but the sharpness of the soldier who had marched into the FBI offices had relaxed into an open collar and comfortable slouch. Blue realized that he was being studied as well. "What?" he asked.

"Blue, where in the fuck did you come from tonight? I think if I stepped off a space ship on the moon, you'd be there."

"You got that right, buddy, but I really wasn't much help. You pulled our arses out of this fire, I'll give you that. Between me, you and the other fellow, I wouldn't of thought of that soldier idea in a million years, but you did. Your whole escape plan taught me what it's like to be humble, buddy. I don't like it one bit. But I'll get over it.

"We've been through some great times together, but this one, if the Lord spares us, to quote the other fellow, takes the ribbon. But I'll tell you this much, when we get home, we're going to have to divide this story in two, then shrink it in a washing machine just to make it a believable lie."

Blue refilled their cups, complaining and apologizing about the vegetarian tea that they drank in the commune. "Their friend Herbal can't hold a candle to our buddy King Cole back home, can it?"

"Blue," Tinker said. "I'll bet you never drank five cups of tea in your life, so how did you become such an expert?"

"Tea's important back home. You don't have to drink it to see that. Especially at times like this. This is like the time my father got caught in the cave-in at the mine. Nobody got killed, but we didn't know for a while. When the old man finally got pulled out from under all that coal, black as a Protestant's sins, as the other fellow says, the first thing my mother did, even before she let the doctor look at him, was pour him a cup of King Cole. You've just come out of a bit of a cave-in yourself, you know, so I'm doing what the old lady would of done, that's all, because you've still got a ways to go before you're out of this mess, you know."

"What do you mean?" Tinker asked, taking a more appreciative sip from his cup.

"When you have a leak in your tap you call a plumber, but who do you call when you have an FBI agent in your basement? Have you worked that part out yet? You can't keep him like he was some kind of stray dog that followed you home, you know, although I don't think his mother would miss him any if you did. But I bet there isn't a cop asleep in the state of California tonight. They think Wise is worth saving, so that tells you what kind of IQ is out there, the kind that pulls triggers, that's what kind."

"Maybe not. Capricorn told me those weren't FBI agents in that building with Wise, they were bodyguards, thugs that work for Fucdepor Petroleum. The building even belongs to Fucdepor. The FBI haven't been lying when they've been denying knowing anything about a manhunt for me or Capricorn."

"Damn! We'll have to keep that part out of the story when we get back home. The FBI makes it much better. By the way, we could both get out of this city and be on our way now if we wanted to. Do we?"

"Do we what, Blue?" Tinker asked uncertainly.

"Do we want to get out of it, this city, this mess? The two of us and the Plymouth could, you know, get out. A couple of dumb Canadians. You know what I mean!"

"Blue, are you serious?"

"No, but it has to be said, just so we know we're both in this together. Buddy, we are trapped by our own nobility, so we have to lay low and let her blow, to quote the other fellow. We've still got an FBI guy in the basement. The best thing for you to do is go back to the tunnel. It'll give you something to do for eight hours a day in a place nobody will be looking. It'll keep you from making mistakes. Me, I'll just keep on with the band and hope we don't become a major curiosity for the FBI. If I'd of known what you were up to, I could of kept my mouth shut and stayed out of this mess, you know, all those things I said in the newspaper and on the radio. So it's all your fault, buddy, which is just the way I like it. So how do we get rid of a breathing body?"

"We'll have to let him go, Blue, and he'll give a pretty good description of me to the papers, so I better stay away from the tunnel, maybe just stay here. Christ, we didn't even need Wise to make our getaway. Nobody tried to stop us. That's how useless the bastard is," Tinker said. "Having him in the basement must be what it's like to have the clap. You can't tell anybody you've got it and you're too embarrassed to go to someone to get rid of it. The shit we got into back home was never like this, was it?"

"Nope, but it's good to know we're not wanted dead or alive."

60

Dawn was a grey wash in their bedroom when Blue made his way there, noticing, as he sat to take off his sandals, that Karma was already roughing out her eighth life. It was vague and undefined and Blue was too tired to play guessing games. Instead, he collapsed into the bed beside Karma, the events of the past few days swirling around his mind like a flock of gulls over the summer fishing boats of home, noisy and patternless. He finally slipped away from them into sleep like someone sinking without resistance into the sea. There, dreams awaited in which the house they were in was surrounded by an army of FBI agents in flak jackets and bullhorns, calling his name with deadly menace.

—

"Blue! Blue, wake up!"

Called up slowly from sleep by the sound of his name, Blue opened his eyes fully expecting to encounter a bedroom full of police with guns pointed, hoping he would give them a reason to shoot.

The room was empty, but Capricorn's voice, accompanied by a series of sharp raps, came from beyond the four walls and the door that he and Karma had acquired with their move across the street. He was alone in the bed, and the light in the room told him the time was late afternoon. He threw the bedclothes off, pulled on his jeans and opened the door. Capricorn stood there holding a copy of *The Subterranean*, telling Blue they needed to talk.

"Where did Peter? get his information for this article," he asked.

"From Tulip and whatever factory manufactures his weird ideas, I suppose. Why?"

"He says here that I was caught trying to break into the Turd's office, that they even brought a bomb squad in to check the place out. This article got me to rethink the whole phony interrogation. That was one of the questions Wise and those other guys wanted to know, why I was breaking into that office, although they were much more anxious to know where Tinker was. But Blue, I wasn't breaking in, I was locking up the office, taking my time, doing it carefully to keep from scratching the lock so no one would know I had been there."

"So?"

"So if they had a bomb squad check the building out, then maybe—"

"—they weren't looking for bugs." Blue finished Capricorn's thought and the two of them let its implications sink in in silence. He was wide awake now, and barely able to keep up to his own thoughts. "If those microphones are still there, we got ourselves a real Arabian stallion here, something really worth trading, and according the Economics class I took, anybody who's got something to trade can always make a deal."

But to find out, Capricorn told Blue, someone would have to drive the van down to the Fucdepor Towers and park within a couple of blocks of the building, then monitor the radio to see if Reggie-the-Turd's office and phone were still on the Human Rainbow Commune's airwaves. "Public broadcasting at its best," Blue concluded when Capricorn gave him a crash course in radio surveillance and reel-to-reel recording in the back of the van while it was parked behind the commune.

Blue volunteered to be the one to drive the van to the Fucdepor Tower, test the recording equipment and come back. "If it's still working, then I've an idea cooking in my head," he told Capricorn. "We'll see if it's fully baked by the time I get back. In the meantime, take good care of our guest. He got us into this mess, but he may be just the guy to get us out, too."

61

"Open up," Blue instructed a blindfolded Wise. "Come on now, you have to keep your strength up, as the other fellow says," he continued, working the spoon against the FBI agent's mouth. Wise spewed the contents in a series of dry spits. "I know, I know, sunflower seeds take some getting used to."

"Why don't you just kill me and get it over with," Wise snarled.

"I didn't think they tasted *that* bad," Blue said, dipping the spoon back into the bowl. "If I was a Nazi, I would of left the husks on, and then you'd know what tasting bad really means. But we got a bigger problem than sunflower seeds. We called the FBI, eh, and said we were holding you hostage and that we wanted a million bucks for your release. Know what they said? 'Keep him.' Well, I'm a bit of a horse trader myself, so I know when to come down a little in the price of an old minker, but I had to come all the way down to ten dollars and you know what they said? 'Keep him!' Looks like they may be looking for a million dollars from us to get them to take you back, so we don't know what to do with you, see. Now take some more. They're good for you. Besides, when you're finished, we're going for a little drive together, but only one of us is coming back."

Special Agent Bud Wise was in his third day of captivity in the Human Rainbow Commune, a relationship as unappealing to the hostage-takers as to the hostage himself.

The first morning, Blue had made his way to Fucdepor Towers where he parked across the street and settled into the back of the van to test the eavesdropping equipment. Following Capricorn's instructions, he soon heard voices, recognizing one of them as belonging to Reginald Regent III because of the petroleum president's angry interviews after he had been mistakenly arrested as Tinker. Staying at his listening post until the office closed and Reginald Regent III himself had left the building, the subject of Tinker never came up. Instead, Blue had recorded numerous conversations between the president and his underlings, as well as several phone calls. Three of the phone calls were to or from presidents of other oil companies, and judging from their conversations, price-fixing sounded like the thrust of their talks. From his economics class in high school Blue understood that price-fixing was shady business, a way for companies that could not form a monopoly because of anti-trust laws to form a monopoly on prices by fixing the price artificially high and keeping new competitors out of the business. It was the kind of stuff that could be turned into a scandal, he figured, but it had nothing to do with Tinker's problems.

On his way back from Fucdepor Towers, it became clear to Blue that the Fucdepor employees who had been left handcuffed together when Tinker and Capricorn made their escape had pooled their powers of observation, creating a composite sketch of Tinker that was portrait perfect. The sketch of Tinker's face, along with a mug shot of Capricorn, was on the front page of every publication. And an FBI agent was missing – a hostage – so now the FBI, which wasn't involved before, was seriously involved now.

Back at the house, listening to the tapes again, there was clearly nothing that remotely incriminated Reginald Regent III in the orders to capture Tinker, seize his plans for the oxygen engine, then have him disappear.

"I couldn't believe they weren't talking about it," Blue told Capricorn. "The fact that these people weren't talking about it is the same as an admission of guilt as far as I'm concerned. Unheard melodies are sweeter, to quote the other fellow, and what I unheard today was a guilty bastard who wants to kill my best friend saying nothing at all about it."

"We can't take somebody's silence to the police, Blue," Capricorn pointed out. "We need evidence. Maybe tomorrow."

—

Tomorrow brought more of the same. Blue sat out in the van, parking across the street from Fucdepor Towers before 8 a.m., a box of new tapes beside him. The whole day passed without a single conversation in Reginald Regent III's office that hinted that the oil company boss had ordered Tinker to be destroyed like one of the old minkers Farmer and he used to truck around.

The day wasn't a total waste Blue decided as he drove home at the end of the office day humming the lyrics to the ninety-ninth verse of "The Red Lobster." He had had the foresight to bring his guitar along for company on the second day, along with a six-pack of beer and some alfalfa sandwiches that Karma had thoughtfully made for him, and which he fortified with slices of ham from a deli along the way. His guitar, the beer and food made the monotony bearable, providing Blue with the understanding that he would never allow himself to work in an office. After two days of feeling like a fly on the wall of Fucdepor's head office, he felt he knew about as much as he would ever need to know about nine-to-five jobs in a suit and tie, and what he knew was that it was just too frigging boring. He had been right, he decided, to waste his time in school learning about horses instead of history. Good marks would have led him to college, and college would have led to an office just like Fucdepor's where he would be trapped for the rest of his life waiting for a gold watch and pension instead of unleashing his creativity. That understanding was inspirational.

> There's more than one lobster
> under the sea
> So why not torment him
> instead of me
> You're the cruelest thing
> in these waters
> Except for that shark
> Before the fisherman caught her
>
> Red lobster, red lobster....

Blue raced up to the bedroom to write down the lyrics and discovered Karma at work on the eighth painting in her series. It was already far enough advanced for him to identify.

"You were in the First World War?" he asked. "I'll bet that's why you're against the war in Vietnam. Probably had something really bad happen to you so now you hate war period."

"You sound as if you believe my painting," Karma said.

"What I mean isn't what I believe. I'm just trying to look at it through your eyes instead of mine, but if I ever start believing what I see through your eyes, I'll just have to pluck them out, as the other fellow says."

"So what do you see through my eyes?"

Blue examined the painting, dull muddy trenches and soggy soldiers rain-lashed under tombstone clouds. A Red Cross emblem painted on a tent offering the only splash of colour, of hope, in an atmosphere that suggested hell itself had risen to the surface of the Earth and was devouring the bodies that lay half submerged in bloody mud.

"The Red Cross! Of course that's where you'd be, cleaning up the mess, fixing the world. But I guess the reason I sound like I believe your painting is because I wouldn't of minded being there myself. I mean I wasn't even born for the Second World War, and I was born in the wrong country for the Vietnam War, so if I was in the First World War, I would of seen some kind of action, wouldn't I?

"Hey, maybe I got shot capturing an enemy trench or something and they took me back to that tent there where you nursed me back to health and stood there holding my hand while some general pinned the Victoria Cross to my chest, and that's why we got karma, Karma."

"Or maybe we were nurses together, Blue, and because we tried to help people who were hurt in the war our karma spared us from having to get involved in another war like the one in Vietnam."

"That's sick, girl. I'd of never been a nurse. If I was, though, it would be Tinker's problem I'd be trying to fix, not the whole world's. I'd leave that up to you."

"You didn't record anything today that would help Tinker?"

"Nothing. Just a bunch of idiots in suits talking about how to make even more money. I got nothing against money, Karma, but I don't think these people can ever get enough to just stop and enjoy it, and they think Tinker's engine will make them millions more. Why? So that when they die they can say they made ten million dollars or something.

"Hell, when I die I'd sooner say I *spent* ten million dollars. I'd be really pissed off to spend my life earning money then die before I got a chance to squander it all on wine, women and song – to quote the other fellow. That's all I learned after listening to Reginald Regent the Turd all afternoon. He never once mentioned Tinker's name. I'm beginning to wonder if he knows the place is bugged and that's why he won't say anything."

"Who is he going say it to, Blue? I'm sure that somebody like Reginald Regent III doesn't just go around blabbering about ordering plans to be stolen or people to be killed. The only person he is going to talk to about it someone he trusts, like Special Agent Wise."

"Did you come straight from Heaven or have you been around here for awhile?" Blue asked, jumping to his feet and bear-hugging Karma before releasing her to run through the door and down the stairs hollering for Tinker, leaving her wondering what she had said.

In the kitchen Blue opened three beers, passed one to Tinker while he briefed him, put a straw in the second bottle, then beckoning his friend to follow him, led the way to the basement where Wise was tied to the chair. He signalled Tinker to stand in the corner and stay silent then took a chair opposite the FBI agent, waving the bottle under his nose. Wise recoiled at first, then recognizing the odor returned his nose to the bottle, sniffing it curious as a dog.

"Brought a Bud for my bud, Bud," Blue said, placing the bottle on a table beside Wise, putting the straw in Wise's mouth.

"Go ahead, drink. It's not poison, although my mother would debate me on that one, especially when the old man goes on a tear. We're just a couple of guys having a beer together. No need of pretending you're not interested, not with a nose like that. Looks like a road map to every liquor store you ever walked into. So tell me, Special Agent Bud Wise, why didn't you just shoot Capricorn when you had the chance? It would of been easy to stage a break-out then shoot him in the back while he was trying to escape, wouldn't it? He who hesitates loses his prisoner, as the other fellow says. Of course, you wanted Tinker even more than Capricorn, didn't you? Why?

"Maybe you would of been happy just to have Capricorn but maybe somebody else with more power than you wanted Tinker even more. So there you were holding prisoner the very man you've been chasing all these years, and all you can do is try to get information out of him. Must of pissed you off real bad. Then it all goes wrong and where do you wind up? A prisoner of your prisoner. You must be really pissed off now."

Wise said nothing but his cheeks concaved so Blue knew he was sipping at the beer.

"Nothing to say? Not even your name, rank and serial number? How about the rumour that you take your orders from the President? The president of Fucdepor Petroleum, that is. I'm sure there's no truth to it, but you know the way newspapers are. Anyway, that's what today's paper said, that you were given orders by Reginald Regent the Turd to kill Tinker after you stole the plans for his oxygen engine. I'd let you read it yourself, but then I have to take off your blindfold and you'd get a look at my face and, well, you know what the other fellow says about kidnappers, don't you, that when the kidnap victim sees the kidnapper's face, it's the last face he'll ever see. So I'm just trying to keep you alive here in the basement of this factory where we'll just keep on manufacturing oxygen engines until the FBI agrees to fly us and our engines to Cuba.

"You winched there, Bud, old buddy. You winched when I said Cuba. So you think Castro will be interested in the oxygen engine? Or is it the oxygen bomb that you think he'd like? The way I see it, it's our only chance to get out of this country alive, because, as your friends in the CIA will tell you, Cuba is the only safe place on the planet because the Americans can't beat that Castro character at all. Every time you try, he comes out smelling like a rose and the United States comes out smelling like a three-day-old butt of one of Castro's cigars. If he starts making oxygen bombs, well, that will take care of the United States army, and if he starts making oxygen engines, that'll take care of Fucdepor Petroleum, so I figure Tinker's invention and Capricorn's revolution are going to come together to turn the world into paradise, paradise being of course anywhere where the oxygen is clean and free. Some place like Cuba. Know what I like about Cuba? It's an island. People who live on islands understand each other, just like me and Castro."

Special Agent Wise pulled his lips from the straw and began struggling against his own handcuffs which held him captive, holding his head back, trying to peek out under the blindfold.

"You can't give that Communist pig the oxygen bomb! He'll blow up the whole free world! Castro's the Russian puppet who pretty near started an atomic war, if you remember the missile crisis. If he gets his hands on the oxygen bomb it could be all over for—"

"That's where you and I differ, Mr. Wise. You'd be surprised how much the two of us – you and me, that is – have in common. We both hate the Ruskies and all that communism stuff, but when it comes to Castro, well Cana— I better not say that. Too much information, as the other fellow says. What I mean is that in the country where I come from we hate the Communists just as much as you do, but not Castro. I got this friend back home, eh, Farm— can't tell you that either, but this friend I got got a dog and know what he called him? Fidel! After Castro, if you can believe that, and this friend of mine fought the Nazis so that should tell you how much he hates the Communists, but not Castro, boy, not Castro.

"What it is, eh, is that all the little countries all around the United States really wish Castro was their prime minister. Not because he's a Communist, but because he doesn't take any shit from you Americans. In the other countries, like mine, say, prime ministers are always kissing somebody's arse down here so we can keep on working up there, American money being what makes the world go round, as the other fellow says, but when we watch Castro we know we'd vote for him if we had the chance."

"You'll never have a chance to vote for that prick because you need a democracy to vote in and he'll never allow Cuba to be a democracy," Wise spat. "Someday, our government will overthrow him and Cuba will be free, just like it used to be, the perfect American vacationland. But if you bring that oxygen engine down there, it will upset the balance of the whole world. He'll use it to make engines that don't need oil and gas, and ruin Detroit. If we send our army to try to stop him from producing oxygen engines, he'll blow us up with the oxygen bomb! What do you think will become of the world if it's not American? If you get near Castro, do us all a favour and kill the bastard. Kill him! Avenge the Bay of Pigs and kill him!" Wise was ranting as Blue turned to Tinker in the corner who nodded that he had heard enough. Blue left the beer for Wise to finish as the two of them went back upstairs.

The next morning, Blue parked the van across the street from Fucdepor Towers, watched Reginald Regent III step from his limousine, then moved into the back of the van, sitting ready to record any conversation that might occur in Reginald Regent III's office. An hour later, Blue packed up and pulled away from the curb, whistling his melody to "The Red Lobster."

62

Blue put the bowl of sunflower seeds down on the table, telling Wise that it was time to go, "but there's a few preparations to be made yet," he informed his captive, calling up the stairs for some help. An hour later, with Wise tied up in the back of the van, Blue pulled away from the Human Rainbow Commune, glanced in the rearview mirror at the Plymouth following him, Tulip behind the wheel.

A half hour later, Blue pulled the van over to a curb, parked and climbed into the back with Wise.

"Sorry about that bump on the head there, Bud, old buddy, but I forgot to tell you to duck. Headache? Bit of a goose-egg but nothing that'll kill you. I suppose I should of told you to duck, but Bud, old buddy, you were kind of dragging your feet there and resisting and I figured if I didn't run your head into the side of the van, you'd put up a hell of fight. I understand why, of course, so it's nothing personal. If somebody was driving me around San Francisco with practically no clothes on, I be screaming and resisting, too. So I apologize for the bump on your head, but not for the blindfold, or the gag or the handcuffs.

"Know why I don't apologize? Because there was this guy, eh, Bobby Seale, you heard of him right, one of the Chicago Seven. He got treated the same way in a courtroom, gagged and handcuffed. Now, I might of read all about that and not batted an eye, really, because when it comes to police and court business, I try not to make it any of my business, hoping, of course, that they will return the favour and not make me any of their business. Live and let live, as the other fellow says. The last while, though, your side hasn't been following my golden rule, have you? You haven't let me or mine alone at all. Not that Bobby Seale was one of mine. Never met the man.

"But I did meet a guy I really like whose name shall remain anonymous. I have to hide a lot of people when I'm around you, don't I? Anyway, this anonymous friend was really into all this peace and love business that the hippies like to think will change the world because they know a lot less about it than a couple of old horse traders like you and me. So this friend just liked to live on a mountain, meditate, grow a little weed for himself and a lot of hay for his horses and dream about the new Jerusalem, to quote the other fellow. He was looking after a couple of nags up there that weren't worth a tin dime in my world or yours, but in his, those bony excuses for horses were worth loving. I've been thinking about that a lot since then, how he could love something that's not worth anything. Know what he thought freedom was? A bunch of wild mustangs running wild on the range. In my experience, a good mustang that's not free on the range is worth a lot more money than one that is, but each to his own, as the other fellow says.

"Anyway, a bunch of FBI agents raid the place where my friend is living, and they arrest him, handcuffs just like yours. Maybe yours, for that matter. But it wasn't your handcuffs that bothered him. It was when the police took him down from the mountain and showed him what was happening to his people. Bobby Seale in America-the-free tied and gagged to his chair in front of the whole world. It wasn't your handcuffs that changed my friend from a hippie to a angry Black Panther, it was those handcuffs that held Bobby Seale in his chair.

"I still love the guy even though he's changed, and that's not a word I just throw around even with my girlfriend or my best friend. As a matter of fact, it's a lot easier for me to understand Cor— him ... now that he wants to punch somebody in the head than it was when he just wanted to look at a couple of old nags and see something beautiful in them. I have this other friend, a really beautiful girl who tells me that Cor— that this other friend will eventually get back to the top of that mountain I first met him on, but that it would be a rough road, made even rougher by people like you.

"What she says is that what they did to Bobby Seale was a pebble in a puddle. Eventually the ripples made it all the way up the mountain and turned someone who was full of passive peace into someone full of angry action. Nothing we do ever stops rippling, she says, so that's why we should only do the things we would be proud to see rippling on and on forever. She's a believer, eh, believes that peace is inevitable and that someday we're all going to Heaven in a little rowboat, to quote the other fellow. She believes everybody is fated be saved in their own good time. Even you. I'm a Catholic myself, so I just have to believe that if I can get myself off this planet and into Heaven, I've done my job. And I don't think the fact that I have you handcuffed and gagged is going to be held against me when news of it ripples all the way up there, because I think you'll have a lot more explaining to do than me."

Excusing himself, Blue made his way to the front of the van, turned on the radio and listened to the music, waiting. Half an hour later, the deejay interrupted a song to bring a special announcement. Describing a tape recording that had been anonymously dropped off at the station, he announced that it would be broadcast next. Tinker turned up the dial and told Wise to listen.

"Is this Mister Regent?" a voice on the radio asked.

"Who is this?" a second voice answered.

"Special Agent Wise," was the reply, a reply that caused Special Agent Wise to make a muffled screaming denial behind his gag. Blue acknowledged the denial, pointing out that his friend Tinker "is one talented man, isn't he? Listened to you when he was a soldier and when you were in the basement, and now he sounds just like you."

"Wise! I thought you were being held hostage."

"Before I go on, I need to confirm who I'm talking to," Wise said. "Who are you?"

"Reginald Regent III, but can we dispense with the cloak-and-dagger and tell me where you are?"

"I escaped. Actually, I did much better than escape, I took my captors captive."

"Capricorn and Tinker? You have them?"

"I do. Now my sworn duty is to bring the two of them into the FBI office where they will be charged with enough federal offences to keep them both in prison for the rest of their lives. Christ, they even took an FBI agent hostage! Me!"

"Fuck your sworn duty to some silly flag. Have you found the plans to the oxygen engine?"

"When you find yourself in a rat's hole, you usually find everything that belongs to the rat. I have the plans for the oxygen engine. I should bring them into the FBI office as evidence."

"And let the whole world get a look at them?" Reginald Regent III, shouted. "Don't be stupid, man. Here's what you're going to do. You are going to shoot the two of them, head shots to be sure that they are dead beyond doubt, then come to my office with the plans. Once they are safe in my safe, you will return to the scene of your unfortunate captivity and call the FBI. They will confirm the deaths, justified in your effort to escape, pin a medal on your chest, and promote you. I'll see to it. Once enough time has passed, then you can retire or quit, whichever doesn't matter, and take over as head of security for Fucdepor Petroleum. By that time, a substantial amount of money will be added to your account to demonstrate Fucdepor's appreciation for your services.

"Now get rid of those bastards but get those plans to me, not the FBI or any other government agency!"

The rest of the tape, thanks to Capricorn's editing, continued to run with conversations between Reginald Regent III and the heads of three other oil companies discussing price-fixing and how to gouge the American car owner of millions of dollars with unnecessarily inflated prices.

As the radio broadcast went on with Wise squealing behind his gag, the Plymouth pulled to the curb in front of a telephone booth two blocks up from the van. Tulip got out and stepped into the booth, dropped her dime and began dialing.

"Time to go, Bud, old buddy," Tinker said, pulling the FBI agent to his feet, leading him blindly from the van onto the sidewalk where Blue opened one of the handcuffs, placed it around a No Parking sign and snapped it shut again, tying Wise to the metal pole. Blue got back into the van and pulled away. Watching in the rearview mirror, he saw the doors of the television studio open as cameramen and broadcasters, curiosity raised by an anonymous phone, found Special FBI Agent Bud Wise in front of their building. What they found, and filmed, was the special agent in his tie-dyed underwear, face painted in peace signs, the graffiti on his chest and back reading "Make Love Not War" and "Hoover Is No Groover" respectively.

While still handcuffed to the pole, one woman thrust a microphone in his still blindfolded face and asked if he was the person who made the phone call to Fucdepor Petroleum president Reginald Regent III's office. Wise made a fervent denial, but his distinctive voice, the very voice the news people had aired not ten minutes ago, convinced them that he had indeed made the call.

As the van and the Plymouth disappeared from the proximity of Wise's release, the newscasters were asking the FBI agent if he had already carried out Reginald Regent III's orders to kill Capricorn and Tinker.

63

Media interest in San Francisco rapidly focused on Special Agent Bud Wise and Fucdepor Petroleum president Reginald Regent III. Wise had been suspended without pay for the duration of an investigation into his handling of what the papers were calling the Tinker Affair. Both the FBI and the Attorney General launched investigations into Reginald Regent III for corrupting one of its agents, issuing execution orders for Tinker and Capricorn, and for price-fixing.

The heat on the two Human Rainbow Commune members continued to drop like a thermometer in a deep freeze when the chief of the FBI branch in San Francisco held a press conference to announce that Wise's obsessive pursuit of Capricorn over the years appeared to have been a personal vendetta. The statute of limitations had run out on the arson charges in the factory fire in New York for which Capricorn had been a suspect. As far as the FBI was concerned, the Human Rainbow Commune would receive no more surveillance than any other organization that protested the official policies of the United States Government.

As for the inventor known as Tinker, the FBI chief reported, all the agency had been able to establish was that he was an illegal alien and, as far as it was concerned, his presence in the United States was a matter for immigration officials. His invention, if it existed, suggested nothing illegal.

Neither Blue nor Blue Cacophony merited any mention.

"The least he could of done was said that Blue Cacophony was just as innocent as Tinker," Blue moaned as he read the paper. "Now this is going to be just Tinker's story when we go home because he'll have the documented proof and I won't."

"Blue," Karma reminded him, "you've got half a scrapbook of clippings about Blue Cacophony. Your picture's been in the paper and you have a hit song. You have lots to tell people back home."

"I've been singing with a dog, for the love of God. But the FBI, Karma! Tinker's the first Cape Bretoner on the FBI's Most Wanted list since Baby Face Nelson, although there was this one guy from back home who used to ride with the James brothers, and Farmer told me once that the first cattle rustler ever hung in the state of Texas was from Cape Breton. Couldn't remember his name, though, but he swore it was true. Must of been the Texas Rangers that caught him, since there was no FBI back then, but that wasn't a bad way to go, I guess. Getting caught by the Texas Rangers is as good as being chased by the FBI who weren't even around when Jesse James was a legend. Tinker's story's going to shrivel mine like a dick in ice water, to quote the other fellow."

Fretting over his undocumented role in the saga of Tinker and Capricorn was a waste of Blue's time. While he was lamenting the unfairness of it to Karma, Peter? was already coaxing his connections in journalism to feature Blue Cacophony's role in the events that took down one corrupt FBI agent and a petroleum president. Within days, stories about Blue Cacophony appeared in two newspapers, both based on interviews with the band's manager. There's nothing like associating with an exonerated victim to improve one's image, Peter?, who was enjoying the risk-free romance of being in the spotlight without worrying about police search lights, explained to Blue. What other bands, Peter? had asked reporters, had the courage to write and sing songs like "The Ballad of Tinker" while he was the hottest criminal in the country? What other band member went on the radio to talk about Tinker's and Capricorn's innocence? And, he mentioned to one reporter, Blue and Tinker had history, a friendship reaching back to the island nation from which they had journeyed together to explore the United States of America.

Blue read the newspaper accounts of the band's underground exploits while sitting on the front step. For several days now, and for the first time since the commune moved across the street, its members were entering and leaving by the front door, free people. Karma and Tulip, standing on a staging of chairs and boards, had painted above the front door the words Human Rainbow Commune.

"Hello," said someone passing by.

Blue, looking up from the paper, replied, "Hello again yourself."

Lighting a cigarette, Blue asked Karma, who was sitting beside him sketching ideas for her ninth life into a small pad, "Know what this reminds me off?" Exhaling thoughtfully, he formulated the answer to his own question. "Summers back home sitting on the show hall steps watching the cars drive by. A whole convoy of cars driving over street, tooting when they went past and everybody sitting on the step waving back, then they'd turn at the Fina garage and toot on their way back to the Irving garage where they'd turn again. This is not much different, you know. That guy who just went by? Five times he said hello. Coming or going, everybody says hello here just like home. If we don't say hello back they'll think we're stuck up or mad at them. But look at this Ford Falcon," Blue said, drawing Karma's attention to a slow-moving vehicle very unlike the Haight-Ashbury choice of transportation. "This is his third or fourth time going by, but he hasn't been waving. He's parking."

Out of the Falcon stepped a heavy-set man dressed like a construction worker. He made his uncertain way toward Karma and Blue.

"Excuse me, but is this where Al Dempsey, ah, Tinker lives?"

"You a cop?" Blue asked.

"No, he used to work with me in the tunnel. I need to see him about something."

"Hey, Tinker," Blue hollered into the open door, "there's a guy here looking for you."

"Mike!" Tinker called from an upstairs window. "What're you doing here? I'll be right down."

The two tunnel workers walked away from the curiosity they had raised on the front step. Blue kept a close eye on them over the top of a page he had time to read several times before Tinker and Mike shook hands and parted. Mike got into his car and drove away nodding acknowledgment to Blue, who nodded back.

"What was that about?" Blue asked as Tinker neared the step carrying an envelope.

"He brought me my back time. I don't have a job anymore, of course, being illegal and all that, but when Mike saw my picture in the paper and read about me and Capricorn and the commune, he told the boss he would bring me my pay. Good thing, too, because I'm about busted. They didn't have to pay me, you know. The company could have just kept it and there's nothing I could do about it, but they gave Mike my cheque and my vacation pay, anyway.

"But that wasn't the only reason why he was here, Blue. Remember last fall, I told you about this guy at work who was going to invite us to his daughter's wedding? Well, that was Mike, and one of the reasons he was here was that he read in the paper about me having something to do with Blue Cacophony. He's not into rock music, at all, strictly Merle Haggard, Johnny Cash, Ryman Hall stuff, your kind of music. But his daughter is a big fan of rock and roll and Mike thought that if he could get a famous rock band to play at her wedding it would, well you know, he's a father—" Tinker ended, letting his Acadian hand gestures finish the statement for him. "I told him you'd be glad to do it. It's in June."

64

"Tinker," Blue said to his best friend after returning from a rehearsal, "I bet you can't guess where the band is going to be playing."

"I give up."

"Woodstock."

"Woodstock! Wow! That's great, Blue."

"Yeah. Peter? says there's a good chance we'll be hired to play there this summer. Some people were talking to him already. The Dead guys are going, too, so Peter? wants to talk to them about crossing the country together, touring, as the other fellow, but that's not what I wanted to talk to you about," Blue said, slipping the beads aside and taking a chair in Tinker's room.

"What is it, Blue?"

"Well, I ... uh ... I...."

"When it's this hard to talk to about, Blue, it's usually Karma. How are things going with you two?"

"Good, I guess, but I never lived with a woman before so, like I said, that's just a guess, but I think Karma cornered herself this time, Tinker. She hasn't painted a word of her next life yet. Remember her eighth life was during the First World War? Well, she never said anything about getting killed in that war, so if she lived through it, well, she might of lived a long time. A lot of people from that war are still alive, for the love of God."

"I don't get it, Blue."

"What I mean is that if she lived through World War One, hell, even if she didn't, that doesn't leave much time to cram a life in between that one and this one, does it? If she doesn't have a ninth life, then maybe she didn't have any of the others either, so the Catholics win – beat the Buddha, as the other fellow says. But that's not it, what I wanted to talk about, I mean. Remember the time I ran away?"

| 353

"Yeah. You came to my house with a can of soup in your pocket and the old lady let you stay for the weekend."

"It's not how far you run, according to the other fellow, but how well. Tinker, do you remember why I ran away?"

"You pissed in your mother's stove."

"Right. How could I forget that? First time I ever got drunk. Farmer and some guys were feeding the wine to me down by the old mine. Big joke to get a little kid drunk, I guess, but I walked home straight as a poker, figuring the stuff didn't affect me at all. My mother was making something in the kitchen, biscuits or supper or something, and I just pulled a chair away from the table and dragged it over by the stove and lifted the lid, took out my bird and pissed into the fire. There was this big puff of coal smoke and then ... well my mother.... There was no explaining it to her, Tink. I had no choice, I had to run away. I remembered running away, but I couldn't remember why, but I don't think I'll be telling it to anybody around in the near future. They probably won't get it and just tell me I'm gross again."

"You thinking about running away, Blue?"

"I don't think so, but that time I ran away keeps coming back to me. Sometimes I think maybe it's a song trying to get written, and sometimes I think maybe it's not, that it's just telling me it's time to grab a can of beans and split. Something's coming, buddy. I can feel it in my bones. If I'm wrong then you know what the other fellow says, it must be arthritis. But I don't think so. I'm not that lucky these days, and there's a lot of good things that can go wrong, Karma, the band, the record. And then there's—"

"Home," Tinker said.

"Know what all those things are, Karma and the band and all that? Roots, Tinker, little tiny roots growing down through the cracks in the sidewalk right here in San Francisco where you see little scraps of grass trying to come out.

"Roots. I'm a guy who knows about roots, Tinker. I took agriculture, remember, and agriculture is the story of roots. They go down under the earth and gnarl up down there, and you see this weed in the grass and you say to yourself, I think I'll pull up that weed, so you bend down and the next thing you know, you're in a tug of war 'cause all those roots want to hold that flower in the one same spot. Tinker, what if June comes, or July even, and we're still here?"

"I think about that, too, Blue, but I try not to worry about it. Of course, you're worrying about things that might happen. I'm so glad about all the things that didn't happen that I'm not going to start worrying about what might happen. My biggest worry right now is how to make some money. Maybe I'll have to go back on the street singing for my supper."

"That's where I got my start, Tink. Nothing wrong with the street, buddy, long as it's an honest dollar, to quote the other feller, but when you're sitting out there singing your songs and waiting for people to throw money at you, give some thought to how we are going to escape this town and get home in one piece instead of like a couple of knights of old getting drawn and quartered along the way by their own hearts."

"Sounds like a song to me, Blue."

"Saddest one since the other fellow wrote 'I'm So Lonesome I Could Cry'."

—

It was well after midnight when Capricorn walked into the kitchen where Blue was consulting Barney on the lyrics to "I'm So Lonesome It Isn't Even Funny." The title itself was just a working one, Blue explained to Capricorn, but the song, if he could get it written, might tell him a lot about what was going on his life right now.

"Is there a lot going on in your life, Blue?" Capricorn asked.

"Buddy, me, you and Tinker have been on a magic carpet ride with the rest of the commune hanging on and flapping behind like underwear on a windy clothesline, and we never lost one of them, not one. Nobody quit on you, Capi, nobody. That tells me more than I thought I knew about you. Getting people to follow you when you take them off into the mountains and the woods in Colorado to hide where everybody's safe is one thing.

But when they find out they aren't safe, the way Cory did, then it's rats from a ship, as the other fellow says."

"Cory isn't a rat," Capricorn argued.

"Did I say he was?" Blue asked, reflecting on his own words. "That's not what I meant. Cory's the first guy in that whole commune of yours who I believed, even back when he was loving those sad excuses for horses up on the mountain. Still do. Hell, if it wasn't for him risking his own freedom to come here and tell us about Wise wanting to kill Tinker, Tinker might be dead now. What I mean, Capi, is that these people stuck with you. To be honest, between you and me, I stuck with Tinker. I really don't know what I would of done if it was you all alone in that mess. I hope I would of done the same thing, but I don't know. I just don't know."

"I do," Capricorn said, getting up and taking a bottle of Tulip's wine from the cupboard. "And I would like to drink a toast to what I know," he added, pulling the cork from the bottle and reaching for a couple of glasses.

"And just what is it you know?"

Capricorn passed Blue one of the glasses, looking deep into his eyes in a way that made Blue look away. Without answering, Capricorn raised his glass, inviting Blue to clink. They did, then drank.

"There's something else we need to talk about," Capricorn said, pulling out a chair and sitting down for the first time since coming into the kitchen. "The record has run its course, Blue, but it did a lot better than anyone would have predicted. I thought we would be lucky to get rid of the first run, but we had to press off two more batches after that. We're down to our last box now and it's not moving at all. The market is saturated. It's time to wind it down."

"It was a good idea, though, wasn't it? We didn't lose our shirts or anything like that, did we?" Blue asked as Capricorn pulled a narrow notebook from his shirt pocket and began thumbing the pages. He place it in front of Blue.

"On this page is the expenses, the equipment we had to buy, paying somebody to press them for us after hours, packaging. On this page is the money we took in, and that last figure is the profit, but I shouldn't need to explain this to you, Blue. You studied economics, after all."

"Yeah, I sure did. Look, what's this figure? It says over six thousand."

"That's right, Blue. It does say over sixthousand. And I mean *over* because if you look closer it says—

"*Sixty thousand!*"

"Sixty-one thousand, seven hundred and three dollars, to be exact. Once 'Failure To Love' hit the radio stations we could hardly keep up. There's a lot more money to be made selling records than singing on them, Blue. If your album was selling under somebody else's label, Blue Cacophony's share would have been maybe five thousand total, so obviously, you're not the only horse trader in the music business."

"That's twelve thousand bucks apiece, Capi, twelve thousand!"

"Not bad calculating for somebody who avoided math in school."

"First thing Farmer told me was to learn to do head figuring. If you're going to be in this business, he said, you have to be able to work with money in your head while you're standing on your feet looking some guy in the eye. Twelve thousand bucks! I don't believe it."

"Believe it, Blue, because here it is," Capricorn said, placing a canvas bag on the table. "I've bundled it into equal shares but you're welcome to count it if you like."

Blue reached into the bag and pulled out a bundle of bills, flipping it. "I believe you. I'm not even going to check your expenses page there. Twelve thousand bucks! What are you going to do with yours?"

"This money," Capricorn said, pulling a bundle out of the bag, "will go a long way toward rebuilding the commune in Colorado. I'm thinking of driving up there in a couple of weeks and assessing the damage. See if I can figure out what it will take to move back. Maybe even design it better, use an Indian village model, perhaps. I'd like to move the commune itself out of here by June or July. What are you going to do with your share?"

"Get you to hang on to it, along with everybody else's. The band's bringing in enough money to pay the piper, as the other fellow says, and the fiddler, too, come to think of it. I don't know what Nathan and Gerry are going to do when I pass them twelve thousand dollars, and I don't even want to think what Peter? will do. Kill me, maybe. I hope he really means this pacifist stuff. Anyway, the band's doing fine, so if you don't mind hanging on to it for a while longer, I'd appreciate it.

"You know, Capi, I bet we could make twice as much if we recorded 'The Red Lobster.' Just one great closing number and I'm finished writing it."

Capricorn held up surrendering hands. "It was a one-time thing, Blue. Quitting while you're ahead must have come up somewhere in that economics class of yours."

"I get what you mean. Run a horse long enough and it's bound to pull up lame, says the other fellow."

65

"I'm telling you, Mrs. Rubble," Blue said while spearing another pork chop from the platter, "we got this guy back home, Farmer, I probably mentioned him...."

"Wasn't he the man who was in the same army with my husband?"

"Same war, anyway. Anyway, what I was going to say was that if Farmer knew what a great cook you were he'd be at your table all the time."

"He would be at more than her table from what I hear," Kathy quipped.

"What was that, dear?" Mrs. Rubble asked.

"Nothing," Blue said. "It's just that Farmer has this reputation for chasing widows and other women orphaned by love, as the other feller says. But he'd like your cooking, I know that."

—

When Tinker departed Mrs. Rubble's apartment to return to commune life, his former landlady extracted from him a promise that he and Blue would return every Sunday for dinner, a promise the two friends had no trouble keeping week after week, because Mrs. Rubble's fondness for cooking wine didn't affect her fondness for cooking. The first couple of Sundays they had gone alone, returning to the commune stuffed, laughing and a little lonesome for home. It was a pattern Karma and Kathy decided to share, their decision made welcome by Mrs. Rubble who piled on the extra carrots and potatoes required to meet their dietary habits although she made no pretense of understanding.

On the first Sunday afternoon the four set out together for Mrs. Rubble's, Tinker and Blue made no apologies for what might happen there.

"You have to consider Mrs. Rubble's place like the demilitarized zone they talk about in Vietnam, the DMZ, as the other fellow says. If we walk into Mrs. Rubble's and there happens to be a dead animal or two lying on her table, then the only civilized thing for Tinker and me to do is eat it. You girls can have all the bread and vegetables you want, but you are not allowed to squish up your faces when we do the poor woman the honour of eating whatever she offers. It's only polite," Blue explained.

—

"A toast to the holiday," Blue said, lifting his glass of wine to the others. Tinker raised his glass but the rest of the drinkware remained on the table while Karma, Kathy and Mrs. Rubble looked to each other for an explanation of what they had missed. Blue and Tinker held their glasses, waiting to be joined.

"What holiday?" Kathy finally asked.

"The twenty-fourth of May. Queen Victoria's birthday, of course. It's the long weekend that says summer's coming—"

"Blue," Tinker said with slow dawning recognition, "it's not a holiday in the United States."

"Of course it's not," Blue realized. "You Americans really shot yourselves in the foot with that revolution of yours, didn't you. Missed out on a great holiday. Tomorrow, while Canadians are still hugging their pillows, all you Americans will be getting up and going to work. You can blame George Washington for that. Not that I'm a big fan of the kings and queens of England, mind you, they crucified my own people, but I am a big fan of holidays. I'm just sorry that I don't have a real job not to get up to tomorrow so I can enjoy it."

"I've always wondered, why didn't Canada join the revolution?" Mrs. Rubble mused.

"Well, there was no Canada back then, for one thing," Tinker observed. "That came later. I'm not really sure why."

"We wouldn't of joined that revolution for all the tea in Boston, to quote the other fellow, but when we heard that you Americans were having a sexual revolution down here, well, I said to Tinker, let's go right down there and enlist in a worthy cause. So here we are," Blue said, raising his glass again and this time all the other glasses at the table rose to join him in a toast to himself. Putting down his glass with a smack of his lips,

Blue continued. "There's another thing about the long weekend in May that you may not know. It's the holidays that says, 'Gentlemen, prepare to pack your suitcases.'

"In places like Sudbury, Toronto, Windsor, Boston, anywhere where two or more are gathered in Cape Breton's name, to quote the other fellow, every one of them knows that this is the long weekend in May. Even if they're working in the States like me and Tinker, where the holiday doesn't even exist, they're celebrating it in their hearts because they know they are only a few away weeks from home. Just a few weeks away from home, Tinker, old buddy, and then we'll be crossing the c auseway.

"And there's a big back seat in the Plymouth, big enough for two more passengers and a dog," Blue added, eyeing Karma and Kathy for a reaction, unable to detect much of anything. He looked back at Tinker who shrugged back at him.

"Know what we should do after dinner? Drive down to Fisherman's Wharf and try to get somebody with a boat to take us over to Alcatraz. What do you think, Tink, put our foot on that island before we head back to our own?"

Tinker's eyes brightened at the thought, then dimmed. "Can't. We promised Peter? and Doc Silver that we would meet them this afternoon. He's still interested in the engine, I guess. Besides, I don't know if I want to get any closer to a prison than I already was, even a closed one."

"Then it's me and you, Karma."

"Why go over there, Blue? It's so dark and dreary just to look at or think about."

"Dark and dreary is the history of mankind, according to the other fellow, but it's just history. Wouldn't you like to stand in the same cell as Al Capone? If I was visiting the Tower of London, and I bet that's a dark and dreary place, too, I'd want to stand in the same cell as yourself back when you were whoever you were back then."

Smiling, Karma shook her head in refusal. She told Blue that he was welcome to go alone, but that she wanted to work on her painting. Tinker and Kathy offered her a ride back to the commune on their way to the meeting at Peter?'s.

"That leaves just you and me, Mrs. Rubble," Blue said. "Interested in Alcatraz?"

"If you want something surrounded by water, Mr. Blue, we can do these dishes together."

Blue, with only Barney for company, left Mrs. Rubble's, choosing to walk toward the bay while the others pulled away in the Plymouth. The late afternoon was warm and Blue, lost in thought, barely noticed when he had covered the distance to Fisherman's Wharf. A busy pedestrian traffic opened and closed around a street singer who had his guitar case hopefully open for donations. Blue dropped some change into it, giving the singer a knowing nod as he kept on going. Men and women sat on benches with faces basking in sunlight or blowing out cigarette smoke. Several people sat on the wall of the wharf, some dangling a line into the water, seemingly indifferent to whether or not anything happened to it. Most would be surprised to know they were meditating.

Blue leaned over the wall and watched his spit swirl down to the oily lap of water against concrete, then he gazed across to Alcatraz. Karma was right. You couldn't know about what went on there and not find it dark and dreary, practically haunted except that there was too much modern life swirling around the island, like boat engines and skyscrapers, for it to have a convincing ghost.

Blue scratched Barney's head while his attention examined Alcatraz in the distance. A moment later, it was drawn away by the music. The arrangement wasn't anything Blue would have recognized, but the words were definitely those of "Failure To Love." He walked Barney, who, unlike Blue, recognized nothing of the tune, over to the singer, where they stood and listened. When the singer finished, Blue spoke to him.

"It's not anything like I wrote it, but it sounded good enough so that I'm going to leave that money I put in your guitar case. Otherwise, I would be retrieving that substantial investment I made in your career a few minutes ago."

"You wrote 'Failure to Love'?" the singer asked. "Then you must be with Blue Cacophony."

"I'm Blue. This here's Barney. We're the vocalists, but I'm the writer."

"I never heard you play live, but I heard 'Failure to Love' on the radio so I bought the album. I know it's a bootleg, man, but I needed to learn that song. The more I think about the way you think, about the way that there's just one sin in the whole world, then it's easier to understand what's wrong with the world. There aren't a million things wrong with it, just one, our failure to love. That's far out, man. Fixing one problem's a lot more hopeful than trying to fix everything that's wrong with everybody, right? That's what you had in mind, right? I'm Randy, by the way, and I'm sorry about buying your album bootleg, but I'll pay you for it right now by buying you something to eat. I'm almost starved myself."

"Tell you what," Blue offered, "there's not enough change in that guitar case of yours to buy yourself a decent meal. Let me look after your spot. I was thinking a few thoughts when I was standing there looking into the water and I need to be holding a guitar to really work them out."

Telling Blue it would be an honour to have him play it, Randy passed him his guitar and walked away toward some food vendors. Blue sat on the sidewalk, strumming. The words really had begun coming at him, rising from the bottom of the ocean while he watched, but he couldn't hear them. Picking an ocean rhythm from the strings of the acoustic, he tried to help them find their way to him. Suddenly, like a trap breaking the surface after hand-hauling a hundred feet of rope, the final words to "The Red Lobster" roared out of him.

> You may throw me back
> Because you don't want me
> Thinking perhaps
> There's more than one in the sea
>
> If you do that
> Well, I don't wanna boast

But lady, you just gave up
The best catch on the East Coast

Red Lobster, Red Lobster
Don't you dare sob, sir,
'Cause love is you, and love is her
You're the meat She's the but-tur!

By the time Randy returned to his spot near the wharf, Blue was wailing out random samples from the one hundred complete verses of "The Red Lobster." In the guitar case, there was a substantial improvement in the cash flow.

"I can't tell you all that money came from my singing," Blue acknowledged. "Some of it was because people felt sorry for you after I told them how sick you are."

"I'm not sick," Randy said.

"Not yet, you aren't, but if you have to live on the little bit I saw you make, you're going to be. Check around this city. The streets are full of people trying to make money singing or selling flowers or doing magic tricks. There's a lot of competition out there, Randy. I know. I've been there before I made it big. And if you're willing to take a good look at yourself, what have you got to offer, really? You're good looking and you sing well. You don't look like a case full of welfare. You look like you don't need any help at all, not when there's girls in wheelchairs and one-armed fiddlers and everything competing against you. So I told some people that I was just filling in for you while you went to the hospital. TB, I told them, the non-contagious kind. What you got to do is learn to yodel a couple of Jimmy Rodgers songs, and cough like hell when you finish. I'll guarantee you a decent living until you start getting some real gigs. Trust me. I know my horses, to quote the other fellow."

With that piece of advice, Blue asked for a piece of paper, which Randy tore from a scribbler filled with lyrics and passed to him. Blue jotted down the words that had risen from the bottom of San Francisco Bay as if they were lobsters that had swum all the way from the Gulf of St. Lawrence through the Panama

Canal to get themselves to him. Euphoric, he and Barney began working their way back, Barney joining the chorus of Blue's repeated version of his latest, and last, verse.

—

Tinker and Kathy, Peter?, Lee and Doc Silver were sitting around the table in Peter?'s apartment when Blue walked in.

"How'd the meeting go?" he asked.

"Pretty good, Blue," Tinker said. "We were talking about—"

"Whatever it was has nothing on what I have to tell you, buddy. It's complete, finished, toot fini, as the other fellow says."

"What is?"

"'The Red Lobster.' I just put the finishing touches to it today. One hundred frigging verses and one hundred frigging choruses! I can't believe it!"

"Blue's been working on this song for ... what? ... must be two years now, and he's finally got it finished."

"Are we going to hear a few bars?" Doc Silver asked.

"Not yet," Blue told him. "Not before I memorize it all, but I was thinking, Peter?, that maybe we could release it at the Fillmore or someplace. You know, Blue Cacophony's epic masterpiece or something like that, posters, newspapers, the whole shebang. Think about it, okay, because that's all I stopped by to say. Karma's got to hear this good news," Blue said, pausing in the doorway as his departure began. "Maybe we could launch it in Woodstock. You said they were expecting twenty, thirty thousand people there," he added, giving a thumbs up to Tinker as he left.

—

Karma was asleep when Blue entered the room. He turned on the lowest lamp and began to undress, noticing as he did that Karma's ninth life had finally begun. Weeks of sketches and torn pages and her final, blank panel on the wall. It was now a wash of forms that could have been waterfalls or cliffs, but at least it had begun. He slipped under the duvet beside her and began kissing her awake. "I finished 'The Red Lobster' he whispered when she began to moan her way toward consciousness. His words reached into her sleep and her eyes opened, smiling.

"That's wonderful, Blue! When?"

"Well, I didn't go to Alcatraz after all, so I could of asked you to come for the walk with me and Barney. But then maybe it wouldn't of happened, right? Anyway, I was down at the wharf and I heard this guy singing, and guess what he was singing? 'Failure To Love,' if you can believe that."

"I can believe that."

"Here's something you'll like believing even better. He says the song changed his thinking about the world. It's got more hope now or something like that. Anyway, he went to get something to eat and I sat there with his guitar and before I even had time to think about it the words were all there. Me and Barney sang it all the way to Peter?'s where we went to tell Tinker, then all the way home to tell you. And what do I see but some progress of your own on the wall. You got your picture started."

"Started, yes, but I'm still guessing a lot about it."

"Well, I woke you up to celebrate my song," Blue told Karma, who drew him to her.

—

Afterwards, Blue said, "When your painting is finished maybe we can celebrate it the same way."

"I hope so, Blue, I hope so."

"I suppose you're going right back to sleep and I'm going to be awake all night just thinking about 'The Red Lobster'," Blue said, sliding into dreams before Karma closed her eyes.

66

Blue, Gerry and Nathan stretched their necks, uncomfortable in rented tuxedos. Each of them, faced with the manners of their respective upbringing, could not bring themselves to attend a wedding wearing nothing but dust and denim, ignoring the reason they were being paid. Only Barney, wearing a tie-dyed neckerchief, was in character. Getting ready on the stage, Blue surveyed the rented estate where the reception was being held, the couple having already arrived from the church leading a long convoy of gift-bearing guests. With her father picking up the price of the band, Blue figured that the newlyweds would come out ahead on this deal by a few thousand bucks.

The wedding party milled around the food tents, sipping wine; most of them, Blue realized, weren't any more comfortable in their formality than himself. They weren't into long-haired music of any kind, classical or hippie rock, and Blue Cacophony was about to crash their party. The younger people might enjoy the band's sound, he thought, but like most weddings, this one was more populated by friends of the bride and groom's parents than their own. Blue guessed that the bride's guests were Merle Haggard fans, and the groom's were more comfortable with Frank Sinatra.

"We're all set to go here," he said into the microphone, his voice attracting the attention of the guests, including the official photographer who found his way to the stage through the viewfinder, his shutter winking. "You all know what the other fellow says about wedding pictures, don't you, that if the wedding was any good then the pictures will be the only proof it ever happened, even for the people who were there. Especially for the people who were there, I guess, and judging from the size of the liquor bar over there, I'd say we're in for one hell of a wedding.

"Now the only way to start off any reception, of course, is with 'The Wedding Waltz,' and my friend Gerry here is going to play just that for the bride and groom to get things started. Take her away, Gerry!"

The introduction stunned Gerry who was preparing for Blue Cacophony's intro number. "What are you doing, Blue? I'm not ready for that. I'm not even in tune."

"What the hell's the difference," Blue barked back. "Nine out of ten people out there won't even know the difference."

"And one out of three on the stage," Gerry snapped.

"We're having a little technical problem here, ladies and gentlemen," Blue said into the mic, "but Gerry will be with you in just one moment."

Holding the violin between his knees, Gerry tuned it to the challenge Blue had forced on him, then began to play, his one-armed style attracting as much attention as his music, but its romantic tone brought the bride and groom onto the dance platform in front of the stage, and the guests turned to watch.

"What are you doing?" Peter? asked as he, Tinker and Kathy, who had just arrived in the Plymouth, walked toward the band.

"What?"

"What's with these clothes, this music?" he asked, nodding toward the tuxedoed Gerry. "You look like some silly act on *The Ed Sullivan Show*."

"What's wrong with Ed Sullivan?" Blue asked, thrusting his chin forward, ready to physically defend the variety show host.

Tinker and Kathy, official guests of Mike, the bride's father, eased themselves away from the tension that surrounded the stage, especially Blue, and made their way to the food tent. On the dance platform, guests began joining the wedding couple as Gerry's violin grew more and more comfortable in his hand, like an amnesia victim suddenly remembering a previous life.

"Look, Peter?, I know what I'm doing here. You don't have to worry about people finding out that Blue Cacophony was playing 'The Wedding Waltz,' because *The Subterranean* doesn't review weddings. Your reputation and your revolution's safe," Blue said as Gerry's music softly ended to solid applause.

"Let's hear it for Gerry," Blue said, jumping onto the stage and grabbing the mic again. "Now you're probably wondering what's a bagpiper doing at a wedding. It's an instrument usually reserved for funerals, as the other fellow says, but there's those people who say what's the difference between them? Well, Nathan here adds something really different to Blue Cacophony's music, and I'm going to ask him to play something lively to get this place hopping. A waltz's okay for those in love, but what about the rest of us, huh, those of us who aren't getting married today or maybe ever. We need something lively, right, and let me tell you, nobody's ever heard anything as lively as 'The Mexican Hat Dance' played on the bagpipes. Take her away, Nathan."

Like Gerry, Nathan was caught in the spotlight of the wedding guests' attention, barely able to comprehend the situation in which Blue had cast him, but in the few moments it took to prepare his pipes, Gerry ran through the hat dance quietly to trigger Nathan's memory. By the time Nathan had found his way into the popular party tune, the guests had begun to bounce in place, then began dancing the giddy steps that changed the tempo of the reception. People began clowning on the dance platform, forgetting the strangulation of their neck-ties, the ankle-wrenching fact of their high heels.

For the next couple of hours, Blue managed the stage in a way that kept the rhythm of the party going, with Gerry and Nathan finding themselves willing accomplices to the war-time tunes and nasal country of Blue's version of some Nashville ballads, making their own contributions by retrieving from hundreds of hours of practice, the standard music that both had long ago left behind, but would never forget. The wedding guests danced themselves dizzy.

"I have a special treat for you now," Blue told the crowd. "I'm going to have a friend of mine come up here and sing a few songs for you. He's a wedding guest so we don't even have to pay him, but wait until you hear this guy, and if you like what you hear, then you can hear him any day you want because he sings for his supper, as the other fellow says. Ladies and gentlemen, let's have a big hand for my friend Tinker, the best street singer in San Francisco."

Reluctant and uncertain, Tinker joined the band on the stage. Blue passed him his guitar and while Tinker started with "Dock of the Bay," Blue jumped down and made his way to the liquor tent as the lights of the estate lawn suddenly lit up against the falling darkness. He ordered a beer and leaned against the bar, watching the party. Gerry and Nathan were improvising on stage. Kathy pulled the sullen Peter? onto the dance floor. Mike, the bride's father, wandered off the dance floor toward the bar.

"You guys are great!" he said, spotting Blue. "I never figured a famous band like yours would be playing songs people could dance to without drugs. And listen to this guy! He's got a great voice, but I've always known that."

"You did?" Blue asked.

"You should have heard him in the tunnel. Some of us would be working on the face and all of a sudden you could hear this voice travelling through the tunnel while he was tearing apart some machine. Shit, I miss him down there. You guys go way back, I take it."

"Yeah, buddy, we go way back," Blue said, pulling a deep drink from his beer, "and any day now we're going way back where we come from. Back where we belong."

Blue ordered another beer and taking it with him walked away from the bar toward the parking lot where he sat on the hood of the Plymouth, parked among the newer models. Alone, he lit a cigarette, listening to the faint but clear sound of Tinker's voice carrying on the still air, and wished Karma was with him.

—

Two weeks earlier, Blue had walked into their bedroom to discover Karma making inspired progress on the last panel of her nine lives. Sitting on the bed, he watched her, paint-smudged, working feverishly at her painting. Studying the picture, recognition came to him.

"Hey, I know that place. That's the waterfalls at the commune in Colorado, the place where we went swimming that first time. And those people are— us. Wait a minute. What's going on here, Karm? That's me, you and Barney. I thought you were doing your past lives, not the one you're living now?"

Karma's brush had stopped but she kept her back to him.

"Karm? Karma?"

Slowly, Karma turned, her eyes meeting Blue's. He didn't like what he saw in them.

"I'm sorry, Blue, but— listen to me, please. I have to go away."

"No problem, we'll go together." Blue's offer was tinged with desperation.

"I have to go alone, Blue."

"Aw, Christ, what did I do? Whatever it is, I'm sorry, but I'll make it up to you. For Christ's sake, don't leave. We were going away together, remember, going to Cape Breton, the two of us, all of us...."

"You didn't do anything, Blue, but I can't go with you. I've known that since the accident. Something happened, Blue, something wonderful. I haven't been able to talk about it really, because the words just aren't there. Maybe if it happened to you— what I mean is that you have a way of turning things into stories.

"Blue, I don't know if I died in the accident or not, or whether your prayers helped bring me back like you believe, or if it was the doctors who helped me, or if I just woke up from a dream. It doesn't matter. What does matter is the knowledge I woke up with. I don't mean answers, because I don't know what the experience itself means. What I do know now is that everything I believe is absolutely true. We are beautiful creatures, Blue. If you could have seen how we look in the light, you would understand, and that's the only way I can describe what I saw. Light, the most beautiful kind of light, filled with beings. Not strange beings, Blue. Us! I don't know if you're friend Danny Danny Dan was among them, but if he knew what was ahead of him, he would give up that eternal funeral of his and go across into the light." Karma stopped, hoping for a smile from Blue.

"I know you haven't been the same since the accident," Blue replied, "but I can't tell you what the difference is. I noticed it, though, ask anybody. But that doesn't mean we can't stay together, does it? If you want to go away, well, there's Cape Breton or any place you want to go. I'll go, I mean that, Karma, I'll go."

"I believe you would, Blue, but you can't. I need to go by myself because what I need to do isn't about us, it's about me. I need to go for me."

"Go where for how long?" Blue asked.

"India. An ashram in India, and I don't know for how long, Blue, because time has nothing to do with it."

"India! Good God, girl, that's on the other side of the world. How are you going to get there? Where will you stay? Do you know anybody from home to look after you there? And what about us, Karma, what about us? You're throwing me away like I'm some old gelding ready for the mink farm. What about me?"

"This isn't easy, Blue—"

"You're friggin' right, it's not!" Blue shouted.

"Don't yell, Blue, or we won't be able to talk at all."

"To hell with talking!" Blue said, storming out of the room, happy that it now had a door he could slam behind him.

Blue left the commune and ran himself to exhaustion through city streets, stopping finally beside a park he had never seen before. He sat on one of the benches, only then noticing that Barney, panting, had followed him from the house. Blue tried to send his thoughts everywhere but where he had just been. It was fruitless. There was no escaping the fact that a hole as large as the San Andreas Fault had opened up in his life with nothing but blackness gaping before him. Nothing distracted him, not music, not food, not thoughts of home. Karma was breaking up with him and running all the way to India to hide. He tried to nurse his anger to rage, imagined returning to the commune, smashing up the place, pounding Capricorn and all his stupid pagan teachings to pulp, then telling Karma to go fuck herself, packing his suitcase and heading out with Tinker in the Plymouth for home. Screw San Francisco. Screw the commune. Screw Blue Cacophony. And screw Karma the Dharma!

"Screw her, Barney, screw her! I suppose she's going to leave you with the commune while she goes off to India to get all her holy answers! Well, the fact is that I just don't care what she does. Her plane can crash for all I care. I wouldn't even go to her funeral!"

Standing beside the bench, Barney placed his head on Blue's thigh, his brown eyes confused by his friend's anger. Blue stroked the dog's head while two slow tears leaked their way down his own cheeks. Blue bent over and buried his face in the dog's neck to hide the shame of his crying eyes from passers-by. He lost all sense of how long he sat there clutching the dog, but dusk was coming when his awareness returned, a coming darkness to match the empty black place inside him.

"We may be made of light, as the other fellow says, Barney, but the bulb in here just burnt out, old buddy, and it will never be bright again in my life. What are we going to do without her? Write some real Nashville songs, I suppose, or maybe not write any more songs, at all. I really don't care.

"She knew this, Barney. She knew when she woke up from the accident that this was going to happen. That's why she's been mostly far away even when we're close together. She was getting ready to write me a Dear John letter. Well, the writing's on the wall now, isn't it, or rather the painting's on the wall.

"I didn't even think of it, Barney. It never occurred to me that Karma would be leaving me. Know what I was worrying about? Leaving her. I kept thinking what if summer comes and it's time to go home and Karma won't come? How is she going to handle me leaving her behind? I don't know if I could of left her behind, though. Maybe I would of decided to stay here with her, but that was a thought to be chased away like a mortal sin, so I never really let myself think about it. It was just too scary. But what was I worrying about, huh? She had it all planned right from the start. Right from the start of her new life anyway, and all of a sudden I'm just another one of her past lives, something to move away from. Christ, I should of left her first, then I wouldn't have to explain to everybody— to hell with everybody! I wouldn't of left her anyway, would I, Barney? Would I?

"I didn't even ask her when she was leaving. I hope she didn't mean she was going tonight. She can't be gone already. It's getting dark as death out here, and Karma might be gone before I get to say ... what? Christ, Barney, what am I going to say to her? Help me think of something on the way back, buddy, because I'm not thinking so good on my own right now. Come on, boy, and remember that what you saw me doing before, you know what I mean, the tears, well, that's our secret, okay? Nobody has to know that. Nobody!"

67

Karma wasn't gone. She was in their bedroom, meditating. The painting was finished. In it, Karma was in the water, Blue and Barney standing beside the waterfall pool, preparing to join her. Blue sat in the chair and watched Karma's trance-like presence. He didn't notice when she had opened her eyes but was suddenly aware that she was watching him. He shrugged uncomfortably.

"I thought maybe you were already gone," Blue said.

"Would it be better if I was?" Karma asked. "I can move—"

"I mean, I was afraid you were already gone," Blue corrected. "When are you going?"

"I have a ticket for next Friday night. The arrangements in India have already been made. There's a Master there who is taking me as a student. How are you, Blue?"

"You know me. I'll be okay. Barney, too, once he gets back to Colorado where he can chase squirrels in the mountains instead of cars in the city. We'll do just fine."

The next few days were filled with preparations for Karma's departure. Blue was soon conveying the impression that Karma's trip to India was his idea. Alone in their room, he touched her greedily, as if assuring to himself that she hadn't already gone.

On Friday evening, Blue borrowed the Plymouth and drove Karma to the airport. In the departure lounge they said their goodbyes.

Blue was afraid to speak, feeling a lump in his throat that threatened to produce more tears.

"You really have to do this, don't you?" he said finally.

"Yes, Blue, I really do. I know it hurts, but I believe we'll find each other again, sometime."

"In another life, you mean. That's the difference between us, you have all these lives to throw away trying to be perfect while I just have this one, and I'm going to be spending the rest of it wondering what ever happened to you once you got on that plane. India's a big place, the dark continent, as the other fellow says."

"That's Africa, Blue, not India."

"Whatever. Anyway, you'll just disappear into those millions and millions of people and I'll never know where you are or what became of you."

"I guess I'm luckier than you."

"How?" Blue asked.

"Because I'll always know where you are. When I think about you, there's the ocean you love so much and the horses and the people and the stories. My mind will always know where to find you, and if I ever have to find you in the flesh, all I need to do is walk into that diner you're always talking about – the one that you told Mr. Lo always puts two King Cole tea bags in a one-cup teapot – or walk into that tavern or Legion of yours, and ask someone where I can find Blue."

"But you won't."

Karma shook her head. "Probably not, but it's comforting for me to know that I can find my best friend if I ever need him."

"Best friend? When did that happen?"

"You've been that since shortly after we met, Blue. We've been that to each other, more than that, I know, but always that. That won't change ever. I love you."

Then Karma was gone into a tunnel that took her onto a plane that took her to a place halfway around the world, leaving Blue standing there like someone by a graveside. He forced himself to leave, getting in the Plymouth and spending hours driving around the city, country radio blaring, his mind forming decisions, his eyes still too misty to go back to the commune.

—

Blue let himself slide off the hood of the Plymouth, stood and chugged the last of the beer, and walked back to the stage. Tinker was still crooning, backed by Gerry and Nathan, but the crowd was beginning to show its age. Most of the older guests were weaving their way toward seats or cars, guided by wives who thought it was time to go home, leaving behind them the young friends of the bride and groom, and Blue knew that now was the time for Blue Cacophony to show its stuff.

Taking his place on the stage, he changed the band's persona by playing "Failure To Love," letting the wedding guests who still remained know that Blue Cacophony was here at last. The apron of plywood that formed a dance floor in front of the stage filled up. They were open to anything that would keep the party going, and those were conditions in which Blue Cacophony thrived. The band played its material and the dancers made the most of it. After an hour, Blue introduced a new number.

"We got this guy back home, eh, Farmer. He's this horse trader who told me one time that every once in a while he'd be loading a horse he just bought or sold, and all of a sudden he would just know that this was a *horse*, not some burnt-out minker or broken-down Clyde, but a real horse, the kind they make movies about. Well, that's how I feel about this next song. I finished it the other day. Took me two years but what I got me here is a real horse, as the other fellow would say."

Behind him, Nathan and Gerry cast anxious eyes at each other.

In the crowd, Tinker, trying to anticipate where Blue was going, guided Kathy closer to the stage.

Peter? walked toward the stage transfixed.

"This is a song with a hundred verses, and it's never been sung all the way through before. It's never even been rehearsed before so you can imagine how my band feels right now, but with them or without them, I'm going to sing for you my latest composition, 'The Red Lobster.' Give me some noise back there, Nate."

Blue began to sing. There was nothing at first. Stares, shrugs, indifference.

As Blue returned over and over to the repetition of the chorus, it began to take with the crowd. Shoulders that had shrugged were now moving to a sort of timing, but because each listener tended to find something rhythmically different in Blue Cacophony's music, the audience rarely swayed in sync. Soon Blue was being joined by a few dozen voices when he sang:

> Red Lobster, Red Lobster
> Don't you dare sob, sir
> 'Cause love is you, and love is her
> You're the meat And she's the but-tur

Because there had been no rehearsals, Gerry and Nathan were not shackled to Blue's arrangements. Under his voice, the violin and pipes began to find a beat that the wedding guests could dance to, and they did. It became a joyful, drunken, giddy marathon that eventually forced many from the dance floor, but a few hung in as the song approached its last verse which, in Blue's current emotional condition, had taken on prophetic proportions. Karma had cast him back into the sea, and now it was just him and his song.

From the dance floor where he and Kathy were actually dancing to Blue's music, Tinker exchanged winks with his friend, giving him the thumbs up while in front of the stage a hyper Peter? was yelling "It works! It works!" and hollering instructions to Gerry and Nathan to remember what they were improvising.

Blue reached the end of his song, and exhausted dancers staggered from the stage.

"If somebody would bring a few beers up here, we'll get this party started," Blue hollered into the mic, half drunk from earlier beers and high on the moment. "Hell, we have a long way to go. There hasn't even been a decent fight yet, and what's a wedding without a few family friends punching it out. So fill her up for a set, as the other fellow would say."

Blue Cacophony played until weariness overcame the band, and the members wandered off the stage. The wedding party had slowed to a low murmur of survivors still drinking whatever they could find. No one could, or wanted to dance anymore.

Blue, Tinker, Kathy, Gerry, Nathan and Peter? sat around one of the picnic tables, talking about the future as Peter? envisioned it. "The Red Lobster" would become the anthem of the revolution.

"Peter?, I love you, old buddy, but your revolution sucks. Nobody's every going to hear 'The Red Lobster' again. Isn't that what you want? Music nobody hears, only hears about," Blue asked, emptying the bottle in front of him and excusing himself. "I have to see a man about a horse, as the other feller says."

Blue wandered off to find a private place to carry out the business at hand, and discovered that place against the back wheel of the Plymouth. He took a couple of steps toward returning to his friends, but second-thinking it, decided that the best place for him right now was to savour the triumph of "The Red Lobster" alone. He opened the back door and climbed into the back seat of Tinker's car, lay down and went to sleep.

"Is he going to be all right?" Nathan asked Tinker.

"He'll get over it. Blue's not used to losing, but you've all heard him. He's almost convinced he talked Karma into going. For me, that's a healthy sign that Blue'll be okay," Tinker said.

"He's wounded, no doubt about that," Peter? said. "But he's a pro, isn't he? Did you see him up on stage tonight? Not a sign that he wasn't in control."

"Maybe we should keep him on stage then, because when he wasn't singing, he was being a complete bastard," Gerry said, reminding Peter? of the way he had snapped at the band members when he didn't have a microphone in his hand.

"Blue's got two problems," Tinker observed. "He's lovesick and he's homesick. Nasty combination, like throwing up and having the shits at the same time."

"Sounds like something the other fellow would say," Gerry said, running the bow across his violin.

"Blue's not the only one who's homesick tonight, though," Tinker said. "Gerry, would you do me a favour? Would you try playing a few tunes for me if I jig them for you first?" Gerry agreed, and Tinker began making the mouth music which, according to Cape Breton history, was the way the music of the

Highlands was preserved when the British banned the music and the instruments after the battle of Culloden. Later, in Cape Breton, those who had learned to jig the airs in the form of Gaelic mouth music called *puirt-a-beul*, passed them on to new generations who translated them back to the fiddle, the pipes, the piano.

At this point in any party back home, the fiddle would be winding down to the slow airs, and it was the most haunting of those tunes that Tinker chose to give to Gerry, who captured the tunes in his impressive memory then turned them into stringed offerings that Tinker listened to while his gaze and his thoughts drifted far, far from where they were gathered.

68

"I heard the call loud and clear, Tinker," Blue told his friend the next day. Although it was late afternoon, both still showed traces of ill health from the previous night. "It's time to go home when I was sleeping in the Plymouth last night, I dreamed of fiddles, man. It was so real that when I woke up I thought I was at the Glencoe dance hall, not a wedding in San Francisco. I figure that car of yours has absorbed so much music driving to all the dances back home that it's kind of haunted, but in a good way. Then I had to throw up so I climbed out of the car and was heaving my guts out behind it and I could still hear the fiddle, then the music put me right back to sleep. That's a sure sign, as the other fellow says."

Tinker decided that Blue would enjoy telling that story as gospel much more than he would appreciate hearing the corrected version.

"But if you go home now, Blue, what about the band? What about playing in Woodstock?"

"Let me ask you something, Tinker. When I told you that, that we were going to be playing in Woodstock, what did you think?"

"That you'd be playing in Woodstock, I guess."

"Woodstock where?"

"New Brunswick."

"That's because you studied the same geography book as myself, and the way I had it figured, we'd play Woodstock, then drive a couple of hours down the TransCanada Highway to Nova Scotia and four hours after that we'd be home, maybe playing the Cabot Trail Tavern or something, but these frigging Americans can't let anybody have anything to themselves. Turns out there's another Woodstock, some little piss-hole in New York, and that's where the concert is, and get this, the concert isn't until August. If we wait until August to go home, we'll miss the

Broad Cove Concert, and if you miss the Broad Cove Concert, then you've missed the summer, to quote the other fellow."

"Blue—" Tinker started, the address followed by a lingering silence.

"I'm listening," Blue replied. "What's on your mind, buddy?"

"Blue, I'm not going back. Not this summer, I mean."

Blue slapped the table hard with his hand. "I knew it! I friggin' well knew it! Why didn't you tell me this before? I might of been long gone except I was waiting for you."

"I tried to tell you at Peter?'s the night we had the meeting with Doc Silver, Blue, but you were after finishing 'Red Lobster' and ... well, then it just got harder to bring it up, but I've decided. I'm going to go to college here, Blue."

"College! How the hell are you going to go to college here? You're a friggin' illegal immigrant, you got no money and these colleges down here cost a friggin' arm and a friggin' leg, and your grade twelve report card isn't exactly something worth framing, if I remember correctly."

"Doc Silver says he can get me into Berkeley. Kathy and me will have to drive up to Vancouver sometime in July and apply from there, but he'll give me a recommendation, and he says he can find me some obscure scholarships that nobody ever applies for, and a couple of those, along with a job on campus, maybe washing dishes in the cafeteria, and I'll be able to pay my way."

Blue looked at his friend in sad understanding.

"You know why he's doing this, don't you? To get his hands on your oxygen engine. There's money to made there, buddy, lots of it, enough to kill for, if you recall. They want you at that university to pick your brains."

"I'm not going to study science. I want to take up acting."

"Holy shit, Tinker, what's going on here? Have we been in the same city for the past year or what? Living in the same house? Acting? You must be good at it because you sure fooled me. We've been together all our lives and you never once mentioned acting. This is Kathy, isn't it? Her and her friggin' playwriting? A friggin' actor, for frig sakes. Who do you think you are, Paul-frigging-Newman or somebody?"

"Listen to me, Blue. I never knew anything about acting before, but now I do, and I want to try it. Hell, when Kathy and me went away to get ready to break out Capricorn, it was the first time I ever really tried acting. She got tapes about the American army, how to march, how to salute, how to do all sorts of things so I could act like a soldier. Then she wrote scripts that she made me memorize, and now am I ever glad that the nuns made us learn how to memorize poems like 'The Wreck of the Hesperus' in school. Anyway, it wasn't until I got in that building that I knew I could act. Jesus, Blue, I was so scared that I was shitting in my pants. That Wise would have shot me in a minute if he knew who I was, but it was the acting that I liked. When I think about it now, it wasn't the thrill of breaking Capricorn out because, like I said, I was scared, but being an actor, convincing people I met that I was who I said I was, that was the really exciting part.

"It was almost the same when I phoned Reginald Regent III and pretended that I was Wise. That was acting, too. I've been acting all my life in some ways, acting like other singers, like Tom Jones, Johnny Cash, anybody I ever imitated. Blue, I could have spent my whole life doing something else like working in the tunnel, and enjoyed it, but I would never even have known I was an actor except that Kathy showed me that I was. We want to see where it takes us, my acting, her writing. This is an opportunity I'm not going to pass up. I'm sorry, Blue, but I am not going home, not right now."

—

"I'll take the bus up to Vancouver, then take the CNR across Canada," Blue explained to Capricorn. He had spent the past couple of days making arrangements for his departure. "I'd like you to do me a favour, though. I talked to Peter? and Gerry and Nathan about breaking up the band. It was Peter? who took it the worst, of course, seeing his revolution coming to an abrupt end like this, but I'm not interested in it anymore. Me and the fat lady may never sing again, to quote the other fellow."

"What will you do when you go back home, Blue? There's not a lot of work, according to what you and Tinker say about the place," Capricorn asked.

"I'll do what I've always done, buddy, sell horses."

"But you told me horse traders were a dying breed, that your friend, Farmer, was one of the last of them."

"Farmer's old, Capi, set in his ways. Sure, horses are disappearing from all the farms in Cape Breton just like they disappeared from all the farms everywhere else, but a guy has to ask himself where did they all go? What I mean is there's lots of horses in Cape Breton, hundreds of them, a thousand maybe, but they're all at race tracks now. Harness racers. Pacers and trotters. Farmer doesn't pay any attention to race horses because he doesn't know anything about them, and we all know what the other fella says about old dogs and new tricks. So I figure I'll hire on at the race track back home for a summer, learn all I need to know then go into the business of selling them."

"You think you can learn all about horse racing in a summer, Blue?" Capricorn asked skeptically.

"I said I could learn all *I* need to know in a summer. All I need to know is enough to convince buyers that I have what they want, or sellers that I am doing them a favour just taking the old nag off their hands. Of course, if I'm any good at my job, and believe me, Capi, I am, then that old nag will make me about thousand per cent profit when I sell her.

"But there's something I have to tell you. I told the guys that the band was breaking up, but when it came time to tell them about the record, I just couldn't. I don't know, maybe I'm getting soft in my old age, but I just didn't want to see the look on Peter?'s face when he found out that my middle name is Judas. So I'm taking the weasel path. I'm not going to tell them about it at all. You are. Coming from you, with your way of being so moral and holy and all that, they'll be more forgiving. Peter?, anyway. I don't think Gerry or Nathan will care, especially when you pass them each a wad of money.

"You'll be in Colorado about the time I get back to Cape Breton. That's good. Good for Barney, anyway. Take good care of him because it's time for me to get going, Capi," Blue said, picking up his suitcase and a large cardboard-wrapped package. "If the landlord is asking where part of the wall in our room went, well, I'm taking it home with me, a souvenir. If there's a bill, Tinker will tell you where to send it. But listen, if you get into trouble with the FBI again, I know a great place for your commune, if you're not scared to take your followers there, considering that for a little while there while you were in jail I used to be king of this particular castle. I might launch a coop de thaw, as the other fellow says.

"I have one stop to make, then I got to go meet Tinker. He's driving me to the bus station, but let's shake on her, Capi. You turned out to be one of the good guys, after all."

—

Blue wobbled into Mr. Lo's weighted down with his suitcase and his package.

"Sorry I'm late, buddy," he apologized as he slipped into the booth across from Tinker. "I had to see Cory before I left. Told him one time that he'd never go back to horses in that commune in Colorado, but I wanted to let him know that if he ever does, then I'll give him a really good deal, better than that guy that sold them those old nags they had there. So where's Kathy?"

"She says goodbye, but she thinks we should be alone, that maybe you'd rather not see her."

"Give her my best, but that's not true anymore, that I'd rather not see her, Tinker. She's your partner now. Maybe I didn't like it when she was trying to be your partner, and you were listening more to her than me, but now that's all water under the bridge, so to speak. I'm going home and there's nothing I want more. Well, almost nothing, but that's just water and bridges again."

Mr. Lo set the menus in front of the two of them, and they ordered combination plates of his Chinese food, telling him that Blue was leaving the city, going home. Mr. Lo tore up the bill before he even went to prepare their food. The two of them sat looking out the window, around the diner, anywhere but into each other's eyes.

"How long have we got before the bus leaves?" Blue asked.

"An hour, a little longer. It won't take long to get there, don't worry."

"I'm not worried. If I miss the bus, there's always another one leaving this city. Aw, Christ, Tinker, I wish you were coming with me. It's like half of me isn't going home at all. But since you're serious about this college business, I'd like you to have this," he said, pushing an envelope across the table top.

Tinker picked it up and looked inside.

"Jesus Christ!" he gasped, flipping the bills in the envelope. "There must be ... must be a thous— a couple of ... Jesus, Blue, there must be—"

"Ten thousand dollars," Blue clarified, explaining about the success of the record.

"But this is all your money—"

"No. I still have a couple of grand. If I had of landed home with twelve thousand bucks in my pocket, I'd of killed myself trying to party it away. A couple of thousand will just maintain me in a style to which I am accustomed, to quote the other fellow. Can't have you going to college with no money, and when you mentioned washing dishes in a cafeteria, I thought, oh boy, a chore neither of us care for, so I said, Lord, if you can let this cup, and saucer, and dinner plate pass, as the other fellow said in Gethsemane, Tinker would be forever grateful. So as one friend to another, it was possible for me, if not the Lord, to spare you that."

"I'll pay you back, Blue. You know that."

"Yes, I know that, but there's conditions on the loan. No 'Your cheque's in the mail,' as the other fellow says. I want cash in my hand, and I won't be travelling out here to get it, if you get my meaning."

Tinker, thick-throated, nodded his understanding that Blue wasn't going to let him get lost in California the way it sometimes happens.

Mr. Lo brought them their dinners which they ate slowly and not completely, each mulling over the moment and their pending parting.

"Blue," Tinker said, pushing his plate aside. "Since you're going home and I'm not, will you bring something back for me?"

"No problem. If it'll fit on the bus I'll wrestle it across the causeway."

"It won't fit on the bus, Blue," Tinker said, sliding his keys across the table.

"The Plymouth? You want me to take the Plymouth home without you? Tinker, old buddy, are you sure this isn't a sentimental gesture you will live to regret five minutes after I'm gone?"

"No. If I couldn't have earned enough to stay in college, I think I might have been forced to sell it for whatever I could get. It's worth a lot to me, but not much to anybody else."

"Except me," Blue replied. "I'll see that it gets home, and two weeks from now, I want you to stop what you're doing at eight o'clock on Thursday night because it'll be midnight back home, and just listen. Your Plymouth will be parked at the Glencoe dance hall, and if you listen hard enough, you might even hear the music, just like I did the night I slept in it.

"Christ, Tinker, the Plymouth. Driving home. This changes everything."

The two friends, no longer tied to bus schedules, lingered over their food, drinking each other's health with toasts of Mr. Lo's tea, until there was nothing left to say but goodbye.

Tinker watched the Plymouth pull away from the curb, while Blue watched him waving frantically in the rearview mirror until the car turned the corner and Tinker was gone from sight, and Blue was on his way home.

Tinker, standing on the street corner, laughed long after the Plymouth disappeared, wondering how long it would take Blue to realize he had driven off in the wrong direction.

Epilogue

Blue coaxed the Plymouth up the steep hill on the TransCanada Highway. On the other side of the hill lay Auld's Cove, the last place on mainland Nova Scotia.

"Just keep your eyes on the top of this hill here, buddy. Don't blink, because all of a sudden we're going to get to the top, and just when we get there it's going to look like an island is suddenly rising up out of the sea, so just keep your eyes glued to the summit. Any minute now ... any minute ... and there. There it is. Across the Strait of Canso, Barney, old buddy, Cape Breton Island. God's Country, as the other fellow says."

Frank Macdonald is the award-winning author of *A Forest for Calum* (CBU Press 2005) and *A Possible Madness* (CBU Press 2011), both long-listed for the International IMPAC Dublin Literary Award, and both finalists for Atlantic Book Awards. A long-time and award-winning columnist, Macdonald is also an accomplished writer of short stories, drama, poetry and songs. His humorous, often satirical columns in the Inverness *Oran* have twice been anthologized; *Assuming I'm Right* in 1990 became a stage production that has toured Nova Scotia and elsewhere in Canada. His play *Her Wake* won Best Canadian Play at the Liverpool International Theatre Festival in 2010 and, also in 2010, he published *T.R.'s Adventure at Angus the Wheeler's* (CBU Press), a children's book, illustrated by Virginia McCoy.

Frank has participated in a number of book and writers festivals, including The Word on the Street, Read by the Sea and the Ullapool International Book Festival.

Frank lives in Inverness, Cape Breton.